Cadets

First Edition, June 2013

Printed in the United States of America

ISBN-10: 0615805582
ISBN-13: 9780615805580

Pop Culture Zoo Press
info@PopCultureZooPress.com
www.PopCultureZooPress.com
(215) 718-8021

First Printing: June 2013

Cadets

Edward Miller

POP
CULTURE
ZOO
PRESS
Superlative Speculative Fiction and Beyond!

Prologue

Nellis Air Force Base, Nevada, March 2012, 2100 Hours

Captain Robert Williamson was in a foul mood when he entered the radar room. This was turning out to be an even worse day than yesterday. The solar flares were still wreaking havoc on all the communications systems, not to mention the radar, planetary, and deep space early warning systems. The computers were severely compromised, and the whole thing was giving him a throbbing headache. Of all days to have an unidentified object heading toward Earth at alarming speed. Hopefully it wouldn't hit a populated area.

"Any updates, Lieutenant?"

Lieutenant Jenner turned and faced him. She looked like she hadn't slept in days. "Sir, about fifty percent of the systems are operating at full capacity. We're still working on the rest."

"Well hurry it up," he said. "We need to know what we're dealing with here."

One of the officers at the deep space early warning station called out. "Captain, I have the bogey showing now at an altitude of one hundred and ten thousand feet. It appears to be slowing down and is flying in a steady trajectory. If it remains on its current course and angle of descent, it will enter our airspace within the next five to ten minutes."

"Do we know what it is?"

"Negative, sir. It's nothing on our list."

Just what they didn't need. Some unknown object was about to enter their airspace, and because of the glitches, they had no way of telling what it could be. Williamson grabbed the microphone on the desk. "This is Captain Williamson calling the flight duty officer. Scramble Eagles One and Two. This is not a drill. I repeat, scramble Eagles One and Two. We have an unidentified object coming in hot. Do you copy?"

"This is Flight Duty Officer Warrington, Captain. I read loud and clear. Scrambling Eagles One and Two, sir."

The two Eagle pilots had been playing cards in the ready room when the alarm sounded. Williamson saw them rush out and head for the runway, where their F-18 fighter jets were waiting. They were moving faster than a bolt of lightning. In a matter of seconds, the first pilot's voice came over the radio. "This is Eagle One calling the tower. Eagles One and Two are requesting clearance for takeoff."

"This is the tower. Eagles One and Two are cleared for takeoff."

"Roger that, tower. Eagles One and Two on the go."

Pushing the throttle to full, the two F-18s took off, their engines roaring as they passed the radar building. When it was quiet enough to hear, Williamson spoke into the mic. "This is Captain Williamson to Eagle One. We have a projected impact point. Latitude 36 degrees north, longitude 116 degrees west, about ten miles south of Pahrump. Looks like we have a desert impact coming up. Do you copy, Eagle One?"

"Roger that, Captain." The pilot's voice was loud and harried. "Thirty-six degrees north, a hundred and sixteen degrees west. Adjusting course now. Do you copy, Eagle Two?"

"Eagle Two to Eagle One. Copy that. Let's hit the afterburners."

Within seconds, the fighters had closed in on the unidentified object.

"Eagle One to base. I have the object on my radar. It's descending rapidly. Speed Mach 2. Angle of descent 45 degrees. She looks like she's out of control."

"Williamson here, Eagle One. Roger that. Stay with her. Don't lose that bogey!"

Looking at the monitor, he could see the F-18s closing in.

"Captain, it's definitely a craft of some kind," said Eagle Two. "I see sparks jumping off it. I think I can make out an outline."

"Jesus!" said Eagle One. "Do you see that thing?"

There was a moment of silence before Eagle Two replied. "I see it. I just don't believe it."

Williamson watched as the fighters banked hard left trying to keep pace with the object, which had started to reel like a drunken sailor.

"Captain Williamson to Eagles One and Two. Have you activated your wing cameras?"

"Dammit!" said the pilot of Eagle One. "My wing camera is malfunctioning."

The pilot of Eagle Two replied. "Not to worry. I've got your back."

"She's trying to level out," said Eagle One. "I can see the burners firing away from multiple sides."

"Williamson here, boys. Obviously you have a visual. Any idea what it is?"

"I'll tell you what it isn't," came the reply from Eagle One. "It's nothing I've ever seen before. It's rectangular, about the size of a 767 without wings, sir. There's engines or something protruding from the back. Whatever it is, she's trying to nose up. Looks like she's attempting to land, but whoever they are, they're in trouble. What are our orders, sir?"

"Stay with them," said Williamson. "If they make any aggressive moves, defend yourselves."

"Affirmative, sir. You heard the man, Paxton. Arm missiles and stay sharp."

"Missiles locked and ready," replied the wingman.

Williamson made his way to the radar screen. It was probably those damn Chinese messing around again. Or maybe one of those rich tech entrepreneurs gone rogue. Still, something seemed off about this one. He tapped the lieutenant on the shoulder. "Is she still on course to come down in the Mojave Desert?"

"Affirmative," said the officer.

"What's their E.T.A.?"

"Their speed's erratic, sir. I'd say no more than a minute. Two at the most."

He started thinking about options, but static on the monitor interrupted his thoughts.

"Eagle One to base. The object appears to be firing some type of forward thrusters, sir. She looks like she's trying to get her nose up. Now at an altitude of one thousand feet and coming in fast and furious. She'll be on the ground shortly."

"Understood, Eagle One,' said Williamson. "Follow her in. Eagle Two, stay alongside of her. Report back to me as soon as she lands."

"Affirmative," came the reply from Eagles One and Two.

The officer at the radar control monitor called out to the captain. "Sir, radar contact lost. The object has dropped below four hundred feet."

The pilot of Eagle One called out. "She's down, Captain. Hit the ground pretty hard and fast. I'm doing four hundred knots, so she had to be moving at around the same speed. I'm going to pull up and circle back. I'll let you know if I see any movement."

The room got very quiet. Other than the sounds of the equipment, the only thing that could be heard was the sound of the men and women in the room breathing. Then, after what seemed like an eternity, the silence was broken.

"Eagle Two to base. There's something moving down there. I'm dropping to one hundred feet. Almost there. It's pretty dusty. Kind of hard to see. Wait a minute. It's clearing a little. My God! They look like . . . like—"

Then, nothing but static.

Williamson slammed his fist on the desk in front of him. "Damn it. Reestablish contact with the pilots, Jenner."

"I'm trying to, Captain. The solar activity is interfering with our communications."

Williamson picked up the red phone and waited to be connected.

"What's the situation?"said the voice on the other line.

"We have a code zero, said Williamson. "What are my orders, sir?"

"You know the drill," came the reply on the other end. "Lock down the facility. Secure the area of impact. Nobody in or out. All data and recordings stored and sealed. No contact with anyone but me or my department. Have the pilots report to my people for debriefing. Do we have an area of contact?"

"Yes, sir. The Mojave Desert."

"What is your name and rank?" requested the voice.

"Captain Robert Williamson, sir."

"This is your official story, Captain," said the voice on the other end of the phone. "There was a military test of a new type of space probe. It malfunctioned and crashed in the desert. You will say nothing more and will direct any questions to me. I will take it from there. Do you understand my orders, Captain Williamson?"

"Yes, sir. Anything else?"

"Lock it down, Williamson. I'll be in touch." The line went dead.

Chapter 1

One Hundred And Fifty Years Later, 2162, Cadet Training Planet

Ryan Thompson didn't care much for awards or authority, so why did he find himself practically racing toward the boarding area for the flight simulator of the UEDF Nimitz space cruiser? Maybe he needed to prove something to himself. After all, he was eighteen now, and soon would be graduating from the academy, no longer a cadet. Or maybe it was more he wanted to prove something to his father—that he could succeed without his help. And then, there was Amanda. Either way, this would be the final simulation for determining who would win the coveted Golden Cadet Award. Luckily, because of his excellent performance in all the other aspects of the competition, he was assigned the role of ship's captain by the head of the academy, Admiral Jonas Williamson.

Though there were many awards, there was no doubt the Golden Cadet was the most prestigious award at the academy. In every graduating class for the past twenty-seven years, one senior had been chosen to receive it based on overall scores and skills in a battery of tests. Winning the award was considered to be almost a sure road to a successful career as an officer in the United Earth Defense Fleet. But that seemed almost secondary to Ryan. No, he wasn't here for the glory. This was more about saving his soul.

Just as he rounded the corner, one of the new recruits ran up to him.

"Hey," said the kid, who looked around fifteen, "you're Flash Thompson's son. Can you sign my induction papers?"

Ryan cringed at the mention of his father. "You still carry your induction papers around with you?" he said.

"Well, I heard you were boarding the simulation, and—"

"No offense," said Ryan, "but really, I'm late."

Ryan started to leave, but something made him turn back. Maybe the need to prove he *wasn't* Flash Thompson's son, at least not when it came to being there for someone. As he turned, he saw the freshman walking away with his head down.

"Hey!" he called. The freshman turned around. "Come on, you got twenty seconds."

The kid nodded and gave a half smile, running back to him.

"You got a pen?" said Ryan.

The freshman grinned as if he'd just been promoted to captain and grabbed a pen out of his book bag. Ryan quickly signed his papers and then ran off toward the Nimitz, the kid yelling his thanks from behind him.

For Ryan, it was bad enough being the son of the man who'd been the first ever winner of the award, not to mention the Fleet Admiral of the whole UEDF. But the very mention of his name brought back horrible memories of that fateful day, something he spent most of his days trying not to think of.

Finally, Ryan arrived at the boarding dock and made his way through the entrance tunnel. It was hard to believe he was inside a simulator. It was an exact replica of the bridge on the Nimitz, one of the oldest, most legendary ships in the United Earth Defense Fleet. The actual planetary battle cruiser, which was still on the base, was practically an antique now, but perfect for using on test flights. Thankfully, the crew that Admiral Williamson had picked for him was the best of the best and should get the job done. But there was one wrinkle—a *huge* one, as far as Ryan was concerned. His old girlfriend, Amanda, who just happened to be Williamson's daughter, would be his executive officer. Not only that, but she was the other candidate for the award. That was a recipe for team conflict if he ever saw one.

As he proceeded onto the battle bridge, Ryan spotted Amanda talking to her friend Jill Myers, the communications officer. It was hard to miss Amanda's long red hair. Why in the world would the admiral have picked her, of all people, to be his right hand? He had to know the possible consequences of that. Besides, any one of the other cadets on the crew would have made a more suitable executive officer. At the least, they could be flexible. She was about as rigid as they came. If anything, she should have been placed in engineering, where her real skills were, not in command, where you had to think on your feet and make spur-of-the-moment decisions. Now he could only hope she wouldn't slow him down and ruin the mission.

Ryan approached the captain's console and fiddled with the controls, trying to get his bearings. They were about to start the simulation when he overheard Amanda talking to her friend Jill Myers.

"Don't you wonder sometimes," said Amanda, "why we keep running these battle simulations? I mean, we haven't had a single war on Earth for over seventy years. And we haven't once had anything even remotely resembling a space battle. Is it me?"

"You don't get it," said Jill. "This isn't about war or preparations. It's about who dies with the most toys. There's money to spend, so people will spend it. Besides, the higher ups think it's 'for the safety of all' as they say. Don't you watch the UEDF promos?"

"It just kills me how many other things we could do with that money," said Amanda. "Do you know how many medical supplies that could buy?"

Ryan hadn't been invited into the conversation, but he couldn't help getting involved. He felt she was missing the point. He casually made his way over to them.

"Ladies, I'm afraid you're oversimplifying it just a little," he said. "This isn't about toys. And it's not even the money. Do you want to know what this is about?"

"I can't wait to hear this one," Amanda said to Jill.

"Oh, you'll love it," said Ryan. "It's about what happens if you're in command of a deep space exploration mission and an unknown ship approaches your ship and opens fire. But you don't have any training to deal with hostile forces, so maybe you hope for the best and try to talk to them. But guess what? They may not be in the mood to listen. Maybe they want to shoot first and ask questions later."

"And just where are these hostile forces coming from?" said Amanda. "Nobody has ever seen a single alien in our entire history.

Like ever. But just in case, I guess you can never be too ready." She shook her head smiling. "Unbelievable," she added.

"So, I guess those two planets we found never really happened then, right?"

"Ryan, that's not—"

"Both of them had clear evidence of alien civilizations and were devastated by someone or something."

"That wasn't even in our solar system. It was light years away."

"Close enough. And every year we're exploring deeper and deeper into space, so we just might meet some friends we weren't expecting—sooner than you think. Remember the Drake equation?"

"That doesn't prove anything, Ryan."

"Oh, so you're doubting Drake?"

"No, not that. I mean it doesn't mean those planets were wiped out by a hostile force. They could have killed themselves off with war. Nobody knows what really happened. And we haven't heard anything since, and that was what, almost twenty-five years ago?"

"One thing we do know," said Ryan. "Those planets were destroyed by some type of weaponry. Our scientists and military experts all agreed. You can read it in the online archives yourself. You're right, though. We don't know if they did it to themselves with a planetary war or not. But do you really feel like taking that chance as we go deeper into space? Because I sure don't."

Amanda just stared at him blankly. "I still think there are better things we could be putting our energy into," she said.

"Suit yourself," he said, tired of trying to reason with her. "I just don't understand why you came to a military academy. I mean, it is called the United Earth *Defense* Fleet."

Just then, the green lights activated on the bridge. Amanda muttered something he couldn't hear. Then the buzzer went off, indicating that the simulation had started.

Ryan glanced over the brief again. Their virtual craft, the UEDF Nimitz, was a light-speed battleship, and they were patrolling the first three planets of Earth's solar system.

Just as he sat down in the middle of the bridge, Jill called out from communications.

"I'm picking up a distress call from the UEDF Hampton," she said. "Her location is fifty miles off the Mars orbital base. She's a medical transport. They're reporting they're under attack. Three ships have them surrounded and are demanding they hand over their medical supplies or they'll destroy her."

"Go to full alert status." Ryan felt the adrenaline flowing through his body. He glanced at his helm officer, Nicole, another friend of Amanda's. "Nicole, set an intercept course, full sub-light speed." Turning to his good friend and weapons officer, Tanner Blackhart, he ordered, "Tanner, bring all weapons to standby status."

"Ryan," said Amanda, "you do know that Defense Fleet regulations say that we're to request backup and await orders before entering any hostile situation, right?"

Ryan knew this was coming. He had to stop himself from making a snide comment. She was technically correct, but sometimes going by the book wasn't the best course to take. In this case, he wasn't about to sit around and wait for backup when lives were in danger. He'd made that mistake once and swore he'd never make it again.

But then, as he glanced at Amanda standing there with her arms crossed, something made him reconsider. Call it temporary insanity. He decided to humor her and go with her decision, if only to prove a point. Besides, he knew if he didn't make the call, she'd continue to hound him. "You're right, Amanda," he said. "Jill, inform Headquarters of the situation. Have them advise us immediately."

"Will do," said Jill. Within seconds, she had the response. "Captain," she said, "the Fleet Admiral has informed us to wait for assistance. They have two ships en route. They'll be here in twenty-two minutes."

"And so, we wait," said Ryan.

Amanda looked surprised and genuinely touched that he'd actually listened to her. Ryan could even detect a slight smile, and he nodded in acknowledgment and smiled back.

After a few more seconds, Jill turned around. "The Hampton's captain reports that they have less than ten minutes before the attacking ships open fire. She's requesting immediate assistance."

Ryan felt the eyes of the entire bridge crew on him, especially Amanda's. He knew his orders were to wait, but sure wasn't going to sit there and let that ship and her crew be destroyed. Sometimes you had to make a tough decision, even if it's an unpopular one. To him, that was what distinguished a good officer from a great one. He made up his mind. "Nicole, move out. Full sub-light power. We're going in."

As expected, Amanda wasn't happy. "Ryan," she said, "if you do this, you know I'll have to log an official protest and report you for going against orders. I have no choice. Our orders are to wait for backup."

"Do what you have to," he said. "As for me, I'm gonna do what I have to and save that ship."

"It's not just about you, Ryan. Your decision affects us all. I'm sorry, but I have to note the record. You're going to get us all killed."

"Trust me for once." He couldn't worry about official records right now. He knew in his gut this was the right thing to do.

Within minutes, they had arrived at the location of the ship in distress. She was surrounded by three large unknown vessels. Ryan looked to Jill. "Open a channel to those ships. Tell them to back off or we'll open fire." He had no illusions about their chances. One against three is never good odds, but he was hoping he could hold them off long enough for the reinforcements to arrive.

Tanner called out, "They're turning toward us and increasing speed. Sensors show they're powering their weapons."

"Open fire," ordered Ryan. "Prepare for evasive maneuvers."

The officers on the bridge sprang into action immediately. Tanner fired the forward torpedoes. "Tubes one through four away."

Amanda was at the sensor console when she called out, "We have multiple torpedoes coming at us. At twelve o'clock, three o'clock, and nine o'clock."

"Pull her up, Nicole. Full throttle," said Ryan. He could feel the shift in the internal gravity as the ship pulled straight up. Then the ship rocked and shook. Sparks flew from some of the stations as damage reports started coming in. He couldn't believe how realistic the simulation was.

"Ry," said Paul, the ship's engineer and Ryan's other good friend. "We've lost port side thrusters and the outer hull is damaged. Power is down to sixty percent."

"Sensors are showing we got one of their ships," said Amanda. "The other two are turning about for another run at us."

Ryan knew they were in trouble. "How long before the reinforcements get here?" he asked Amanda. "Hey—"

She didn't get the opportunity to reply. The Nimitz rocked again and smoke filled the bridge. Then suddenly, the red lights came on and the simulation ended. Ryan stood up and was about to ask why, but his question was answered for him. Admiral Williamson was entering the bridge.

"The simulation is over," said the admiral. "I've just received a message from Fleet Headquarters that we're to put the academy on a level two lockdown. This is real, folks. Not a drill." Looking at Ryan, he shook his head. "Cadet Thompson. In my office. The rest of you are dismissed."

Ryan knew he was in a heap of trouble. He also knew that a

level two lockdown meant that the deep space outpost on Pluto must have detected a possible threat to Earth—something large and incoming. The admiral didn't say whether it was an asteroid or an alien presence, but with a lockdown on such short notice, he was willing to bet anything it was probably the latter. He thought back to those two devastated planets. Despite what he told Amanda, he didn't really expect to see any repercussions of that in his lifetime. As he looked over at her leaving the simulation area, he was half tempted to ask her how her theory about wasting time with battle simulations was looking right about now. But he didn't. Instead he just gazed at her, studying the look of concern on her face—the same concern he now felt.

Chapter 2

A Matter Of Discipline

Ryan made his way to Admiral Williamson's office. His mind was racing. The only other time there had been a level two alert was when an asteroid had been heading toward Earth a few years back. Fortunately the UEDF was able to divert it off course. But with that one, there'd been plenty of warning, with escalating levels of alerts for nearly a year. This one seemed to have come out of thin air. Whatever it was, he'd find out soon enough.

Of course there was also the little issue of his choice to break the rules during the simulation. But that was a decision he was going to stand firmly by. The problem with the military was that you weren't supposed to think for yourself. They expected you to blindly follow orders. If that was the case, why didn't they just build a bunch of drone warriors and command them remotely?

Arriving at the admiral's office, he approached the assistant's desk. "Cadet Ryan Thompson reporting," he said to the familiar face. "I'm here to see the admiral."

Looking up from her desk, Lieutenant Andrea Rhimes smiled. "Ryan, it's been almost two weeks since you've been here. I guessed twelve days in the pool we held, so I was right on target." She grinned as she hit the intercom. "Cadet Thompson is here to see you, Admiral." She glanced up at Ryan again. "At this rate," she said, "I'll be rich."

Ryan smiled at her. "Glad to oblige, though I do think should be entitled to half your winnings, shouldn't I?"

Admiral Williamson's voice bellowed over the speaker, "Send him in, Lieutenant."

"Yes, sir. You heard the admiral, Mr. Thompson." She saluted in jest.

Saluting her back, Ryan couldn't help smiling. "As you wish, Lieutenant!" Andrea Rhimes always managed to cheer him up. He wondered how she stayed so upbeat day in and day out. Cautiously, he stepped into Admiral Williamson's office and snapped to attention. "Cadet Ryan Thompson, sir!"

"Cut the crap, Ryan. It's just the two of us in here." The admiral stood up, walked around his desk, and started to pace. Ryan knew this wasn't a good sign. After all, this wasn't the first time the admiral had reamed him out, and it probably wouldn't be the last.

"Do you know how hard it is to get a spot in this academy? Only seven hundred and fifty students a year get into this place. What the hell is wrong with you, Thompson?"

Ryan started to open his mouth, but the admiral held up his hand.

"Can it, Ryan. I've heard it all before. I'd wise up if I were you. One of these days your attitude is going to get you killed. Not to mention your shipmates. What in God's name were you thinking during that battle simulation? You ignored procedure, took your cruiser into battle against unbeatable odds, and got almost half your crew injured or killed."

"Sir. If you w—"

"Stow it, Thompson! That was a hypothetical question. I'm not done yet."

"Begging the admi—" Seeing the look on the admiral's face, Ryan figured he'd better shut up.

Williamson looked surprised. "Is that a hint of self-restraint I see or do my eyes deceive me? We might just make you a soldier yet." Pausing for a moment, the admiral took a deep breath and returned to his desk. "Sit down, Thompson. Listen . . ." His voice grew softer, almost fatherly, as he continued. "Ryan, I've been watching your progress over the past three years. Hell, your father is my best friend. You're as close to being family as it gets, but damn it, Ryan, you have to follow regulations. I'm no longer just a family friend. I'm your senior officer, and I can't protect you when you screw up. What the hell were you thinking?"

Ryan paused.

"That's a real question this time," said Williamson.

Realizing that the admiral knew him as well as anybody, Ryan decided to go with his gut. "Admiral, we have a duty to protect the citizens of Earth. It's our sworn oath to defend our people even in the face of death. You know me, sir. I'm not the type to sit on my butt and wait for the cavalry to show up. I made that mistake once, sir." He paused a moment to collect himself. "I won't make it again."

The admiral's demeanor softened even more, and Ryan knew why. "Listen, Ryan," said Williamson. "We've been over this. What happened to your mother wasn't your fault. You did what the authorities told you to do. You've got to let it go. For your sake and for your career."

Williamson was right. It wasn't his fault. Not exactly. But still, if he'd done what he wanted to, he might have been able to save her. But now, all he could do was avoid making the same mistakes again, which is why he chose to put human lives ahead of blindly following orders. Obviously, Williamson didn't want to hear it anymore, so what was the use trying to explain himself?

Gathering his thoughts, Ryan said, "Is there anything else, sir?"

The admiral paused for a moment. Ryan was waiting for the other shoe to drop.

"Damn right there's more. We're in a level two situation now, son. You do know what that means."

"Do we know what it is yet?"

"That's a negative, but according to our outpost on Pluto, it's something we haven't seen before. I'll leave it at that."

"Aliens, sir?"

"Something we haven't seen before. I think that's what I said."

"I suppose we'll find out soon enough, sir."

"Thompson, we're about to enter the big leagues fast. And in the context of this fun little situation we find ourselves in, it'll help you to remember that this is the military, son. When you command a ship, it says United Earth Defense Fleet on it, not Ryan Thompson's ship of fools. There's a reason we have a chain of command. For Christ's sake, Ryan, you're the son of the Fleet Admiral, and not only that, but the best goddamned one who ever lived. One day soon, maybe sooner than you think, you're going to be out there for real. All our lives will depend on everyone following orders. Am I being clear?"

Ryan tensed at the mention of his father. It took everything he had to keep from saying something he'd regret. Clenching his teeth he responded. "Yes, sir."

Williamson continued. "Good. Now I guess you're wondering why I put you two together."

"The thought crossed my mind."

"Good. Well, keep thinking about that."

"I will sir. Anything else?"

"Yes, one last bit of advice. Ryan, your dad knows better than anyone when to take chances. But he also knows the importance of regulations. He knows how to look at the bigger picture. I want that same thing from you, and I know you can do it."

"I'll do my best to make you proud, sir." He hesitated, then decided to go for it. "I do have a question, though."

"Shoot."

"You were talking about regulations, sir. Seeing how Cadet Williamson is your daughter, should the competition end in a tie, regulations say that the commanding officer makes the final decision. Are you planning to recuse yourself if that happens . . . sir?"

Williamson stared at him.

"Are you implying that my decision would be skewed because my daughter is your opponent? Is that what I am hearing?"

"It's just that—"

The admiral leaned closer to him. "If I were you, son, I'd be more concerned about Cadet Williamson. From what I saw today, she wasn't too thrilled with your actions during the simulation. And you know what she's like when she's pissed off. If you want something to worry about, I'd be worried about her kicking your butt. That's all, Thompson. Dismissed!"

Ryan saluted. "Yes sir!" He started to walk out, but he couldn't resist turning around. "Sir, with all due respect, I think I made the right choice today. And, honestly, given the same information, I'd make the same one tomorrow. I know I'm right for this role . . . sir."

"The best cadet will win, Thompson. You can take that to the bank. And if you keep making choices like that, there won't be a tomorrow. Now get out of here before I throw you in the brig."

"Sir, yes sir!" Ryan tried to suppress a laugh. As he turned to leave, out of the corner of his eye he noticed the admiral shaking his head.

Making his way up the corridor, Ryan began to contemplate the admiral's words about the lockdown. What was that he said?

Something we haven't seen before.

Of course, the admiral didn't seem to be *that* concerned, at least not in a panic. He almost seemed more concerned about his actions during about the simulation. Then again, the admiral always did play things close to the vest, and after all, it had been a level two alert. Other than that planet-threatening asteroid, the only alerts he knew of had been level three or four. Someone or something was out there and heading towards Earth. Either that, or this was going to be one helluva drill.

Chapter 3

Cadet Training Facility, Finals Week

Amanda sat at the table eating lunch and looking at her notes for next week's finals. She was having a hard time concentrating and was still thinking about how Ryan had ignored her input during the battle simulation. It was like she was invisible, like he thought she was in over her head or something. And maybe she was, but as far as she was concerned, her option was the safer one and the correct one in that situation. His would have gotten them all killed.

As if all that wasn't enough, now there was this level two alert. Ever since she was a little kid watching movies about aliens that abduct humans and destroy entire planets, the thought of actually meeting an alien species had unnerved her. Maybe it was fear of the unknown. It sure hadn't stopped her from wanting to enter the fleet, though. The exploration and the sheer beauty of space, the amazing scientific discoveries, and the possibility of understanding more about our universe were absolutely captivating to her. Most of all she loved building things, so, all in all, the UEDF was the perfect place for her. If only her father hadn't given her a hard time when she said she wanted to be an engineer. Not enough advancement opportunities, he said. At least with officer training, there'd be a broad array of career options. The fact is, he never believed in her abilities. She used to experiment with spare parts at home and he'd call it a waste of time.

Her daydreaming was cut short when Jill came up and sat next to her.

"So what do you think about this lockdown?" said Jill, peeling a clementine.

"That smells good. I don't know what to think, but we better find out soon. My mind is almost too full to worry."

"Oh my God, are you still obsessing over that simulation?"

"That and everything else," said Amanda.

"Don't worry. I'm sure your dad laid into him. Were you surprised? I mean, we all know he's a cowboy. What surprises me is that you two ever dated."

"He was different then. We were as close as could be. Then when his mom was killed, he just turned cold on me. I gave him some space but he just drifted away. Now it's like he hates me."

"He doesn't hate you, Mandy. Guys just change."

"No like that. Not overnight. I understand he was sad, but what did I ever do to him?"

"Maybe he associates you with his mom. You should go for Paul anyway. He has black hair and blue eyes. He's an engineer. He's quiet, which is cool."

"Why don't *you* go for him then?"

"He's not my type. You know I go for the crazy ones. Plus I have a boyfriend. At least I think I do."

Just then, Amanda's attention was diverted to the other side of the cafeteria, where Ryan entered the room with Paul and Tanner at his side.

Jill smacked her on the arm. "Better decide fast."

Amanda could feel her face turning red. "Hey, you're supposed to be helping me. Do you have any idea how hard I've been training? Between the gym and the library, I've barely had time to sleep. And now we have this stupid lockdown to worry about."

They were interrupted when the third part of their trio, Nicole Gordon, made her way to the table. Nicole appeared to follow Amanda's eyes as she spotted Ryan and his friends. "So we're all guy watching today?" said Nicole. "I guess it beats worrying about lockdowns and training. I'll call them over."

Nicole waived her arm in the air and Amanda grabbed it. "Nicole, wait. Don't . . ."

It was too late. The guys spotted Nicole and began heading toward their table.

"You did it now," said Jill.

"Ryan," said Jill as they approached, "don't you think you owe Amanda an apology for getting us all killed?"

"Jill, forget it," said Amanda. "It's over."

"It wasn't over a few minutes ago," said Jill.

Amanda cringed and just wanted to hide under the table.

"I didn't get you guys killed," said Ryan. "We still had a chance."

"Yeah," said Tanner, "we didn't bring out the big guns yet."

"What do you think," Nicole said to Paul. "Do you think we should have waited for reinforcements?"

"I'm not sure," said Paul. "I'm an engineer, I just build the stuff."

"Guys, can we drop it?" said Amanda. "I mean this lockdown is a bigger issue right now, don't you think?"

"Your dad said it's something we haven't seen before," said Ryan. "What do you think that means?"

She was almost surprised he even spoke to her. "He told me the same thing," she said. "It doesn't sound good."

"I'm voting for aliens," said Tanner. "That would be pretty cool, actually."

"Tanner, can you be serious for once?" said Nicole.

"I am. We don't know if it's bad, so why all the worrying? It could be a bunch of little dudes like ET. Or apes. Maybe all we need are bananas."

"How did you ever get in this academy?" said Jill.

"Weapons, baby. Weapons," said Tanner.

"Guys," said Ryan. "Seriously, we don't know what this is. But I'd bet anything it's not an asteroid. Sooner or later, they'll need to tell us, and we may need to be ready for anything."

"They won't involve us," said Tanner. "If anything they'll make us incommunicado. We'll go into mushroom mode."

"I think he's right," said Amanda. "Already we have a level two alert that nobody's telling us anything about. Don't you find that strange? A level two alert and then silence? Complete and total silence?"

They all stood there staring at one another, contemplating it for a few seconds. Then Amanda just about jumped out of her seat when the bosun's whistle sounded. An important announcement was coming.

Chapter 4

Strange Invaders

Admiral Benjamin "Flash" Thompson entered his office at the UEDF Headquarters. Though it was five years ago, it seemed like yesterday when, at 40 years old, he'd been the youngest person ever to reach the rank of Fleet Admiral. That was just one of the reasons he'd earned the nickname Flash, which, according to his buddy Frank, was inspired by the name of a superstar jock in the Spider-Man comics. Ironically, he never read comics. He didn't have time, even as a teen. He couldn't help his success. It just seemed like everything he did was at full speed. It was the only way he knew how to work. And of course he always finished ahead of everyone else. Some people said he was lucky, but he always told them it was funny how the harder he worked, the luckier he got.

As he sat down in his chair, he looked at the picture on his desk. It was the last picture taken with his wife and sons before she was killed. If there were only one day he could change, it would have been the fateful day he chose to tend to work matters over family—the day he should have taken Ryan to the academy.

He started looking through the daily reports. It appeared that this was just another routine day, when his communication system started beeping. "Command Headquarters, Thompson speaking," he answered.

The young officer on the viewer was fidgeting and seemed a bit anxious. "Ensign Cooper here, sir."

"I know who it is, Ensign. Your name comes through on the feed. I'm assuming you have a message for me."

"I . . . I just received a level one contact from our deep space outpost on Pluto, sir."

Thompson had to be sure he had heard right. "Are you sure it was a level one contact?" This would have meant that they had a confirmed visual of an incoming extraterrestrial presence.

"Yes, sir," replied Cooper. "When we issued the level two alert, we only had a sensor reading. They were too far out to get any visuals. But we've got them now, sir, and it's plain as day. I'm going to send you the actual transmission from Lieutenant Haywood as well as the video feed he sent me. Coming your way now, sir."

As the video feed came across his screen, Thompson stood up. The hairs on the back of his neck tingled as the image of a fleet of unknown ships appeared. They were much sleeker than Earth's ships, and they appeared to be longer. Their design was obviously alien. "Ensign Cooper, keep this to yourself. Do you understand me? This is a level one protocol."

The ensign nodded. "Any other orders, Admiral?"

"Yes. Contact Lieutenant Haywood and tell him to rig his base for silent running. I do not want his position compromised. Get that to him immediately."

"Understood, Admiral. I'll contact him now. Cooper out."

Twenty-seven years in the fleet and nothing had ever come close to this. Sure there were the two planets they had found during the first years of obtaining light speed. They were Earth-like planets that had been devastated by obvious signs of an attack and were now barren. It was unknown whether the devastation had been caused by the inhabitants or by an alien attack. The political leaders back on Earth had been divided on the question of adding defense capabilities to the Earth Space Fleet. Debates had flown back and forth as they tried to determine whether or not to turn the deep space exploration units into a military branch. Deciding to err on the side of caution and create more jobs for the civilian population, the leaders of the world had finally agreed to start the United Earth Defense Fleet and arm all deep space ships, with the caveat that their primary purpose would still be exploration.

Now in his fifth year as commander of the UEDF, Thompson found himself in a position that no military officer had had to deal with since the world had barely averted World War III in 2090. His mind was racing with all the procedures that had to be set in motion. "First things first," he said to himself. He pressed the intercom that connected him to his assistant. "Ensign Morgan, get me the president of the Global Council. Tell him we're upgrading from a code two alert to a code one level one emergency."

Morgan's reply was immediate. "Yes, sir," she said. "Contacting him now. I'll put him through as soon as I reach him."

"Thank you," he said. While he waited, he replayed the video of the unknown ships. He wondered who or what was inside them. What did they want? His thoughts were interrupted by his assistant.

"Admiral, I have President Hawking on a secure video feed. I'm putting him through to you now."

President Hawking had recently been elected. The contest had been heated, and he had narrowly defeated his opponent, Neville Ashcroft. Many on the planet wanted to scale down the military. Luckily for Thompson, Hawking understood the need for defense.

"Mr. President, I'm sorry to bother you, but we have a situation."

"What's the issue?" said Hawking.

"We have a code one level one situation. I need your permission to prepare the fleet for a full response."

There was a brief moment of silence on the other end. "Admiral, are you absolutely sure? Do you have visual confirmation?"

"Yes, Mr. President. Forwarding it to you as we speak. I think we need a meeting with the Defense Council immediately. I do not want to waste any time. At their current speed, we estimate these ships will be here in less than two weeks. The best course of action would be to send the fleet to intercept them."

The president seemed to be mulling over this information. "Do we have any idea of their intentions? Has any attempt been made to contact them?"

"Not yet, sir. We wouldn't want to alert them until we can ascertain their motives. I'd rather discuss all of this with you in person before we meet with the defense ministers and the Global Committee. If you could call a meeting for 2200 hours, that will give everyone twelve hours to get to the conference room at the Pentagon. Let's meet an hour ahead of time."

"I'll make it happen, Admiral. I'll see you at 2100 hours."

"Understood, sir." The communication ended. Thompson took one last look at the picture of his wife and sons. Pressing a link on his holograph viewer, he pulled up a file he prayed would not have to be implemented. The top secret file opened, and the heading *PLANETARY DEFENSIVE MEASURES* jumped off the image at him like a bad dream. He deactivated the viewer and started to make preparations for the upcoming meeting. No doubt, it was going to be a long and trying day.

Chapter 5

A Momentous Decision

Admiral Thompson entered the vast chamber used for official meetings and took his seat. It appeared that all parties were in attendance. The secretary of the Global Committee stood up and called the president to the podium.

"Ladies and gentlemen of the committee," said Hawking. "We have called this emergency meeting due to an unknown deep space contact. Without further delay, I am asking the head of our Defense Fleet to speak."

Thompson stood up and made his way to the podium. There was an obvious air of tension in the audience, which included the six defense ministers, one from each participating continent, along with other constituents, including deputy assistants and the vice president. The Global Committee had been formed in the year 2100, following the global nuclear crisis of '90.

Once everyone quieted down, he surveyed the crowd and started speaking. "Ladies and gentlemen. As many of you know, we have a deep space outpost at the far edge of our solar system. The long-range scanning base is in orbit above Pluto, with a small sub-surface base on the planet as well. At 0800 hours today, we received a call from one of the officers on watch. If you will look at the screen above me, you will see what our scanners picked up."

A gasp emerged from the defense ministers as they watched the screen. Questions started to come in rapid-fire fashion. "Who are they?" said one man.

"Are they headed our way?" said another.

"Do we know what their intentions are?" said a woman at the far end of the room.

The admiral held up his hands. "Please. I need all of you to listen. We do not have any answers as of this time. They are not yet in communication range. Even if and when they are, we do not know if we can communicate with them."

Another attendee shouted out, a gruff sort of man Thompson had seen somewhere before, maybe at a conference. "So, what do you know?" he said.

Thompson was grim. "We know nothing. What I'm proposing to do is send the majority of the fleet to meet them before they get here. At their current speed, they'll be in our solar system in ten days. It is imperative that we ascertain their intent and do so before they reach Earth. Now, I'm asking for a vote. By the laws of the committee, we must have a majority in favor for any action to be taken. I've spoken with the president, and he agrees that this is the best course of action. Can I see a show of hands? Who's in favor of sending a greeting party?"

The minister from Europe, a Frenchman, interjected, "Wait a moment. I call for a discussion."

Thompson wasn't surprised. There were always a few politicians who resisted military confrontation, more often than not, the Europeans. Defense Minister Legrande was one of them.

Well, he figured, he might as well get this over with. "The chair recognizes Minister Legrande," said Thompson. "State your point."

Standing, the minister paused and looked at each of the members of the council. "My esteemed colleagues, it is my position that we are moving too fast. Who is to say if these ships are headed for Earth? They could be passing through our system. Perhaps they are headed elsewhere. If we confront them, we could be causing the very attack that we are fearing." The room filled with the murmuring of the defense secretaries and their deputies.

The next person to request the floor was Vice President Curtis Roberts. Thompson shot a quick glance at President Hawking. The president returned the look with a slight nod. Thompson knew the only way Hawking had been able to win the election was to ally himself with a candidate who was the opposite of him. Roberts was just that. "You have the floor, Mr. Vice President," said Thompson.

The vice president echoed the sentiment of Minister Legrande. In fact, he went one step further, indicating that sending an unmanned ship would be the best way to attempt contact.

There were two other ministers who voiced their concerns as well, but the majority was leaning toward Admiral Thompson's point of view.

After forty-five minutes of debate, Admiral Thompson decided to make another brief statement. "If one ship was headed our way, I'd concur with Minister Legrande. But with fifty ships coming toward us? I'm concerned. Let's not forget the two devastated planets we found. I'd rather be prepared for the worst case scenario. Are there any others who wish to speak?"

Seeing that the rest of the ministers remained seated, he continued, "No one? Then at this time I call for a vote."

In the event of a tie, the president would decide. Each member had mobile devices to vote at their seats. Within seconds, all the votes had been submitted. The secretary of the committee looked at the vote and gave the results to the admiral.

"By a vote of nine ayes, five nays, and one abstention, it is the decree of the committee to intercept the oncoming ships," said Thompson. "I will take my leave and return to Headquarters to prepare the fleet for departure. If I may make another suggestion, Mr. President?"

The president nodded. "By all means, Admiral."

"The fleet systems are already on level one alert. I would do the same for all of Earth's land forces as well as the planetary laser cannons and missiles, sir."

"Understood, Admiral. I will see to it. And Admiral?"

"Yes, Mr. President."

"God speed and a safe return."

"Thank you, Mr. President." Thompson left and made his way back to Command Headquarters. It was time to scramble the fleet.

Chapter 6

Recall

Ryan was counting down the days before the final competition for the Golden Cadet Award. Even with the base on lockdown, the academy was still running its normal routine, with one exception. Nobody was allowed to approach the planet, and nobody was allowed to leave. Other than that, it was business as usual. Of course, there was an air of trepidation throughout the base.

Ryan's focus for the moment was on doing well in the final competition. Winning the award guaranteed you a posting of your choice. You could pick an assignment on any ship or station within the fleet. And to top it off, instead of starting out as an ensign, the recipient of the award graduated with the rank of second lieutenant. In order to win, you had to have the highest grade point average, the best scores in all simulations, and high grades in hand-to-hand combat. He knew Amanda would be just as determined as he was. And she'd never let him forget it if she won. In many ways, he wished he were facing anyone but her in the competition. But he couldn't get distracted by any of that.

As he entered the gym, he was surprised to see Paul and Tanner.

"This has to be a dream," he said. "Both of you here at the gym? To what do I owe the pleasure?"

"We are here, Mr. Thompson," said Tanner, "to assist in your training, and to ensure you don't bring shame to our gender by letting Amanda beat you in the physical endurance part of the competition."

Ryan laughed. "I think I'll manage, but thanks for caring."

"I have to ask, Ry, how the hell did you let her get away? I mean, she's one hot redhead if I have to admit."

"Tanner, are you sure you really want to go there?" said Paul.

"Trust me," said Ryan. "You don't. She's beautiful, but, just . . . don't."

"There you go dodging the question again," said Tanner. "You should run for office."

"Changing the subject," said Paul, "when are we going to get the next announcement?"

"Yeah, what's up with that?" said Tanner. "We got an announcement saying, 'Stay tuned for an important announcement.' Who sends an announcement to announce an announcement?"

Ryan was about to comment when the loudspeaker blared with the sound of the bosun's whistle.

"Attention, all cadets. This is Admiral Williamson. All cadets and instructors are to report to the main auditorium at thirteen hundred hours. This is a must-attend event. No excuses for any reason. That is all."

"Okay," said Tanner. "So we had an announcement to announce the announcement to tell us to go to the auditorium for an announcement. When the hell are they going to tell us something?"

Looking at his watch, Ryan said, "I don't know, but that's an hour and thirty-five minutes from now. We better get showered and get moving."

Ryan left with Paul and Tanner to head to the showers. Then it was back to their quarters to dump their things.

An hour and a half later, they were sitting side by side in the main auditorium. The admiral walked onto the stage and stood in front of all 2,250 cadets, as well as the 250 academy personnel. From the look on his face, Ryan knew it wasn't good news. Their families had been close since Ryan was a kid. He remembered seeing that look on the admiral's face only two other times: once when he was seven years old and Amanda's grandmother had died, and the other time at his mother's funeral. He scanned the crowd, looking for Amanda. She was sitting with her friends a few rows ahead of him. The admiral started to speak.

"My fellow officers and cadets, I've just received news from Fleet Admiral Thompson that what appears to be a fleet of extraterrestrial vessels are in fact headed toward Earth. Approximately fifty of them.

We have a video from the long-range scanning outpost on Pluto that shows them quite clearly. If you'll watch the screen . . ." The admiral activated the view screen and played the video.

Ryan's eyes were glued to the large view screen. He was mesmerized by the video. Even though the images were crystal clear, his mind couldn't fully grasp what he was seeing. There were a few gasps and cries of disbelief from the other cadets. Everyone was on the edge of their seats, as the admiral shut off the video and continued.

"The president and the Global Committee have ordered the fleet to intercept and attempt to communicate with the inhabitants of these ships. Our orders are to recall all active officers to Earth immediately. For security reasons, everyone's orders have been sent to your quarters. The academy will be on a full level one alert. All cadets will start preparing our training ships for active combat readiness in the event they're needed by the fleet."

Everyone started whispering, and the admiral held up his hand.

"I am sure all of you have many questions. I do not have answers for you at this time. What I do have is the procedure that all of us will follow to the letter. As soon as I dismiss you, go to your rooms and check the transmissions I've sent you for your status and assignments. I will be remaining on the base to coordinate all efforts and keep you informed. That is all. Dismissed."

Ryan stood up and made his way toward the admiral. The possibility—even likelihood—that his family could be in grave danger hit him hard. While he had his issues with his father, he didn't want him to die, plus he had two older brothers serving in the fleet and was worried about them as well. He wasn't ready to talk to his father, but maybe there was another way. Knowing he'd need a secure transmission to send any kind of message, he approached the admiral. "Sir, is it possible I can contact my brothers? I haven't heard from them in weeks."

Williamson nodded. "Thompson, give me an hour and meet me in my office. Any message you send will take a few hours to get there and may miss them entirely. I assume you do know that."

Ryan looked at the admiral. "Yes, sir, I know. I just want to try, so I can wish them luck."

"Then I'll see you in an hour. Oh, and I almost forgot, there's a communication on your computer from your father."

Ryan's face dropped at the mention of his father. Just what he was hoping to avoid. He was watching the admiral walk away when he felt a hand on his shoulder. It was Amanda. From the look of worry on her face, he gathered she'd heard his conversation with her father.

"Your family," she said. "Don't worry, Ryan, they know how to take care of themselves."

He looked into her green eyes and knew she was sincere. But all he could think about was her father's reprimand the day before about following rules.

"I'll tell you one thing," he said. "If they do run into any trouble, you can bet I'm not sitting here on my hands doing nothing about it."

"Come on, Ryan," she said. "There's nothing we can do. Think about what you're saying. We have to keep our heads here."

He wanted to say something to her. Maybe even have a real conversation for once. But he couldn't let her in again. So instead, he just nodded.

He thought back to when she kept trying to pacify him after his mother's death. The more she tried to tell him everything was okay, the angrier he got. It wasn't okay. It would never be. And maybe inside, he was afraid of losing her too, or anyone else he loved. It just seemed like the safest thing to do was pull away completely, backwards as that seemed. But if getting past the memories of those times meant cutting Amanda out of his life, that's what had to be done. He regretted that decision since then, but now it was too late. Now, for the first time in Earth's history, the very real possibility of intergalactic war was looming. And he never felt so alone. The sad part was, Amanda probably felt the same.

He shook the morbid thoughts out of his head and decided it was time to get to his room and find out what his orders were. He made his way to his quarters, where Tanner and Paul were waiting. He walked silently to his desk and took his Slider out of his holster. What a wonder of technology. He was still baffled how it worked. The device was a combination computer, holograph movie viewer, and mobile communicator, and could shrink small enough to fit in your pocket or be worn on your wrist, or be stretched into almost any size, up to about a 19" monitor. He remembered reading about the old days when people had separate computers, televisions, and telephones. Now even children have their Sliders with them wherever they go. Through the wonders of satellite, he could even use it to peer down at his old house on Earth and see what his neighbors were up to.

He brought up the admiral's transmission and let the Slider read his face as he spoke the standard decryption code. Then the orders came up on the monitor. He stretched the Slider to a larger size so he could see it better. Reading his assignment, he was surprised that the admiral had put him in command of the crew that was to overhaul the UEDF Nimitz. And this was the real Nimitz this time, not just a simulation. "Well, I'll be damned," he said. "I guess the admiral does believe in me. It looks like I'm in command of the Nimitz."

Tanner smiled, "Guess who's your second officer as well as weapons officer."

On the other side of the room, Paul looked disappointed. "The Nimitz? Guys, she's been retired for ten years! Add fifteen years of service, and that makes her twenty-five years old. Other than the lame test flights we take on these old buckets, they've been neglected forever. Do you have any idea how hard it's going to be to get those engines running again? It's a good thing I'm going to be there to do it."

Tanner broke into laughter. "You mean you're on it too? Hey, Ry, it looks like we're all on the same ship!"

Ryan wasn't in a laughing mood, but gave a half-hearted smile. It appeared that Tanner had caught on. "Why the sour look, Ry? You have command of an amazingly cool ship, and we're all on it together. It'll be one big happy—"

"Happy?" said Ryan. "Take a look at who our first officer is."

"I saw," said Tanner. "Ry, you have to get over this Amanda thing. It'll work out. Besides, there are worse execs to look at."

"That's not the point," said Ryan. "There's more to it. There's tension between us as it is. And then when you consider we have completely opposite views on just about everything . . ."

"Dude," said Tanner, "I think he did it to try and make both of you better," said Tanner.

Paul put his hand up. "Maybe this isn't—"

"No, he has to hear this," said Tanner. "Ry, I'm not that stupid. Everyone knows you guys are the top two cadets. Both of you are great officer material. Maybe he thinks the two of you together are better than each of you apart. Making up for each other's weaknesses and all that."

"And she does look a hell of a lot better than you," said Paul, apparently trying to lighten the mood.

"Hey, I'll be the comic relief around here," said Tanner to Paul.

"You guys really don't get it," said Ryan. "I say left, she says right. And we have more baggage than a family of ten on vacation. How is that a good thing for any kind of mission?"

"Ry, it's just an overhaul job," said Tanner.

"Any . . . kind . . . of mission," repeated Ryan. "Anyway, I don't want to be part of a psychology test while our fearless admiral plays head games. It's not good for us, and it's not even good for Amanda. Do you think she wants to be second in command to me? I can answer that. No, she doesn't. I'm gonna set this straight once and for all."

"So what's your plan?" said Tanner.

"I'm going to have a little talk with the admiral," he said.

Tanner and Paul looked at each other. "Not your best idea, Ryan," said Tanner.

Ryan was done talking for now. He left them standing there with dumbfounded expressions and headed to the admiral's office.

Chapter 7
Executive Officer

Amanda was still in a state of shock. Thinking about the possibility of mankind meeting another species is one thing, but being faced with the reality of it was quite another. There were so many ways this could be headed. The entire academy was abuzz with the news. Some people were excited, others were scared, and some were in denial. Amanda found herself somewhere between curious and terrified.

She opened her jewelry box and dug through it, looking for an old amulet necklace she was pretty sure was still in there. It was a family heirloom passed down from her great-great-grandfather. Apparently, it was supposed to protect the wearer and her family in times of danger. At least that was what she'd been told when she was thirteen. She kept it purely as a good luck charm, but considering all that was going on, she figured it couldn't hurt to put it on.

As she was struggling with the catch, Jill walked into the room and was staring at the necklace with her mouth open.

"What on earth is that you're wearing?" she said. "It's hideous."

"I'm not wearing it as a fashion statement. It's a good luck charm, which I figure we can use some of."

"Well it better be good for something," said Jill. "Where did you find it? Dracula's castle?"

"Close. My dad's side of the family has owned it for a zillion generations. Well, more like two centuries. My mom gave it to me as a gift when I turned thirteen."

"I hope you got a TV with it, too. I mean, that *is* kind of cool though. The only thing my family passed down was neurotic anxiety."

Amanda laughed while Jill studied the face of the amulet closer.

"It's unique, I'll give it that," said Jill. "Is it gold?"

"Would you believe one hundred percent pure platinum?"

"Okay, now I love it."

"Seriously, it is. My great-great-grandfather told the family it was from ancient times, like thousands of years ago. He said it belonged to the lost tribe, whoever they were."

"Please tell me that you don't really believe that," said Jill. "Plus, how can there be *the* lost tribe? There's probably thousands of lost tribes. And second, what were they doing with platinum necklaces?"

"Considering all that's going on," said Amanda, "I'll believe anything."

Jill took the amulet in her hands and looked down at it. "There's some kind of weird crest. And the gemstones around it are in a totally haphazard pattern. It looks like it was designed by Salvador Dali. Either that or a blind jeweler."

"I know," said Amanda. "I tried looking the crest up in all the history and anthropology programs and couldn't find anything. But if it's said to bring good luck, I'm all for wearing it."

"Suit yourself," said Jill. "I doubt it'll do anything against any alien invaders. Do you think they'll stop and say, 'Oh wait! They have the all-powerful necklace! Let's turn back!'? I think you may have watched too many science fiction movies, girl, seriously."

Amanda laughed. "Well it's no worse than anything else we have to throw at them."

"You got me there," said Jill. "Anyway, I came here to see what ship you're on. I'm on the Nimitz. So is Nicole. Please tell me you're commanding that ship."

Amanda was so sidetracked thinking about the aliens that she almost forgot she hadn't checked her orders yet.

"Let's find out," she said. She brought up the file on her Slider, and her mouth dropped. "Are you kidding me? This has got to be a mistake. There's no way I'm going to do this."

Jill looked at her. "What's wrong? You're not on our ship?"

Amanda closed up her Slider. "Yes, I'm on the ship—as the executive officer. Ryan's the captain. I can't do this."

"Relax," said Jill. "It'll all work out."

"I can't do this again, Jill. Not only does he not want me there, but how am I supposed to compete with him while I'm serving as his assistant? This is my dad's doing. First he talks me into going for command when he knew I wanted to be an engineer. Then he does everything in his power to knock me down."

"Mandy, I'm sure it's not like that."

"It's exactly like that, and I'm going to call him on it."

She marched out the door, leaving Jill standing there.

As Amanda stormed into the entrance area to her father's office, Lieutenant Rhimes saw the look on her face and didn't even attempt to stop her. Hitting the intercom, she called out, "Admiral, red alert. Your daughter is on her way in, and considering the look on her face, I'd say she's seen her orders, sir."

Amanda entered her father's office, immediately came around to the side of his desk and threw her Slider with his orders down in front of him. "Seriously? Is this some type of sick joke? Because if it is, I'm not getting the punch line. I've worked hard to get where I am. All of you tried to talk me out of joining the fleet because I was the only girl in the family! Mom, you, and both my brothers. Then, after I *finally* signed up for the academy, I decided I wanted to be an engineer. But *no,* you said. Take command training. At least in command training you have room to advance. Your words, Father, not mine. Then, after I've worked my butt off to prove I'm just as good—no, in fact *better* than either of my brothers—you do this to me?"

She paused to take a breath and then noticed her father was sitting there calmly, as if he were listening to a concerto. Finally, he glanced up at her.

"Are you done? Feeling better now? Did you get it all out of your system?"

"No," she said. "I want answers. I'm one of the top two cadets in the class and Ryan gets his own command and I don't? And I'm under him?"

"You're both where I need you to be. Listen, Amanda. I may be your father, but I'm also your commanding officer, and you're crossing a line you don't want to cross."

The admiral stood up and moved closer to her just as the intercom beeped. "You'll never guess who just walked into here looking to talk to you, Admiral," said Lieutenant Rhimes. "It's the other half of your master plan."

"Well, isn't this a glorious day of surprises," he said. "Send him in."

Amanda couldn't believe her father was going to try to explain this with the both of them the room.

Ryan walked in and his mouth dropped. He obviously wasn't expecting her to be there either.

"Well, now," said her father. "It's so nice of the two of you to come here to see me today. I believe you may disagree with your posting, am I right?"

Amanda knew better and said nothing.

Ryan, just as she suspected he would, spoke out. "Sir. I must pro—"

The admiral held up his hand. "Not now, Thompson. Obviously you're gravely misinformed. This isn't a democracy. This is the military. You obey your orders or wash out. That goes for the both of you. And it case I'm not being clear enough, let me spell it out. Neither of you have to like each other. In fact, you can despise one another on your personal time. But I have you together for a reason, and that reason need only be known to me."

He paused briefly and slowly looked at each of them. "Listen, you two are the best damn cadets we have. Yes, you're about as different as a cat's tooth and a rat's ass, but you're both well trained, and both of you scored through the roof in your combined training exercises. But the fact is, you're stronger together than you are apart."

"That's a matter of opinion, sir," said Ryan.

"Damn right, Thompson. And lest we forget, my opinion is the only one that counts on this base. I'd suggest that you come to terms with that."

"Yes, sir," said Ryan. Amanda wasn't quite ready to acquiesce so easily. She still felt double-crossed.

"And I suppose you think it's wise to put your 'two best cadets'"—she made quotation marks with her hands—"on the same ship? I mean what if we have to engage in an emergency mission?"

"As if they'd let us go anywhere," said Ryan. "On the Nimitz, no less."

"In case you two have failed to notice," said Williamson, "humanity is about to either make a first contact with a benevolent alien race, or enter an intergalactic war with monsters out to kill us. Now your job is to get those ships ready. Are you in or out? Because I sure as hell can't risk anyone letting one-upmanship or personal feelings get in the way of our mission in a crisis situation. And that goes for my best friend's son . . . and my daughter. So, what will it be?"

Amanda glared first at Ryan, then at her father. She still felt let down, but she wasn't about to let her feelings toward either of them get in the way. She swallowed and thrust her shoulders back.

"I'm in," she said. Then she looked at Ryan to see what he would do.

Ryan stared directly at the admiral. "I'm in, sir. May I be dismissed, sir?"

"Dismissed, Thompson. Get some rest. We all have a lot of work to do to get these ships into combat-ready shape."

Ryan turned to leave, then hesitated and turned to face Amanda. "Well, I'll see you at 0600 hours then," he said. He saluted the admiral and spun around to leave the room.

"Sure," she said, not looking at him. As Ryan left, she noticed her father smiling. If this was his idea of a joke, she wasn't getting the humor.

"May I be dismissed . . . *sir?*" she said.

"Absolutely," he replied.

She exited his office, making sure to slam the door.

Chapter 8

Mobilization

Fleet Admiral Thompson looked at the view from the monitor. It was a sight to behold. Fifty-five battleships from all of the major countries, flying in formation in deep space. With the earth as a backdrop, it almost resembled a work of art.

Earth Defense Fleet was running through their final checklists as they prepared to meet the alien fleet. The flagship was the UEDF Constitution, and Thompson was commanding her. She was the newest and largest ship in the fleet.

Sitting in the center of the bridge, Thompson looked around at his crew. All of them were immersed in their duties. They were highly experienced, a truly elite team, and most of them had been with him for years.

At the helm was Lieutenant Vinnie Romano. Romano had been Thompson's helmsman for the last five years.

His weapons officer, Lieutenant Carson Diego, had come on board along with Romano. The two were close friends.

The chief engineer, Captain Reggie Fowler, a Brit, had served with Thompson on and off over the last twenty years. He was one of the original members of the light-speed engine design team.

Another longtime friend and Englishman, Niles Thames, was Thompson's executive officer. Thames had gone to the academy with Thompson and had served alongside him for nearly three decades.

Last was the newest member of the bridge crew, Thompson's communications officer, Lieutenant Kyra Barnes. With her long dark hair and bronze skin, and standing around six feet tall, she looked like she could have been an Amazon warrior.

It was time to address the fleet.

"Lieutenant Barnes, open communications, fleet-wide," said the admiral.

Barnes's long bony hands flew across her console. "Fleet-wide communications open, Admiral."

Thompson leaned back in his chair. "I want to take a minute to personally thank each and every one of you for your service. Today we embark on a journey like never before. What happens over the course of the next few days will be a new experience for all of us. Hopefully, we'll engage in peaceful and groundbreaking communication with a new species. But, if this is an attack on our home and our families, then we must not fail. I am proud to lead this fleet, and I know there's not a crew in the world I'd rather be heading into the great unknown with."

He turned to Romano. "Full thrusters ahead. Take the lead."

Facing Barnes, he ordered, "Have all ships set up in a wing formation. Let's move out. One-tenth sub-light speed. Once we clear the moon, have the fleet increase to one-quarter light speed."

"Understood, Admiral," said Barnes. "Sending message to the fleet now, sir."

The ship moved smoothly to the head of the fleet. Watching the rest of the ships on the video monitor, Thompson could see them falling into formation.

"Barnes, contact Headquarters. Have them inform the president we're en route."

"Sending message now, Admiral," said Barnes. "Receiving confirmation. Sir, all ships fully operational and in position."

"Very well, Miss Barnes."

Romano called out, "Admiral, we'll be coming up on the moon in twenty minutes."

"Thank you, Mr. Romano," replied Thompson. "Miss Barnes, direct the fleet to adjust speed to one-quarter sub-light. Have all ships engage on our mark. Inform them we will rendezvous at Sector 57. Once we get there, we'll wait for the unknown fleet to move into communication range."

"Aye, sir," said Barnes. "Sending the message now."

Looking over to the weapons station, Thompson said, "Diego, run full-scale diagnostics on all the weapons systems."

"Will do, Admiral. Starting full-scale diagnostics now."

Thompson sat back in his chair. His thoughts drifted to his son Ryan. It had been three years since their relationship had gone south. He wondered if he would ever have the chance to repair the rift between them.

As he resumed checking the data from the outpost on Pluto, he noticed the projected flight path of the oncoming fleet. Triangulating the position they were coming from, he saw that they would have passed the two devastated planets that had been discovered all those years ago. Now he was even more concerned that they might be about to meet the aliens responsible for that devastation.

Chapter 9
Personal Message

Ryan was sitting alone in his dorm room. Tanner and Paul were busy at the library going over the specs for the Nimitz. He was still annoyed about Williamson's decision, but he had much more important things to worry about—things like completely overhauling the Nimitz.

What bothered him even more was what was going to happen next. Or more precisely, what wasn't going to happen. Getting the ships back in battle condition was his objective, but what would the outcome be? He knew that if things didn't go well, they would send seasoned officers to get the ships. Or maybe the cadets would even fly the ships to the outpost on Pluto to meet up with the officers. But what if things went really badly? What if the UEDF was somehow defeated and then the aliens discovered the cadet location? How would he handle an actual battle with an unknown alien fleet? All these possibilities made Ryan feel like he was standing on the edge of a cliff. Well, he thought, whatever was going to happen, he'd know soon enough.

Just as he was getting ready to head over to the gym and work out, he received a priority message from Admiral Williamson. Trying to figure out who he'd pissed off this time, he answered the call. "Cadet Thompson reporting, Admiral. What can I do for you, sir?"

"Thompson, I told you yesterday about the message from your father. You still haven't opened it. As you know, he outranks all of us. It's for your eyes only. It will only play once, and then it will automatically erase. I . . . suggest you view it."

Ryan wasn't in the mood to listen to more lecturing, but he took a few deep breaths to remain calm, something his shrink had taught him after his mother's death.

"Listen, Ryan," said the admiral, no doubt sensing his hesitation, "I know you and your father haven't quite gotten along for the last few years. And I'm not here to tell you what to do in your personal life.

What I do know is that I would die for my children, and so would he. This isn't some damn drill, Ryan. This is the real thing. Life and death. It's not a good time for grudges, son. Anyway, my orders were for you to read this message. See to it that you do."

"Is that all, sir?" Ryan asked.

The admiral sighed on the other end of the call. "That's all, Thompson." The line disconnected.

Ryan sat there for a few minutes trying to prepare himself for the sound of his father's voice. His older brothers were both members of the fleet so he thought maybe he should listen to the message after all. Reluctantly, he opened it. It was a video of his father.

"Ryan, I know we only talk when it has to do with the fleet or your schooling at the academy. Maybe one day you'll forgive me and we can both move forward with our lives, maybe not. Regardless of that, the fleet is heading out on what could very well be a dangerous mission. I just wanted you to know that if something should happen to me, not a day goes by that I don't think of you and that I love you, son."

The video went dark and the program deleted itself. A million thoughts were floating in Ryan's head. Why now? Why was his dad trying to sound like a real father now? Where was he before? He thought of that horrible day and slammed his monitor shut so hard he was surprised the screen didn't break into pieces.

He needed to take a walk and get some fresh air. He had a ship to get ready and needed a clear head to make it happen.

Grabbing his jacket, he headed out the door and made his way to the one place where he felt at home and could be at peace: the observatory. He always found looking at the stars comforting. Gazing up into the heavens and talking to his mother was what he needed now to calm himself and find inner strength. After all, soon there would be no time for contemplation. The whole world would be different, because they would have met an advanced alien intelligence. And they'd have either learned from it, or been destroyed by it.

Chapter 10

Encounter

Admiral Thompson checked the time on the ship's chronometer. It had been two hours and fourteen minutes since the fleet had stopped. The waiting was grinding on the admiral's nerves. "Barnes, how much longer until they're in communications range?"

Barnes turned to face him. "Five minutes, sir."

"Contact the fleet. Have all ships bring engines back on line. Inform them to go to alert status one. Place all weapons on standby and activate all outer cameras."

"Aye, sir. Sending message fleet-wide."

Diego called out from the weapons console. "All forward torpedo bays are fully loaded. Missile launchers are on standby. Lasers are online and at optimum power."

"Very good, Mr. Diego."

Thames stepped beside Thompson and put a hand on his shoulder. "I sure hope whoever these guys are, they aren't heading for Earth. That many ships wouldn't be coming just to drop by and say hello."

"Damn right, Niles. Let's keep our fingers crossed and our weapons ready."

Thames looked down at his hand. Thompson forgot Thames had lost two of his fingers in a warehouse explosion. "Sorry," said Thompson. "Bad choice of words."

Thames smiled and crossed the fingers of his other hand. "Not to worry, sir. And let's hope Earth isn't their final destination."

Barnes piped up. "Admiral, the unknown fleet will be in communication range in thirty seconds."

Thompson looked at the monitor. "Begin transmitting standard greetings on all bandwidths using all known languages."

"Aye, sir." The lieutenant activated the standard broadcast system, which automatically began transmitting greetings. "Communication initiated," she said.

They watched and waited. Would these beings recognize any of the languages? Or would they suddenly sense a foreign presence and launch an attack?

After only a minute or so, Diego shouted, "Admiral, they appear to have stopped."

"It seems they have picked up our transmission, Admiral," said Thames.

"Yes, it does," said Thompson. "The question is, do they have any understanding of what we are transmitting?"

Almost as if in response to his question, Barnes shouted, "Admiral, we are receiving an incoming transmission."

"Put it on the speakers, Lieutenant."

The bridge went silent. This would be the first time mankind would hear the voice of another species.

At first there was nothing. Then there was a loud noise that sounded like a crowd at a football field. Apparently, a message was coming back in many languages simultaneously.

"Set the incoming channels to English only," said Thompson.

"On it, Admiral," said Barnes.

As soon as she made the switch, a message could clearly be heard.

"I repeat. This is Supreme Commander Granthaxe of Altarra," said the deep, blaring voice. "With whom is it I speak?"

"English?" said Thames. "They speak English?"

Thompson picked up the transmission mic. "This is Admiral Thompson of Earth," he said. "May I ex—"

"Earth!" The alien commander's voice dripped with venom. "If you think you can deter my forces, you are severely mistaken, Admiral Thompson. I will ask you once and only once. What did you do with our envoys?"

Thompson looked around at the crew. Everyone was shrugging their shoulders and looked as confused as he did.

"Forgive me, Commander Granthaxe," he said, speaking slowly and clearly. "I do not know what envoys you speak of. Perhaps you can give me more details."

"So. You take me for a fool, Admiral Thompson. Do you think we would travel all this distance to confront those who captured our envoys and believe you know nothing of this? We are not so easily deceived. I ask you again. Where are they? What did you do with them? For the sake of your species they had better be alive!"

Thompson glanced over at Thames and didn't have to say a word. It was clear. These beings *were* headed for Earth. He redirected his attention to the strange visitor as he picked up the mic again.

"I can assure you, Commander, I know nothing of your missing envoys. Maybe they never made it to Earth."

"Do not insult me, Admiral Thompson! We have proof that they not only made it to your world, they were attacked. Their ship was hit with some type of weapon that rendered their systems inoperative. They managed to survive a crash landing and spoke with those of your kind. Then they were taken prisoner. We have the audio of the entire encounter, that is, until your people confiscated our envoys' communication devices."

Thompson was pacing back and forth listening to what the alien commander was saying. The commander must have been mistaken. Maybe he could reason with him.

"Commander," said Thompson, "I have been a member of this fleet for over twenty-seven years. I can assure you that I have never heard of anyone outside our solar system contacting Earth, or for that matter landing there. In fact, throughout our history, there has never been any concrete proof of any other life forms, let alone yours, visiting Earth."

"Your kind thinks the universe exists to serve Earth," said Granthaxe. "I assure you it does not. The event I speak of happened in the days of the past. Our envoys traveled over thirty of your years to make that trip."

The past? How far back, Thompson wondered.

"Unless you are more specific with a time and place, Commander, it will be hard for us to track down any useful information. We don't even know if any of your envoys—if they did make it to Earth—are even alive on our planet. Or if any of our people that knew about it are still alive. Especially if this happened many years ago."

"Useless banter!" said Granthaxe. "Do you think me fooled? It is obvious that you are either lying, or were deceived by those who lead you. We are coming to find and reclaim our missing comrades, Admiral. In capturing our envoys, you have committed an act of war. One of ours who was on that ship was our future queen. If you cannot assist us, I'd advise you to stand clear. You have five of your minutes to do so, Admiral Thompson. There shall be no other warnings."

The transmission went dead.

Thompson couldn't imagine what all this was about, but he was going to find out one way or another. Could the commander have been right? He only hoped he could get some answers from the executive branch, or perhaps some of the more clandestine areas of the government. He looked to Lieutenant Barnes at the communications station.

"Barnes, send that entire conversation to Command Headquarters," he said. "Priority one, obviously."

"Yes, sir," said Barnes. "Sending now."

He made his way over to Thames. "Thoughts, Niles? Seems we're in new territory here."

"It's a hell of a lot of information to try and digest, that's for sure. Of course we know about all those UFO reports in the twentieth and early twenty-first centuries, and all the conspiracy speculation. But we don't even know what time frame this is from, or what country."

"Agreed. We have to get an investigation started on Earth. And we also need to notify the Global Committee. Should be interesting trying to get anyone to reveal classified information."

Thompson tried to put all of the facts together. Obviously the Altarran commander believed their government was holding his people prisoner. But why? If only he was able to provide a little more information. What language did the alleged capturers speak? What time frame was this? If the commander wanted his people so badly, he should be willing to cooperate.

"Barnes," he said. "Try to raise the commander again."

Suddenly the weapons officer, Diego, interrupted them. "Admiral, I'm picking up multiple signatures on radar. They're firing at us!"

"Evasive maneuvers," shouted Thompson. "Barnes, have all ships break formation. As soon as you send the order to the fleet, inform Headquarters we are under attack."

"Aye, sir," replied Barnes. "Sending now."

Thompson watched the video feed and nodded approval as all of the ships from his fleet managed to evade the incoming missiles. Either the opposing commander had underestimated the speed of Earth's fleet, or he was very crafty and this was a tactic to find out how fast and maneuverable they were. Either way, Thompson wasn't going to sit still and wait for the next move.

"Barnes! Have the fleet go to attack pattern three-V, as in Victor. Commence attack dead ahead. Speed one-half sub-light."

While Barnes was transmitting the order, Thompson shouted instructions to his helmsman. "Mr. Romano, take the lead."

"Aye, sir," replied Romano.

With cat-like speed, the UEDF Constitution bolted forward, flanked on either side by the Lexington and the Armstrong in a V-shaped formation. Thompson watched on the monitors as the remainder of the fleet broke into the same pattern. They closed in on the Altarran ships.

Thompson noticed Diego staring at his radar screen in disbelief. "Admiral, they're not breaking formation," said Diego. "They're still moving forward."

"Prepare to fire when we reach a distance of twenty thousand feet. Mr. Romano, as soon as we fire, break off the attack pattern. Barnes, inform the Lexington and the Armstrong to follow our lead."

"Yes, sir," replied all three officers.

Thompson watched intently as they continued to close in on the Altarran fleet. The alien vessels were much longer and the bows of their ships were bent forward. Odd, he thought, they looked like dragons without wings. They almost seemed defiant in their pattern. They didn't seem to care about being shot at as they slowly plodded forward.

"Don't you find it strange that they're not breaking formation?" he asked Thames.

"Honestly, I find it absolutely insane," Thames replied.

"We'll be at twenty thousand feet in twenty-five seconds, Admiral," said Diego. "I have a firing solution. Permission to fire, sir."

"Permission granted. Fire when you reach twenty thousand feet."

Turning to Romano, Thompson ordered, "Pull her up, maximum thrust immediately after we fire."

"Aye, sir," replied both officers.

"Firing full spreads, bays one through four," shouted Diego.

Thompson could feel the internal gravity straining as the Constitution pulled straight up. At the same time, he could see the Lexington and the Armstrong break to the port and starboard sides respectively.

"Time till impact," ordered Thompson.

Diego responded immediately. "All torpedoes tracking true. Impact in six, five, four, three, two . . ." Diego paused.

Thompson and the entire bridge crew were watching the main viewer. Then, a tremendous explosion filled the screen. A devastating assortment of weapons surrounded the alien fleet. It almost looked like a huge pyrotechnic show.

"Welcome to the Fourth of July," said Thompson. The rest of the crew cheered.

As the explosion dissipated, he couldn't believe the images on the main viewer. The alien fleet was intact.

"Diego, what the hell happened? Talk to me."

"All the torpedoes exploded prior to impact," said Diego. "I am reading no damage to the Altarran ships. They must have some type of energy field or shields protecting their hull, Admiral."

"Barnes, keep forwarding this information to Headquarters."

Barnes looked up from her communications station briefly. "Yes, sir," she said. "Along with the audio, I'm sending a live video feed as well."

"Sir!" Diego sounded concerned.

"What is it?" said Thompson.

"They're breaking formation. It appears they're moving toward the fleet at high speed. Sensors are detecting multiple weapons fire from all of their ships."

"Evasive maneuvers," ordered Thompson.

The ship banked hard to port as Romano tried to evade the missiles heading for them.

Barnes called out to the admiral, "Sir! I'm receiving reports of multiple hits on the fleet. At least twenty ships have reported being hit."

Thompson surveyed the bridge. He could see the concern on the crewmembers' faces. They needed to regroup and come up with another plan of attack. "Barnes, have the fleet break off the attack. Inform all ships to go to light speed and rendezvous at Mars orbital base."

"Aye, sir. Sending message to all ships."

"Mr. Romano," said Thompson. "Hard about. Set course Mars orbital station. Activate light speed."

The UEDF Constitution, along with thirty-four other ships of Earth's Defense Fleet, left Sector 57 and headed to Mars orbital base to regroup. Admiral Thompson sat back in his command chair searching for answers. He had just had his ass handed to him by an angry and aggressive alien fleet. They had fired everything they had at the Altarrans and hadn't even put a dent in them. It appeared that the Altarran ships were protected by some type of shielding they couldn't break through. It was becoming clear that the United Earth Defense Fleet, and with it the Earth, was in serious trouble.

Chapter 11

Earth Defense Fleet Academy, 0600

Ryan was on his way to the hangar where the UEDF Nimitz was housed. At his side were Tanner and Paul. It was only 0500, but they wanted to get an early start. He didn't expect the rest of the crew to be there for at least another hour.

As they turned the corner, he could see the entrance to the hangar. Ryan was surprised to see Amanda, Nicole, and Jill already waiting for them.

"Looks like the gang's all here," he said, turning to Paul and Tanner.

Tanner and Paul exchanged glances and kept walking. "This should be interesting," said Tanner.

They reached the secure door where the girls were waiting.

"Morning, Captain," said Nicole. "Your bridge crew awaits you."

Jill laughed. Amanda looked uncomfortable.

Ryan saluted them all in half jest and gave a slight smile.

He entered the combination into the keypad on the door and put his hand against the scanner. The door opened, and they all entered the hangar. The lights came on as the six cadets made their way up the ramp into the ship.

As soon as they entered the bridge of the Nimitz, Ryan looked around in awe. It was one thing being in a simulator version of the ship, but this was the real thing—the former flagship of the whole fleet, though it had seen better days. They were all gazing at their surroundings like they'd just entered a chocolate factory. A very old and abandoned chocolate factory. Ryan figured he may as well get everyone started. This was the first non-drill exercise he was leading, but he had to get used to it sooner or later.

"Paul," he said, "how about you and Amanda check out the engine room. Run diagnostics and see what needs to be done and what improvements can be made. Jill and Nicole, I guess it makes sense for you to check the communications systems as well as the helm and navigational computer. Tanner, you know your bit—weapons systems and ship's sensors. We only have a short amount of time to get this ship in combat-ready shape, so we better get started."

"And what are you going to do, fearless leader?" said Tanner.

Ryan laughed. "I'm going to get the duty list together for the other forty-four cadets on their way and get their assignments ready for them so they can hit the deck running. Does that meet with your approval?"

"Works for me, Ry—I mean, Captain."

Ryan took a long look around the bridge, his gaze stopping on Amanda. She seemed deep in thought, like her mind was elsewhere. He couldn't help but wonder where things had gone wrong with them, though he sort of knew. It had been so long that he'd almost forgotten the sequence of events. And once he'd shut her out and moved on, it was like the door had closed, never to be reopened. They were enemies without a cause, she on one side of the door and he on the other.

Realizing everyone was staring at him, he straightened himself out and got back to business. "Well, we all know our duties," he said. "Let's get to it."

They had all started to head their separate ways when Ryan decided he needed to set things straight once and for all. "Amanda," he said, "can I talk to you for a minute?"

Amanda looked a bit puzzled, but she waited as the rest of them headed off to their respective departments. She wasn't that much shorter than he was, but somehow she was looking up at him. His mind went blank, and he couldn't quite get the right words out.

After what seemed like a minute of awkward silence, he finally figured out what he should probably say. He was still trying to get the words out of his mouth when the shrill of the bosun's whistle came from the com station.

"This is Admiral Williamson to all cadets. I have just received a report from Fleet Headquarters. At 2300 hours last night, the Earth Defense Fleet, headed by Admiral Benjamin Thompson, was attacked by a race that calls themselves the Altarrans. The initial report is not encouraging. It appears that the fleet has confirmed that twelve of our ships have been destroyed and eight severely damaged."

Nicole let out a gasp from the communications station. "My sister—"

Williamson continued.

"I have no information yet as to which ships were destroyed or how many survivors there are. Our orders are to continue overhauling our ships, as we may be needed to pick up survivors. The fleet is regrouping at Mars to plan their next move. As of now, there are no plans for our ships to be used for battle. It is now looking like a total blackout for the academy. This does not mean that you are to stop what you're doing. We may need these ships for the very survival of our species. Stay focused. Keep your heads. I will have more information forthcoming. Williamson out."

There was dead silence on the bridge of the Nimitz. Ryan looked over at the com station. Amanda and Jill were trying to comfort Nicole. He knew he had to say something.

"Listen up, guys." He made sure to pause a moment until they all turned to look at him. "I know we all have family, either out there or about to be. All we can do is hope they stay safe. But for now we need to get these ships up and running because we may be the only ones that can rescue the survivors. What do you say we all get to our stations and get busy? We've got a bunch of work to do. And if we really want to help the fleet, then let's get moving and help win this thing."

They all agreed and grabbed their instruments. Nobody said a word, as one by one they headed to their stations. Ryan could see the look of fear in their eyes. He understood because he was just as scared, but he couldn't afford to show it. He walked over to Amanda.

"I guess we can talk later. For now, you better get down to engineering. I'm sure Paul is waiting for you. He's gonna need all the help you can give him."

She looked up at him but said nothing. He could see an expression of sadness and helplessness, and something else he hadn't seen in her in a long time, at least not when looking at him. Vulnerability. He stood there for a moment watching her walk away, then returned to his duties.

Chapter 12

Uedf Nimitz, Main Engineering

Amanda made her way down to the engineering section. Her mind was still reeling over the announcement she'd just heard. Her worst fears were coming true—hostile aliens. And powerful ones, apparently. Engineering appeared to be empty. As she entered the main engine room, she called out, "Paul? Are you here?"

"Over here," Paul said.

Following the sound of his voice, she saw a pair of legs protruding from under the solar coils. "Need a hand?" she said.

"Actually I could use two hands," he said. "Grab me a sonic wrench from my toolbox."

She opened the neatly organized toolbox and extracted the wrench. "Did you hear the announcement down here?"

Grasping the wrench in his first two fingers, Paul came out from underneath the coils. "I sure did. That's why I jumped right on these engines. It seems like we're gonna need to work a miracle, and it doesn't look like we have a whole lot of time to do it. I sure hope you came here to help me, because these engines are on life support."

"That's why I'm here," she said. "When you're done working on those coils, you need to check the light-speed accelerator."

"Oh," he said. "And you know this *because?*"

"I was the last one to command this ship on live training maneuvers."

"You're kidding me. The Nimitz?" Paul looked as if she'd just said she invented the ship.

"Yep. I have captained ships you know. I remember there was a miniscule hesitation when we jumped to light speed. I noted it on the ship's log. I'll bet you the accelerator hasn't been checked since then.

For training it's fine. But if this ship has to save lives or go into battle, that little delay can make a big difference. Like life and death big."

"Okay, well let's take a look at it," he said. He powered up the engineering console and started a diagnostic on the light-speed drive. The constantly changing status whizzed by on the display and ended with a one-line report that proved Amanda's point. "Damn, Amanda. I'm impressed. The delay in the accelerator was one thirtieth of a second. I can't believe you noticed it."

Amanda smiled. It was good to feel appreciated. She knew there was something she liked about Paul. "I've spent most of my life on ships," she said. "Plus, I originally considered taking engineering, but my dad insisted I focus on command instead."

Paul nodded. "Well he *is* an admiral. I guess he wants you to follow in his footsteps. But if it's any consolation, I think you'd be great at both."

She didn't know what came over her, but she lunged forward and hugged Paul, who looked completely uncomfortable. "That's for believing in me," she said.

"Oh I believe," said Paul, looking flustered.

Amanda figured now would be a good time to ask Paul a question that had been bothering her for years. "Can I ask you a serious question?" she said. "And you promise you'll answer it?"

"Sure," said Paul. He appeared as if he had no idea where she was going with this. And of course, he probably didn't.

"What's the deal with Ryan and his dad? Why is he so pissed off at him?"

"You really don't know?" he said, looking both surprised and relieved by the question. "Wow, I thought you'd know better than anyone."

"Nope. All I know is the day his mother was murdered was the day he stopped talking to everyone. And by everyone, I mean me. And I guess maybe his dad too. Even though his dad was hardly around anyway."

"That's the reason right there. Did you know his father was supposed to take him to the academy for his induction?"

"Did I know? That's all he talked about. Next thing I heard, his mom was killed the day of the induction. We were all devastated by that. But I never expected Ryan to take it out on me. Or his dad."

"Well it gets kind of tricky there," said Paul.

"Tricky how?"

"Well, his dad kind of bailed on him. It was bad enough his dad was away all the time, not that there was any choice, being the fleet admiral and all, but then of all days, he decided to go to a weapons briefing that day at the last minute instead of being there for Ryan. Ryan's mom had to take him instead. And you know how that ended up."

"But that's not his dad's fault," said Amanda. "It's just fate. Besides, my family was told Ryan's dad had to attend that conference. I remember that now."

"Yeah, that was the story that everyone was told. But according to Ryan, his dad didn't have to go. He was given a choice. But because he always insisted on sacrifice for the good of the fleet, to set an example, he *chose* to go."

"For the good of the fleet?" said Amanda, shaking her head. "In peacetime? Don't get me started there. But it's still fate. It's not like his dad wanted his mom to die."

Paul nodded. "No, but you haven't heard the details yet. After his mom took him to registration, she decided to make a stop at the hospital with Ryan to visit a friend of hers."

"Yes, I know. That's where that lunatic tried to kill his ex-girlfriend and ended up killing Ryan's mom when she spotted his gun. It was all over the news."

"Ryan could have stopped him, Amanda. He said he could have tackled the guy before he shot, but the hospital guards told him to wait. There was a standoff, and the gunman stood in the hallway aiming the gun at Ryan's mom. Ryan hesitated for just a few seconds, but by then the guards grabbed him and held him back to keep him safe. Meanwhile, the gunman just panicked and shot her and ran. Ryan watched his mom die right in front of his eyes while the guards held him back."

Amanda was horrified. She'd never heard this part of the story.

"He didn't tell you this?" said Paul.

She shook her head. "He hardly talked to me at all after that," she said. Amanda started to feel nauseous. "I can't even imagine. No wonder he hates authority. But still, it wasn't his dad's fault really."

"You have to understand," said Paul, "Ryan was never close with his dad. His dad was virtually nonexistent in his life, and the one time he planned to make up for all the disappointments, he backs out. If his dad was there, his mom wouldn't have died that day, simple as that. And the more he hears about his dad's stellar reputation, the more it reminds him that it was really the academy that killed his mom."

"So why did he even join the academy?"

"That's the great mystery, isn't it?" said Paul. "Best I can guess, it's the only tie he has left to his mom, who took him to the induction. Except every day he's here, he's forced to deal with comparisons to his dad. Some crappy twist of fate, right?"

Amanda began to choke up. "I could have helped him," she said. "Why didn't he tell me? I know I could have helped him."

"You still don't get it, do you?" said Paul.

"No, Paul, I don't. Why did he shut me out? Did he tell you?"

"Not exactly, but it's kind of obvious."

"Not to me."

"Amanda, Ryan's mom was really all he had. All he's known is loss. His mom was killed. His dad was absent. His brothers were older and away at the academy. To him, after his mom's death, it was probably safer to just clam up emotionally. I know that sounds messed up, but he sort of half-explained it to me once in one of those rare drunken stupors when we were up all night talking. Well, maybe not so rare."

"No, I get it," said Amanda, ignoring Paul's comment about the drunken stupors.

"You do?"

"Yeah, it makes sense. You know you missed your calling, Paulie. You should have been a shrink."

Paul smiled a warm and comforting smile. "Doctor Paul at your service."

For the first time, Amanda started to see what Ryan's topsy-turvy mind was telling him. It was like a great mystery was unlocked.

"You know I think I can still help him," she said. "If he'll let me."

"Amanda," said Paul, " you can't say anything to him about this. You guys are just starting to talk again. He may push you away even more if you try to corner him about it. Not to mention that if he finds out I told you, I'll never hear the end of it. Promise me, not a word, Amanda."

She thought about it for a few seconds. "I promise," she said.

Paul looked like he wasn't convinced.

"You have my word, really. Anyway, let's get back to work. After all, we do have a planet to save. It's going to take hours to calibrate the light-speed accelerator."

Paul nodded. "I'll work on the coils and you handle the reactor room."

"Works for me," she said. Within minutes, she was inside the main reactor room, where the power to run the light-speed drive was generated. It was deep in the belly of the ship and had the most protection, as it was surrounded by four walls of heavy-duty armor.

The reactor room was also the most dangerous part of the ship. In order for the vessel to obtain light speed, the reactor has to be working flawlessly. Combining matter and antimatter in such close proximity called for precise calculations and a finely calibrated reactor.

Amanda was in the middle of adjusting the flow chambers when Paul walked in. She didn't hear or see him. He slapped her on the back. "I brought you some coffee. How's it coming along?" he asked.

Startled, she screamed and dropped the sonic calibrator. She turned around and glared at him. "My God, don't ever sneak up on me again like that or I'll rip your freakin' head off!" Then she caught herself and smiled. "Thanks for the coffee," she said. "I could really use some."

"Schizophrenic much?" he said, laughing. "Relax. I almost spilled it. Here's your coffee."

Taking the steaming cup from him, she eased up a bit. "I'm sorry, Paul. I guess I'm just spooked with all this stuff going on."

"No worries. Everyone's jumpy. I just came from the bridge and you should see Ryan trying to deal with all the cadets. Plus he just got an update from your father. More news coming in about all those ships we lost today."

She was almost afraid to ask Paul what he'd heard. "Is his family all right?"

"Yeah," he answered. "They're okay. But from what I heard, the fleet got their butts handed to them. It doesn't look good."

"My God," she said softly. "What are they planning to do?"

"I'm not sure. I guess you heard they hightailed it back to the Mars orbital station. If they can't figure out how stop the alien fleet from there, the aliens will be at Earth in a matter of days."

She couldn't imagine what Ryan would do if he lost the rest of his family, and she didn't want to think about it. "Did my father tell him what our next move is?" she asked.

"Not really. Still the same as earlier today. We're supposed to continue getting these old ships back into battle condition. But if you think about it, what chance would we have in these old buckets anyway? Hell, if the unshakable Flash Thompson and his fleet can't stop them, we're screwed. I mean, think about it," he continued. "It would be like going to a laser fight with a butter knife."

Amanda thought hard about what Paul was saying. It was looking less and less promising by the minute, and time seemed to be closing in on them. One thing she knew, though, was that she wasn't a quitter. She shot Paul a determined look. "Well, I don't know about you, but I'm not ready to stick my head in the dirt and give up."

Truth be told, she wasn't sure if she was talking more about getting the ships ready or about Ryan.

Chapter 13

Hit And Run Tactics

Admiral Thompson looked at the thirty-four other captains in the room and studied their faces. Most of them hid their fear well, though a few looked agitated and some seemed to be outwardly frightened. Considering what had taken place in the last week, it was understandable that there would be some doubt and mixed emotions amongst the fleet. What bothered him the most, though, was the empty eighteen seats. He knew that they were all waiting for him to say something that would calm their fears. But he was never one for deceiving those under his command. He had always believed in telling it like it is.

"I'd like to thank all of you for your courage yesterday," he said. "We faced the unknown, and we faced it with strength and fortitude. Now we have to figure out a way to stop the Altarran fleet from reaching Earth."

He looked around the room at the fully attentive faces and continued.

"I spoke with the officers at Research and Development. Unfortunately, they have very little to go on. They suggest we try to overload their force fields using a concentration of force approach, focusing our weapons on one ship at a time. With that in mind, what we're going to do is combine that with tactics we're calling hit and run. The fleet will be divided into four attack groups: three groups of nine ships and one group of eight. Captains Hartwell, Irons, Ratchet, and myself will lead the groups. We'll coordinate the attacks from four different locations."

Thompson walked over to a large monitor on the wall where a simulation of the Altarran fleet was displayed. There was a circle around the picture with arrows pointed at four areas of attack.

"We will attack from equal points of the circle. We'll attack at 90 degrees, 180 degrees, 270 degrees, and 360 degrees. All of the attacks will be coordinated to take place simultaneously in an attempt to confuse the enemy. Any questions so far?"

"Sir," said a voice from the back of the room.

"Captain Wilcox? Question?"

"Admiral, I understand the combined attack on specific focus points. But how do we avoid being shot at by their other adjacent ships?"

"That's where the hit and run comes in," said Thompson. "It's vitally important that we fly in formation, get our shots off in unison, and scatter immediately, breaking formation and coming back to base. If we scatter widely enough it should confuse them. It's a risk, and they may pick some of us off, but God willing, we'll minimize damage and cause some of our own. More importantly, we have no other choice."

Thompson heard a few whispers, but everyone quickly quieted down.

"Further questions?" he said.

The room was silent. Satisfied that everyone was in agreement and understood the plan, Thompson looked at the officers in his command. He nearly choked up with a sense of awe and gratitude. Heroes, every last damn one of them.

"All right then," he continued. "We'll attack when the Altarran fleet passes Jupiter. The planet's gravitational pull should disrupt their radar. I'll assign each group leader their attack point. We'll leave in 24 hours. At the current speed and course of the Altarran fleet, they'll just be passing Jupiter then." Pausing, he looked at each commander and turned off the monitor. "Good luck to all of you. Dismissed."

The officers in the room all snapped to attention and saluted him. Bursting with pride, he returned the salute and made his way back to the bridge of his ship, where his officers, who must have sprinted in order to get there ahead of him, were already awaiting his orders.

"Lieutenant Barnes, inform the squadrons that we're ready to begin Operation Hit and Run," Thompson ordered.

"Aye, sir," Barnes replied. "I'll inform you as soon as I receive confirmation from all squad leaders."

"Thank you, Lieutenant." Turning to Romano, Thompson asked, "Have you coordinated course and speed to match the other attack groups?"

"Affirmative," said Romano. "Course set and locked in."

"Good," said Thompson. "We'll be the first to leave as we have the longest flight. We'll be going around the Altarran fleet and coming up on their six."

Thames came up alongside him. "I see you picked the longest and most dangerous path for us, Admiral."

Looking at his longtime friend, Thompson nodded. "Would you really expect me to take the easy way and have another commander take our path?"

"No, Admiral," said Thames. "In fact, I knew the minute you came up with this half-witted idea we'd be running the end around. I wouldn't want it any other way."

"Of course you wouldn't. You're almost as crazy as I am."

"Sir," called out Barnes. "I have confirmation from all squad leaders. They are ready and waiting your orders, sir."

"Put me through to the fleet, Miss Barnes."

"Yes, sir. Placing you on fleet-wide com channel now, Admiral. You're all set."

Thompson stood and gathered his thoughts. "Before we embark on this mission," he said, "I want you all to know I appreciate—and am truly grateful for—your commitment, your character, and most of all, your courage. I'd be lying to you if I said we were certain this attack will work, and I think we all know there are risks involved. But I do know one thing. We are going to give them absolute hell. We're going to throw the best we have to offer at them. And under no circumstances are we going to give up fighting. I know I don't need to tell you what's at stake here. We have friends, family, and about ten billion people back on Earth counting on us. Good luck, soldiers. I'm proud to be your Admiral. It's an honor. Thompson out."

Barnes cut the transmission and looked into his eyes. "Well said, sir."

"Thank you, Miss Barnes. Open a channel to President Hawking."

The lieutenant's hands moved effortlessly as she adjusted the frequency to contact Earth. "I have the president on the com."

"Mr. President, this is Fleet Admiral Thompson. We're about to attack the Altarran fleet. Have you found out anything about their claims that their people were here in the past?"

"No, Admiral. Nothing yet. There's nothing in our current records of any such event. And you know as well as I do that many of the older records were destroyed. We do know that back in the 20th and 21st centuries there were a number of covert government agencies, but that's about all we know. They could have been involved in anything, and I'm sure they were. We're still researching all possibilities, but it isn't looking good. You'll have to do the best you can to stall them. Good luck, Admiral. If anyone can handle this, I know you can."

"Thank you, Mr. President. We'll forward a report of our attack as soon as we return. If you don't hear anything . . . well, you know what to do."

"That won't be necessary, Admiral. God speed." The transmission ended.

Thompson looked at Thames. "Well he sure has confidence, though the news doesn't sound very promising."

"No, Admiral, it certainly doesn't. Though I must say I find it ironic, sir."

"Ironic ? How so?"

"All those years we played with fire. Almost caused our own destruction. Finally, after coming within minutes of destroying ourselves, the world finally unites and forges a true peace. Then what does our government do? They destroy all files relating to collusion and covert operations. I guess they thought if no one knew, there would be less chance of it coming back to haunt them. Well it's haunting them now, isn't it, sir?"

Despite the dire circumstances, Thompson couldn't help laughing. "It sure is, Niles," he said. "All in the name of preserving peace.

Sweeping everything under the proverbial rug. Oh well, I guess they did what they thought was the right thing. Damn idiots."

"Admiral," said Barnes. "We've received clearance from the station for departure."

"Thank you, Miss Barnes. Inform Mars orbital station that we're ready for departure. Then tell the rest of our squadron to follow in order at five-second intervals."

"Aye, sir. Sending messages now, sir." After a few seconds, Barnes had received the all clear. "We're clear for departure. All ships have responded as well, sir."

"Understood," said Thompson. He opened a com link to engineering. "Chief, I assume we have full power and are ready for departure?"

"We are ready and able, Admiral," replied Fowler. "You have full power."

"Thank you, Chief. Thank God for small favors." Looking to his helmsman, he said, "Release docking clamps."

"Docking clamps released, sir."

The sound of the clamps breaking free could be heard throughout the ship. Normally, this familiar signal lifted the crew's hearts, but this time the image of an executioner mounting a scaffold popped into Thompson's head. For all he knew, these would be his last moments alive.

"Prepare to fire port maneuvering thrusters," he said, realizing that he had waited just a bit longer than usual to give the order.

"Ready on your mark, sir," replied Romano a little breathlessly.

Thompson felt a little catch in his throat. He and his bridge crew had been together so long that they were able to anticipate his every move. At a time like this, that would really come in handy. If only they could get out of this alive. He took a breath.

"Now," he ordered. The massive ship pushed away from the station. "As soon as we reach a thousand-foot clearance, shut down port thrusters and fire aft thrusters."

Seconds later, Romano called out, "Shutting portside thrusters. Firing aft thrusters now, sir!"

"As soon as we reach standard distance, prepare to fire light-speed thrusters," Thompson ordered.

A few minutes passed while the ship pulled away from the station. Romano looked at the admiral. "Sir, we are at the required distance. Preparing to engage light speed on your command."

Thompson leaned back. He always hated the feeling in his stomach when the ship first transitioned to light speed. "Now," he ordered. The sound of the engines powering up echoed throughout the ship. There was a brief instant where time seemed to stand still. After all these years he still couldn't get used to it. Then, without warning, he felt that forward motion where you lose all sense of balance or feeling. There was no time to think, let alone throw up.

In the blink of an eye, everything was back to normal—or at least as normal as light-speed travel could be. The shift, though, was always the worst part.

Thames looked at the admiral, laughing. "Still enjoy light-speed transitions, sir?"

Thompson chuckled back and shook his head. "No," he said. "I sure as hell don't." He checked the ship's chronometer. "Two hours until we reach our point of attack."

Thames leaned closer to the admiral and whispered, "What's your gut say about this situation? Propaganda aside, of course."

"Truthfully, Niles? We may get a few of them, but in the long run, if we don't find a way to get through that force field of theirs, we're in deep trouble. We're going to need a Plan B at some point, assuming we make it that far. My hope is that this buys us some time. I just hope they don't obliterate us all first."

"I concur with that, Admiral," said Thames.

The next couple of hours passed quickly. The crew kept busy running checks on all of their systems. Finally, Diego broke the increasingly tense silence.

"Two minutes to contact, sir. All forward torpedo bays loaded with full spread. Lasers powered and ready."

"This is it, ladies and gentlemen," said Thompson. He had a brief mental picture of a sheriff facing his arch enemy on a dusty street. Except this was high noon at 370 million miles. "Diego, hold fire for forty-five seconds. Target the closest ship to us as soon as we exit light speed."

Diego never took his eyes off his console. "Aye, sir. Forty-five seconds. Concentrate all fire on closest target," he replied.

Thompson could feel his heart beating as the countdown continued. Romano called out, "Twenty seconds to target." Thompson ran the situation over and over again in his mind. If they were lucky, each of the four squadrons would destroy one enemy ship, and all thirty-five UEDF vessels would escape unscathed. Then again, he had never been one to believe in luck.

The sound of the Constitution's engines straining as they were powered down from light speed to thrusters was deafening. The hull creaked as the mighty ship slowed. Thompson stood up and watched the eight other battleships from his unit coming up alongside each other. It took only thirty seconds for all eight ships to arrive, but it seemed like an eternity. Once his squadron was all in place, he gave the most important order of his life.

"Mr. Diego, target the closest Altarran ship and commence firing. Empty all forward tubes and fire all laser cannons."

Diego had already set his targeting sensors to fire at the closest enemy ship, and he was armed and ready. "I have a targeting solution. Firing tubes one through four. Forward laser cannons locked on and firing, sir."

Thompson could feel the giant ship recoil like a snake about to attack its prey, as each torpedo bay launched four deadly torpedoes at the Altarran vessel.

Barnes shouted from the communications station, "All ships reported firing full torpedo spreads, sir."

"We're being targeted, Admiral," said Thames from the sensor station. "Enemy fleet breaking formation. They're firing weapons."

"Admiral," shouted Barnes, "I have confirmation the other three squadrons have attacked as well. All of our ships are retreating and scattering as ordered, sir!"

Thames let out a yell from the sensor station. "Direct hit, sir! It worked. Their ships is breaking up. Even their shields can't take over a hundred direct hits and withstand it."

"Let's get the hell out of here," ordered Thompson.

There was an enthusiastic cheer from the crew as they heard that they'd destroyed one of the Altarran ships.

"Admiral," said Diego, loud enough to cut through the cheers, "multiple torpedoes closing in on us."

"Evasive maneuvers, Romano. Pull her up. Full throttle."

The crew held on as the massive ship tried to evade the incoming torpedoes, or whatever they were. The first three missed, but the fourth one caught them toward the rear of the ship. Alarms rang out and damage reports started coming in from the lower decks. The ship slowed as the engines shut down. The admiral punched the com link on his chair.

"Engineering, what's going on down there? We need power now. We're sitting ducks."

There was a crackle of static before Fowler answered. "Sorry, Admiral. That blast knocked the generator offline. I'll have it back on in about thirty seconds."

"That's thirty seconds too long," said Thompson.

"They're coming around to finish us off, sir," said Diego.

Thompson knew they were in serious trouble. Even in the heat of battle, his first thought was that he'd never see his sons again. Had that been Kelly's last thought before she was murdered too?

"Incoming fire, sir," yelled Diego. "Contact in ten seconds."

Punching his com link, Thompson called to Fowler, "Chief, I need power now!"

"Almost there," came the strained voice of the chief.

Thompson sat back, unable to do anything but wait and prepare for death. Without warning, there was a deafening sound and the ship rocked from the force of an explosion, throwing him off his seat like a rag doll. The last thought in his mind was of his crew. Then everything went blank for a few seconds.

Something was strange, though. When he shook off the cobwebs, he could barely believe he was still alive and the ship was still in one piece. A direct hit like that should have obliterated them. He stood and weakly called out to Barnes, "Damage report."

"No major damage reported, sir!" said Barnes.

Just then, Fowler shouted, "Admiral, the engines are back online!"

"Romano," said Thompson, "Get us the hell out of here, now!"

As the engines engaged, he noticed a pained expression on Thames's face. "What is it, Niles?"

"The reason we're still alive," said Thames, "is because the Lexington flew directly into the path of those torpedoes meant for us. They absorbed most of the impact."

Thompson couldn't believe what he was hearing. "Any survivors?" was all he could get out.

"I doubt it. It's possible, but we left so fast there wasn't enough time to check."

Thompson fell back into his chair. There had been one hundred men and women on that ship. How many of them had sacrificed themselves to save him and his crew for the overall good of the mission? He was devastated. The entire bridge went silent as they made their way back to the station orbiting Mars. They were running out of time. More important, they were running out of ships.

Chapter 14

Update

Ryan entered Admiral Williamson's office. Today was the day the cadets were to take the Nimitz out on a test flight. He knew that his father's fleet had just returned from their current attack and he was anxious to get the latest update. It was hard to believe that it had only been five days since the level two alert. It seemed that the whole world had changed and everything before was now null and void. From this day on, nobody would know a world without alien invaders. The days of the lonely, isolated earth were gone, as if they had never existed.

He was due on the Nimitz in an hour. He smiled at Lieutenant Rhimes and she immediately hit the intercom without a word. She didn't seem herself. "Cadet Thompson is here to see you, Admiral," she said quietly.

"Send him in, Lieutenant," came the voice on the other end.

Normally talkative and jovial, Rhimes was all business today. She was obviously aware that Ryan's father was currently engaged in battle. Did she know something he didn't? "The Admiral will see you now, Cadet Thompson," she said.

Ryan made his way through the door and into Admiral Williamson's office. He stood tall and gave the admiral a brief salute. "You asked to see me, sir?"

"At ease, Ryan. Take a seat." Williamson looked somber.

Ryan sat down. He had a bad feeling from the tone of the admiral's voice and the expression on his face.

Williamson paused briefly before speaking. "I received a transmission from Headquarters. Earlier today, the fleet intercepted the alien ships yet again. Somehow—I don't know how—we managed to destroy four of their ships, but we lost another eight."

There were a million thoughts racing in Ryan's head, and his emotions were running wild. "My brothers," he said. "Did you hear anything about their ship?" He paused for a moment and then added,

"And my father?" He surprised even himself with that one, and by the look Williamson was giving him, the admiral was surprised as well.

"We'll have all that information shortly. Ryan, your dad is fine. He's trying to get reports on which ships were lost and if there were any survivors. We won't really know about the survivors until we hear from the deep space outpost on Pluto. The point is, we don't know about your brothers."

Ryan shook his head as if he were trying to wake up from a dream. "What went wrong?" he asked.

"It seems the alien ships have some type of force field we haven't been able to penetrate. For now, your father ordered the fleet to retreat to Mars orbital station and regroup. They tried a strategy they called hit and run, but it was more run than hit."

"So what's next?"

"Well, they'll have to run the data through the brass at the station and do simulations to see if we can find a way to penetrate those force fields. Until we hear otherwise, we're to remain on total blackout. We can receive transmissions, but nothing outgoing. Obviously your father doesn't want to compromise our position."

Ryan was beside himself. Here he was sitting and waiting again, unable to help. "With all due respect, Admiral," he said. "I think we should get our ships ready as quickly as possible and get moving."

"And do what, Ryan? Get ourselves killed in record time? You want that on your hands? Your father is one of the best military minds on Earth. If anyone can figure it out, he can. In the meantime, he gave specific orders that we're to continue to work on these ships and wait for further instructions."

"And what if he can't, Admiral? What if they can't find a way to penetrate their force field? Then what?"

The admiral stood up and glared at him. "Listen, for once in your life, son. This is about the very survival of mankind. Nobody is more aware than your father—and I— about what's at stake. If this goes badly, we'll need a place to fall back and regroup. So, we sit tight and wait. Besides, we may need this planet to have somewhere to rebuild. You jump the gun, and we lose that chance."

Ryan knew the admiral was right. He understood the rationale behind the idea, but he sure didn't like it. He'd sworn that he would never again sit idly by and do nothing. And now he was being ordered to do just that. Using all the will power he had, he took a deep breath and accepted the situation for what it was. "Is that all, sir?" he said.

"That's all, Thompson," said the admiral. "If you want to do something productive, see to it that you get the Nimitz in the best shape possible. And Ryan?"

"Yes, Admiral?"

"Your father told me that you have more potential than he ever had. So stay strong, son. Don't sell him short."

Ryan didn't know what to think. On one hand it bothered him when his father praised him, but somehow it also made him feel stronger. This time, he chose to take the high road and be gracious.

"Thank you, Admiral," he said. "And sir?"

The admiral gave him a curious look.

"Thank you for being real with me."

"Hey, that's me. Mister real."

Ryan saluted crisply and made his way out the door.

Chapter 15

Doubts

Amanda walked into the dorm suite living room. They were about to leave for the Nimitz's test flight. Nicole was looking at her Slider, which was stretched open to the "book size" setting.

"What are you reading, Nikki?" asked Amanda.

"Just the last communication from my sister. She's on the Lexington. She said that their weapons didn't even penetrate the alien ships' hulls. Jesus, Amanda, how are these old retired ships going to make a difference? Our entire fleet of modern ships can't stop them."

Amanda didn't have an answer, but she knew she had to say something positive. "I'm sure with all the engineers and research people working on it, we'll come up with something," she said.

"You don't really believe that, do you?" said Jill. She was sitting on the edge of the couch with her mouth open. "I mean they're tearing through our best ships like a great white against a school of . . . minnows or something. The only thing they're gonna come up with is to tell us to sit tight and pray they don't find us."

Amanda noticed that Nicole was getting upset. "Nice going, Jill. You know her sister's out there."

"I'm sorry," said Jill. "But so are my father and brother. And your two brothers. Trust me, I'm scared to death that I'm never gonna see them again. I just don't believe in false hope."

"Exactly," said Nicole. "Even if we get these ships up and running, the only thing they'd be good for is for us to run and hide somewhere and hope they don't find us."

Amanda had heard enough. "My God, don't throw in the towel so fast. If all of our ancestors gave up every time the odds seemed impossible, we wouldn't even be here having this conversation. I mean, why bother living if you're just going to give up? The way I look at it, we joined the academy for a reason—to better humanity. Not to abandon it. That's why we exist. We *can't* give up."

"You know why we joined," said Jill. "We both had scholarships, our fathers are in the fleet, and honestly, the money's great and we're able to explore the galaxy. It seemed like a great idea at the time. But I wasn't expecting this—to go to war."

"Jesus, Amanda," said Nicole, "I never thought we'd really have to fight anyone either, and neither did you. There hasn't been a war in over seventy years."

Amanda was beginning to realize that they'd all been a bit naïve, including herself. "That's enough," she said. "Yes, I thought war was a thing of the past. And I sure didn't think we'd find life out there, especially life that wants to kill us. But that's how it turned out, and it's time to make some tough choices. We don't know what's next. We may have to fight. Or we might have to help rebuild our society. Or we may just stay put while the UEDF works this out. Whatever happens, we'll get through this together. And if we have to fight, well . . . then we'll have to give ourselves the best chance of winning, or at least surviving. We can't just curl up and die. Now come on. We have to be on the Nimitz and ready to go in less than an hour."

As they made their way out of the dorm and headed across the compound to the hangar, Amanda thought about all that had taken place over the last week. While she was putting up a brave front, the idea of meeting a hostile alien race terrified her. What if this really was the fall of Earth? What if this was how it all ends? How long could she and the others on the cadet planet survive?

Obviously, being the admiral's daughter, she knew the protocol for this situation. If Earth were to fall and it was deemed that their weapons couldn't defeat the enemy, then they'd stay put. Unless their position was compromised. Under that scenario, they'd leave the planet and try to rebuild elsewhere. But there weren't too many elsewheres to go. At least not that could sustain life long term, maybe ten years tops with their equipment.

She pushed those thoughts away and put her mind back to the task at hand: getting the Nimitz ready for her final test flight. That was something she *could* handle.

Just then, her communicator buzzer went off. It was her father.

"Amanda," he said. "Please have Nicole come and see me immediately. I know she's with you. I have some news that I need to deliver to her."

"What is it?" she said.

"Just have her see me."

The line went dead.

Chapter 16

The Beginning Of The End

Even though they had just regrouped there, Admiral Thompson had given the order to abandon the Mars orbital base. Unlike the facility on Pluto, which was underground, the Mars base was an orbital platform and a sitting duck against the Altarran armada.

The last transport was loaded and ready to leave. Wondering whether this would be his last ever visit to the red planet, Thompson told Barnes to have the remaining ships set course for Earth. "We'll rendezvous and set up a last line of defense," he said. "Inform the transports to head back to Headquarters."

"Understood, Admiral," said Barnes. "Informing the fleet now. As soon as they confirm, I'll inform the transport ships of your orders."

"Thank you, Barnes." Then he turned to Romano. "Set course for Earth orbit. Orbital altitude. One-quarter sub-light speed."

Romano made the course changes and punched his console. "Aye, sir. Course and speed set."

"Admiral," said Barnes. "I have President Hawking on the communications link. He wants your report and recommendations. You're live now, sir."

"Mr. President," said the admiral. "I think it's time you activate full planetary crisis procedures. Code red. We're down to twenty-seven ships and we've only managed to destroy four of theirs. We'll give you as much time as we can, but they'll be in range of Earth in about six hours at their current speed."

"I understand, Admiral," said Hawking. "Code red it is. I'll call an emergency meeting and place all planetary defenses on attack status. We'll evacuate all heavily populated areas and have worldwide shelters opened and ready. I know you're doing all you can, Thompson. Good luck to you and your fleet."

Thompson sat back in his chair. They were going to need more than good luck to win. They were going to need a damn super hero or something.

"Sir," said Thames, "sensors are picking up increased activity from the sun. It appears that a large mass ejection is imminent. I expect it to reach us within the next four to eight hours."

Thompson just shook his head. Damn solar flares. "Great," he said. "What next? A swarm of locusts? Okay, everyone, you know the drill. Go to manual controls as soon as the flares start. Shut down all computers until the electromagnetic particles subside. We'll have to do this the old-fashioned way."

As acknowledgements came from the various bridge officers, Thompson took a moment to reflect on the situation. He wasn't afraid of dying. It was a part of the job that everyone knew could happen. What he was afraid of was failure. His entire life was about overcoming obstacles, always finding a way to defeat the odds. Losing was never even a thought in his mind. It was hard to believe he could really be in a position where winning might not be possible. And yet it was his very drive to win, to always be on top of his game, that had destroyed his family. Now, irony of ironies, here he was in an unwinnable situation, and all he could think of was Ryan. And what could have been.

Thames interrupted his thoughts.

"Admiral, sensors are detecting multiple explosions back at the Mars orbital station. Confirming the Altarran fleet is the cause. We've lost all computer contact with the base. We should have visitors soon."

"Understood," said Thompson. "Maintain speed and course." He was hoping to gain more ground before the Altarrans caught up, but it was not to be.

Things were tense over the next few hours as Thompson and his crew kept checking to see if the Altarrans were catching up. After what seemed like a lifetime, the remaining 27 ships reached their rendezvous point. Thompson stood up and walked over to the communications station.

"Barnes, have the fleet set up in an X formation. That way we can concentrate all our firepower dead center of the Altarran fleet when they arrive. Also, in the event any ship is damaged beyond its ability to defend itself, or if I order a retreat, have the ships make their way back to the base on Pluto and remain there with the rest of the survivors."

"Will do, Admiral," said Barnes. "Informing the fleet now."

"Admiral," said Thames, "I've just picked up the Altarran fleet. They'll be in weapons range in ten minutes."

"This is it, ladies and gentlemen," said Thompson. Looking to Barnes, he said, "Have all ships power weapons. Target the lead ship with the first salvo, then repeat firing at the next one. Have all ships repeat the attack pattern for as long as we can maintain formation. We hold this line until they break past us or destroy us."

"Yes, sir," replied Barnes. "Sending message now."

Thames came up alongside Thompson. "I guess we're about to find out how your General Custer felt."

"That's one feeling I could live without."

Just then the ship's warning systems activated. *WARNING. SOLAR ACTIVITY DETECTED.*

"Dammit," said Thompson, "All departments, switch to manual overrides. Disconnect computerized systems."

Moments later, Diego called out, "Sir! The Altarran fleet. They seem to be experiencing some type of systems failure. I'm not registering any frequency from their shields or their light-speed drive. They must be offline, sir."

"It must have something to do with the solar activity," said Thompson. "Ladies and gentleman, maybe we just found our advantage. Open fire. All ships."

Within seconds, Diego called out, "Direct hits! Three of their ships are breaking up!"

Thompson couldn't believe it. Maybe they would catch a break after all. "Barnes, have all ships open fire. Target multiple ships. Let's get these sons of bitches."

"Informing the fleet now, sir," said Barnes, barely containing her smile.

During the next couple of minutes, Thompson watched with a combination of pride and relief as the tide began to turn in the fleet's favor. They had managed to destroy four more Altarran ships. Then, seemingly in an instant, the Altarran fleet got their power back up and began returning fire. Thompson stood helplessly as the Altarrans gained the advantage again, destroying ship after ship. In the chaos, he couldn't tell how many ships were lost, but it was turning into a massacre. Suddenly, he was thrown to the ground as his own ship took a partial hit. This time, there was no Lexington to block the hit, and alarms sounded all over the Constitution.

"Status!" yelled Thompson.

"We're outgunned thirty-five to nine," said Diego. "We've lost eighteen ships, sir."

"Hull breach to the rear of the ship," said Thames. "Two torpedo bays damaged."

Thompson knew it was time to call it quits. Maybe he could buy some time for the ground forces.

"Barnes," he said, "have the remaining ships bug out fast. Raise the Altarran commander. Tell him we're breaking off our attack. Tell him I wish to discuss terms for surrender."

Barnes, usually quick to reply, hesitated briefly. Thompson could feel the eyes of his bridge crew on him. "Yes, sir," she finally said. "Hailing the Altarran commander now." She turned to her controls to broadcast the disheartening message and then looked up. "I've told him we wish to surrender, sir."

There were a few moments of silence. The only sounds Thompson could hear were his own heartbeat and the breathing of the bridge crew. Finally, Barnes turned around to address him. "Sir, I have Commander Granthaxe on speaker."

Thompson stood up and addressed the alien. "Commander Granthaxe, I've ordered my fleet to stand down. I would like to discuss terms—"

"Silence! There are no terms, Admiral Thompson. And it is *Supreme* Commander. I should destroy you and your ship for your crimes against the citizens of Altarra. But alas, perhaps terms, as you say, may yet save you. My terms are the same as they were upon our meeting. Produce my missing envoys."

"Forgive me, Supreme Commander," said Thompson. "I know you don't believe me. But we are trying to look into your claims. We can help you find them. You'll have much more success with our help. But we need more time."

"Time," Granthaxe said, as if he were contemplating what the word meant. "I will give you time. I have a fleet of troop carriers ten of your Earth days behind me. You have until then to find my envoys or get me the answers I seek. Once our troops arrive, by my word they *will* land on your planet and we *will* take control. If your people resist, it shall be the last action they ever take. I warn you, if you try to leave your orbit or attack us before my carriers arrive, we will launch an immediate attack, beginning with your most populated areas. Those are the terms of the cease-fire. Accept them . . . or not."

Despite the harsh terms, what Thompson needed was time, and that he got. He answered the commander calmly and deliberately. "Your terms are fair and generous. I am returning to Earth to forward your demands and start a formal investigation concerning your missing envoys. I will contact you every 24 hours with updates on our search."

"I will only warn you once, Admiral Thompson. Do not take me lightly. If you try anything foolish, we do have the power to incinerate the surface of your planet, city by city."

The line went dead. Thompson sat down and gathered his thoughts. He glanced over at Thames. "Niles," he said, "get me all the data and film from the moment the Altarran ships lost power. I want to know exactly when it happened and how long it lasted. We need to get that information to the braniacs at R&D fast."

"Yes, sir. I'm compiling all the information as we speak. When I'm finished, I'll download all of it and send it directly to Headquarters."

"Barnes," said Thompson, "get a message to the president. Have him contact the outpost on Pluto and have any survivors or any of our ships there stay put and continue to stay dark."

"Yes, Admiral," Barnes replied.

"Romano, set a course for Headquarters. Let's get on the ground and see what we can find out."

"Course already set. Preliminary landing procedure set and awaiting your orders, Admiral."

"Take us home, Romano. Nice and easy." As the Constitution began her course change, she passed the front of the lead Altarran ship. The outer camera caught the insignia on its side. Thompson's eyes went wide. "I don't be—"

"Niles, replay that shot of the insignia on the Altarran ship and enlarge it."

Thames pulled up the image and froze it on the screen. "Enlarging picture now, Admiral."

Thompson couldn't believe what he was seeing. "You've got to be kidding me."

"What is it, Admiral?" said Thames.

"I'll explain later, Niles. There's something I need to confirm first. In the meantime, get that image along with all the information about the solar flares and have it on my desk as soon as we land."

"Yes, sir." Thames seemed puzzled, but he knew better than to question him right now. He turned away and started gathering the information.

Thompson sat back in his chair and wondered if it was too late. Maybe, just maybe, there was still a fighting chance. One thing was certain, though. This was going to be a hell of an interesting ten days if what he just saw was true.

Chapter 17

Uedf Nimitz, Test Flight

Ryan entered the bridge of the UEDF Nimitz. He'd participated in countless simulations, as had the rest of the senior class. But this was different. This was real. You don't get a chill down your spine entering the bridge of a simulation ship. Not like this, with lives depending on how successful you are.

Adding to the stress was the news about the Lexington. Nicole was inconsolable after learning about her sister's ship being destroyed. People said they could hear her screaming from outside the admiral's office. Though it was doubtful there were any survivors, he and the others tried to convince her that there was still a chance her sister might somehow be alive, and that it was the courageous act of all onboard that had enabled the fleet to fight another day. In a way, this horrible situation brought his whole crew closer together, though he wished there'd been a less depressing way to have made that happen.

Ryan walked to each station and looked at the controls. All cadets in command training had to know how to man all bridge stations in the event of emergencies. Funny, he'd been waiting for this day for years. But not like this. He'd never dreamed he'd have to lead in such dire circumstances.

He could only hope that his father would pull off a miracle and find a way to beat these invaders. If there was ever a time he was rooting for his father, it was now. Good family man or not, there was no doubt he knew how to lead a fleet and keep his calm. At least that's what everyone said about him.

As Ryan thought about it, even though it drove him crazy being compared to his father, in reality it make him work that much harder. And, truth be told, his dad was the model for how he tried to act as a leader. In a way, it had always made him feel unstoppable. But now, with the whole planet in danger and everything turned upside down, he no longer felt invincible. Quite the opposite, he felt infinitely small and unimportant. It seemed that's how everyone was feeling these days, like a bunch of ants scampering around while a giant shadow closes in on them. And, somehow, it was up to him to get them thinking otherwise.

Hearing steps, he turned around to see Tanner and Paul heading his way. "Hey, guys," he said. "Ready to see what this baby can do?"

"Sure am," said Paul. "Just don't push her too hard at first. Let the old engines warm up a bit."

"Just what we need," said Tanner, "a ship with arthritis."

"Don't worry about the engines," said Ryan. "We'll take it slow and steady."

Tanner planted himself at the weapons console. "Yeah, like an old lady running from a mountain lion. By the way, I hear we have all practice torpedoes. I guess they're afraid we'll go rogue or something."

Ryan laughed. "I doubt that. More like they need to save them for when we really need them. We don't have too many on this base."

"That's comforting," said Tanner. "Since you're in the know, any news from the admiral about the fleet?"

"Yeah, he wants us to head an armada to go help out the UEDF forces?"

"You're kidding," said Paul. "Really?"

Tanner looked genuinely shocked.

"Of course not," said Ryan. "He said for now we're to continue as planned. To be honest, I don't think they'd ever send us into battle under any circumstances. Truth is, we'll be lucky if they ask us to pick up survivors."

"No," said Paul, "we'll be lucky if your dad finds a way to beat these assholes and they don't need us as all."

"Damn right on that," said Tanner.

Ryan smiled and nodded. They had a point. This wasn't about him or them, or who saves the day. It was about winning.

Paul looked at his watch. "Well, guys, I'm off to engineering. Time to run a preflight check and start warming those engines."

After a few hours, when all the checks had been run and passed, everyone returned to their stations. Ryan looked around at his bridge crew, Tanner at weapons, Amanda at the exec console, Jill at communications, and Nicole at the helm. Paul was down in engineering. They all looked confident, but cautious. Finally, he gave the order to lift off. He was anxious to see how the ship would do, not to mention how the crew would work together. He was putting a lot of faith in Nicole as the pilot, especially knowing what she'd just been through with losing her sister. But she had an amazing reputation as a skilled pilot, and she did extremely well in the simulations. Another real test would be how well Amanda and Paul did in engineering to get the ship in running order. This was quite a challenge, even for crack engineers.

He watched out the large circular window as the Nimitz rose from its platform. The takeoff was incredibly smooth, almost too good to be true. As they progressed outside the planetary atmosphere, a smiled formed on his face. He had no idea of the pride he would feel at the accomplishments of his crew. Damn it, they did it! They got this old thing running.

Before he knew it, the Nimitz had entered orbit. And a perfect, beautiful orbit it was. They ran the ship through test after test. The engines performed to spec and the weapons systems were dead on. Despite all odds, this ship was ready for action. Satisfied that all tests had been passed, he gave the order to head back to base.

It had been a perfect flight with an excellent takeoff. Upon an equally smooth landing, Ryan looked around at the team Admiral Williamson had assigned him. He was beginning to understand just what Williamson had meant. A team that works well together can accomplish amazing things.

Ryan already knew that Tanner was great with weapons systems and Paul was a hotshot engineer, but what really impressed him was Nicole, who not only excelled, but had to put on a brave face doing it. It was hard to believe this was only the second time she'd flown a ship in a live test. While she'd spent many hours in the simulators, that wasn't the same as the real thing. She made it look as if she'd been flying for years.

Jill was also at the top of her game. She had all the different communication systems down pat. Plus she knew every single code they threw at her.

Then there was Amanda. He was beginning to understand that she was more than just his old girlfriend and a competitor for the award. Yeah, she still did everything by the book, but she knew more about those old engines than even Paul did. And Paul was considered to be the best engineering cadet in the academy. Ryan glanced over at her and saw that she was making notes. Then she noticed him and looked down.

It was time to give the bridge crew his assessment of the test. He was about to go through the flight data with them when they received a priority message from Admiral Williamson.

"Attention, all cadets. You are all ordered to cease all duties and report to the main auditorium immediately. As of this minute, the academy is going dark. All cadets are to report to the auditorium for further details. Williamson out."

Ryan could almost feel everyone's tension as he looked around. What now? Could it get any worse? As he saw the looks on his ship-mates' faces, he knew had to say something to lift their spirits. That's what a good commanding officer is supposed to do. But what to say?

As always, he decided to shoot from his gut.

"Before we leave here," he said, as everyone turned to face him. "I just wanted to say, this entire crew did an unbelievable job." He looked around at his crew, and at Amanda, Nicole, and Jill to make sure they knew he meant them especially. "I know we may have started off on the wrong foot," he continued. "That was my mistake. I can assure all of you, it won't happen again." He paused for a moment to let his words sink in. "We may be going dark now," he added. "But inside, I know that each of us is ready to take on any mission, if and when we're called to action. For now, we'll do what they want, even if it means laying low. And we can hope that soon, they'll want what I know we can do. It ain't over yet, guys. Remember that, no matter what we hear today. And there's no team I'd rather serve with than all of you. Now, let's power down everything and get going."

He watched as everyone nodded in acceptance. And as they made their way out of the Nimitz and headed for the auditorium, none of them spoke a word. Ryan looked up to the sky and thought of his mother. He also wondered if his father and brothers were now with her. The fact that the admiral had ordered the academy to *go dark* meant one thing and one thing only. Earth's Defense Fleet had been defeated and the academy was to close off all contact with the outside world.

Chapter 18

Final Report

Amanda entered the main auditorium with the bridge crew of the Nimitz. Unlike the last time they'd made this trip, the six of them sat together. It felt kind of nice, and considering all that had taken place over the last six days, she needed all the togetherness she could get. This was one crew she never in her wildest dreams thought would form a bond.

Even Ryan had changed. And in a way, so had she—or at least her perspective. A week ago, she wouldn't have considered sitting next to him. Now, in light of everything going on, it hit home that none of us were really all that different, and that life was much deeper—and much more precious—than she had realized. And now that she knew the truth about Ryan's horrifying experience, his attitudes made sense.

Her thoughts were cut short when her father appeared onstage at the podium. She braced herself for the worst. Seeing the look on his face, she knew the news wasn't going to be good. Her hands were sweaty and she felt dizzy just anticipating the thought of what the news might entail. Could the entire Earth be soon to come to an end? All her friends and family back home? She felt frozen in time as she watched her father standing there in silence, looking somber.

"I wish I could be the bearer of better news," began her father. "Unfortunately, at 2100 hours last night, the United Earth Defense Fleet surrendered."

Amanda couldn't breathe, as cries of anger, fear, and disbelief came from all directions. She glanced over at Ryan, who looked like he was holding back tears. She wanted to reach out to him, to comfort him, but this wasn't the time or place for that.

"I have received orders from Admiral Thompson," continued her father, "and I will go over these with all of you during the next 24 hours."

Voices started calling out. "How many ships were destroyed?" "Do we know anything about survivors?" "What about Earth?"

Amanda was half in a daze. At least Ryan's dad was still alive. Thank God for that.

"Please," said her father, holding up his hand. "All of you quiet down. I understand your concerns. And I am aware that many of you have family on board those ships. Data is still coming in. The minute we have answers, I can assure you that I will personally notify each and every one of you. For now, we are to continue with a full blackout. I know that's difficult for you to accept; this is difficult for all of us. But these are our orders, and trust me when I say that it's for the good of humankind. I should add that there's a very real possibility that the future of the human race could lie with us. Before I dismiss you, I want you to understand that I am counting on your total cooperation. That's all. Dismissed."

There was silence for a moment, but then the murmur of the crowd picked up. Everyone got up and started to leave. Amanda was about to talk to Jill and Nicole when her father approached her. "Yes, Dad . . . um . . . Admiral?"

"I want both of you in my office immediately," he said, motioning to her and Ryan.

"What's this about?" she asked.

"Not here," he said.

Amanda nodded and turned toward Ryan. She noticed a look on his face she'd never seen before. He looked lost. "Ryan? Are you okay? Did you hear my father?"

"Yeah—I mean yes, sir. I'm ready. I'll be right there."

"Good," replied the admiral. "I'll see the two of you in a moment." He turned and walked away.

Amanda took a chance and grabbed Ryan's arm softly.

"Come on, Ry," she said. "If it's okay, I'll walk with you. If you don't need it, I do."

He gave her a slight smile and walked beside her.

They left the auditorium in silence and made their way to her father's office. Though neither of them said a word the entire way, it was the most they had communicated in years. Words didn't need to be said. She was dying to know why her father wanted to see the two of them. What could this be about? She started to think of all the horrible possibilities. Were the aliens on their way here? Then she had an even darker thought. Was it Ryan's dad? His brothers? *Her* brothers?

When they arrived at her father's office, Lieutenant Rhimes waved them right in. She was working on her Slider viewer and seemed to be overwhelmed. Her father motioned to them to take a seat.

"I'm sure you're wondering why I called you here together."

That was the understatement of the century.

"Ryan," he continued. "Your dad asked me to give you a personal message. I sent you the file. I hope you'll watch it."

"Can I ask what's on it?"

"No, you can watch the video when you get to your quarters."

"Will do, sir."

Amanda thought Ryan seemed way too calm, considering all that was going on. Or maybe he was just in a daze like she was. But why was *she* here? She was almost afraid to ask.

"Dad," she finally said, "are Tyler and Keene all right?" She was terrified about the thought of losing her brothers.

"Tyler's ship was damaged but made it safely to Pluto. Keene's on Ryan's dad's ship and I know he's fine—or as fine as anyone can be at this point. That's not why I called you here. I want the two of you to look at this picture I'm going to put on the main viewer."

He moved over to his console and clicked on it. On the main view screen appeared a large picture of the front of a ship.

"I don't get it," said Ryan. "What is it?"

"Neither of you recognize that insignia?" said Williamson.

Amanda wasn't sure at first, though it did look familiar. Then it hit her and she gasped.

"What is it?" said Ryan.

Amanda held up the amulet on her necklace to show him. Ryan's mouth dropped and it looked like his eyes were about to bug out of his head.

"The insignia looks the same!" said Ryan.

"That's because it *is* the same," replied the admiral.

"What ship is that?" asked Ryan.

"That's the ship of the commander of the Altarran fleet."

Amanda grabbed hold of Ryan's arm. "My God. Don't you get what this means? It's true?"

"What's true?"

"My great-great grandfather said this amulet belonged to some lost tribe. We thought he was crazy. And now we find out it's connected to these aliens. The question is how did an ancient tribe come upon an alien amulet?"

She looked at Ryan, who looked as confused as she was.

"This isn't adding up," said Ryan. "Okay, either this amulet belongs to the aliens and they gave it to an ancient tribe, or a lost tribe met the aliens and made the amulet to match the insignia on the alien ship. It still doesn't explain the connection. And I thought Jill said you were wearing a good luck charm or something."

"Yes," said Amanda. "It's supposed to be used in times of extreme danger."

"What this means," said Williamson, "and the only thing it means at the moment, is that these aliens were here on Earth before, just as they said. They've accused us of something, and now we know they may just be right."

"So where do we go from here?" said Amanda.

"For one," said Williamson, "we need to figure out how this amulet got in the hands of our dear old Robert Williamson. Either he got it from these aliens directly or he somehow got it from the tribe. What we don't know is when this tribe was around, what their role in this was, or if they even still exist.

"Do you have family records or something?" said Ryan.

"Unfortunately, we do not. But if he left any government records mentioning this tribe or anything else we give a hoot about, that would surely come in handy about now. It just so happens that your dad is researching government records as we speak. Of course we're on a communications blackout, so we can only hope his trail leads to the right place."

"Fat chance of that," said Ryan. "It doesn't sound like something that would be on official government records."

"Who said anything about official?" said Williamson. "Sit tight, and don't underestimate your dad."

"Well, I guess we're back to doing what we do best then," said Ryan. "Sitting and waiting."

"Not quite, Ryan," said Williamson. "I didn't call you two in here just to share news so you could sit on your thumbs and ponder the universe. I called you here to put you into action."

Amanda nearly fell over. She was about as shocked as Ryan appeared to be.

"Ryan," said Williamson, "your dad said that when the solar flares hit, they seemed to interfere with the Altarran ships' systems. He thinks there's something to that. Unfortunately, it's not like we can make solar flares on demand. But if we can research the—"

"Could you repeat that, Dad?" said Amanda. She had been trying to process everything, but she couldn't believe what she just heard.

"I said it's not like we can manufacture solar flares," said the admiral. "But if we can—"

"I can," said Amanda.

"You can what?"

"I can create solar flares."

Both her father and Ryan were looking at her like she'd lost her mind. "Impossible," said her dad.

"Seriously, Amanda," said Ryan. "How could you do that? We're years away from anything like that."

"Okay, it's hypothetical," she said. "But I did a paper on it when I was still trying to be an engineer. CME Reproduction Techniques— you can look it up. If I had access to the right system, given enough time I think I can do it."

"Time, time, time," said her father, "a wonderful asset that I'm afraid we do not have."

"But we have to try," said Amanda.

"She's right, sir," said Ryan.

Her dad looked at the two of them as if he couldn't believe they both actually agreed on something. "Alright," he said. "Approved. I'll give you and your crew full access to whatever resources and systems you need."

Her dad looked right at her. "And by the way," he added, "I remember that report, now that you mention it. Didn't understand a damn word of it. But I do know you, Mandy, more than you know. When you put your mind to something, you don't quit until you're done. You go do this. And Ryan, maybe you can get the crew working on whatever's needed to make this happen."

"I'd be honored to, sir," said Ryan.

As they left the admiral's office, Amanda realized that for the first time in the last few days, she felt optimistic. Maybe, just maybe, they might be able to help turn the tide.

Maybe, too, there was a lot more to the amulet and the alleged missing Altarrans. Could the leaders of Earth have been so foolish back then? Would they have been so shortsighted that they thought nobody would come looking for their missing comrades? Maybe we were in the wrong, and now it's payback time. And what was her great-great-grandfather's role in all this? All she knew was that he worked for a top secret government agency, and then supposedly he went crazy with all sorts of weird theories. But maybe he was crazy like a fox. Maybe he knew something others didn't.

In any case, she couldn't wait to tell Jill and Nicole about the amulet. Especially Jill. What was it she'd said about too many science fiction movies? One thing about science fiction movies though, was that the good guys always win. But in this case, who were the good guys? In some ways, Amanda was more confused now than ever before.

Chapter 19
Attack Plans

Ryan entered the engineering compound with Amanda. They were discussing Amanda's theory, and he couldn't believe what he was hearing. All he could do was shake his head and laugh.

"So what you're telling me," he said, "is in order to test your theory, we need to override the safety protocols of the light-speed generator, then shut down the engines less than a half of a second before a catastrophic failure."

"Yes," she said. "Then when we dump the energy from the overload, we find a way to put it into a matter stream array and aim it at the target. Easy peasey."

"And everyone says I'm reckless and crazy. That's just plain sick. What did your professor say about your thesis?"

Amanda looked down at the floor. "She said it was an interesting theory and well written."

"And . . ." said Ryan.

"And that it would be too risky to do in reality. But this isn't a normal situation."

Suddenly he could remember what it was about Amanda that drew him to her when they were younger. She was naïve in a way, but so passionate about things. And she truly was brilliant with anything mathematical or scientific, sometimes to the point where nobody understood what she was talking about. Most of all, he liked her positive energy, and that was something he hadn't seen in a while. It made him realize how much he missed it. How much he missed *her*.

He realized he was staring at her and turned his view to the table where the bridge crew was waiting for them. Everyone looked up. It was hard to read their faces. It was a combination of nervous anxiety at what his and Amanda's meeting with Williamson was about, and shock that he and Amanda were actually walking together.

"Okay," said Tanner, "I want to know right now, who are you and what did you do with the real Ryan and Amanda?"

"Forget that," said Jill. "What did the admiral say?"

"Relax, guys," said Ryan. "There's no new news about the fleet or anyone's families. But we did hear two important pieces of information that may put us back in the game."

"What do you mean *back*?" said Tanner. "We were never in the game."

"Will you shut up for once?" said Jill, elbowing him.

"Well we're in it now," said Amanda.

Everyone quieted down.

"Apparently," Ryan continued, "the Altarrans' shields can be disrupted by solar flares. And that weird amulet that Amanda has? It turns out, it belonged to the missing Altarrans, since it matches the insignia on their ship. So it looks like they did land on Earth after all. Except it was at least a hundred and fifty years ago."

Ryan was wondering why Jill was staring at Amanda wide-eyed with her mouth open. He glanced over at Amanda, who looked like she was trying to suppress a grin.

"So basically," said Tanner, "all we proved is that Amanda's great-great-grandfather wasn't a nut job after all. But we're still screwed because whoever captured their people is dead now, and so are their people. Which means so are we. So, how exactly does that put is in the game? Or is it the 'kill all the humans' game you were referring to?"

"We don't know for sure," said Ryan. "We're still investigating to see if there are any clues. But it's a lead."

"You mentioned two bits of information," said Paul. "What's the other?"

"The solar flares I mentioned. We can use that to our advantage."

"Um, and just how can we use that?" said Paul.

"Yeah," said Tanner. "Last I checked, we can't manufacture solar flares."

"Amanda can," said Ryan.

Tanner and Paul looked at each other.

"Oh, now I feel so much better," said Tanner. "Why didn't you say so before? And here I was worried."

"Somehow I knew you'd be skeptical," said Ryan. "But hear us out."

"Us?" said Tanner. "Ry, have you lost your mind? One minute you can't talk about your old girlfriend, and now you think she can do the equivalent of walking on water?"

Ryan shot Tanner a look.

"I'm going to say this once," said Ryan. "We have orders from Admiral Williamson. We have two options here. We sit and wait, just like we have been, or we get to work on Amanda's idea. If she says it can work, I believe her."

"Okay, what's the plan?" said Paul, breaking the tension. "How can we manufacture solar flares?"

Ryan looked over at Amanda, who explained her theory. As expected, everyone had blank stares, even Jill and Nicole.

Paul was shaking his head. "Ry, I don't know, man. This doesn't sound too feasible. It sounds kinda risky."

"Kinda risky?" said Tanner. "We'll all be blown to bits!"

"What other choice do we have?" said Ryan. "If we can stop these guys, we need to try. We may be the last line of defense. No, correct that. We *are* the last line of defense."

"I can do this, guys," added Amanda. "You have to trust me. I wouldn't put all our lives at risk. But I need your help."

"Amanda, I don't know," said Paul.

"She was right about the engine delays," said Ryan. He didn't want to rub it in, but he had no choice.

Paul shook his head. "Okay," he said. After pausing a few seconds, he added, "I'm in."

"I'm in too," said Jill.

"Count me in," added Nicole.

Tanner just stared at Ryan. "You know, I asked my 106 year old great-grandfather once what he liked most about being 106. He said, 'no peer pressure.' Lucky for you, Mr. Thompson, I'm not 106. Alright, I'm in."

"Good," said Ryan. "Thanks, all of you. So, here's the deal. Admiral Williamson is giving us full run of the engineering department to try Amanda's theory. What I want you guys to do is set up shop here full-time. Amanda and Paul will run the show. The rest of you help out any way you can."

He paused briefly. He wanted to make sure he was being totally clear. "If, and I say if Amanda and Paul can pull this off, I'm going to ask Admiral Williamson if we can head to Earth to use this weapon on the Altarrans. If you guys are with me on this, I want you to spread it around to the rest of the cadets. We're going to need everybody to be on the same page."

Tanner said, "On that, you can count us in, *Captain*."

"Damn right," added Paul.

Jill and Nicole were looking at Amanda.

"If I can get this to work," said Amanda, "we can beat them. I know we can. We would catch them off guard. Of course, I'd much rather try and bring about a peaceful solution, if possible. But if that fails, this is our only option."

"That's good enough for me," said Jill.

Nicole shrugged her shoulders. "Well . . . if all you guys are in, than I guess I am also."

"Then it's settled," said Ryan. "Glad we got done the easy part."

"The easy part?" said Paul. "What's the hard part?

"Convincing Amanda's dad to let us go. But that's my problem. Listen, guys. I have to go check something out. I'll be back in a while. You guys get to work."

As Ryan was leaving, Tanner walked out with him.

"You need something?" said Ryan

"You sure are sharp, Captain," said Tanner, laughing. Did you figure that out all by yourself?"

"I'm good like that some times. What's on your mind?"

"Remember a couple days ago when we were working on the Nimitz and I told you I was going to bring my own torpedo on board if needed?"

"Yeah, I remember. What about it?"

"Well, I was thinking. If Little Red Riding Hood can really bring down the big bad wolf's shields, I can deliver a special knock-out punch."

"What the hell are you talking about, Tanner? What kinda knockout punch?"

"Come on, Ry. Think about it. Remember when we first came here? Nobody is allowed on the western mountains. Do you remember why?"

"Sure. The place is loaded with uranium and plutonium." Ryan stopped, realizing what Tanner was getting at. "You can't be serious, man. That stuff's been illegal for over seventy years."

"Are you for real, Ry? You of all people worrying about what's legal when the earth is in danger of being destroyed?"

Even Ryan had to chuckle at that.

"I'll tell you what, Tanner," he said. "If Amanda can figure out a way to get past their shields, and if I can talk her father into letting us actually take these ships to Earth, then by all means, feel free to bring a nuke along for the ride."

"I knew you'd see it my way. Well, just in case you can talk the old man into letting us go through with it, I'm gonna find a transport and take a ride to the western side and pick up what I need. I'll see you for dinner."

As Tanner headed off, Ryan made his way back to his room. It was time to watch the message his father had sent him.

As soon as he entered the dorm, he took his Slider out of his holster and stretched it out to form a monitor. He tapped the file and watched the screen as his father came into view. He looked like he hadn't slept in days.

"Ryan, I just wanted to let you know that both your brothers are safe. I'm not going to leave you a long-winded message, but I thought you should know, in the event that things don't work out, I'm sorry for what

happened to your mother. I realize that I put my career above my family. That was wrong. I just hope that one day you'll forgive me. Take care, son. This may be the last time you hear from me."

Ryan closed up the Slider. A million different emotions were flooding his mind. He couldn't believe he was choked up over the thought of losing his father, but he was. All those years of avoiding his dad. All that anger. It figured, now that he finally wanted to talk to him, he might not get the chance. He was beginning to understand the sacrifices his dad had made, and the loneliness he must have felt out in the field. It didn't excuse what he'd done, but at least he understood it more. All he could do was not make the same mistakes himself in the future. That is, if there was a future.

The more he thought about it, the more he was beginning to see a recurring theme in life. For everything we do or don't do, there's an effect—and a much broader effect than the action at hand. He decided it was time to have a talk with Admiral Williamson. He needed to plead his case, because whatever action they took now would have an impact on the whole world.

Chapter 20

The Weapon

Amanda was running the numbers and checking her calculations when Paul entered the testing chamber. "Did you get the override codes?" she asked. "We'll need them in order to run the initial test."

"Got 'em," said Paul. "Though I gotta tell you, the master engineer was pretty pissed off. In fact he didn't believe me when I told him we had authorization. I actually had to contact your dad and have him personally tell the chief to give me the codes."

"I'm sure he wasn't happy at all. He gave me the same treatment. Needless to say, he didn't believe me either."

"You talked to him already?! Why didn't you tell me?"

"You didn't ask me. Seriously, I thought you might have better luck as the *official* engineer."

Paul laughed, ignoring her comment. "Well I can't understand why he wouldn't believe you. I mean, all you want to do is purposely overload a perfectly good light-speed generator, which in turn will cause a catastrophic engine failure, which will lead to an implosion of the matter-antimatter stream, which could blow this entire building into tiny little pieces. Does that pretty much sum it up? Because I have to admit, even I think you just might have gone off the deep end here."

Amanda smiled. "Thanks for the compliment, Paul. You really want to know?"

"Uh, yeah?!"

"Back when I was taking engineering classes, they asked us to write a thesis on a project. We had a couple of ideas to choose from. One of the assignments was to come up with a way to use the power from the engines to manufacture a weapon using natural resources. I knew how much havoc solar flares caused on our ships and figured a way—theoretically, of course—to reproduce the core elements of solar flares. I figured if I'm going to be forced into making a weapon, at least it'll be one that's not destructive. At best, it would just fry all the computer systems and shut down communications. I mean—"

She nearly jumped out of her skin when a hand grabbed her shoulder from behind.

"Doctor Frankenstein and Igor, how goes the doomsday machine?" It was Tanner.

"Holy Jesus!" she said. "Where did you come from?"

He looked like he was trying to keep from laughing. "I had Scotty beam me up," said Tanner, "but I must have given him the wrong coordinates. He was supposed to beam me into the Victoria's Secret dressing room."

"Your loss I guess," said Amanda. "Anyway, we're almost ready to run the first test. How are you coming with a way to deliver the dispersion of the electromagnetic particles, gamma rays, and solar gases? Did you measure the isotopic composition of the SEPs and the ionization potential?"

"I'm glad you asked that question. Although I didn't understand half of what you said, I believe if we use the torpedo launchers and good old fashioned CO_2 cartridges as we dump the power buildup from the overload, it just might work."

"Forget it. I'll measure it myself. We need an exact probabilistic model if this is going to work."

"Relax, Amanda," he said. "I'm kidding.I mean about not understanding. Sort of. But I did look up the stuff you told me and ran the measures. We're cool. And as for how to deliver your sunshine payload, what I just said will do the trick." He paused for a second. "Wait a minute," he added. "What the hell is an exact probabilistic model? It's either exact or it isn't. That's an oxymoron."

She shook her head and smiled. Tanner was a pain in the ass, but he was no dummy.

"You know what I meant," she said. "Anyway, about your idea—CO_2 cartridges. Actually, that sounds like it might work."

"You sound surprised," he said.

"We're about to run the first test of the engine overload," she said. "Care to come watch? *Quietly?*"

Tanner shook his head. "No, thanks. I think I'll mosey on over to the other side of the base. If I don't hear an explosion and the world as we know it doesn't end, I'll be back in an hour to check up on you guys."

After Tanner had gone, Amanda and Paul powered the light-speed generator and waited for it to overload. "In all honesty," she said, "I'm hoping we never have to use this."

"But isn't that why we're doing it?" said Paul.

"Well, yes, but what I'm really hoping is that we can try and talk to the Altarrans first. If we actually get this to work, maybe I can try to contact them first about the amulet. Maybe start some type of communication with them so we can end this peacefully."

Amanda watched the monitor as the meter rose.

"Amanda, I'm just saying . . . what if they see your amulet, and then it *really* pisses them off? What if they see it as proof we killed their people? Then they kill you and everyone before we even get a chance to use this thing."

"I don't think they'd do that. I think they'd look at it as proof we can help find their people. Don't you see? It's a show of faith that we're making progress."

"Yeah but find them where? Nobody's seen them in our entire lifetime, so what chance could we possibly have? Where do we look—under our beds? Our cabinets? All it would do is buy us a little time at best, and more likely get us all killed faster."

"Paul, listen to me," she said. "If I thought for one second that would happen, I wouldn't have suggested it. I just think we owe it to them to try to help. After all, we did capture their people. And if it doesn't work, then we can use this weapon and fight back."

"Amanda, honestly, I admire your compassion," said Paul. "But we may not get that chance. And besides, the whole 'who's right and who's wrong' idea doesn't matter at this point. Earth is nine days away from total disaster. That's all that matters. Think about it. We can't afford them thinking it's a stall tactic and going ballistic on us. At least now we have a chance of maybe finding something."

Amanda nodded. "I guess so," she said. "But let's keep it in the back of our mind as a last resort."

"Fair enough," said Paul.

She knew that Paul was right, but she didn't want to admit it, especially to herself. She'd always thought about how wasteful the wars of old were, and how they could have been avoided. Now they had an object that could possibly head off any further destruction, and it seemed a tragedy not to use it.

Paul brought her back into the moment. "Okay, we're ready," he said. "I'm powering up the engines."

"Got it," said Amanda. "All equipment up and running. Pushing the generator to maximum output."

They watched via the monitors at the engine, which was in a double-shielded room a quarter mile away. Between the high radiation levels and the possibility of an explosion, this was the only reasonable way to run the test.

About an hour into the test, the engine passed its maximum power limits. In another ten minutes, the engine would explode. Amanda and Paul waited for what seemed like a lifetime, until finally they were approaching the sixty-second countdown.

"Okay," said Amanda. "When we get to the one-second mark, shut down the engine. The power dump will be automatically ejected and we can measure the effects."

When the countdown made it to the one-second mark, Paul shut down the engine. Amanda watched as the energy buildup was automatically ejected into a containment area, where the particles could be broken down and the data would show whether the effect was the same as that of a massive solar flare.

She brought up the data on the computer and studied it intently.

"Damn it!" she said.

"What?" asked Paul.

She sighed. "I guess my professor was right."

"About . . ."

"She said that my idea could conceivably work, but the engine would have to explode. I disagreed."

"Explode? Did you say explode? And when were you going to let me in on this?" Paul said. "I mean, that's not a small detail."

"It's not that bad," said Amanda. An idea popped into her head.

"Not that bad? Exploding, bad; living, good. I'm not sure there's an in-between, Amanda. That's like saying 'Other than that, Mrs. Lincoln, how did you enjoy the play.'"

"No, I have an idea. I know it may sound crazy and a little dangerous, but I think it could work."

"You *think*? You thought this would work too."

"Trust me," she said, smiling. As Paul stood there looking like a deer in the headlights, Amanda thought more about her idea. That, and how to convince everyone it could work.

Chapter 21

Permission Requested

Ryan was gathering his thoughts as he waited to see Admiral Williamson. He was hoping he'd be able to convince him to authorize his crew to use nuclear weapons. Obviously somebody had to do something and the cadets just might be the only option left. Of course, it all depended on whether Amanda could come through with her plan to replicate a solar flare.

Ryan could see that the admiral was immersed in a sea of holographic images all over his desk. Peeking at a few of them, he could see that they appeared to pertain to the ships in the UEDF. "Is that the casualty list?" he asked.

"Yes, it is," said the admiral, shutting them all down with one touch.

Ryan didn't want to ask, but he couldn't help himself. "How many?"

"Twenty-two hundred and forty-one confirmed dead. Three hundred and fifty-nine missing. Eight hundred and eighty-three injured. Thirty-one ships destroyed, fifteen damaged." The admiral paused and took a breath, then continued. "Only nine ships left without damage in the fleet."

Williamson threw the files back down onto his desk. "We had fifty-five battleships and we couldn't stop them. Hell, we barely slowed them down." He stood up. "As you can see, Ryan, I have my hands full. What can I do for you?"

"I can see that, sir. Sorry to interrupt, but I'd like to discuss an idea I have. An idea that could make the sacrifice of all those men and women not be in vain."

"Listen, Ryan. I know where you're going with this. You know damn well that I cannot allow you or any of the cadets at the academy to go into battle. It's not even a decision I can make. It's not only against regulations, it's illegal."

"I'm well aware of regulations, sir, and I am in no way asking you to break the rules."

"Well that's good to hear."

"Right, sir. I'm quite prepared to do that all by myself."

"Ryan—"

"Of course, all of this depends on whether or not Amanda and Paul can make her idea work. But if they can pull it off, we'd really like your consent."

"We? What do you mean we, Thompson? Consent for what?"

Almost as if on cue, Lieutenant Rhimes's voice came across the speaker. "Admiral Williamson, your daughter is here to see you."

The admiral gave Ryan a strange look. "Now I know this must be a dream. You and my daughter teaming up together against me? This I have got to hear." He pressed the intercom. "Send her in, Lieutenant."

Amanda burst into the room. She was obviously out of breath.

"How did the test go?" said Ryan, before she could utter a word.

"I'm going to have to run it again tomorrow," she said. "I need to make some more adjustments."

"When my daughter says she needs to make adjustments," said the admiral, "that means there's a problem—usually a big problem."

"Not funny, Dad." Looking at Ryan, Amanda asked, "Did you tell my father yet?"

"I was trying to when you walked in," Ryan said.

"Tell me what?" said Williamson.

"Sir," said Ryan, "as I was trying to say, if Amanda can get this theory of hers to become a reality, we intend to take the ships we overhauled and outfit each of them with the weapon we're working on. Then we're hoping to catch the Altarrans by surprise and stop them, sir."

"And what makes you think you can stop them when our entire fleet couldn't?"

"They wouldn't be expecting us, sir. By the time they'd spot us, we can have their shields down and blast away. All their focus will be on the ground or on the defense fleet ships."

"You're not ready for that kind of work, Thompson, and neither is my daughter."

"The point is, sir, there is nobody else. If not us, then who? These aren't normal times."

"He's right, Dad," said Amanda.

The admiral looked sternly at her. "And you agree with this foolish idea?"

"Yes, Father. I do," said Amanda."

"It's something we have to do, sir," added Ryan. "We'd like your blessing, but we'll do it without it if need be. That's how sure we are of this."

Williamson sat close-lipped as his face got redder and redder. After an awkward thirty seconds or so, during which Ryan wasn't sure if he was contemplating locking them up, the admiral pounded his fist on the table.

"Well, that settles it," said Williamson. "If you're going, I'm going with you."

Amanda had an ear-to-ear smile on her face.

Ryan didn't.

"Sorry, sir," said Ryan, "but you can't."

Williamson laughed. "I'm sorry, I must have had something in my ears, because I thought I heard you say I can't. Now I *know* that's not what you said."

"Sir, begging your pardon, that is exactly what I said."

"Thompson, you do realize that I am the only *real* officer with ship's captain experience on this planet, correct? When in a combat situation, there are no do-overs. No mulligans. No checking the guidebook as I know my daughter is prone to do. And no loose cannon hunches. You either make the right call, or you die. End of story. So what, pray tell, is your reason for not wanting me on that ship that my precious daughter is on? *My* ship, I might add."

Ryan knew he had to frame his response carefully. He remembered something his father had told him when he was thirteen and wanted to go to the academy to be a ship's captain. He said that to be a good leader, you had to be able to get people to do what you want them to do because *they* want to do it. Strange that at a time like this, with all the marbles on the line, his father's words were the ones guiding him.

"Sir," he began, "I know we don't have the experience you do. Not many people do. But I've seen our crew, and I've seen what your daughter can do in engineering. We believe in each other, sir. You taught us that. You told us we were better together than apart, and you were right. Until six days ago, no officer had ever died in space fighting a war. We're all in new territory here, sir. But the fact is, if we don't do something, tons of people are going to die. Innocent people, children younger than us. Millions of entire families wiped out. But here's why you can't join us, sir."

Williamson was quietly listening, hands folded. Ryan continued.

"If we fail . . . if we don't make it, you're the only command officer left. The sophomores and the juniors are going to need someone to lead them and keep things together. This planet could be the last hope for the human race. You would need to stay here and keep everyone safe, sir. Because you're the best qualified . . . and the most experienced to do it."

Ryan watched as the admiral thought for a moment. Amanda took Ryan's arm. For a split second, he thought he even saw the admirals' eyes getting watery, but then the admiral's usual controlled demeanor returned.

"Well," said Williamson, "that was a well thought-out response, I'll give you that. And I'm glad my words meant something, I really am. But the fact is, I cannot legally give you the

order to go into a combat situation. If I don't go with you—
and you've just made an excellent case why I can't—then I'm
afraid I can't give you the order to go on your own. The fact is,
if you leave against orders, I would be under obligation to file
disciplinary action, leading to court martial and expulsion from
the academy. I can't play favorites, son. That goes for you too,
Amanda."

"So you're saying you're ordering us not to go, sir?"

Ryan wanted Williamson to really think this through and take
responsibility for his decision, even though he had every intention of
breaking the order if need be.

"What I'm saying," said the admiral, "and I want you both to
listen very carefully . . ." He stared at the two of them, "is that this
conversation never happened. Is that understood?"

Ryan read the admiral loud and clear. He stood tall and straight-
faced and gave Williamson a crisp salute. "Understood, sir," he said.
Then he turned to leave the office, Amanda in tow.

"Well that was interesting," he said quietly to Amanda, once
they were in the hallway.

Amanda's mind seemed elsewhere, though. "Yeah," she said, half-
heartedly. "By the way," she added, "about those adjustments . . ."

Chapter 22

Amanda's Crazy Idea

Amanda had spent most of the night running and rerunning the data. This time, she had it right. Now came the problem of explaining her idea to Ryan and Paul. She started to tell Ryan as they left her father's office, but had quickly thought the better of it and changed the subject. After all, it was an extremely dangerous proposition, but it was the only way to make it work.

When she arrived at the engineering compound, Paul and Ryan were talking. "I'm telling you," said Ryan, "you should have seen her. She basically told her father that she agreed with me. I'm glad she showed up."

"I'll bet you were," said Amanda grinning from ear to ear.

"You know, I rarely agree with Tanner," said Paul. "The reason being, well, he's Tanner. But it sure is strange watching the two of you guys lately."

Amanda just smiled. "Well, you know that old saying. Stranger things have happened."

Just then, Tanner popped up from behind one of the consoles.

"Speaking of stranger things," said Paul.

"Hey, lighten up, folks," said Tanner. "You gotta have fun out here or you'll lose your mind."

Ryan interjected. "Tanner, in your case, it's already hopelessly lost."

"Be that as it may," said Tanner, "I'm here with news for Red Riding Hood."

Amanda rolled her eyes. She hated when he called her that. Tanner continued.

"I've run some tests on my idea for delivering the dispersion of all that mumbo jumbo of particles you talked about. And you'll be glad to know that in a computer simulation, it worked like a charm. Please . . . no applause, everyone. Just throw liquor and women."

"You're a pig," said Amanda. She smiled. "A smart one, but a pig."

"Wanna roll in the mud?" said Tanner.

"That's great news, really," she said, ignoring his comment. "Hopefully we'll be able to put together a working model soon enough." She went to the computer and called Paul over. "I've reworked the numbers, and I have it all on file for you to look at."

Amanda watched nervously as Paul stared at the screen scanning the data.

"I don't get it," said Paul. "You're taking the engine to overload. We'll blow to smithereens. I hope that's not your plan."

"Not overload," said Amanda. "Actually a tenth of a second before overload."

Paul looked dumbfounded. Tanner said to Ryan, "And you say *I've* lost my mind?"

"Wait," said Amanda. You haven't heard the rest."

"Oh, you mean the part where our ashes get scattered all over the place?" said Tanner. "You can skip that part."

"How are we going to trigger anything at a tenth of a second?" said Paul.

"She wants to strap a Rolex to the controls," said Tanner.

Amanda was getting impatient and just stood there silent.

"Guys," said Ryan. "Let's hear the rest." Amanda was surprised, but grateful that Ryan had backed her up.

"Anyway," she said, "we can use the ship's computers to shut down the overload. We can automate the engine shutdown at a tenth of a second, which should allow enough buildup of the particles to be successful."

"But the engine will be too hot," said Paul. "We wouldn't be able to engage light speed after that. We'd be sitting ducks. Not to mention the engine's still likely to explode. Don't you remember our tests during light-speed training last year, when one of the engines was just about to overload and blew up?"

"That engine did overload," said Amanda.

"It was borderline," said Paul. "But are we really gonna split hairs and take that chance?"

"Look," said Amanda, I'll admit it's risky. But we can test it. On a more positive note, even without light speed we'll still have thrusters and sub-light drive and should be able to put enough space between us and the Altarrans until the light-speed engines restart."

"Should?" said Tanner. "This sounds like you're should-ing all over yourself with this one."

"We have no other choice," said Amanda. "Besides, I've thought this through. We just have to get the timing perfect."

"Ya think?" said Tanner.

"There's one other problem," said Ryan.

"What's that?" said Amanda.

"Even if this works as you planned it, we're only gonna get one shot off from each of our ships before we have to bug out. Let's not forget that they outnumber us almost three to one. Even with their shields down, their ships are more powerful than ours. Not to mention, they *will* return fire, you can bank on that, so we can't stand there and trade punches with them. We're gonna have to get our shots off, move out, get our light speed back up before they do, and make multiple runs at them."

"So, let me get all this straight," said Paul. "We run the engines to near explosion; time them to shut down at one tenth of a second; pray to God that they don't explode; fire our solar flares at the enemy, followed by our weapons; and then crawl away at sub-light speed hoping to get far enough away before their systems go back online. Then . . . we come back and do it all again. Did I get that right?" He took a deep breath.

"That's it exactly," said Amanda.

Paul stared at her for a few seconds.

"Works for me," he said.

At first she thought he was kidding, but she could see that he was serious.

"Guys," said Tanner. "This is a suicide mission. There are so many ways this could go wrong, we'd need a computer just to tally them up."

"I don't see a flood of ideas coming our way," said Amanda. "Do you have a better idea? Does anyone? Because I'm all ears."

"Well then listen to this," said Tanner. "No! Besides, from what I can see, you're all legs."

Ignoring him, Amanda said, "Seriously, guys, I know this is dangerous, but it will work. I ran the simulation over a hundred times last night."

"Listen, Amanda," said Tanner. "I'm not saying that it won't work. I'm just saying that it's dangerous as hell. In a perfect situation, maybe it's repeatable. But we're not gonna be in a perfect situation. We're gonna be in space, under the most grueling circumstances and a lot of pressure. Not to mention an unpredictable enemy. One teensy little mistake and we're all dead."

"And, if we don't try, everyone on Earth is dead," said Ryan. Amanda was relieved that someone else had spoken up, as she was starting to doubt herself. "Let's at least run the test on the actual engine in the test chamber," he continued. "If it works, we can try it out on the Nimitz. To be safe, we'll run it via remote testing a few times. If that works, then we'll try it with a skeleton crew. If we're all still alive after that, then I say we run with it."

Amanda looked at Paul and Tanner. Paul still seemed okay with everything. It was Tanner she was worried about.

"Okay," said Tanner. "I'll go with the majority. Let's just hope the skeleton crew doesn't end up as skeletons. And speaking of which," he said, "who's gonna be flying this baby?"

"Oh my God," said Amanda. "We have to tell Nicole and Jill."

Chapter 23

Search For The Truth

Admiral Thompson was running out of time and ideas. With less than seven days to go before the Altarrans' ultimatum expired, he was on his way to visit an abandoned base that was a widely recognized hotbed of extraterrestrial folklore. Along with a staff of twenty clerks and the minister of defense for the United States, Ian Rupert, the admiral was preparing to land at Nevada Base 51, or as it was called in its heyday, Area 51.

At first glance, there was little to see. The landscape was barren for miles. But what did one expect to see in the middle of the desert? The panoramic view did make Thompson wonder why the military would put a supposedly top secret base in a wide-open place, but then he recalled hearing that the airspace was tightly controlled and the entrance was well hidden. Not to mention, they used to refer to the airspace as *Dreamland*, as even top-clearance escorted visitors had to wear blindfolds when approaching. Most of the actual base was underground, and allegedly all its contents had been destroyed. At least that was the official line. Apparently, there were also a number of other underground bases here, connected by a secret subway system.

They came upon what appeared to be two hangars and one large administrative building. They headed for the latter. Thompson was still steaming, and not just because of the weather.

"You mind telling me," he said to Rupert, who was sitting across the aisle from him to the left, "why I was never informed that a top secret base—one that was supposedly shut down and cleaned out over a hundred and fifty years ago—could still possibly be holding key information about alien contacts? I mean, I'm only in charge of Earth's defense fleet. Just putting that out there."

"Oh sour grapes, Admiral," said Rupert. "It's unbecoming. I would think you'd be above that sort of thing. Nobody has set foot here for well over a century. And why would anyone want to?"

"That's not the point."

"The problem with you field commanders is you think there's always something going on over your head. Well, I have news for you. If there's something you need to know, you'll know it."

"Really?" said Thompson. "What about those two civilizations I found? You remember them? I sent a full report to the government. I provided evidence that both planets were destroyed by unknown weapons unlike anything we've ever seen. Wouldn't that constitute need-to-know? Or maybe that slipped your mind."

Rupert gave him a dismissive look. "As I recall, there was no proof whatsoever of an alien attack."

Thompson looked at his assistant, Ensign Morgan, and she rolled her eyes. "Well it looks like we have one now, doesn't it?" he said, loud enough for Rupert to hear.

The plane shifted, and Thompson saw they were making their final descent. It occurred to him that if they didn't get some answers here, soon everyone on the planet would be making a final descent.

As the plane touched down, he asked Morgan to coordinate the rest of his team in disembarking from the plane. He left first with Rupert, and they made their way to the main building, a plain white administrative office. The others followed behind.

When they got there, the building was locked up tighter than a drum, but Rupert had the old access codes and surprisingly—or maybe not surprisingly—they still worked. Rupert pushed the door open and Thompson followed him inside. Ensign Morgan led the others in after them.

The room was dark, as expected, but Rupert had a handheld floodlight, which he switched on and aimed around toward the bare walls. It was dead empty in there. In the dim light, Thompson could see a door at the far corner of the room.

"That's the door to the stairs, according to my map," said Rupert. "We need to head down to the basement." His voice echoed in the empty room.

Thompson followed him through the door and down the stairs. Once there, Rupert placed the floodlight down and unfolded it so that it formed a small floor lamp. It provided dim but adequate lighting for the room. As the rest of the team descended the stairs, it sounded like a herd of elephants.

Thompson looked around. Even in the muted light, he could see that the basement was completely empty, save for a lot of dust. Not only that, but it appeared to lead to another large room that also looked bare. Rupert picked the lamp back up and they proceeded to the next room.

The more they walked, the more Thompson realized how vast the base was. The small administrative office upstairs was just a decoy. Underneath, the basement had to be at least two city blocks long, and it was built like a maze. Hallways broke off and went in all different directions, even diagonally sometimes. It would take forever to explore. Hell, at this rate, he wondered if they'd find their way back.

Thompson was losing patience. "I assume there's more than a maze full of empty basements here. I mean, if you want to play hide and seek, this is a helluva place to do it. But it's not like we have all the time in the world."

"Admiral," said Rupert, "do you think I would take you on a wild goose chase?"

"Do you want me to answer that?"

"This facility, for your information, held the most precious secrets ever denied. And while most of it has been removed, our records show there were old files left here when they closed it. Many old files."

"They must be invisible ones."

"Spare me your impatience, Admiral. When you achieve my position, you'll have full privileges, but for now, let's just say it's above your pay grade."

Thompson looked back at Morgan and whispered, "God, I hate politicians."

She chuckled. "Shush. If he hears you he'll talk even more."

But Rupert wasn't listening. He had some type of device that resembled a laser pointer. Thompson watched as he pointed it at an electrical outlet on the wall. Within seconds, a portion of the wall opened and a lighted passageway appeared.

Thompson wasn't sure if he was impressed or annoyed. "What's next, the yellow brick road?"

They made their way down the corridor one by one. After about five minutes, they came to what appeared to be a dead end. This time the minister removed a device that looked like a tuning fork. He hit it against the wall and within seconds, the entire wall had disappeared and a vast room opened up.

"No wonder they had an economic crisis back then," said Thompson. "This place had to cost the taxpayers a damn fortune." The room was filled with boxes upon boxes, piled from floor to ceiling. They had to be at least five rows deep. He turned to Morgan. "Why don't you pair everyone up into teams and have them start looking through these boxes?"

"Will do, sir," she said.

"Anything referring to an extraterrestrial landing," he said, "I need it sent to me immediately. From the look of it, it's going to be a few days at least. See to it that supplies are brought in for the duration, and some proper lighting. For now, I'm going to look for the offices and see if I can find anything that may be of any use. Then I better get back to Headquarters. You're in charge, Morgan."

"Got it, sir."

"Oh, and contact me personally if you find anything that jumps out at you."

"Lord, I hope nothing jumps out at me," she said. "Don't worry, I'll send you updates every twelve hours. Safe trip back to Headquarters, sir."

Glad to have things in Morgan's reliable hands, Thompson continued down the corridor with his own flashlight and came upon another large room. This was obviously some type of medical area.

There were hospital beds and some very old medical supplies. Some of the beds resembled old-fashioned critical care units with heart monitors and brain monitors. Experimentation maybe? Either way, the place gave him a bad feeling. He was beginning to think the Altarran commander was right. Maybe his people did land on Earth and were captured. Considering all the files and equipment they had in here, it wasn't too much of a stretch to think that someone, perhaps the Altarrans, or maybe even other aliens, could have been kept here.

Continuing down the hall, he made his way into another area that looked like a row of offices. One in particular caught his eye. The nameplate was still on the door: General Robert Williamson, CO. Could it be? The door was partially open. He entered the office. Other than a chair and a desk with a bookshelf over it, the room was empty. Something about the desk sparked a memory, though. It resembled one that his great-grandfather had owned and passed down to the family, a mahogany secretary with a fold-down desk and a number of hidden compartments. Perhaps this one had similar compartments.

Sitting down in the extremely dusty chair, Thompson started opening the drawers. "Come on, General," he said out loud. "You weren't so crazy after all. Please tell me you have something else for us besides that damn amulet."

After about five minutes of looking and quite a bit of sneezing, he had found nothing. If he was going to find something from Williamson, this would have been the place. "Dammit," he said, "why couldn't you give us something more to go on, you old bastard?"

After he put the final drawer back in place, he decided to feel around the molding above the desk, just below the bookshelf. It was elaborately designed, which sometimes meant there were compartments built in. He kept pushing on the different sections until he felt one give way a little. He applied some pressure to it, and lo and behold, a secret compartment popped out, spewing dust right into his face. When he was done sneezing and coughing, he saw something.

Inside the compartment was a piece of paper in a clear plastic bag. The paper looked to be in surprisingly good shape. "Well, what do we have here?" He took it out and carefully unfolded it. One side of the page was blank. Turning it over, he noticed some writing at the top. It was plain and clear. He stared at it, trying to make sense of it.

The Queen is with her loyal subjects
Inside the truth is sealed
Only the worthy who see the ten
Shall have the path revealed

What the hell did that mean? He kept going over the passage in his head. What queen? The truth is sealed inside where? And what did "the ten" refer to? None of this made any sense. He wondered if this was some kind of cryptic message or the ravings of a lunatic. And why would he have kept it hidden where nobody would find it? Or maybe that was the point. Maybe he wanted to hide it until he could send it to someone, but never got the chance. That sounded more likely than anything. "What was it, Williamson?" he said. "Were you nuts or were you trying to leave someone a hint?"

Thompson heard footsteps coming his way. He folded the note quickly and put it into his pocket just as the door opened. It was Rupert, shining a flashlight on him. "Well, Admiral," said Rupert. "Did you find anything of interest? I thought I heard talking."

Thompson stood up, his body hiding the secret compartment. "Not a damn thing," he said. "I tend to talk to myself when I reach a dead end. You should try it sometime. I checked every drawer and every nook and cranny in here. It looks like we're out of luck unless there's something in all those boxes we found."

"Let's do hope they find something then," said Rupert. "I'd hate to think we may have come all this way for nothing. As for me, I'm afraid I have to return to Washington. I'll leave the instructions needed to get in and out with your assistant. Shall we go, Admiral? I'm sure you have more pressing issues waiting for you at Defense Fleet Headquarters."

"All right, Minister," said Thompson. "To the transport it is."

Making sure that Rupert wasn't looking back, Thompson followed the minister out of the room and back toward the area they had come from. For some reason he didn't trust Rupert. Then again, he didn't like politicians in general. But something in Rupert's demeanor just felt all wrong to him. It was as if it was a bother for him to be here, almost as if he couldn't care less whether anything useful was found at the base. Or, for that matter, that there was an impending alien invasion of the planet. He was just too casual about it all. Or maybe that was part of his public office training.

One thing the admiral did know was that General Williamson had left the piece of paper there for a reason. It was the only paper in the entire desk, and it was in a hidden compartment. Now he had to figure out what that reason was, and the clock was ticking.

Chapter 24

Preliminary Testing

Ryan was in the cafeteria having lunch with several of the cadets who'd been put in charge of overhauling the other ships. He'd been keeping them up to date on Amanda's progress with the weapon. It was day three of Earth's ten-day truce, and, needless to say, everyone on the base needed some good news soon.

Ryan was waiting to hear the results of the latest test. He was glad Jill and Nicole were on board with the plan. To his surprise, they had taken it easier than Paul and Tanner had. Something about wanting to avenge Nicole's sister. He was looking at his watch when his personal communicator beeped. It was Amanda. Hopefully, this was the news he was waiting for. He clicked it on.

"Amanda?"

"Ryan," she said, through a lot of background noise, "I need you to come to the engineering compound as soon as possible. We tried the test."

Her voice sounded shaky, but he couldn't make out whether it was joy or terror, and he could hear yelling in the background. Or was it screaming?

"Please tell me it's good news," he said.

"Yes," she said. "It is! I'm rechecking the data as we speak, but it worked. Ryan, do you hear me, it worked! Hurry up and get here so I can show you the results."

"On my way."

Dammit, she actually did it! They all did.

Before leaving, he quietly told a few of the other captains the good news and asked them to spread the word. They were going to run the test a couple more times in the lab and then try it out on the Nimitz. If all went according to plan, he was hoping they could get all fifteen ships ready to leave within three or four days. The trip to Earth at full speed would take close to seventy-two hours. They'd be cutting it close, but if everything went perfectly, they'd just make it to Earth before the Altarran troop carriers got there.

When he arrived at the engineering compound, he could see his entire bridge crew celebrating, including Jill and Nicole. It looked like New Year's Eve. Amanda turned around and ran to him.

"It worked!" she said. "We ran the test five times. Every single time we pulled enough electromagnetic particles and gamma rays to produce a solar flare. In fact, the last test we threw in a bunch of software, computers, and a small probe. And we fried everything!"

She was glowing. It had been a long time since Ryan had seen her like this. He held out his arms and she embraced him. As he looked down at her face beaming up at him, he couldn't help thinking how wonderful it felt holding her in his arms. "We did it, Amanda," he said, softly. "*You* did it. I knew you would. Never had a doubt."

Over Amanda's head, he could see Tanner looking at Paul. "Do you think the flare could separate those two?" said Tanner.

Nicole elbowed Tanner. "Can it," she said. "Before we use the flares to fry your last remaining brain cell."

Amanda let go of Ryan. Her face was red and she had a shy smile. Paul, on the other hand, was too busy going over all the data to be bothered with all the chatter. "It looks amazingly good," said Paul.

"How soon can we set it up on the Nimitz and give it a go?" said Ryan, looking at Amanda. "Time's running short, and we have to make sure it'll work on a ship during actual battle conditions in deep space."

"It'll take us about eight hours to set everything up," said Amanda. "While Paul and I are preparing the engine room, Tanner, Jill, and Nicole can start getting the firing system ready. I'd say we should be ready to test it on the Nimitz by 0600 hours tomorrow." She glanced over at Paul. "Sound right to you, Paul?"

"Absolutely," he said. "In fact, if we all ate on the ship and worked non-stop in teams, we could probably be ready by midnight."

While Ryan was in a hurry to get the work done as soon as possible, he didn't want to risk a tired crew. "I think 0600 is good," he said. "Let's do this once and do it right. Like a wise old man told me recently, we don't get any do-overs here." He glanced at Amanda and smiled. One day maybe she'd tell her dad he was actually listening when the admiral spoke.

One by one, they agreed and started setting the plan into motion. They grabbed their tools and gear and headed to the Nimitz.

Amanda caught up to Ryan as they made their way to the hangar. "This will work, Ryan. I know it. I just want to tell you, I'm really glad you believed in me. It means a lot."

"It wasn't too tough," he said. "The minute you said you knew of a way to duplicate solar flares, I knew you'd find a way. That's what you do, Mandy. You know, I remember when we were little. You could fix anything. Now, if all this works like we think, you could just end up being the person that saved Earth. How cool would that be? I guess your dad couldn't complain about you being an engineer if we pulled that off, now, could he?"

"I guess not," she said, smiling.

They entered the hangar and boarded the Nimitz. Things were starting to shape up. For the first time in over a week, Ryan believed they actually had a shot at pulling this off. Not a huge shot, but at least a chance. But more important, for the first time in three years, he felt alive. Truly alive. It figured he should feel this way at the very time they were about to come closer to death than ever before.

Chapter 25

Final Testing

Amanda finished running the mechanism for the kill switch from the light-speed generator to the main engineering console. The switch was needed in case they lost computer systems during an attack and had to manually stop the override. Hopefully, they would never need to use it.

She peered over at Paul. He was busy connecting the extra lead shielding needed to compensate for the overflow of radiation that would result from the overload of the reactor.

"How much longer until you're done?" she said.

"When it's done, I'll know. I'd worry more about whether they'll get the autopilot system working on time."

Amanda checked the time. "Good thought. I better go check. When you're done down here, give me a holler."

"Nicole will love that," he said. "She likes being interrupted when she's in deep thought."

"Now you sound like Tanner," she said.

Amanda made her way out of the engineering section and continued to the bow of the ship. As soon as she entered the bridge, she knew something was wrong. She could hear Nicole talking to herself. One thing Amanda knew for sure about Nicole: if she was talking to herself, there was a problem.

Nicole's feet were protruding from under the helm console, but her mouth was working just fine. "God darn, archaic autodrive systems. I don't know how this crappy setup ever worked in the first place."

"Problems?" said Amanda.

Nicole jumped and hit her head on the console. "Ow! Damn it, Mandy!" She crawled out from under the console rubbing her head and laughing.

Amanda reached out her hand and helped her up.

"Hey, at least I didn't grab your feet like last time," said Amanda. "Anyway, what's the issue?"

"The issue is that this ship was retired from active duty ten years ago. And since these old ships are only used for low-orbital test flights, they never bothered upgrading the autopilot systems."

"That's crazy," said Amanda. "Then why have us use it during the simulation?"

"That's the problem," said Nicole. "They figured the simulation would be enough. They never expected to actually need these ships for active duty. Of course, it takes next to nothing to maintain the systems properly, but no! Idiots! Fricking idiots!"

Tanner was listening at the weapons console. "Way to tell them, Nicole! I have to say that was eloquently put. I see Jill's teaching you well."

This time it was Jill who smacked Tanner.

"Hey! If you guys are really into double teaming me . . ."

"In your dreams," said Jill.

"Hey," said Tanner, "Walt Disney said dreams can come true if you have the courage to pursue them."

"I'm not hearing any of this," added Nicole.

At that moment Ryan walked onto the bridge. Amanda had updated him while the others were talking. "I hear we can't get the autopilot to work," he said.

"Yep," said Nicole. "The entire system is fried. And to make it worse, we don't have any spare parts for these old units."

"Well that screws us," said Tanner. "So much for our test flight."

"We'll need to run it live," said Ryan.

"Live?" said Tanner. "You mean test this thing with real people?"

"We have no other choice," said Ryan. "We'll just have to be that much more diligent in our simulations."

Amanda was glad Ryan was holding strong, but even she was a bit concerned about this.

"If any of you don't want to do the live test flight," said Ryan, "now is your chance to back out. But either way, I'm going to be on that ship, even if I have to run all the positions myself. So, anyone want to back out?"

Amanda looked around at the bridge crew. No one said a word. One by one, they all went back to work.

She felt a lump in her throat. She knew what they must be feeling—too young to die and too scared to run. They must have been trembling inside just like her. But somehow they found it in themselves to focus, even on a makeshift plan that was one step short of suicidal. There just wasn't any other choice here. To think how far they'd come in just a few short days. Something special was definitely happening, something that if they managed to survive all this, would bind them together forever.

She turned to Ryan, who looked equally touched. "I'm heading down to engineering," she said, as if it were a normal work day. "I want to run one last check on the engines and the light-speed generator. I'll fill Paul in on what's going on."

"Sounds good," he said. "Let me know as soon as he's done. Meanwhile, I'll try to get clearance from your dad for our test flight. I'll also ask him to launch a few communications satellites and see if we can fry them. Wish me luck."

"You'll need it," she said. "Let me know if he gives you a hard time."

He smiled. "But that's my job, to give *him* a hard time."

"Trust me," she said, laughing. "Nobody can do it better than daddy's little girl."

She thought of all the hard times she'd given her father. If Ryan only knew the half of it. As she watched him walk off, she went in the opposite direction to head for engineering to see Paul.

When she got there, Paul was putting the welding equipment away. That was a good sign. It meant he was done with the shielding and they were ready to go.

Paul looked up. "We're all set," he said. "Now all we need to do is leave the ship and watch the absolutely perfect results from the safety of our monitors."

"Well . . . not exactly," she said.

"Umm . . . you care to explain to me what 'not exactly' means?"

Amanda started to pace back and forth. Her palms were sweating. Finally, she decided to just blurt it out. "Well, you see, it's like this. The autopilot system doesn't work and there are no spare units available . . . so . . . well, I'm sure you get the point."

"Um . . . well . . . no. I don't. You mean we can't do the test?"

"Paul," she said. "We're doing a live test. Everyone's in. Well, I'm hoping 'everyone' means you too."

She watched as Paul stood silent and blank-faced, almost as if he were contemplating what to eat for dinner. It occurred to her he'd be great at poker.

"You know," he said, "my mother always told me this would happen."

"Your mother told you *this*? What, is she a psychic?"

"No." He smiled. "She told me if I didn't start going to church instead of trying to build and fix things all the time, God wouldn't have my back."

"You're kidding, right?"

Paul laughed. "Actually she really did say that. Anyway, when does our test start?"

"So, you're in?"

"Of course. What the hell. We've come this far. If we're gonna do this, then let's do it."

She forced a smile. Poor Paul was trying to keep it together, just like her. But inside, she knew he had to be as nervous about the odds as she was. Even with all the simulations and preparation, things somehow always managed to go wrong when in a live space environment. Hopefully this wasn't one of those cases. Out of instinct, she held out her arms for Paul, and he came forward to hold her—just two scared kids comforting each other. No words needed to be said.

When she left engineering, she called Ryan to give him the news. He had news for her as well.

"Mandy?" he said. "Looks like it's a go."

"You mean you talked to my dad? He said yes?"

"Well, more like he didn't say no. He said he didn't want to hear any more and would be unreachable for the next thirty minutes. Then he proceeded to tell me all the things we'd need to do if we were going to do such a test. So, I take that as a yes. Sort of."

Typical, she thought. She could never get a straight answer out of her dad.

"So what's our next step?" she said.

"Well, we need to do a final systems check and take off within the next thirty minutes."

Thirty minutes! Everything that had taken place in the last week ran through her mind in an instant. So much had happened. Suddenly all her calculations, all her testing, seemed inadequate. Now, her whole life—and everybody's—came down to what would happen in the next hour. This must be how death row prisoners feel awaiting the electric chair.

Chapter 26

Uedf Nimitz, Live Test

Ryan was starting to feel the pressure. Commanding a live mission—especially one with so much at stake and so many dangers looming—was in no way, shape, or form like leading a crew in a simulation, or even on a critical maintenance detail. And this was no ordinary test flight. They'd barely had time to regret their decision when it had been time to take off. So far, so good, though. Despite everyone's anxiety, the Nimitz had taken off without a hitch and all systems were running at one hundred percent capacity. The real test was yet to come. Soon they'd find out one way or another whether Amanda's risky plan would work.

"This is your friendly weapons officer, Tanner Blackhart, reporting," said Tanner, breaking the nervous silence. "I'm detecting several extremely menacing-looking communication satellites dead ahead, Captain."

As long as Ryan had known Tanner, he'd always been like this. The more difficult or dangerous a situation was, the crazier he acted. Of course, in a simulation, it wasn't too hard to do, but it was good to know that even in a live situation, he was still the same old Tanner. Ryan wished he could be like that sometimes, but it wasn't in his nature. Besides, he was always too busy trying to hold the fort together.

"Target the satellites, Tanner," he ordered. "When we get to five thousand feet, prepare to fire the solar disrupter."

Tanner smiled. "Solar disrupter, eh? Why, thanks, Ry. You used my name. Told you it was cool."

"Well let's hope it disrupts."

Ryan could see they were getting closer to their target.

"Locking the targeting sensors now, Capt'n," said Tanner.

"Jill, patch me through to engineering," said Ryan.

"Main engineering is on the line . . . *Captain.*" Jill was smirking, obviously mimicking Tanner.

"This is Ryan to main engineering. Do you copy?" He felt awkward being so formal, but he was sure Admiral Williamson was secretly listening to the test flight, and he wanted his acceptance.

"Engineering here, Ry—I mean, Captain," said Paul. "We're ready to engage overload within sixty seconds of target."

Ryan looked to Amanda at the sensor array. "Say when, Amanda."

"Paul," said Amanda, "according to my sensor readings, begin overload in . . . ten seconds."

"Copy that, Amanda. Overload in seven, six, five, four, three, two, one. Engaging engine overload . . . now."

Ryan could feel the vibrations run through the entire ship as the light-speed generator was set to maximum output. As the power surge continued, the vibrations got stronger, making his whole body numb.

"Steady as she goes, Nicole," he said, his voice shaking with the ship's movements. "Hold course and maintain speed."

Nicole's eyes never left her console as she replied, "Course and speed steady as she goes."

The entire ship was shaking. Ryan was starting to sweat as he heard the sound of metal contracting. He thought he heard a bolt or two pop. "How much longer, Paul?"

"Thirty seconds until catastrophic overload. At ten seconds, I'll be activating the automated timing system. That will shut down the overload with a tenth of a second cushion. Let's all say a prayer. 'Cause if this doesn't work, we'll all be blown into subatomic particles, in which case I'll see you on the other side."

Ryan was using all of his inner strength to remain calm. He could feel the tension on the bridge. "Thanks for the vote of confidence, Paul. From all of us on the bridge, we truly hate you."

"Seriously folks," said Tanner, "you all need to calm down. Do you have any idea of all the things that can happen in one-tenth of a second? A hummingbird can flap his wings ten times. A laser can travel hundreds of feet—"

"Tanner, shut up," said Jill. "You're not helping."

Ryan grabbed hold of his chair as the Nimitz rocked and the vibrations got stronger and louder.

Nicole yelled out from the helm. "I'm having a hard time holding her on course."

Ryan had to yell over the noise. "Hold her steady, Nicole. Just a little bit longer."

Ryan's heart was beating out of his chest. He could barely hear Paul over his com link as he counted down. "Prepare to fire in five, four, three, two, one."

The ship felt like it was about to fall apart, when suddenly the vibrations stopped. The bridge crew let out a loud cheer, as Ryan, with barely time to breathe a sigh of relief, yelled to Tanner over the noise.

"FIRE!"

"Solar disrupter fired!" said Tanner, stepping back from the targeting array.

Ryan actually felt the ship buck when the weapon was discharged. He watched the monitor. The near overload of the light-speed generator dumped an enormous volume of particles and gasses into a controlled energy beam. Within seconds, the powerful discharge reached the archaic collection of communication satellites along with a couple of out-of-service small transports.

He held his breath and looked at Amanda. She was staring intently at the sensor array, waiting for the data to come through. They'd made it past the explosion danger. Now to see if the experiment worked. The entire bridge was silent, waiting to hear her report and watching her face closely for any sign. Any hint.

Finally, her eyes widened.

"Oh, my God," she said.

"What?" said Tanner. Don't keep us in suspense, for Chrissakes."

Then a grin formed on her face as she looked up at Ryan.

"It worked!" she said. "All satellites are offline. Both transport ships have shut down." She pumped her fist up in the air as she ran directly to Ryan.

The rest of the bridge was also up on their feet and cheering, except for Nicole, who was flying the ship.

Ryan stood up as Amanda jumped into his arms. He looked into her eyes and saw pure elation. He couldn't help thinking what a total jerk he had been to her the last three years. He hugged her as tight as he could, and whispered in her ear, "I'm so proud of you. You did it. You really did it." He put her down and looked around the bridge. Everyone was congratulating each other. Either nobody noticed their exchange, or if they did, they were so overwhelmed with joy that they didn't care—which was just fine, as far as Ryan was concerned.

Jill called out to him. "Ryan," she said. He voice had a serious tone. "Um . . . Admiral Williamson is on the com, sir. He wants to speak with you and Amanda."

Ryan looked over at Amanda, who shrugged her shoulders.

"Put him on video," said Ryan. He figured if they were going to get reamed out, it may as well happen in front of the whole crew.

Jill hit a button, and the video display turned on. Williamson's face, as usual, was hard to read.

"To all the cadets on the Nimitz. This will be a brief, but important message. I want you all to remember, and let sink in, what you have just done. You have willingly chosen to undertake this highly risky, extremely dangerous test, and put yourself in harm's way, with the greatest of intentions, mind you—nothing less than to find a way to save the human race. Your attempt, which all of you chose to do, without my explicit orders I might add, was foolhardy beyond belief. But it was also the most daring, brave, and well-executed goddamn thing I've ever seen in my life. Thanks to you, mankind may very well have a chance to beat these bastards. I'm proud as hell of all of you. As for you, Ryan and Amanda, I'd like to see you both in my office for a debriefing once you're on the ground. Williamson out."

The screen went blank.

"Did I just witness that?" said Tanner.

"So, what's next?" said Paul.

"I guess now we have to get all the other ships set up and ready to move out," said Amanda.

Ryan nodded. "That, and convince everyone else *and* your father to let us go."

"You'll need my help on that," she said. "Trust me." She smiled at him.

Ryan had to laugh.

"What's so funny?" said Amanda.

"Nothing," he said. "Just that you always said you wanted to save the world and make it a better place. Well you'll have a helluva chance now."

He smiled as he turned to Nicole at the helm. "Take us in, Nikki. Nice and easy."

"Captain," said Nicole, beaming. "Taking us in."

Ryan sat back in the command chair and took a deep breath. Now the hard part would begin.

Chapter 27

In Harm's Way

As his jubilant but anxious crew exited the hangar, Ryan was taken aback by the large crowd of cadets waiting. They all cheered as he and the rest of the team descended. Apparently, word about the test results had spread, and it seemed there was a renewed sense of hope in the air.

He called his bridge crew together as soon as they'd made it past the mob.

"Okay, guys," he said, "here's the deal. Amanda and I are going to meet with her dad and put together a plan of attack. Jill and Nikki, you guys get the word out and have all the cadets meet in the auditorium at fourteen hundred hours."

Ryan gestured to Paul and Tanner. "I'll need the two of you get all the engineers and weapons officers together and give them a crash course on the system and how to get it up and running. Then get all the crews working on this for the other ships. Whatever you do, guys, be sure to personally check every unit to make sure they've all been installed properly."

"Got it," said Paul. "I'm heading over to the engineering library first. I'm sure most of the engineers are there now, looking over the schematics Amanda and I posted on the server."

"I'm gonna tag along with Paul," said Tanner. "Not to worry, skipper. We won't rest until there's a solar disrupter in every household . . . or at least every ship."

Ryan laughed, as he motioned to Amanda. "We better get going. Your dad's waiting, and you know how he gets."

Amanda joined him as they made their way down the long corridor to the admiral's office.

As they entered Williamson's reception area, Ryan was surprised to see the admiral waiting right there. The assistant's desk was vacant.

"Where's Lieutenant Rhimes?" asked Ryan.

"Taking a much needed rest. I gave her the day off. In times like this, people die, Thompson, and her husband was reported missing. She's good people. So was he."

"Oh no," said Amanda. "She must be beside herself."

Williamson was stone-faced as usual. "Let's step into my office, we have more pressing issues to discuss." Then he softened up and almost looked human as he held Amanda's shoulders. "Listen, Mandy," he said, "I'm as upset as you are about that, but there's nothing we can do."

She nodded as they all proceeded into Williamson's office. The admiral sat behind his desk.

"I have all the data here," said Amanda. "I also sent you a complete breakdown."

"No need to see it again, I've already sent it to an engineer I trust," said Williamson, "the last senior guy on the base."

"Did he get back to you?" said Ryan.

"He sure did." The admiral paused.

"Well, are you going to tell us?" said Amanda.

"He said it looks sound. Dangerous as hell, but sound."

"And?" said Amanda.

"There is no 'and.' You guys did one hell of a job."

Ryan decided that now was the time to make his case. "Sir," he said. "If you don't mind, I'd like to revisit our previous conversation about taking the fleet of ships we have, arming them with the solar disrupter, and heading out towards Earth."

"What previous conversation?" said Williamson.

"Sir—"

"You must be referring to the one that never happened, just like this one isn't happening."

The admiral got up and started to pace back and forth. "I've given this plenty of thought, Thompson. In many ways, you're right, I'll give you that. There is no other way, or no other answer I can think of. If I try to forward the information to Fleet Headquarters, the Altarrans would probably intercept the message and that would be that. Even if I encoded it, it would still give away our position."

"Sir. I under—"

"Damn it, Ryan. Please be quiet and let me finish."

"Yes, sir," said Ryan. "Sorry, sir."

"As I was saying, even if we did send the information to Head-quarters, they don't have enough ships or time to make it work. So that really only leaves one choice."

"Us," said Amanda.

"I want you to contact the other cadets," said Williamson, who seemed to be in a bit of a daze, "and ask who's willing to go with you. Don't make threats or promises. If you can get enough of them to man all fifteen ships, I won't stand in your way. God knows I don't want to put my daughter in harm's way, or you either, Ryan, but damn if it isn't the only choice we have. And you're right, I can't go, because if it . . . doesn't go as expected, these people here need me."

"Sir," said Ryan, "you're making the right decision."

"I made no decision, Thompson. I want both of you to know that I cannot sanction this mission, and on the official record, it happened without my consent. I can help you with whatever information you need, but I cannot endorse this mission. Understood?"

"Yes sir," said Ryan.

The admiral looked at his daughter.

"Yes, Dad," she said.

"Dad?" said the admiral.

"Well, we're not on official business, are we?" She smiled, and for the first time, Williamson smiled back.

Ryan could see that the admiral was torn up inside, but the hardened man, whose weathered face made him look old beyond his years, appeared as a rock—an unmoving, proud, supportive rock. But inside, the man was all love. And that's all anyone could ever expect from an admiral. Or a father.

"Sir," he said, "we're going to leave one battleship here with you. Also, in the event that you have to evacuate the base, enough transports to take the remaining cadets to a safe place."

"Just leave the transports, Ryan. You're going to need every last one of those ships to succeed."

"Guys," said Amanda, "I have another idea."

Ryan and Williamson both looked at her, wondering where she was going with this.

"What if we could end this peacefully?" she said. "I mean, you told us that they came here looking for their lost envoys. And I do have an amulet that matches their insignia. Maybe if I mention the amulet to them, we can open up negotiations and end this without any more bloodshed. After all, we did cause this in a way."

Ryan just shook his head. "Are you serious? We'd give away our position and the whole plan would be shot. Don't forget they killed over two thousand men and women from our fleet because a few of their envoys are missing? And we didn't cause anything, our ancestors did—allegedly. But they didn't seem to care about that, from what the report said. These creatures have no conscience, Amanda; they're not gonna say, 'Yeah, maybe you're right.'"

The admiral was just looking at them like he was watching a tennis match. Amanda's face turned beet red. "You don't know that," she said. "And what happened to trusting my opinion?"

"I trust your opinion with engineering, but this is different. The only option here is to blow them away before they do it to us. All's fair in war, Amanda. Besides, you're the one who came up with the weapon in the first place."

"You know, just when I was starting to think that you *might* actually have an open mind, you revert to being a Neanderthal. Why do we have to go in guns blazing? Couldn't we broadcast the message from—"

"Why?" he said. "I'll tell you why." He couldn't believe, after all that had happened, the naïve Amanda had returned. "Even if they *are* right, we have no clue when this happened. It seems like it was a helluva long time ago. If, and I say *if*, their people did crash land on Earth, they're long gone and we can't bring them back. How can you not get that? We have no bargaining chip. All you'd do is prove for sure to them that we did something to their people. Think about it."

Amanda didn't look like she was buying it. "But if we appealed to them," she said, "and showed them the amulet in good faith, it might make a difference. They might listen. The odds are better of that, than of our mission working. Sometimes, you just have to have a little faith in humanity."

"But that's the point. They're not human, Amanda!"

"No, but you can't think everyone's out to intentionally cause evil, either. Sometimes bad things happen, Ryan. Unfortunate things."

"Unfortunate?"

"But it doesn't mean it can't be fixed with a little understanding," she added.

"This isn't about me, Amanda."

"Isn't it? Because I think you're making this a personal vendetta to make up for what happened at the hospital."

Ryan felt his fists clench.

"Don't even—"

"Hold up there, children," said Williamson.

Before Ryan could respond, Amanda turned around and stormed out of the office.

Williamson just shook his head and looked at Ryan. "Now you've done it. You pissed her off all over again. Just when it looked like you two might actually grow up."

Ryan stood there dumbfounded. He wasn't even sure what had just happened, and he certainly didn't get Amanda's position. Or rather, he didn't get how she couldn't understand his. He looked at the admiral.

"Begging the admiral's pardon, but why did she even design a weapon that would disable the Altarrans' shields if not to use it to win this war?"

Williamson looked directly at him, his face a little softer. "Son, sometimes you just have to figure things out for yourself. My daughter has always believed there can be a peaceful outcome to any altercation. Just because we're members of the military doesn't mean we shouldn't try to put an end to a dispute peacefully."

"So you're telling me you don't think what she's suggesting is insane?"

"Sure it's insane. Everything we've been talking about is insane. Listen, Ryan. There comes a time when there's no black or white decision. Oh there's a right answer and a wrong one, but you don't find out which is which until the game's over. Welcome to leadership, son. Now, you've got a whole lot of work ahead of you and not a lot of time to get it done. Why don't you get out of here and get to it."

"Will do, sir."

"Dismissed, Thompson."

Ryan saluted, turned around, and left the office. He knew the admiral was right. Time was against them. But he couldn't get Amanda out of his mind. She just didn't understand that sometimes you need to seize the opportunity, and discussions just aren't an option. That's why governments don't negotiate with terrorists. But she had a bleeding heart, and he supposed he couldn't fault her for that. Except, in this case it could become a hazard to the mission. He couldn't let that sidetrack him though. They had a fleet to get armed and ready, and then they had a small army of cadets to convince to go to war.

Chapter 28

Counterpoint

As Amanda entered her dorm, she could hear Jill and Nicole blabbering away. They sounded excited. She slammed the door as she walked in, and they both stopped to stare at her. She threw her files on the table and slumped down on the sofa next to them. "Why, why do I do this to myself?"

Jill looked at her. "Okay, what happened now? You guys left the ship an hour ago looking like Romeo and Juliet."

Amanda sighed. "We were talking to my dad about getting the fleet armed and ready to head to Earth. I mentioned to Ryan that maybe, just maybe, we could try and talk to the Altarrans before shooting at them. You know?"

"Uh oh," said Jill. "I'm sure that went over well."

"All I wanted to do," said Amanda, "was to try to end this peacefully. I mean, I have the amulet. Maybe if we reached out to them and told them that, we could at least open up a dialogue. Maybe we could avoid a possible disaster."

"It sounds reasonable to me," said Nicole.

"Tell Ryan that. All he could talk about was why it wouldn't work."

Nicole shook her head. "What was his argument?"

"He said it would give away our positions. But if he had let me finish, we could have discussed ways around that. But no, he was too busy on his warpath to even consider it."

"Maybe we can convince him to at least think about it," said Nicole.

"There's no convincing him of anything. Meanwhile, he's putting all of humanity at risk because he won't take time to listen."

"Well," said Jill, "you better figure out a way to put on a common front with him in the next sixty minutes."

"Why is that?"

"Because we have the entire academy attending a special meeting. A meeting where you and Ryan are the speakers."

"Just great," said Amanda. "I was so worked up I almost forgot about that."

"Yeah, well, you better figure something out," said Jill. "Because you and Ryan are the leaders here, and you're going to have to stand united if we have any chance of pulling this mission together."

Amanda stood up and took a deep breath. "You're right. I'll be okay. After all, we still have a ton of work to do to get the ships ready."

"Are you sure you're okay?" said Nicole.

"Never better," said Amanda, shooting Nicole a false smile as she headed to her room to get ready.

Within thirty minutes, they were headed toward the auditorium. Amanda was running ideas through her mind, searching for the right words to say to the class. Either way, she still wasn't giving up the idea of finding a peaceful resolution. She owed humanity that much.

As she entered the auditorium, she could see that the place was full. She overheard some of the conversations as she walked down toward the front of the auditorium. There seemed to be a combination of excitement and fear. It appeared that all three classes were in attendance.

Just before she reached the stage she saw Tanner and Paul in the first row. Tanner waved to her. "Let's have a hand for Doctor Doom," he yelled out, "the mad scientist and creator of the solar death ray."

She ignored him.

As she headed to the stage, she rubbed her sweaty palms on the side of her pants. Ryan was already there. She walked onto the stage and took a seat next to him. As he got up and walked to the podium, the noise level dropped. She got up and stood beside him. She watched as he looked out at the audience. She had to admit, he seemed calm and in control, emitting an air of self confidence. In a way that just aggravated her even more, though, considering what was at stake.

"My fellow cadets," he said. "All of you are aware of the events that took place last week. Our home, Earth, is at a cross-roads. You all know my father, Fleet Admiral 'Flash' Thompson." Ryan paused as many in the audience hollered out and applauded at the mention of Ryan's father. It was the first time Amanda had heard Ryan speak of his father in public, especially using his nickname.

"We all know that our fleet fought bravely. Unfortunately, the enemy has shields protecting their ships. Just before my father's fleet surrendered, he found out that the Altarrans' shields were briefly disrupted by the effects of a solar flare. Well, as luck would have it, Amanda Williamson, who is standing next to me, has developed a weapon that will replicate the effects of a solar flare. What this means is that we now have a weapon to disable their shields!"

The crowd began cheering loudly. Amanda glanced over at Ryan, who was beaming as he applauded her. He truly seemed proud, and had a look of sincere respect. That just confused her even more. If he respected her work, why didn't he respect her opinion?

He turned the podium over to her, and she looked out at the audience. She was amazed by the camaraderie in the crowd. It was true what they say about people pulling together in times of great stress, even with practically impossible odds. She looked back at Ryan. She could see he was waiting for her to do something to rally everyone—though he did appear a bit nervous, as if he wasn't quite sure what she would say.

Here goes, she thought. She grabbed Ryan's hand and thrust hers and his together into the air, as the crowd screamed and yelled in response.

"United and together," she said over the deafening noise, "we can save our planet and end the fighting. The only thing I want to know is: Are you all with us?!"

The audience jumped to their feet and roared their approval, their fists all pumping in the air. To her surprise, they were raring to get started and ready to go. While she was sure that word must have leaked about the engineers working on some special project, she wondered if they knew the full dangers of the mission. If not, they'd soon find out.

Ryan looked at her as the crowd noise continued. "Thanks," he said, grinning. "This is exactly what we needed. Look at them all!" He seemed to be enjoying this a little too much.

"Yeah," she said off-mic, "so why do I feel like I just signed everyone's death warrants?" Then she got closer and whispered in his ear. "You can say and think what you want, but I'm telling you now, you may be captain, but you're not the only one who can break the rules. I was left that amulet for a reason. If I get the chance to bring a peaceful solution to this nightmare, I'm going to take it. Trust me on that, King Ryan."

She turned her attention back to the crowd and pumped her fist into the air as the audience continued to cheer and applaud.

Chapter 29

Final Preparations

Ryan and his crew had been on the go for eighteen hours a day for the last two days. They had a three-day trip ahead of them to get to Earth. That left them two more days to get all the ships armed and ready. Of the fifteen ships they had available, they still had six to finish. Everything would have to go perfect if they were going to make their deadline.

He knew Amanda was working with Paul in the engineering sections of the remaining ships, and Tanner and Jill were working with the weapons consoles. Meanwhile he had been spending most of his time going over strategy with the other ships' captains. It was time to take a break and meet up with his crew for dinner.

Other than for work-related discussions, Amanda seemed to be keeping clear of him. He wished it were different, but he just couldn't get through to her. He remembered reading that there are three occasions when you have no choice but to make a stand and use force: when your back's against the wall with nowhere to run to; when you're in life-threatening danger and you can't trust what the enemy will do; and when the cost of defeat is so high that you can't take a chance. And this situation involved all three. Who knew how they'd react if presented with the amulet? The fact is: If you're cornered by an armed robber and you have a gun, you shoot him first. You don't stop first to ask about his family upbringing and try to appeal to his good nature. He'll shoot you in mid sentence. If only Amanda could understand that.

He was approaching the cafeteria now, and as he entered through the doors, he noticed Paul and Tanner at the far table. He took a seat next to them.

"How's it coming, guys?"

"It's coming along splendidly," said Tanner. "That is, of course, if you don't mind not sleeping. Or eating field rations for breakfast, lunch, and dinner."

Paul was more serious and looked exhausted. "It's gonna be close. Down to the wire, Ry. If we're going to have any chance of getting there before the Altarran troop carriers, we're gonna have to work just about straight through the next two days."

Ryan was only partially listening. He found himself wanting to ask them if they'd seen or talked to Amanda. "That sucks," he said mechanically. "I was hoping we'd get there long before the Altarrans."

"Fat chance of that," said Paul. "We'll be lucky to get there before they actually start their attack on Earth."

Ryan noticed that Tanner looked like he was deep in thought. "Tanner, what's on your mind?"

"That's always a loaded question," said Paul.

"If we arrive before they start unloading their troops," said Tanner, "maybe we should target the troop carriers first. If nothing else, it will stop their ground invasion. That certainly would show ET we mean business."

"That's actually an amazing idea," said Ryan.

Tanner laughed. "Hey, just because I like to goof off and have a little fun does not an idiot make me."

"Okay, Yoda," said Paul.

"Laugh now," said Tanner, "but they may be arriving with Storm Troopers. But not to worry, Amanda's death star will get 'em all."

Ryan and Paul were still laughing when Amanda, Jill, and Nicole walked in. "Care to share the joke with the whole class?" said Jill.

Ryan cringed. Just what he needed was something to fuel Amanda's fire.

"It was Tanner," Paul said. "For once he actually made sense."

Jill had a blank expression. "Now I know we're doomed," she said.

As the girls sat down, Ryan tapped Amanda on the shoulder. She clanked up at him, looking tired.

"Can we talk somewhere?" he said.

"I'm right here," she said. "Let's talk."

"I meant alone, if that's okay with you."

"Come on, Tanner," Paul said, standing. "I think they just put some steaks out."

Tanner jumped up. "Steaks? Where?"

As Paul and Tanner left the table, Jill and Nicole tactfully disappeared too. Amanda was just looking at him as he fought with the right words.

"Listen, Amanda," he finally said. "I know we've had our differences. But I want you to know that I do respect your opinion. I just don't agree. I mean, we both know that the Altarrans are going to attack Earth. They say they're looking for their lost envoys, but who knows how long ago that happened or if it even did?"

"It happened," said Amanda. "And I have the proof it did. The amulet. Somehow, my great-great-grandfather either met up with them or was there when they landed. But our stupid leaders back then hid the truth from everyone or our government would know about it."

"Okay," he said. "Maybe you're right. I believe you on that. I do. But that was over a hundred and fifty years ago. How are we supposed to fix that? They were either killed back then or died later, but there's nothing we can do about it now."

"Yes, we can. I have the amulet. I can explain to them that we don't have any information from back then, but I can at least show them that we want to try and resolve this issue without anyone else dying."

"But what if it inflames them even more? They may not react how you think. The point is, if we have any chance of this mission working, we need to do this together. We'll be leaving in the next day or two. I need to know that you won't go rogue and go off on your own."

"Can I expect the same from you?"

"Yes. I mean I'm okay making decisions together, but if I'm captain I may have to make some tough calls. I'm just saying it'll be a hell of a lot easier if you're with me."

"Look, if we have to fight, I'll fight. I'd just rather we try to end this without any more people dying."

"So would I. I think we both want that. We just have different views on how to do that. So can we work together on this?"

Amanda shook her head. "Ryan, the problem is, you've already made up your mind. Once we get there, and the Altarran ships are in our sight, do you really think you'll be listening to anything I say? Do you think you'd want to talk about how to reach out to them? Be honest."

"Honestly, probably not. Not if lives are in danger."

"But that's the exact time when it's important to communicate. Do you know how many wars could have been avoided if people would just talk? If they could just agree to work together on solving the problem they're fighting about in the first place?"

"We're talking now," said Ryan. "Are we getting anywhere? No. I rest my case."

"No, you made mine." She pushed her food away, got up, and left the table.

Ryan didn't say anything else. He sat there in silence and watched her walk away. Deep down, somewhere inside him, he wanted to go after her. And he hated himself for not doing that, but he just couldn't. Maybe he was afraid he'd give in to her whims and let her contact the Altarrans. But that could prove to be the deadliest of decisions. He had to remind himself that Amanda was brilliant and passionate, but emotions could sometimes lead to bad decisions in times of war. Meanwhile, he had a mission to run.

If all went well, they would finish the last of the ships in time to make their departure cutoff. Then it was one final briefing with Admiral Williamson. After that, they'd be off to the great unknown. Ryan was beginning to wonder if they really could pull it off and win this thing, or if they were on a collision course with death, headed toward their final hours. In the end, he wasn't sure if he was more afraid of what the Altarrans would do . . . or what Amanda would do.

Chapter 30

Earth Bound

Ryan heard the alarm and reached over to shut it off. It had been a grueling three days of twenty-hour shifts, and he could barely function. He shook the cobwebs out of his head. They were supposed to be ready to leave in the next eight hours, and, last he heard, they were still running way behind schedule. They only had three days until the cease-fire would end and the Altarran troop carriers would arrive at Earth. At full speed, they could just barely make it to Earth on time.

He crawled out of bed and jumped in the shower. He had a full plate scheduled for the day. The first matter at hand was a meeting with Admiral Williamson. The sophomores and the juniors, who would be staying on the planet, were busy getting the ships loaded and ready for departure.

Funny how things turn out, he thought, as the hot water hit his face. Not so long ago his only worry was whether or not he would win the Golden Cadet Award. Now, less than two weeks later, he was preparing for intergalactic war.

After drying off and getting dressed, it was off to the admiral's office.

As he entered the admiral's waiting area, he stopped to give his condolences to Lieutenant Rhimes. "I'm very sorry about your husband, Lieutenant."

Her eyes were red and it looked like she hadn't slept in days. "Thank you, Ryan. The admiral's in there waiting for you. And, Ryan?"

"Yes, Lieutenant," he said.

"You make damn sure to give those bastards hell."

Ryan looked at her and nodded. "I'll do my best, ma'am."

He saluted her and entered Williamson's office. Amanda was already there, waiting.

The admiral was sitting at his desk. He pointed to an empty chair next to Amanda. "Take a seat, Ryan. There are a few details before you leave."

Ryan sat. He looked at over at Amanda. "Morning," he said to her. He wasn't quite sure how she'd react.

She looked at him, but didn't answer. Her face seemed devoid of emotion and she appeared exhausted. Then again, everyone was.

The admiral stood up. "Your initial stop will be Pluto," he said, getting right to business. "The underground base there is on total blackout. You'll need a special code to get through to them, which I've sent to your Slider. Without it, you will be shot as if you were an alien with tentacles and three horns. Broadcast the code immediately upon your approach."

Ryan nodded. "Thank you, sir."

"The two transports you'll have with you are to pick up the survivors at the base and bring them back here. We have a full hospital here, so don't leave the wounded stranded there picking scabs off their butts. Make sure they get on those ships. And stay healthy yourselves or you'll end up coming back with them, and I'm not ready to see your faces that soon. I'm pulling fifteen medical technicians from our facility to go along with you—one for each ship."

"Thank you, Admiral," said Ryan. "I was going to ask you about having medical personnel for the ships."

"Hell, Ryan. Did you really think I'd send you off to battle without medical support? Next I assume you were going to ask about weapons."

"Well—"

"Glad you asked. On the base, they have munitions, and lots of them. I've sent you encrypted orders from me, directing them to stock your ships with torpedoes and anything else you may need."

"Thank you, Admiral," said Ryan. "For everything. We won't let you down, sir."

"Don't thank me, Ryan. Thank Amanda. Without that solar weapon, we'd all be sitting here playing checkers and singing Kumbayah while we counted down our last days. We may still do that, but at least now it'll be more interesting." The admiral looked at Amanda and added, "It's just a shame she talks so damn much, I can't get a word in."

Ryan looked at Amanda sitting next to him. For the first time, she smiled, though she did look embarrassed. "Really, Dad," she said. "I'm sure R&D could have figured it out if they knew sooner."

"Regardless," said Williamson, "you made it happen and I'm damn proud to say you did."

The admiral walked toward Ryan. "Thompson, this is the most important thing I'm going to tell you. If you fire the weapon and it doesn't work, you are to retreat immediately and hightail it to Pluto for further instructions. Do I make myself clear? No heroics."

"Absolutely, Admiral. If the weapon fails, trust me, we'll retreat. I may be impulsive, sir, but I'm not crazy."

"Yes you are and I'm damn glad or you wouldn't be leading this mission. And remember. Radio silence. Only use the codes I gave you to make contact."

"Yes, sir. Will do, Admiral."

Williamson was staring at him with a touch of sadness. Ryan couldn't quite read his expression. "Everything okay, sir?"

Williamson nodded and held out his hand as Ryan stood up to shake it. "Good luck, son," said the admiral.

Amanda jumped up and threw her arms around her father. "I love you, Dad," she said. Ryan could see tears welling up in her eyes.

"I love you too, Mandy," said Williamson. "Now get out of here and make an old man proud."

Amanda kissed her father on the cheek and left the room. Ryan started out as well, but the admiral called him back. "Thompson."

"Yes, sir, said Ryan. "Is there something else?"

Williamson moved closer to Ryan and stopped right in front of him. "Yes there is. Something vitally important, even more than the other thing I said was the most important. In fact you can consider this your number one priority."

"What is it, sir?"

"Bring my daughter back to me safe and sound. That's an order, Thompson." He paused, and then added, "Please."

Ryan snapped to attention and saluted the admiral. "You have my word on that, sir."

With that, he turned sharply and left the office. As he headed toward the hangars where all fifteen ships waited, he looked up into the sky and said a prayer. He prayed he could make good on his word.

Chapter 31
Searching For Answers

Admiral Thompson was at his wits' end. The team at the Nevada base was still searching for answers and it didn't look like they were going to find anything anytime soon. Sure, they'd uncovered a few secrets that had apparently been kept from the public through the centuries, but so far they hadn't found anything that seemed remotely related to this case. At one point, Morgan had called him and said they'd found photographs and reports of verified UFOs, but no mention of an alien capture, and certainly nothing about an amulet or any kind of landing. Of course, they still had a lot of boxes to go through.

Meanwhile he'd just about exhausted all his searches concerning the cryptic note he'd found hidden in General Williamson's desk. He looked at it again.

The Queen is with her loyal subjects
Inside the truth is sealed
Only the worthy who see the ten
Shall have the path revealed

"The Queen is with her loyal subjects," he said to himself several times, as if repeating the phrase would somehow magically cause it to make sense. He'd searched all of the old military codes and couldn't find anything that matched. He'd even researched cryptograms and ciphers—anything he could find involving queens and subjects. Most of it was nonsense. And the phrase "inside the truth is sealed" didn't help at all. He'd thought perhaps it meant inside the general's desk, but he'd left instructions to have it dismantled and they hadn't found anything. As for "the worthy who see the ten," that wasn't much help either. There were some biblical references, but they were useless. His thoughts were beginning to blur and he was running out of patience.

Just then, his communication link beeped. Finally, the call he was waiting for.

"Please tell me you have some good news, Morgan."

"Nothing that will help us yet, Admiral," she said. "We're only halfway through these boxes. We did find a few filled with microfilm and microchips, but we don't even have the equipment to decipher any of it. It's ancient technology."

Thompson sighed. "Damn it. I should have thought about that. I'll have a team of experts on old military protocol there within an hour or two. That's gonna cost us time."

"Well it hasn't exactly been business as usual, sir. It's hard to think of everything."

"Sure it's hard," he said. "But it's the small details that'll kill you every time and it's my job to think of them. Anyway, I have a meeting with R&D in thirty minutes. Let me know when the experts get there."

"Will do," said Morgan. "Good luck, sir."

"From your mouth to God's ears, Morgan. Thompson out."

He practically flew outside, where a transport was waiting to take him to the research and development buildings located on the opposite side of the base.

As the vehicle pulled off, his mind was racing. He was wracking his brain still trying to make sense of the bizarre message. He was good at puzzles, but he wasn't getting anywhere with this one. He decided maybe the best thing was to put it out of his mind for a bit. Maybe then something would come to him in a sudden burst of inspiration. At least that's how it always seemed to work for him in the past.

Within minutes, the transport had arrived at the research facility. As soon as he left the vehicle and made his way to the building entrance, he was greeted by Commodore Osaki, the lead engineer for the R&D department. With Osaki was one of his assistants, a woman who looked to be in her late thirties, with tied-up hair and glasses too big for her face, though she had a certain beauty about her.

Thompson shook Osaki's hand, then the woman's, and the three of them exchanged pleasantries and made their way toward the lab. "Any luck on the solar flare emulation?" said Thompson.

"Unfortunately, nothing of substance," said Osaki.

The commodore's assistant seemed to have another opinion. "If I may interject—" she said in an accent Thompson couldn't quite make out but was pretty sure was French.

Osaki gave her a disapproving look and she stopped talking.

Thompson was in no mood to worry about hurting people's feelings. There were more important issues at hand, and he wanted to hear what this officer had to say. "And you are?" he said.

"Captain Laurent, sir," said the woman in a most certainly French accent. "Marie Laurent. I used to teach engineering at the academy. I just transferred here last month." She took off her glasses and put them in her pocket, making her look even more attractive.

"Yes, she's very new," said Osaki, as they entered the lab, "so please pardon—"

"Can it, Osaki," said Thompson. "I want to hear what Captain Laurent has to say. It's not like we have anything else to consider at this point." Looking back at Laurent, he said, "Please continue, Captain."

Laurent stepped forward and gave Osaki an I-told-you-so look. "Admiral," she said, "while teaching at the academy, I had a student—very bright, who was very much ahead of the other students. She wrote a thesis on resourceful artillery. We asked all new students to design a weapon using only auxiliary resources from our engines and other equipment."

Osaki couldn't help himself. "Captain, we've discussed this. Even you said that it was a dangerous and risky idea. If we—"

"Commodore," interjected Thompson, "if you interrupt again, I will demote you to a lieutenant. I will not have another officer silenced when we're in a code red situation. *Are we clear?*"

Osaki didn't say a word. He just nodded and took a couple of steps back.

"Please continue, Captain," said Thompson.

Laurent gave Osaki a smug look. "As I was saying, Admiral, this young lady wrote a brilliant thesis. And it was about the very thing you are asking. She theorized that a solar flare could be manufactured by overloading the light-speed generator and shutting it down milliseconds before detonation."

Thompson was listening intently. He could see why Osaki thought it was risky. "And what was your take on it?" he asked Laurent. "Is it feasible?"

She shrugged her shoulders. "It could work, with slight modification. I just told the student that her shutdown time might be too early, but yes, it could work in theory. It's very dangerous though. The odds—"

"Odds don't matter right now," he said. "Who was this student? Do we have her report?"

"I have the report. Amanda Williamson is the girl. Her father's an admiral at the—"

"Yes, I know him well." Thompson had to smile. He should have known it was Amanda. Without hesitation, he said, "I want the entire R&D department recalled. Nobody, I repeat, nobody is to leave this building. I want every resource this department has on this project."

Osaki, who looked embarrassed, stepped forward. "I'll get everyone recalled and on this immediately, sir."

"Thompson had seen too many people like the Commodore over the years—brown-nosers and bureaucrats. Meanwhile, the R&D staff had wasted seven days spinning their wheels because Osaki was being too cautious in an urgent situation. "I wasn't talking to you, *Captain* Osaki," he said. "I was talking to the new department head, *Commodore* Laurent. You work for her now."

He looked at Laurent. "Commodore Laurent, I want updates every hour on the hour. Understood?"

Laurent smiled nervously at him. "Yes, sir," she said. "Every hour."

Thompson nodded and left the lab to head toward the transports. He couldn't get over the fact that Osaki had withheld an idea that was the one thing that could help them against the Altarrans. The entire facility had been tasked with only one thing—to find out how to produce solar flares—and a solution had been put right in the man's pocket. Sure it was a long shot, but a long shot beats no shot.

He thought he'd drilled that into every soldier's head by now. It figured it was a student who came up with the idea. And not just any student. Amanda. He wasn't surprised. She was brilliant. He'd always felt she should have gone into engineering, but he knew Jonas wanted her in command training. Well, if her idea worked, this would be a good a time as any to change an old friend's mind.

Chapter 32

Change Of Plans

Ryan looked at the clock. If they left now, they would get to Earth *maybe* an hour or two before the cease-fire ended. But it didn't seem they were anywhere near ready.

Paul and Amanda were working along with the other engineering cadets trying to install the solar disrupter on the last ship—the Churchill.

"How much longer until you guys are done?" Ryan asked.

"At least another eight hours," said Amanda.

"We don't have eight hours," he said. "If we don't leave in an hour—two at the most—we're screwed."

The way she jumped up from behind the sonic coils brandishing a thermal welder in her hand, he thought she was going to pounce on him. She lowered her protective visor.

"Listen, Ryan, we've working nonstop for the last three days and your interrupting us every ten minutes isn't gonna make us go any faster. Don't you think we know what's at stake? We'll be done as soon as we can."

"Amanda, that's what I'm saying. As soon as you can is too late."

"So what do you want me to do about it?!"

Paul jumped in between them. "That's enough. Everyone is tired and upset. I've got a better idea."

Ryan looked at Paul. "What's that?"

"Let's switch ships."

"Switch ships?"

"Yes, let the crew of the Churchill take the Nimitz. We'll take the Churchill. We can make the Churchill the flagship and we can work on the engine en route."

"Are you crazy?" said Amanda. "It's difficult enough to do this in a safe environment. You want to do this in space? While we're traveling at light speed?"

"But you're the one who gave me the idea," said Paul. "You said that in the worst case scenario, it could be done."

"Exactly. I said worst case scenario. I meant if we were already en route and something went wrong. It's not something I'd plan to do on purpose. If we make a mistake or something goes wrong while we're at light speed, we'll all be space dust in seconds."

"Is that anything like pixie dust?" said Tanner, who had just entered the room.

Everyone was too focused to even respond.

Ryan thought for a moment. As much as he was annoyed at Amanda, her idea made sense. In dire circumstances, sometimes you needed to take a chance, even if the odds were against you. It was something his father had drilled into his head from day one. "Okay," he said. "Let's do it."

"Do what?" said Paul.

"Let's do Amanda's idea."

"Hey, I was the one who brought it up," said Paul. "She doesn't even want to do it."

"Don't speak for me," said Amanda.

"I'll notify Shelby," said Ryan. "He was assigned to the Churchill. I'll have him and his crew take the Nimitz. We'll switch the flag to the Churchill, and we'll finish installing the solar disrupter on our way to Earth. Are we all together on this?"

Paul nodded. "Sounds like a plan."

"Sounds like fun," said Tanner. "I'm in."

Amanda took off her visor and packed away her thermal welder. "Sounds like suicide to me," she said. "But let's do it."

"Ry," said Tanner, "since we're taking the Churchill, I better get over to the Nimitz and pick up Punch and Judy."

"Well, you better get them now. I want to be ready to depart in two hours."

"Your wish is my command. On my way, Ry."

"Wait, who the hell are Punch and Judy?" asked Amanda.

"Just a couple of Tanner's homemade torpedoes," said Ryan.

The next two hours passed quickly. All fifteen ships were cleared for departure. Ryan was on the bridge with Tanner, Jill, and Nicole. Amanda and Paul were in engineering. Ryan decided now was a good time to address his crew. He motioned to Jill to switch on the internal mic.

"Okay, everyone," he said, "it's time to do this. I know we spent a lot of time on the Nimitz, but right now the Churchill is our new home. May it serve us well. While Admiral Williamson won't be seeing us off, he's privately arranged unofficial clearance for departure. So we're on our own—only not. Now, it'll be up to us as the flagship to lead this fleet through some pretty rough times. I don't know about you, but I'm not ready to die yet. So trust me when I say, we *will* win this thing. Let's make it happen."

"Let's make it happen!" yelled out Tanner, as the others joined in and then went to their stations.

"Take us out, Nicole," said Ryan. "Standard orbit until the entire fleet is with us."

"Standard orbit. Engaging now."

Ryan sat in the command chair and watched the viewer as the Churchill climbed into orbit, followed by the rest of the fourteen battleships and the two transports.

Ryan called to Jill. "Have all ships line up in a wing formation. Tell them to engage light speed on our mark. Then patch me through to engineering."

"Sending message to the fleet now," Jill said. "All ships acknowledged. Putting you through to engineering now."

Amanda replied immediately. "Main engineering here. We're ready to engage."

"Confirmed," said Ryan. He looked to Nicole at the helm. "Prepare to engage light speed in ten seconds."

"Confirmed. Ten seconds."

Ryan listened as the computer counted down. *Five, four, three, two, one.*

"Now," shouted Ryan.

He waited for the initial kick of the engines. He was trying to remember the last time he had actually experienced light speed in the simulator and wondered how this would compare. As he clenched the sides of his chair and waited, it felt as if they were standing perfectly still. It was eerily quiet and he could hear the breathing of the other crew members. Then, in an instant, he felt his whole body being pulled forward with a jerk, and yet it felt like he was being stretched, as if part of his body didn't want to move. He felt dizzy, much worse than in any simulation, and everything around him blurred into one big distorted view. He could actually see his own image reflected over and over, mixed in with images of the entire bridge for as far as the eye could see. Then there came a giant snap, like he was being catapulted forward by a huge slingshot. He felt like his stomach was in his mouth. Seconds later, everything was back to normal, although the residual effects were making him nauseous.

As he shook off the cobwebs, Ryan looked around. He could see by the looks on everyone's faces that the rest of the bridge crew felt pretty much like he did. He called out to Tanner, who, with Amanda off in engineering, was manning the sensor station. "Does everything look normal?"

Tanner hesitated briefly. "Define normal," he said. "We have a fleet of nauseous teenage cadets careening about space at light speed, on the way to use an unknown and never-before-used weapon to fight a formidable enemy that has far superior numbers. Other than that . . . yeah, pretty normal. All systems are running tried and true, Mon Capitan."

"Thanks, I think," said Ryan.

Ryan sat back and thought about what awaited them. Truth be told, he was scared to death, though he'd never show it.

He was almost knocked off his chair when the ship started to vibrate without warning. What the hell was happening? Alarms suddenly went off on the bridge. "What's going on?" he called out. "Talk to me."

"Ry," said Tanner. "I'm detecting an overload in engineering."

"Jill," said Ryan. "Patch me through to engineering fast."

"Right away. You're on."

"Paul, Amanda, what the hell happened down there?"

There was a slight hesitation. "This . . . this is Cadet Rawlings, sir. There's been an explosion in the reactor room. Paul is unconscious. I've called for a medical tech."

"An explosion! Where's Amanda?" All sorts of things were racing through Ryan's head.

"In the reactor room sir. She grabbed a radiation suit and ran in there. I couldn't stop her, sir."

"She what?" said Ryan. "Get her out of there now. Those doors will automatically lock, and if the problem isn't fixed when the countdown hits thirty seconds, the core and anyone in that room will be ejected into space."

"I know that, Captain," said Rawlings. "But she outranks me, and she ordered everyone out of the area . . . and . . . well . . ."

"And what!" screamed Ryan.

"Well . . . um . . . the door's already locked. Nobody can get in or out . . . sir."

Ryan fell back into his command chair. Everything was falling apart before they had even started. He had to do something, but what? He jumped out of his chair and called to Tanner, "I'm heading down to engineering. You've got the bridge."

Tanner stood up grabbed him as he tried to pass. "Ry, man," he said, "there's nothing you can do. In fact, if you're too close when the reactor's jettisoned, it could kill you."

Ryan didn't have time to even consider that. He broke free and was off and running. "Sorry, Tanner," he said. "I can't just sit here and let her die."

He flew off the bridge, reality hitting him like a ton of bricks. He really did care about her, more than he'd wanted to admit. And he sure wasn't about to let her die because of his orders . . . because of his impatience. He was also worried about poor Paul, but the only thing that could be done there was to wait for the medics. At least Amanda he had a chance of saving. The question was how. He had to figure out a way. He'd already lost a part of himself and wasn't about to lose another. It had taken all the inner strength he had to get past the nightmare of his mother's death. If Amanda died because of his decision to work on the engines in flight, he would never forgive himself.

Chapter 33
Life And Death

Amanda knew she was running on borrowed time. The doors had sealed shut as soon as she'd entered the reactor room. To make matters worse, the mechanical voice of the computer kept blaring in her ears.

Warning. Core overload in ten minutes. Automatic ejection system will activate at one minute.

"Wonderful," she said to herself as she looked around for the containment field mechanism. "I knew this was a bad idea. Sure, work on a light-speed engine while engaged in light-speed drive. Should have listened to me, folks."

As the alarm blasted and she scanned the room, she couldn't get Paul's bloody face out of her mind. Luckily, he'd still had a pulse when she checked it. Now it was up to the medics. Just minutes ago she'd been working on the wiring when she'd heard a persistent whining sound, indicating that someone had failed to align the containment field properly. But before she could warn Paul, the explosion had hit. Poor Rawlings had tried to stop her from running to the reactor room, but to no avail. If she'd evacuated and the engines had blown, the whole fleet would have had to stop to help them abandon ship and the mission would have been lost. That was still a possibility, but if she could only find the containment field . . .

Just then, she spotted its glowing blue light peeking from behind a safety divider by the far wall.

Grabbing her tools, she began trying to align the containment field. It was getting hotter and she was starting to sweat inside the suit. She struggled to get a grip on the alignment mechanism inside the field with the long tool, and her hands were shaking. Looking at the gauge on the wall, she could see the temperature was up to a hundred and twenty-five degrees. The suit should protect her to about two hundred and ten, but only for a few minutes. Not that she'd ever reach that state, since she only had about five minutes to fix this problem before she'd be ejected into space to die an agonizing and lonely death.

Her thoughts were starting to get fuzzy and she was feeling disoriented and nauseous. Between the extreme heat and high radiation, her vision was impaired as well, which made it extra difficult.

Checking the timer on the wall, she saw that she had a little over two minutes until she and the reactor were ejected into space. "Come on, dammit," she said, trying to get the field perfectly aligned until the whining noise stopped. The tool kept slipping off the adjuster. "Crap. I need something narrower." She reached into her toolkit. She could barely see and had to go by feel. Meanwhile the countdown kept blasting in her ears.

Core will eject in ninety-five seconds.

Sweat was burning her eyes, and she knew she was getting dehydrated as she felt shaky. The radiation alarm on her suit went off, which made her heart pound even more. That meant she had sixty seconds to contain the overload before it reached critical mass. She reached into the containment field and made another adjustment, her hands trembling. The countdown continued. *Fifty-six, fifty-five . . .*

Then the temperature alarm started blaring, adding to the countdown and her radiation alarm. If the radiation didn't kill her, the noise would. It was beginning to hurt her ears, clouding her senses further. She dropped her sonic wrench and had to quickly feel around for it. She couldn't see anything. The air was so dense between the heat and the radiation that she operating totally blind. Her hopes began to disappear with her vision.

Twenty-one, twenty, nineteen . . .

It had to be well over two hundred degrees in the room if the temperature alarm was sounding. She remembered something she'd learned in class: your blood starts to boil at two hundred and twelve degrees. She was seconds away from finding out what that felt like.

Ready to give in to defeat, with a last half-hearted attempt, she made one final adjustment. She could sense she was about to lose consciousness, and could barely turn the sonic wrench. A noise startled her. This was it. It was the sound of the outer locks disengaging so the room could be jettisoned from the ship. She braced herself.

There was nothing to describe the feeling of dying alone. No goodbyes, no last kiss. She closed her eyes tight. *Five, four, three.*

She held her ears to drown out reality.

Two . . .

Then silence.

Her whole body was trembling.

A long alarm sounded, followed by:

Containment field stable. Overload aborted.

She hadn't even noticed that her last adjustment had caused the whining noise to stop.

She fell to her knees in tears. "I did it. I did it Ryan, I did it." Then she collapsed on the floor face down. Though she didn't have energy to even lift a finger, she could hear the automated systems flushing out the radiation and the cooling fans coming on. She kept going in and out of consciousness. She thought about her father, and prayed she would see him again. In the foggy recesses of her mind, she thought she heard someone calling her name from a faraway field. Then she realized where she was, and thought she heard someone pounding on the lead doors. She tried to lift her head to see. Could someone be coming to help or was it a dream? Her face fell back to the floor, breaking her faceplate. The last sound she heard was her oxygen hissing as it left her protective suit. Then she finally gave in as she lost consciousness.

Chapter 34

Medical Emergency

Ryan had been pounding on the double lead doors the whole time the alarms were going off, knowing his life would be in danger if the reactor had ejected. He'd been momentarily elated when the all clear alarm had sounded. But now he was in a panic again as he listened for any signs of life from Amanda on the other side of the huge opaque doors. He thought back to the all clear warning. How had it been phrased again?

Overload averted. Containment field stable. Doors will unlock when conditions are deemed safe.

What the hell was taking the doors so long? He thought back to the day his mother died. He remembered how helpless he'd felt. It wasn't that he hadn't wanted to try and save her, but the guards had held him back. This was a different situation, but with the same potential outcome staring him in the face, and he was just as helpless.

Ryan was still banging on the outer blast doors and yelling Amanda's name, trying to listen for a reaction out of her to see if she was alive. But so far, there was no response. He knew how high the temperature had gotten and that she was likely dead, but he wasn't ready to accept it. He wished he could see inside. As he was preparing himself to give up hope for the only girl he'd loved in his entire life, he heard the automated computer.

Environment stabilizing. Door sequence activating.

The outer blast doors suddenly opened, but the reactor doors behind them were still closed. Ryan slammed the emergency com unit button on the wall just inside the blast doors. It connected him directly to the infirmary.

"Doctor Basha here," she said. "Have the doors opened?"

"Just the blast doors," he said. "Doc, I need you down here at the reactor room immediately."

Ryan knew they were working on Paul, but the doctor's assistant could monitor him in the meantime. At least Paul was stable, last he'd heard.

"On my way, Captain," said the doctor.

Ryan looked at the readouts on the monitor outside the reactor door. By his calculations, it would be another five minutes until the computer deemed it safe enough to unlock the inner doors. He noticed a display button and activated it to see if he could see Amanda.

When the monitor came on, he was horrified. He could see her in the middle of the room, lying face-down on the floor. Her faceplate was shattered and there was blood on the floor. God, please don't let her be dead.

He heard the sound of footsteps behind him. He turned around to see Doctor Anya Basha running his way at a full sprint.

"What's the situation, Captain?" she asked.

"She's unconscious and the doors won't open for at least another few minutes."

Basha looked at the monitor and shook her head. "That's too long. If she's not breathing, I have to get to her now."

Ryan knew what had to be done. Even if the environment wasn't stable, he needed to get in there. It was a chance he was willing to take.

"Doctor, stand back, please."

Once the doctor was at a sufficient distance, he entered the code on the door panel that he'd never in his wildest dreams expected to use: the emergency code that overrode all systems. A computerized voice answered him. *Override code accepted. Place right hand on panel to verify.*

He placed his right hand on the panel. The voice confirmed. *Thompson, Ryan, command override accepted.*

As the latches on the door started to unlock, Basha called out to him. "The temperature inside there is about a hundred and seventy degrees," she said. "Still high levels of radiation. Get in and out fast."

Ryan ripped off his shirt and used it to cover his nose and mouth. The doors opened and he rushed in. Immediately his eyes started to burn. It felt worse than any sauna he'd been in and he could barely breathe, but he continued on. He saw Amanda on the floor. She wasn't moving. Kneeling down, he gently picked her up and exited the room as quickly as possible. Once in the cooler engineering area, he put her down and entered the codes to shut the doors.

Basha quickly took Amanda's vitals. Removing her headgear, she grabbed a hypo from her bag and gave her a shot in the neck. Then she pulled a small breathing device from her bag and placed it over Amanda's nose and mouth. "I need to get her to the infirmary, now."

"How is she, Doc? Is she alive? Will she be okay?" Ryan was beside himself as he helped Basha pick Amanda up and put her on the gurney.

"Her vitals are weak and she's extremely dehydrated, but alive." Basha paused to check Amanda's pulse again. "Weak, but steady. A good sign. I gave her a shot of DPA."

"DPA?"

"Diethylenetriamine pentaacetic acid, for the radiation exposure. The sooner we get her to the infirmary and get some fluids in her, the more I'll be able to tell. The test will be the impact to her cognitive systems, her brain function."

Ryan followed Basha to the infirmary, where the doctor's assistant helped place Amanda in one of the beds. As soon as Amanda hit the bed, the doctor attached all kinds of tubes to her and the automated scanners started gathering information.

"What's it showing?" said Ryan. He was pacing back and forth.

"Not much yet, said the doctor. "Her vitals are better than they were. I'm sure the cooler temperature and fluids are helping."

Ryan watched as an automated device took a blood sample.

A voice called out from one of the beds on the other side of the room. "That's okay. I'm fine. Thanks for asking. Don't worry about me."

Ryan walked over to Paul. "What the hell happened, man? You scared the crap out of me."

Paul shrugged his shoulders. "I really don't know. First I heard the vibrations. Then next thing I know, I see Amanda about to yell something and an explosion knocks me on my ass. That's the last thing I remember until about five minutes ago, when I woke up in here." He looked over at Amanda. "What happened to her?"

"She was in the reactor room, and—"

"The reactor room?!"

"Well, there was an overload in progress and she went in to stop it just before it went into lockout mode. She was seconds from being ejected. Damn if she didn't find a way to stop it. She's in pretty bad shape, Paul."

"I'm sorry, Ry. She better pull though. If anyone can, it's Amanda. Wait, what kind of overload?"

"I'm pretty sure the monitor said it was the containment field."

"The containment field? Are you sure?"

"Well, when Rawlings told me that you were hurt and Amanda was inside the reactor room, I took off from the bridge so fast I really don't remember, but I'm pretty sure that's what it said."

"Ry, that's suicide trying to align that while it's active. She'd be dead in an instant. It couldn't have been that."

"Containment field . . ." said a female voice from behind him. Ryan turned around. It was Amanda, half sitting up! ". . . aligned . . ." Her voice tailed off, then she fell back to her pillow.

Ryan's face lit up as he ran to her bed. "You're okay!" he said. She was barely conscious as she looked up at him with half-closed eyes.

"Okay?" she said, lifting her head to look down at the tubes and bandages. "This?" She reached her hand up to point to him. "Next time," she said, in a strained voice, "listen . . . to . . ." Then she started coughing uncontrollably.

Doctor Basha stepped in. "Captain," she said, "I need to ask you to leave. Both my patients need to get some rest."

"But—"

"You may be the captain of this ship," said the doctor, "but in the infirmary, I'm in charge. Now, as I said, both my patients need to get some rest. I'll have a report to you within the next eight hours."

Ryan looked at the five-foot-tall doctor and wanted to laugh. She was glaring at him with her hands on her hips. "Do you have any idea when either of them will be ready for duty?" he said.

"If they get through the next twenty-four hours without any symptoms or setbacks, I'll let you know. "

"So then—"

"Run along, Captain."

Ryan nodded and smiled. "Of course, Doc."

He looked at Paul and Amanda. "Get some rest, guys. I'm really glad you're both still with us. I mean that."

Paul waved. Amanda was asleep.

As he left the room, Ryan thought about Amanda, and about the mission ahead. They had two days of traveling before getting to Pluto. Paul seemed in better shape, but it was Amanda he was really worried about. He prayed she'd make a full recovery. Besides the obvious, he needed them for Pluto, and he most certainly needed them before they reached Earth. This was going to be impossible enough as it was, and if they had any chance of pulling this off, they were going to need their top engineers. Not only that, but when the chips were down, Ryan had come to rely on Amanda's genius. Most of all, though, he just wanted his friends back.

Chapter 35
Deep Space Outpost, Pluto

Ryan was on the bridge checking the latest status reports from all the ships in his armada. Fortunately there were no major issues other than the near disaster with his own ship. There were some minor problems, like the Napoleon's environmental systems acting up, and the Columbus was having trouble with their sensor array. But those were easy to fix, and all in all, they'd been lucky.

The doors to the bridge opened and Ryan had to do a double-take. It was Amanda! She'd been in sickbay for almost two days and was showing signs of recovery, but now she looked downright healthy. Not bad for someone who'd almost died. Paul fared even better and was already back in engineering. As Amanda approached, Ryan stood up and started clapping. The rest of the bridge crew followed suit. She responded with a half smile and looked slightly embarrassed.

Tanner was at the sensor station and stepped aside to let her resume her post. "Welcome back, Big Red," he said. "I've kept your seat warm."

"Thanks, Tanner," she said. "I appreciate it."

Ryan walked up to her. "Glad to have you back. How are you feeling?"

"Much better," she said. "You really don't all have to make a big deal. I'm fine." She looked over at him and smiled. "Really," she added. "I am." Maybe she was warming up after all.

"Okay, everyone," he said, as he watched Pluto emerge on the monitor. "Back to business. We're at our communications point."

Ryan took out his Slider and brought up the codes for contacting the deep space outpost on Pluto. He also needed them for requesting permission to dock. "Open a secure channel," he said to Jill. "Send the following sequence: *Bravo, One, One, Zero, Alpha, Tango, Romeo, Charlie, Foxtrot, Zero.*"

"Sending code now," she said.

Less than a minute later they received a reply.

"Deep space outpost. Code received and clearance granted. Proceed to dark-side landing platform."

"Nicole, you heard the man," said Ryan. "Take us around to the back door."

"Roger that, Captain," said Nicole. "Setting coordinates for the rear landing platform."

"Jill, send a coded message to the rest of the fleet to follow us in. Tell them we're going to the dark side of Pluto. One by one."

"Sending message now," she replied.

"Beware the dark side, young Jedi," said Tanner. "It is twisted and evil." Ryan shook his head and laughed. "You and your two-hundred-year-old movies," he said.

"Yeah, but they keep releasing new versions," said Tanner. "The new one's in holograph format."

Ryan looked at him.

"I'm serious," said Tanner. "Lucas's great-great grandson supervised it himself."

As they approached Pluto's noxious atmosphere, Ryan watched on the main viewer as all fifteen battleships and the two transports made their way to the landing platforms. The ship began to buck suddenly. With winds exceeding two hundred miles-per-hour, it was difficult to maneuver, even with the stabilization controls. He had to hold tight to his command chair as the Churchill shifted from side to side like a runaway elevator. Even the monitors kept getting clouded up, as the external temperatures were reading at minus 400 degrees Fahrenheit. Thank God for thermal shields.

"You really need a sweater out there," said Tanner, breaking the tension.

Finally the intense shifting stopped, and Ryan breathed a sigh of relief as he felt the Churchill settle onto the terrain. "Thank you, Nicole," he said to himself. The ship still shook in the surface wind, but nothing like on the descent. He watched the monitors as the other ships touched down. As soon as the last ship had landed, the ground platforms lowered until they were well below the surface of the planet. At last, things were quiet.

Ryan looked at Amanda and Tanner. "Okay, I'd like you two with me. The rest of you stay put for now." Turning to Jill, he said, "Inform the captains of each ship to stand by for further orders."

"Will do," she said.

Ryan left the bridge with Amanda and Tanner. They continued down the corridor until they reached the main exit. As they approached, he stood for the automatic facial scan and the door opened. There were six armed officers waiting on the other side. One of them walked up to Ryan and blocked his path. "Where's your commanding officer?" the guard asked.

Ryan looked at him with a straight face. "That would be me."

At that moment the commander of the outpost showed up. "Lieutenant John Haywood, commanding officer. Care to explain to me what's going on here?"

"Cadet Ryan Thompson, sir. With me are Cadets Amanda Williamson and Tanner Blackhart."

"You've got to be kidding me," said Haywood. "Cadets? Thompson and Williamson? How do the kids of our top admirals end up here? What the hell happened? Did the Altarrans attack the academy?"

Tanner cleared his throat. "I thought you should know that I'm Susan Blackhart's son. She was the head librarian at the public library in Lancaster, Pennsylvania."

"What?" said Haywood.

"He's a little odd," said Ryan, "but damn good with weapons, sir."

"I feel safer already," said Haywood. "Now maybe you can enlighten me about what's going on."

"It's a long story, but we have a weapon that can help against the Altarrans."

"A weapon? Well I'll be damned. Come to my office. We'll all have a seat and chat. I have the best damn hot chocolate on Pluto. Come to think of it, the only damn hot chocolate on Pluto."

For the next hour, Ryan explained in detail all that had transpired. He told Haywood about the solar disrupter and the overhaul of the outdated ships.

He could see that Haywood was listening intently. After Ryan was finished, Haywood looked at him and shook his head. "That's one hell of a story. Never would have dreamed in a million years cadets could have thought of that. But then, you ain't no ordinary cadets, are you? I'll be damned if it'll work, but who am I to argue? So I assume you're here with orders?"

"I am, sir." Ryan held up his Slider. "From Admiral Williamson. He told me only you would have the codes to open the file."

Haywood took Ryan's Slider and waved it over his console. Then he gave it back and entered his passcodes on the console viewer. Ryan stayed seated and waited patiently while Haywood watched the screen.

Haywood stood up and turned off the viewer. "That's damn impressive, Cadet Williamson. I have to admit, I thought Cadet Thompson here was exaggerating."

"It should work, sir," said Amanda. Ryan could see she was uncomfortable with compliments.

"All right," said Haywood. "These orders are confirmed and authentic. I'll have the survivors, including the wounded, brought to the transport ships and flown to the academy. As for munitions, we have enough of a stockpile to arm you guys to the teeth. But to do that we'll need to just about empty all our reserves. I'd love to give you guys all of it, but we need to maintain a supply for our ships, not to mention for the base. We'll have you ready to go within four hours."

Ryan stood up. "Thank you, Lieutenant. I appreciate your assistance."

Haywood's communicator beeped. "Haywood here."

Ryan listened in as an excited voice came across the communicator. "Walker here, sir. We've got something on the long-range visual feed. We think it's the troop carriers, sir. You'd better get down here and see this."

"On my way," said Haywood. Barely turning around, he added, "Okay Cadet folk. You three with me."

Ryan followed Haywood with Amanda and Tanner right behind him. They entered a large room filled with monitors displaying various sectors. His eyes immediately went to the middle monitor.

Amanda gasped, "Oh my lord."

Tanner, for once, was speechless.

Ryan couldn't believe what he was looking at. Three enormous ships were headed their way. He'd never seen a ship that large. They seemed to go on forever.

"How big are they?" asked Haywood.

Walker turned around. "According to the sensors, two miles in length and one mile wide. The height of each ship from highest point to the bottom is fifteen hundred feet."

"Holy shit," said Tanner.

"How long until they reach us?" asked Ryan.

Walker turned around to answer him. "At their current speed, about three hours and fifty minutes."

"Um, Ry," said Tanner. "How many troops and ground weapons do you think a ship that size could carry?"

Ryan tried to calculate it in his head.

"Too many," he said.

"It also depends how large the aliens are," said Amanda.

Ryan looked at Haywood. "Lieutenant, we need to get those weapons on board and we need to do it fast."

Haywood nodded. "Walker, I want all hands on deck. We're going to load these ships in record time."

"Yes, sir," said Walker.

"Thank you, Lieutenant," Ryan said to Haywood. "If you'll excuse me, we've got to get back to our ships."

"Go," said Haywood. "And good luck. Lord knows you'll need it."

Ryan made his way back to his ship with Amanda and Tanner right on his heels. His mind was racing. He had to figure out a plan of attack and he had very little time to do it. Clearly he hadn't counted on such a large volume of enemy troops.

Chapter 36

Plan Of Attack

Ryan entered the conference room on board the Churchill. His bridge crew was already there waiting for him. They had two hours left before the troop carriers passed Pluto on their way to Earth, so time for planning was limited.

"Okay, guys," he said, as he entered. "We need to talk about our alternatives here. Let's look at what we're dealing with."

He played the video from the satellite images they'd seen on the base. For Amanda and Tanner, it was a replay. But Jill, Nicole, and Paul were visibly shaken.

"What do we do now?" said Paul. "Those things are like floating cities."

"There's got to be a way," said Ryan.

"How?" said Paul. "The hulls alone would have to be so thick that even with their shields down, it would probably take our whole artillery to even make a dent."

Tanner stood up. "Ry, I think if we used my torpedoes we could destroy at least two of them. Maybe even all three."

"Torpedoes would be like throwing rice at them," said Paul.

"Not my torpedoes," said Tanner.

"Wait a minute," said Amanda. "I hope you don't mean your Pop and Jody or whatever they're called."

"Punch and Judy," said Tanner.

"Whatever," she said. "What's exactly is in those torpedoes?"

Ryan gave Tanner an odd look. "Tanner, those are only to be used in a worst case scenario."

"Well this seems like a pretty shitty scenario, doesn't it?" said Tanner. "Or did I miss something and those things really aren't the size of San Francisco?"

Amanda asked again. "I repeat, Tanner. What kind of torpedoes?"

"Listen, Amanda," said Ryan. "These are last case scenario weapons. If and when the time comes to use them, we'll discuss it, but as captain I reserve the right to make the final decision. For now, let's think of additional options."

"So that's how you play it?" she said. "You keep your executive officer in the dark?"

"Guys," Paul said. "Can we focus on the real problem?" He pointed to the monitor.

"Right," said Ryan. "So, who has an idea? And that means you, too, Amanda. We need to stop these troop carriers from making it to Earth, but we can't use all of our munitions up on these three ships. That would leave us defenseless against the fleet in Earth's orbit."

"I have an idea," said Tanner. Ryan turned to look at him, as did everyone else. "What?" said Tanner. "Hey, nobody takes me seriously. I'm a serious kinda guy. Well, maybe not always, but that's because you guys are boring. Well, except for you two." He pointed to Ryan and Amanda. "You're always a source of entertainment. But seriously, I *am* the best weapons specialist in the academy, and—"

"Tanner," said Ryan.

"What?"

"Your idea."

"Oh yeah," said Tanner. "Here it is. We let them pass us."

"Let them pass us?" said Ryan. "That's your idea?"

"Are you insane?" said Jill.

"Wait," said Tanner, "hear me out. We let them pass us, but we break into three groups of five ships. Then we come up behind them with our weapons hot. And then, we blast their engines from behind."

"Would that work?" said Paul.

"Look at the video. Look how exposed those engines are. Even with their shields up, we have the disrupter. They'll never see us coming. If we knock out their engines, they ain't going nowhere."

Amanda jumped in. "You know something? That's actually a good idea. But the timing would be critical. We'd have to plan it down to the last second."

Tanner took a bow. "I didn't say it would be easy. But we'd have the element of surprise. They'd never know what hit them. And best of all, maybe we could hightail it outta there before they can respond."

"Tanner, you're a genius," said Ryan. "Let's see if we can work out the details. Amanda and Paul, you guys work out the timing. We have less than two hours to make it happen. Let's do this."

Amanda, Paul, and Tanner left to start running simulations for planning the attack.

It took two hours for them to finish loading all the torpedoes. Ryan checked the time and ran the scenario over in his mind. They would have to power the solar disrupter before getting into firing range. Then, with less than three seconds before the overload, stop on a dime, shut down the overload at the tenth of a second mark, and then fire the disrupter and their weapons. Timing would be everything. If they arrived even a few seconds late, they might not have time to fire off their shots. If they were a few seconds early, the Altarrans might just spot them and fire back. That would be a disaster.

Ryan entered the bridge. He was waiting to get the word from Lieutenant Haywood letting him know when the Altarran troop carriers passed the base. According to their projections, they should arrive any second.

"Are those calculations ready?" he asked Amanda.

"Very close," she said.

"Take your time," he said. "Not like we're in a hurry or anything."

"They'll be ready," she said.

"Captain," said Jill, "I have Lieutenant Haywood on a secure channel."

"Put him through," said Ryan.

"Haywood here, Thompson. The Altarran troop ships are just passing us now. Their current speed is one-quarter sub-light."

"Copy," said Ryan. "Thanks for all your help."

"Good luck, Thompson. Give 'em hell. Haywood out."

Ryan turned to Amanda. "Well, you're up. We're waiting on those calculations."

Amanda looked up. "On my mark," she said to the bridge crew, "have all ships engage their solar disrupter. As soon as we engage, we need to get each group of ships into position. All ships must be at the coordinates I've assigned them within twenty-five seconds of liftoff. Once they're in position, each group needs to head to their target area at one-half light speed for thirty seconds. Got that? One-half light speed for thirty seconds. That'll give us a five-second window to stop and fire the disrupter, followed by our torpedoes."

"Jill, you copy that?" said Ryan. "Inform all ships to bring main engines online."

Jill opened a channel to the entire fleet and told all ships to power their engines. "Captain, all ships report ready." She turned to Amanda. "Mandy, your com link is open. All ships are awaiting your mark."

Ryan noticed how quiet the bridge was. This would be their first real action and he could feel their tension.

Amanda looked up from her console. "Now! All ships lift off and get into position."

Ryan watched the rear monitor. He could see all the ships climbing off the surface of Pluto. It was a beautiful sight, watching the fifteen ships in perfect formation with Pluto in the background. For a brief moment, he felt like a spectator. Turning to Jill, he said, "Inform all ships to power their weapons."

"Message sent, sir," she said.

Amanda was studying her monitor intently. "All ships go to one-half sub-light speed. Bring solar disrupter online."

Ryan watched as the fleet broke into three groups of five ships and each group bore down on their target.

"Holy shit, would you look at that," said Tanner.

Ryan couldn't believe the image on the monitor, even though he was expecting it. This was the first close-up view they'd had of the alien troop carriers. Seeing them from a distance was one thing. But within close proximity, it was an awe-inspiring sight, even from the rear. They truly were like floating cities.

"Stay focused," said Ryan.

Tanner called out from the weapons console. "Solar disrupter activated. We are closing on target."

"Twenty seconds until we reach target," said Nicole from the helm.

"Twenty-five seconds until solar disrupter is activated," said Tanner.

Ryan held on tight as the ship started to vibrate from the overload in the reactor.

Yelling to hear himself over the noise level, Tanner counted down. "Five seconds to target area."

"All stop," yelled Ryan.

Nicole cut the engines and hit the reverse thrusters to bring the Churchill to a dead stop.

Ryan could hear the stress of the engines and the hull creaking as the Churchill came grinding to a halt. The sudden shift of the internal gravity threw him to the floor. Between feeling like he weighed five hundred pounds and wanting to puke his guts out, the effect was almost intolerable. He had to shake it off. They only had five seconds to react.

"Enemy ship targeted, Ry," said Tanner. "Firing solar disrupter."

Everyone's eyes were fixated on the main viewer as the immense troop carriers seemed to slow down.

Ryan stood up. "Fire tubes one through four. Full spreads!"

He could feel the recoil of the ship as four torpedoes were fired in rapid succession from each tube. His mind ran the numbers as he watched on the main viewer. Sixteen torpedoes times five ships. Eighty of them directed at each Altarran troop carrier, forty per engine. Ryan prayed to God that it would be enough to take out their engines.

"Tracking torpedoes," said Amanda.

It only took a few seconds, but it seemed like an eternity to Ryan as he waited to hear if they had hit their targets. He had a feeling, though. Before Amanda could say a word, he knew they were dead on.

Amanda pumped her fist in the air. "Direct hits on all three carriers."

Ryan felt a sense of pride as cheers could be heard all throughout the ship. Just then, Jill let out a scream from the communications console. "Oh no!"

"What is it?" said Ryan, his heart pounding.

"The Nimitz . . . she's . . . gone."

"What do you mean gone?"

"No communications. And look at those particles on the monitor. She just exploded. I don't understand. She wasn't hit by enemy fire."

Ryan looked at the viewer and his heart sank. "Damn it. Have all ships break off attack," he said. "Full speed. Set course for Mars."

Jill seemed as if she was in a trance for a moment, then she reacted. "Sending message now."

Amanda looked up from her sensor station. Ryan could see the pain in her eyes. "We stopped the troop carriers," she said. "All three took heavy damage to their engines. They're dead in the water."

It should have been a moment to celebrate, but it was a bitter-sweet victory. "We all did our jobs well," he said. He couldn't think of anything else to say.

He looked around at the crew, *his* crew. Even though they had succeeded in disabling the Altarran troop carriers, the mood was somber. They had just lost one of their ships. Fifty of their friends and classmates were gone in an instant.

He'd always wondered how it would feel to lead an attack and suffer casualties. Unfortunately, there was nothing in the handbook to explain how to handle the gut-wrenching experience of watching your friends die—friends under *your* command who trusted you to keep them safe. What made it even more jarring was that the ship that had exploded was the ship he and his crew were supposed to be manning. Had they been on time installing the weapon, it would have been them on the Nimitz. Odd, he thought, how every move that you make, or don't make, can spell the difference between life and death. And usually, there's no way to tell which ones are which.

His stomach was in knots. The reality of war had just hit home like a Category 5 hurricane. And something told him the worst was yet to come.

Chapter 37

Confrontation

Ryan could see Mars on the main viewer. They were almost there. Barring the occasional update from other ships in the fleet about minor technical malfunctions, the three-hour flight had been quiet and routine. Or as routine as you could get after witnessing the death of your classmates and knowing you were about to face a formidable alien force. But for now, all they could do was focus on the task at hand.

"We're ten minutes from Mars, Captain," said Nicole, breaking the anxious silence.

"Understood," said Ryan. "We'll set up in a wing formation. Put us on the point. Keep Mars between us and Earth. I don't know how powerful the Altarran sensors are, but I'd rather play it safe. Jill, inform the fleet and have them get into position."

"Sending message now," said Jill.

Ryan stared at the main and side viewers. Seconds after Jill's broadcast, he could see all the ships moving into formation. All but one glaring exception—the empty space where the Nimitz should have been.

"Have all ships run full diagnostics on all systems," he said to Jill. "Let them know I want to be ready to head for Earth as soon as possible."

Ryan was running a few different strategies through his head when he noticed Amanda approaching. "So what's our plan?" she said.

"Truth? I'm not sure yet. They don't expect an attack, so that's one good thing in our favor. And they're probably overconfident, since they had no trouble with the best the fleet had to throw at them."

"Can we do the same thing we did against their troop carriers?"

"What, disable their engines from behind?"

"Well, I was thinking we could come in with the solar disrupter ready to be discharged, only we'd have to use light speed so we arrive ready, sort of like a cobra strike."

"And you thought fixing a light speed engine in space was risky? I mean, not that I don't believe you could figure it out, but—"

"I can do it, I just . . ." She paused for some reason.

"Second thoughts?"

"No, I just wish we could talk to them first and avoid all this."

"Amanda, we don't get second chances here. And—"

"I know," she said. "I get it. We're outnumbered."

Ryan was surprised by her response.

"What if we took out half their ships and then tried to talk?" she said.

"We'd be talking to some pretty pissed off aliens."

"Yes, but we'd have the upper hand."

Ryan took a deep breath.

"Why don't we first figure out how we can take out the first batch?" he said. "Then let's see if we're still even alive to talk to anyone. Agreed?"

She hesitated for a moment, then nodded.

"Now," said Ryan, "how are we gonna get the timing right? If we're a second late, we could end up either crashing into Earth or overshooting them by hundreds of thousands of miles. It still sounds like we're pretty far from a realistic plan here."

"Trust me," said Amanda. "I got us this far, didn't I?"

Ryan laughed. "I suppose you did."

"I can calculate the speed and distance with Nikki. Then we can run the numbers for each ship. If we do this right, we'll be there and gone before they know what hit them."

"Sounds good if it works," said Ryan, "but it's the 'doing this right' part that has me nervous. About how long are we talking from Mars to Earth at light speed?"

"Hard to say. We're over eighty-seven million miles from Earth at least, but the distance varies. Plus, we have to account for the relative velocity of time dilation."

"Care to say that in English?"

"The longer the distance, the more we have to account for the movement of both planets. The computer will crunch it though."

"Let's say we get the numbers right. Can we use autopilot?"

"Well, that's another issue," she said. "For some ships, yes, and even those will need some work to get them up to speed. But more than half of our ships' autopilot systems aren't even operative."

"And what do we do for those?"

"That's where you come in."

"Me?"

"What I need you to do is find out which ships don't have a working autopilot. I'll need to contact those ships and explain to them how to synchronize their navigational computers with their helm controls."

"Will do," said Ryan. "Meanwhile, you and Nicole go do your thing. How much time do you need?"

"Two hours," said Amanda.

"Got it. We'll touch base then."

Ryan turned toward the weapons console. "Hey, Tanner, how many more times can we attack before we run short of torpedoes?"

Tanner did a quick tally. "We're good for at least two more runs at them," he said. "Will that do?"

"It'll have to." This didn't leave room for any error, but then again everything else had been down to the wire, so it was par for the course.

Paul called the bridge from engineering. "Ryan, I've run a full diagnostic on the engines. Best case scenario, we can run the overload sequence two more times before we fry them. Worst case, we may only get one more shot. After that, we'd be screwed because all we'd have left would be sub-light drive and our maneuvering thrusters."

"Then we damn well better make each attack count."

By the time he had identified which ships lacked autopilot systems and forwarded the names to Amanda, an hour had gone by. He was waiting like an expectant father for another hour when he heard the doors to the bridge open. Amanda and Nicole entered.

"I could really use some good news about now," he said.

"We have the data," said Amanda. "I'm downloading the calculations into the helm. I've also sent all the information to each ship in the fleet. We should be all set to go in ten minutes."

Ryan nodded. Ten minutes. All the planning and all the events over the last few weeks, and it all came down to ten lousy minutes.

"Okay," he said. "Jill, inform the fleet that we move in exactly . . . nine minutes. We need to time the takeoff perfectly so we arrive together."

It felt surreal watching the crew go about their business looking like real pros. To think that just a few short weeks ago their biggest worry had been passing exams. Things sure had changed. It amazed him how quickly they'd all bonded and how far they had come in such a short time. He remembered reading that a study of the most elite teams showed that they all shared four beliefs: a belief in the mission, in their leader, in themselves, and, most of all, in each other. If that was true, then this was the most elite of teams, with the grand-daddy of all challenges: how to survive another day and save Earth. Yes indeed, a far cry from his life just three weeks ago.

After a few short minutes, Amanda called over to him. "We're ready to go, Ryan."

"Jill, put me through to Paul," he said.

"Patching you to engineering now."

"Paul, full power to engines. Prepare for light-speed drive."

"Engines hot and ready," said Paul. "We're good to go."

"You heard the man, Nicole. Punch it. Light speed, now."

"Engaging light-speed drive, Captain."

Ryan gripped his chair. He wasn't sure if he was more worried about the light speed transition or what was waiting on the other side. Either way, his stomach rose up into his throat as soon as the jump began.

It was hard to believe they were traveling at one hundred and eighty-six thousand miles per second. No matter how many times Ryan tried to grasp it, he still found the idea mind-boggling.

He was watching the clock. One fraction off and they could end up on the wrong side of Earth, or worse, crash into the planet. Not only did they need to have pinpoint accuracy, but their timing had to be perfect. Hoping for the best but still anxious, he could feel his stomach tightening.

At exactly eighteen minutes into their flight, the computer activated the overload in the reactor and the now-familiar vibrations started. The closer to the sixty-second countdown it got, the more violent the rumbling became. With the count at fifteen seconds, the braking thrusters were activated and the ship came to a screeching halt. The internal gravity slammed Ryan forward against his restraints. It was like a roller coaster ride on steroids. But now the real hell would begin. The moment of truth.

Over the roar of the braking thrusters, Ryan could hear Tanner yelling, "Firing solar disrupters. Targeting systems activated. Firing torpedoes."

It was like chaos, with everything happening at once. From the sensor station Amanda yelled out, "Incoming weapons fire."

"Hard about," ordered Ryan. "Prepare to bug out."

Suddenly the ship lurched violently. Alarms were blaring on the bridge. "Were we hit?" asked Ryan.

"Near miss!" yelled Tanner.

"We dodged a bullet," said Nicole.

"Get us outta here, Nicole. Now!" yelled Ryan. He knew it would be a few minutes before they regained light-speed ability, but hopefully the disrupters had done their job on the enemy.

As the ship bucked with Nicole's maneuvering, Ryan tried to look at Amanda's console. "Did we hit any?" he said.

Amanda was deep in concentration. Finally, she yelled out, "We got them!"

Ryan noticed sparks coming from Amanda's console and sprang into action, running from his seat and jumping in front of her just as the device erupted into flames and shorted out.

As he pushed her out of harm's way and to the floor, the console blew up with a deafening sound. The force of the explosion threw Ryan into a bulkhead, ramming his head against it and knocking him to the ground. Dazed, he could see that Amanda was all right even though she was lying next to him on the floor.

Fighting to maintain consciousness, he could see the crew working to put out fires from short circuits around the bridge. Amanda was trying to say something to him. Her mouth was moving, but all he could hear was a loud ringing in his ears.

He noticed that her amulet had broken open and was lying on the floor next to him. Something had fallen out of it. Ryan struggled to move his finger and managed to point to it. He tried to speak, but he couldn't. Then the room started spinning and everything went dark.

Chapter 38

Contact

Amanda felt like she'd been hit by a freight train. One second she was watching her sensor array, the next she was lying on the floor. Everything seemed to have happened at once. She knew they'd barely escaped the direct hit. Then she'd felt herself being tackled and the next thing she knew, there was an explosion. She crawled toward Ryan, who was passed out face-down on the floor. God, please let him be okay.

Tanner and Jill came running over.

"I'm okay," she said. "Go call the medics."

She kept calling Ryan's name, but he wasn't responding. She went to turn him over, but noticed her amulet on the floor next to his hand. It had broken open and there were two small flat black objects beside it. The necklace must have fallen off during the explosion, unless it was from when Ryan tackled her. Poor Ryan was probably trying to get to the amulet after he fell. She turned her attention back to him, praying he was alive.

He was unconscious, but he was breathing, though his breaths were labored. His shirt was torn and he appeared to have burns on his chest and arms. As she turned his head, she could see that he was bleeding from a deep gash on his forehead. She quickly forced herself up to grab a first aid kit and sat down on the floor next to him. If not for him, it would have been she who had suffered the brunt of the explosion.

"Damn you, Ryan," she said, choked up. "Oh God, please don't die." She was about to apply pressure to the gaping wound above his right eye when the bridge doors opened.

She jumped up and saw the medical team. "Over here!" she yelled.

They rushed over and Doctor Basha checked his pulse and looked into his eyes. She then felt around his head and neck and examined the burns on his chest.

"Was he like this when you found him?" she said.

"Yes . . . well I turned him over," said Amanda.

"Never do that. If he had a spinal injury, you could have made it worse. They covered that in your emergency medical training."

"I'm sorry. Is he okay?"

"His pulse is steady," said Basha. "Some second-degree burns. Internal injuries are always a possibility. I've got to get him to the infirmary." The tech helped the doctor put a neck brace on Ryan, and they immobilized his back so they could put him safely on the gurney. Then they whisked him away.

It dawned on Amanda that with Ryan out of commission, she was next in command. Funny how all she had wanted before was to beat him, and now she'd give anything to have him back in command. Or to have him back, period. She didn't even want to think about losing him.

She was tempted to go to the infirmary, but she knew she was needed on the bridge. As she scanned the room to survey the situation, she noticed that a damage control team had arrived and was trying to put out some small fires.

"Jill, I need a damage report from all departments," she said.

"Damage reports are just starting to come in," said Jill. "I'll get them to you ASAP."

"Thanks." Amanda made her way to the helm console and put a hand on Nicole's shoulder.

"You okay?" said Nicole.

"I'll live. I'm just hoping Ryan's all right. Do we still have full flight control and light-speed ability?"

"Somehow it looks like we do," said Nicole. "I'm waiting for confirmation. For now, Ryan ordered me to head back to Mars. The rest of the fleet is supposed to meet us there."

"Okay," said Amanda. "Stay on course."

She looked around. The damage control teams were preparing to leave the bridge when Cadet Rawlings approached. "The sensor array is shot," he said. "We'll need to repair it. I just wanted to let you know before I run."

"Run where?" said Amanda. "How long will it take?"

"I need to go help Paul run a diagnostic on the reactor and the light-speed generator. I'm guessing that'll take an hour, and then another hour for the sensor array. See you soon, Amanda . . . I mean, Captain."

"Amanda is fine," she said.

As Rawlings and his team left the bridge, Amanda thought, *You wanted a chance to try and end the fighting. Well, here it is.*

Another two hours went by, and finally all the diagnostics were run and repairs made as needed. Amanda used the time to think of options, and one in particular was making more and more sense.

"All systems are go for light speed," said Nicole.

"All stations ready," said Jill.

Amanda strapped herself in to get ready for the light-speed jump and closed her eyes. She was so focused on Ryan and the mission ahead that she barely noticed the jump this time. Once they reached light speed, her thoughts drifted off as she thought about the events over the last few weeks.

In practically no time, she was brought back to reality by a beep from the bridge.

"We'll be at Mars in ten minutes," said Nicole.

Amanda looked around and everyone was up and busy.

"Jill," she said. "Do we have confirmation from all of our ships?"

"We still haven't heard from the Zhukov," said Jill. "The Kennedy reported heavy damage and said the survivors were abandoning ship and heading toward Pluto. All other ships are accounted for."

"Do we have a number of verified kills?" asked Amanda.

"Thirteen," said Jill.

"Odd," said Amanda. "The Zhukov must have overshot their target or run into some type of trouble. Check for their automated distress beacon. It should have ejected if something happened."

"Activating the search sequence now," said Jill. In seconds, she let out a gasp.

"What?" said Amanda.

"I found it. The beacon data shows there was a failure in their autopilot system that took them off course." Jill paused and turned to face her. "It's not good, Amanda. They crashed."

"Crashed into Earth?"

"No, according to the coordinates, they collided head on with 1999 RQ36. You know the size of that asteroid, Amanda. There's no way there could be any survivors."

"Damn these old ships! Just great. The asteroid just misses Earth, courtesy of the UEDF, and then they have to hit it." Amanda couldn't believe they'd lost another ship. And more classmates. It didn't make her feel overly safe on the Churchill either. But it didn't have to be this way. Nobody else had to die. This convinced her of it. It was time to put an end to this violence before any more cadets lost their lives.

"Nicole," she said. "Take us around to the other side of Mars. I want to get into position to contact the Altarran commander."

Tanner approached Amanda. "Permission to tell it like it is?"

"Don't you always?" said Amanda.

"Listen," said Tanner, "you have lots of really good ideas, I'll admit that. But this ain't one of them. If you contact them, they just may track the transmission and find our ships. Then we're screwed. We can't outrun them in these freakin' floating trashcans."

"You know something, Tanner? That was very diplomatic, and it actually makes sense. But don't worry. I've got it covered."

"Covered how? This I can't wait to hear."

"The fleet will be moved to Saturn. I'm going alone."

"Oh. Well, then," said Tanner. "Why didn't you just say so? That's much different. Suicidal much?"

"I'll be less of a threat."

"Oh, I'll say," said Tanner. "One little transport ship against twenty-two advanced battleships. What could happen there, right? That's an awesome plan. I love this plan . . . I'll put that on your tombstone, 'She was less of a threat.'"

"Tanner, it's not like I'm going to waltz in there by surprise. When I tell them about the amulet, I'm betting they'll talk."

Tanner was staring at the broken amulet with the two black objects that Amanda had gathered in a box. "I'm sure they'll love the fact that it's broken. Where'd those come from?"

"Those black things? I think they were inside the amulet. But I have no idea what they are. Here. Take a look." She put the two small black objects into Tanner's hand.

"Wait a minute," he said. "I've seen stuff like this before, in the archives library with Jill."

"You have? What are they?"

"They're some type of information chip. Micro-something or other. Jill would know."

Amanda called Jill over.

"You ever see anything like this before?" said Amanda.

Jill examined them closely. "How old is this amulet?" she asked.

"Not really sure," said Amanda. "It's been in our family over a hundred and twenty-five years. I have no idea how old it is."

"This one looks like an old-style microchip," said Jill. "The other one, I'm not really sure. That one's a little different. It could be a microfilm. Unfortunately, we don't have anything on board that I can use to read them. Back at the academy in the old archives library, they did. The only reason I remember is because Tanner and I did a thesis about the evolution of military information storage."

"Let me take them to Paul," said Tanner. "Maybe he and I can figure something out."

No sooner had Tanner left with the objects than Nicole called out. "We've reached the other side of Mars," she said. "We have a clear communication path to Earth."

"Jill," said Amanda. "Can you find any unusual frequency channels? Something that might be foreign?"

"Searching," said Jill.

Amanda waited as Jill fiddled with the controls.

"I've detected a frequency that could be them," said Jill. "It's off any of our normal ranges."

"Okay, here goes," said Amanda. "Let's see if we can open a channel to the Altarran fleet."

Jill hesitated, then pressed a button.

"Channel open. You're live."

Amanda took a deep breath. She'd been memorizing this introduction ever since she'd read the file her dad had posted on the Altarrans, soon after she'd found out the amulet matched the alien insignia.

"This is Captain Amanda Williamson of the United Earth Defense Fleet," she said. "I'd like to speak with Supreme Commander Granthaxe."

She listened and waited.

"I'd like to speak with Supreme Commander Granthaxe," she repeated.

Finally she heard static. Then a booming voice came from the speakers.

"It is an unwise captain who dares to speak after breaking the truce," said the alien commander, practically shattering her eardrums. "Your people shall suffer in proportion to your insolence."

"Supreme Commander," she said, almost forgetting her fear of aliens, "you gave us no choice."

"I gave you time! And all you have given in return is trickery. Now, you have no time, Captain Amanda Williamson. By my order, we make preparations as I speak."

"You delivered an ultimatum to our planet that we couldn't satisfy," she said. "You wanted answers to something that happened years before any of us were born."

"Then the sons and daughters shall pay for the deeds of the fathers. You were unwise to attack us."

"Commander, wait."

"Supreme Commander!"

"Okay, Supreme Commander. I believe I have something that you may want to see. Something I believe to be of great value to you." She left out that it had broken in half.

"There is no value but that of my people forsaken on your wretched planet. Aside from that, there is only one gift your people can bestow."

"And what is that?"

"To die. A life for a life, magnified a billion-fold. Soon you will observe as we commence bombardment upon your planet," said Granthaxe.

"Supreme Commander, before you make that mistake, I have another gift that you may be interested in."

"A gift of fools no doubt."

"Let me remind you that we do have the weapons to disable your shields. But I'd rather we both put an end to this useless waste of life. The gift I speak of is a necklace that may be of interest to you, with an amulet. It bears the same image as the crest on your ship. It has three diamonds above your crest, surrounded by gems. Does this sound familiar to you?"

There was silence for a minute. "Describe this amulet." The commander didn't sound happy. "Tell me more, now!"

"There are three gemstones in a triangular carving," she said. "But the gemstones are in an uneven spot on each side of the triangle. Above the gemstones appear to be objects shaped like stars, with diamonds at the center of each."

"Stolen from our envoys," said the commander. "Proof of your crimes and you use it to bait me!"

"It was left to me by my family. It's not a trick. I'd be willing to bring it to you," she said. "On a small transport ship. No weapons."

She waited for an answer.

"Bring it to me," he said. "Alone. I shall hold off on my attacks until you arrive."

"If I bring it to you," she said, "can I have assurances that you'll spare us and work with us?"

"You have assurances . . . that we will destroy your planet if you don't. Those are the only assurances I can offer. When can I expect you?"

Amanda thought about it. He just *had* to listen if she brought it. She was already opening up a dialogue. She could feel it.

"I'll be there in eight hours," she said. "You have my word."

"Your word means nothing to me."

"I'm sorry you feel that way, Supreme Commander. I hope to prove to you wrong."

"I expect to see you in eight hours, Captain Amanda Williamson."

Amanda swallowed. "I'll be there," she said. "Eight hours."

"We will broadcast coordinates," said Granthaxe. "Oh, and since you find favor with assurances," he added, "I will give you one more. While you may have surprised us with your last cowardly maneuver, let me assure you, the next time we will be waiting with surprises of our own. And if we all die together, then so be it. But, by the gods, it will not be before I fire every last weapon that we have upon your Earth. Your next trick, Captain Amanda Williamson, shall be your last."

The communication abruptly ended.

Amanda looked around at the shocked faces on the bridge.

"Well, that went well," said Tanner.

"Actually," said Amanda, "it did."

"Jesus, I was kidding. What part of that went well? The part where he said he'll wipe out life as we know it or the part where you agreed to come visit him with his precious amulet that's broken in half?"

"Hey at least he agreed to meet me face to face."

"Face to face? Are you forgetting the rest of it, like what happens next? And how do you know they even have faces?"

"Oh my God, don't even say that." That was something she hadn't even thought of.

"That's what you're worried about, what they look like?"

"We have no other options, Tanner," she said.

"What about the plan we came in with in the first place? Whatever happened to that? 'Cause that sounded a far sight better than this."

"Tanner has a point," said Jill.

"If we do that," said Amanda, then we risk everyone dying. We have to give this a shot at least."

"And this doesn't?" said Tanner? "'Cause I thought I heard him say we have no assurances, and you are, after all, tricking him yet again by bringing him a broken amulet. Who knows what was inside it before those chips?"

"I need you to trust me," she said. "I believe he'll listen to reason."

"Yeah, he sure sounded like it . . . *Captain Amanda Williamson.*"

She had to laugh at Tanner's overdramatic imitation of Granthaxe. But inside, she, too, was afraid of what might happen. And Tanner wasn't helping.

"Aren't you all forgetting something?" said Nicole.

Amanda looked at her, as did Tanner and Jill.

"Those troop carriers are the size of small cities," she said. "We may have knocked them out for a bit, but there's a good chance they'll get up again. And we all know what their mission is. If we go in for another strike, even if we're successful, we won't have ammunition to go against those carriers. So Amanda's right. Convincing the commander seems like our only option."

Amanda hadn't even thought of that, but Nicole was right. Even Tanner was quiet now. She looked up as Tanner and Jill nodded their approval of her plan.

So this was it.

"Well," she said, "I better get ready."

She turned to leave the bridge, her stomach in knots. Not only was she possibly facing her last hours, but the fate of the entire world rested on whether she could get Granthaxe to listen. No pressure, Amanda. Worse yet, she was hours away from facing her deepest fear, a true close encounter of the fifth kind with a hostile alien race. That alone was giving her the shakes. She knew she should be focusing now on what to say when she got there. Instead her mind was filled with all the ways they might kill her.

Chapter 39

One-Way Trip

Amanda had to do a few things before leaving. Tanner may have been a joker, but he was highly skilled, and she trusted him—mostly.

"You have command until I get back or Ryan recovers, Tanner," she said. "I've got some loose ends to tie up before I leave."

"Loose ends," he said. "Sure. But before you go, I need a favor."

"That depends," she said. "What is it?"

"Promise me you'll stay calm when you get there. No screaming. This isn't King Kong. We need you back, preferably in one piece and alive. And most important . . . can I have a hug?"

She smiled and hugged him. "You bet, Tanner."

"You can do this," he said. "If anyone can, you can."

Those simple words of confidence were what she needed to hear most. And especially coming from Tanner, they helped.

Amanda left the bridge and headed to the infirmary. Ryan was lying in one of the beds. He was either sleeping or still unconscious and had bandages covering his chest. She hated seeing him that way and was pretty sure he'd hate her seeing him like this.

She knelt down close to him and whispered. "We don't always agree, Ryan." She felt the tears coming and couldn't help laughing. "Yeah, understatement, I know." She took a deep breath and continued. "But you mean a lot to me. And I know you're gonna be pretty pissed at me when you hear what I'm about to do, but I've got to try. It's only me now." She paused to stroke his face. "You get better. And thanks for saving me. Maybe now it's my turn to save you." She bent over and kissed him on the cheek.

Reluctantly, she took the lift down to the cargo hold. Upon entering, she made her way to one of the small transport ships and got on board. There were normally two-day food rations on the transports, which should do fine. The way she figured it, in two days she'd either be back or dead. Sitting down, she began a pre-flight checklist.

Before leaving, she grabbed a thermal sealer to repair the amulet. She wanted to make sure that it was in one piece when delivering it to the Altarran commander.

Activating the communication console, she called the bridge. "I'm depressurizing the cargo bay and preparing to take Transport One to rendezvous with the Altarrans. If you guys don't hear from me within two hours of docking on the Altarran ship, prepare another attack run and do whatever's necessary to put an end to this war. I'm leaving the cargo bay now. I'll be running silent. Williamson out."

Tanner replied, "Hey, Big Red. I'm deploying communication satellites in orbit above Mars, and I'll release more above Jupiter when we get there. That way you can bounce the signal to us in the event you need to get in contact. If you run into any trouble, just give a holler and we'll come running."

"Perfect," she said. "If you keep this up, you're going to ruin your reputation as the class clown."

Amanda powered up the transport and began the eight-hour flight. This was going to be the longest eight hours of her life. Thank God this wasn't two hundred years ago or it would have been eight months for the trip to Earth. To pass the time, she began recording all that had taken place over the past five days. She wanted to have everything documented in the event she didn't make it back or was kept as a prisoner of war.

She also recorded a message to her father to share with her family, assuming any of them survived whatever Granthaxe would have in store. She left messages to each of her friends as well. Last, but not least, she recorded a heartfelt message to Ryan, repeating what she'd whispered at his bedside.

Having finished all her messages, she sent them out with the ominous header: *To be viewed in the event of my death.*

The remaining time she spent going over various scenarios in her head, preparing what she would say to Granthaxe and wondering how Ryan was faring. Eventually, she found herself dozing off, exhausted by the traumatic events of the last few days.

She was startled when the silence was broken by a booming voice over the speakers.

"This is Supreme Commander Granthaxe. We have you in visual range. Bring your vessel directly in front of our ships. You will see an opening. If you deter from your course or make any threatening moves, my ships have orders to fire."

"I read you loud and clear," said Amanda. She maneuvered the transport toward the imposing line of Altarran ships, all facing her like a firing squad. There was a large gap directly in the center. "I see the opening now," she said. "Correcting course and angle." As she proceeded forward into the gap, a large docking area descended from an enormous labyrinthine vessel. It dwarfed any of the UEDF ships that she knew of. "I'll be inside shortly," she said.

She was starting to sweat, and her legs were trembling. She had been busy or asleep for most of the flight. Now here she was, about to be the first human to dock with an alien ship, a CE-5 encounter. Bringing her ship close to the docking area, she cut power and glided in using her forward and side thrusters to maneuver. As soon as she entered the inside of the vessel, she hit her reverse thrusters and landed gently on the deck.

"I'm inside your ship," she said.

"We are aware of your presence," said Granthaxe. "Remain in your ship as we close the docking bay doors. We will provide oxygen to the area for you to breathe. I will inform you when it is safe to exit your vessel."

"How did you know we require oxygen?" she said.

"Ha! Do you think humans the only species to thrive on the breath of the gods? Do you think Earth the only such planet? You amuse me with your insignificance. Your kind is like a young child, a seedling."

The sound of the outer doors closing startled her, followed by a deafening hiss. Now she was really starting to have a panic attack. This was it. There was no turning back now.

The noise stopped. "You may leave your vessel," said Granthaxe. "The docking area is safe. I will arrive momentarily. Have the amulet ready for my inspection."

Amanda took a deep breath and put the amulet around her neck before exiting the ship. The area was dark, dimly illuminated by some sort of green hue. As soon as she closed the cockpit door, she heard the sounds of the alien ship's door locks disengaging. She was standing about fifty feet from the largest double doors she'd ever seen, which she could barely make out in the darkness. She could hear heavy foot-steps approaching, the ground shaking with each step. She braced herself, as she remembered Tanner's words. Don't scream, Amanda.

As the doors slid open with a loud whoosh, she saw a huge shadow, followed by two hulking figures that had to be at least twelve feet tall. It was too dark to make out any details, but they walked upright like humans. One seemed to be about a foot taller than the other. She could see that they had two arms, two legs, and one head, which was a good sign. But their glowing eyes frightened her. She could hear her own heartbeat as they came closer and she could start to make out their shapes. Her mouth dropped at the sight of them. They were incredibly muscular and had to weigh close to five hundred pounds. They could crush any human with ease. She looked down as her nerves were getting the best of her.

Maybe this wasn't such a great idea after all, she thought. She was trying to remain calm and not hyperventilate.

"The amulet, Amanda Williamson," said the larger one. His voice, coming down from at least seven feet above her, was as loud in person as over the speakers. "Hand it to me."

She hesitated and slowly looked up into his eyes. It was hard to believe that she was looking at a creature from another planet, pos-sibly another galaxy.

"My God," she said, "you really do exist."

Granthaxe looked down at her. "Of course I exist. What is that supposed to mean?"

"I'm sorry, I meant—"

"Does the amulet exist, Amanda Williamson? Because if it does not, then we will see who exists and who does not."

She gingerly placed the amulet in his very large hand.

"It was damaged during battle," she said. "I repaired it as best I could."

Granthaxe's icy glowing eyes stared down at her in silence, then he looked at the amulet in his hands. She couldn't tell what he was thinking, and was trembling waiting for a response. Any kind of response.

Finally, he turned to the other creature.

"Lock her in the holding area," he said.

She started to panic. "Wait," she said, as the other creature's huge hands grabbed her as if she were a Barbie doll.

Amanda watched Granthaxe leave the room. She turned to the creature that was holding her.

"What is he planning?" she asked, but the creature didn't respond. Before she knew it, she was being placed in a small brig-like room with no furniture. The door slammed shut and she heard the locks click. She sat down on the floor and tried to figure out what her next move should be, or if she would even survive the rest of the day.

Chapter 40
General Order 61

Fleet Admiral Thompson was having his morning cup of coffee as he watched the clock on the wall. The Altarran truce had expired, and to his surprise, he hadn't heard anything from the supreme commander. There was no movement detected on any of the Earth-based radar sites either. He was about to check with the observatory concerning any activity from the Altarran fleet when his com link beeped.

"Sir," said the voice on the other line, "it's Lieutenant Robbins from the observatory. You've got to see this. I'm forwarding images we just recorded. Sending now."

Thompson watched his monitor intently. A video appeared showing multiple Altarran ships being destroyed. He jumped up from his desk, spilling his coffee. "Hell, yeah!" he yelled. "She did it! That girl's damn crazy idea worked."

He shut off the video and hit his intercom. "Morgan, get me Commodore Laurent immediately."

"Funny you should ask that," said his assistant. "She's actually on the line waiting to talk to you."

Thompson opened the channel to the R&D building. "Commodore," he said, "I've just seen video confirming that Amanda Williamson's idea worked. In fact, it seems like her father, God love him, must have picked up all the survivors from Pluto to man the old retired fleet at the academy. I saw the Churchill on that video. Brilliant idea. I'll have to commend him when I see him."

"Actually," said Laurent, "I was calling you to tell you we've also developed a much better version of her weapon. If you'll come to the compound, I'll show you."

"On my way." Thompson cut the link and called to Morgan to have a driver ready. For the first time in days, he felt a sense of hope. He wasn't sure how many Altarran ships had been destroyed, but the fact was, the fleet now had the capability to disable their shields at will. He headed outside where his driver was already waiting for him.

Within minutes they had reached the security checkpoint at the research and development complex. The guard at the gate recognized the admiral and waved him through. Upon arriving at the building, Thompson made his way inside. Laurent and Osaki were waiting for him. Osaki looked none too happy to be the new commander's subordinate. Thompson ignored him, looking directly at Laurent.

"Okay, Commodore," he said. "What have you got for me?"

Laurent smiled at him. "Good day to you as well, Admiral. Come to the monitor and I'll show you."

He followed her to the large monitor.

"This is a video of the weapon we tested late last night," she said.

She turned on the monitor, and immediately a video appeared showing a room full of electronic equipment. It looked like a small warehouse full of every type of electronic device imaginable. They were all activated, with lights blinking everywhere. In an instant, a beam of light flashed throughout the room, and immediately all the devices malfunctioned. It was as if someone had pulled the master plug. Some of the smaller devices began smoking.

Laurent turned off the monitor. "Not only have we duplicated Ms. Williamson's weapon," she said, "we've made it perfectly safe. The only drawback is that it can hold only three charges. After that, you must come back to the base and recharge it."

"Great work," said Thompson. "When can you install these on our remaining ships?"

Laurent grinned. "I thought you'd never ask. I've taken the initiative already and had them installed today. All your remaining ships have the weapon. Powered up and ready to go, sir."

Osaki stepped forward. "Admiral," he said, "I must protest. This weapon has not been tested on an actual ship in actual battle conditions or in the vacuum of space."

"I don't care, Captain."

"Sir, according to proper protocol, this weapon has not been deemed safe or properly tested and cannot be used."

Thompson leered at him. "You're forgetting General Order 61."

"General Order 61, sir?"

"General Order 61. It allows any senior commanding officer to override any and all regulations when engaged in planet-threatening situations without a clear line of communication."

"Indeed, Admiral," said Osaki, "but we have a communication device available to us."

Thompson looked at Osaki and then over to the communications console where a nervous-looking young ensign was trying to pretend he wasn't listening.

Pointing to the console, Thompson said to Osaki, "You mean that communication system there?"

Osaki followed his gaze. "Yes," he said. "I think you should contact the defense minister immediately."

The admiral walked closer to the console. "Ensign, please stand up and move away from the console."

"Yes, sir." The young ensign jumped up and moved a good twenty feet away.

"You know something, Osaki? I think there's something wrong with that system. I don't think it works."

Thompson smiled at Laurent. She was grinning from ear to ear. He was beginning to like her. The fact that she was attractive didn't hurt either.

Osaki gave him a strange look. "There is nothing wrong with that system. It works fine."

Thompson removed his sidearm and fired his laser at the communication system. Sparks jumped out from it and a gaping hole appeared dead center of the console.

He looked at Osaki. "It looks to me like it has a big hole in it. I'd get that fixed."

Osaki looked at him in disbelief. "You can't do that."

Laurent was trying to suppress her laughter, but wasn't doing a very good job of it.

"Do what?" said Thompson. "All I saw was a horrible malfunction." He looked at the poor ensign, whose legs were now shaking. "Isn't that what you saw, Ensign?"

"Y-yes, sir," said the young officer. "A malfunction."

Thompson turned to Laurent. "All nine ships are locked and loaded and ready to go?"

"They're at your beck and call, sir."

"Good. I'm going to round up the crews and prepare to leave as soon as we can get our ships manned. Good work, Marie. In fact, if we make it back alive, I owe you dinner."

Laurent smiled at him. "You're not getting away from me that easy, sir. You're going to need me on board with you in case any problems arise."

Thompson laughed. "Oh, so that's how it's going to be. Okay, you're with me. Let's move out."

Thompson left the building with Laurent and had his driver take them to the hangars. He was feeling more upbeat by the minute. Not only did they have a chance, but they could actually win this war. A far cry from his thoughts when he'd woken up this morning.

Chapter 41

A New Plan

Ryan was groggy when he came to. His head felt like it weighed a hundred pounds. He looked around and saw that he was in the infirmary. Then it all came back to him: the near torpedo miss, the sensor console exploding on the bridge, falling to the floor and reaching for the amulet. Amanda! Last he remembered she'd been knocked to the ground. He sat up. When the room started to spin, he closed his eyes.

"Feeling a bit woozy?" said Doctor Basha.

"You can say that. How long have I been out?"

"A little over fourteen hours."

"Amanda?" He was almost afraid to ask.

Basha looked at him hesitatingly.

"I need to know," he said. "How is she?"

"She fared better than you did," said Basha. "She's fine."

"Thank God. Are we still in Mars orbit?"

"Not anymore. We're orbiting Jupiter."

"Jupiter? What the hell are we doing there? My last orders were for the fleet to regroup at Mars."

"First of all, Cadet Thompson, I may be a doctor, but I'm also a captain in the defense fleet. Please try to remember that when addressing me."

"I'm sorry, Doc, but my head's killing me and I need to know why we're in a completely different place from where I ordered our crew. No offense."

"You have second degree burns on your chest and your forearms. You also have twelve stitches above your right eye and a low-grade concussion. Under normal conditions, I'd have you rest for a couple days. But today's your lucky day."

"Yeah, it sure feels like it. Why lucky?"

"Considering the current state of affairs, I'm declaring you fit for duty."

"And just what is the current state of affairs?"

"I suggest you ask your crew. I'm just the doctor. Now I'm leaving you with some meds for the pain and salve for the burns. If your vision becomes blurry, get back down here immediately."

"Anything else?" he said, taking the medication from her.

"Yes. If we're still alive in twenty-four hours. I want you back here for a checkup."

He tried to muster a smile. "Thanks, Doc," he said. "For everything."

"Don't thank me," she said. "Thank Cadet Williamson."

"I'll do that now."

"Well, that may be difficult," she said. "Your crew will explain."

"What do you mean difficult?"

"Your crew will explain."

Ryan knew he wouldn't get any further with Basha. He lifted himself off the bed and left the infirmary. He still heard a slight ringing in his ears as he made his way to the bridge.

As he entered, he was surprised to see Tanner sitting in the command chair and Amanda nowhere in sight.

Tanner made eye contact with Ryan. "Ry! How the hell are you feeling?"

Something wasn't right. Ryan could sense the tension in Tanner's voice, and it was odd how quiet the bridge had got when he had walked in. "I'll live. But I'm confused."

"Well, you did get hit pretty hard," said Tanner.

"No, I mean about what's going on here. First, why are we orbiting Jupiter instead of Mars? Second, why is Rawlings manning the sensor array? And last, where the hell is Amanda?"

"Very good questions, Ry. To answer, we're orbiting Jupiter because Amanda ordered the fleet here. Rawlings is currently filling in for her. And, well, the reason for that is that Amanda decided to meet with the Altarran commander."

"She *what*? Meet him where? When?"

"On his ship. She took the amulet and a transport and left about six hours ago."

"How the hell could you allow her to do that?"

"There was nothing I could say or do to stop her, man. She was captain. You were unconscious in the infirmary."

"But you couldn't talk her out of it?"

"Well, after we realized the troop carriers could still rebuild their engines, and seeing how the odds were so much against us, it seemed like the only choice left. We agreed with her, Ry."

Ryan took a deep breath to process everything. He was torn between anger and concern for Amanda. One thing he knew for sure. He wasn't going to sit around and do nothing. He was going after her.

"Jill," he said, "inform the fleet that we're moving out in thirty minutes," he said.

Jill hesitated, then said, "Contacting the fleet now."

"Ry," said Tanner. "There are a few things you need to know."

"You mean there's more?"

"Well, yeah. We ran diagnostics on all the ships and Paul has been checking the data. The light-speed engines are in rough shape. We may get one more trip out of them, but if we try to overload them again, they'll blow."

"So what are you saying?"

"I'm saying we can't take down their shields anymore."

"Well this just keeps getting better by the minute, doesn't it?"

Ryan wondered what kind of chance they'd have against the Altarrans without being able to take down their shields. The answer was . . . not much.

"Well," said Tanner, "I do have a bit of good news."

"What, that we've all been given superpowers?"

"Close. We still have my nukes. In fact, we have more than the two onboard our ship."

Ryan couldn't believe what he was hearing.

"How many more?" he said. "And when were you gonna tell me this?"

"A lot more," said Tanner. "Listen, I didn't want you to take the heat for my idea. I got together with the rest of the weapons officers about a week before we left and told them about my plan. Just to be safe, we put one on every ship."

"You're telling me every one of our ships has nukes?"

"Uh . . . yep."

"Do you think they can break through their shields?"

"Are you kidding me? Well, I don't know for sure but I'd bet all I had on it. Then again if I was wrong I wouldn't be able to collect, so no. But I mean yes, I think it would definitely break through their shields."

Ryan thought about it for a minute.

"Well, at least this gives us a fighting chance," he said. "Now all I have to do is figure out a way to get Amanda back. Nicole, set a course for Earth. One-tenth light speed."

"Yes, sir," she said. "Setting course and speed. Ready on your mark."

"Jill, have all the ships replied that they're ready for departure?"

"Affirmative. All ships report ready."

"Put me through to Paul in engineering."

"Patching you through now, sir," said Jill.

"Paul," said Ryan, "Tanner tells me our light-speed engines are just about gone and the reactors can't contain another overload."

"That about sums it up. We've got one more trip left in these old engines. So if we're gonna do this, it's now or never."

"Well, let's do it then."

Looking at Jill, he said, "Inform the fleet we're moving out. Once we're out of orbit, we'll be going to one-tenth light speed."

"The fleet is on standby," she said. "They're waiting on your orders."

"Take us out, Nicole."

"Affirmative, sir. Taking us out of orbit now."

As the ship took off, Tanner approached Ryan. "If you don't mind," he said, "I want to head down to engineering. Paul and I have been trying to find a way to view those old microchips from the amulet. We've got a few hours before we meet up with the Altarrans and I'd like to put them to good use."

"Good idea. Maybe we can get some answers before we get there. If we can show something to the Altarrans that may vindicate us, maybe we can put a stop to all of this, just like Amanda wanted. *And* get her back safe and sound."

Ryan watched as Tanner left the bridge. He hoped Amanda was right. They could use a break right about now.

"Sir," said Nicole, "we're out of orbit and clear of Saturn's moons."

"Take us to one-tenth light speed, Nicole."

"Yes, sir. Engaging now."

It seemed as if the ship hesitated briefly before springing forward. Ryan looked at Nicole. "What was that?"

"The helm control seems sluggish," she said.

Ryan nodded. "I think we've pushed these old ships way past their limits. We're definitely only gonna get one more shot at the Altarrans, so this better work."

Ryan sat back and wondered if Amanda would still be alive when they got there. He wasn't the religious type, but he held his head down and silently said a small prayer. Not only had he made a promise to her father, he'd made one to himself—a promise never to let anyone he cared about be taken from him again. And especially not her. They had a three-hour flight ahead of them. Somehow he had to figure out a way to get Amanda back before they were left with no choice but to send the Altarrans into oblivion. It all depended on what they could find on those microchips. The one thing he prayed wasn't on there was evidence the missing envoys were tortured or killed. Then all bets were off.

Chapter 42

Supreme Commander Granthaxe

Supreme Commander Granthaxe was alone in his quarters, deep in thought. The events of the last two weeks had not played out as he had envisioned. This plan, *his plan*, had been in the works for twenty-five years. Confounded humans. Since his scientists had developed sunlight drive and powerful energy shields, he had planned this mission along with his father, King Morthaxe. They all said if anyone could avenge the queen's capture by the humans it would be his son. Now, after what had seemed like an easy victory, the prospect of failure loomed ahead.

The troop ships had not yet arrived. He was beginning to fear that they had been destroyed by the humans. Each carrier was bringing with it one hundred thousand warriors, not to mention countless weapons and vehicles, enough to destroy a planet ten times Earth. But now, Granthaxe, Prince of Altarra, could very well go down in history as the fool who had lost an entire armada—not to mention half the Altarran military—in an effort to save the queen.

His thoughts were interrupted by a knock on the door.

"Enter," he said. The door opened, and he acknowledged Chief Science Officer Kyron, who bowed her head and knelt to the floor. "What information do you have for me concerning the amulet of the gods?" he said.

"Supreme Commander Granthaxe," said Kyron, "I have confirmed the legitimacy of the amulet. Not only is it authentic, but the queen aligned the gemstones before parting with it."

"And what do the gemstones tell us?" said Granthaxe.

"The amulet was entrusted to the bearer in friendship," she said. "But," she continued, "the planetary leaders are . . . *not* to be trusted, sir."

"As I thought," said Granthaxe. "While a scant few of these humans may be of good conscience, their rulers are nothing but malicious scoundrels. And *all* of them bear the mark of deceit. Bring Amanda Williamson to me."

Kyron stood. "As you wish, Supreme Commander. I shall bring her personally."

Granthaxe was growing impatient as he waited. Why had the human lied to him and not revealed that she had helped the queen? She must know the whereabouts of his missing envoys, or at the very least, where and when they had last been seen alive. He heard the approach of footsteps and opened his door. He looked down at the frail child-like being in front of him, her skinny arms held by Kyron and the guard. How could a species so small and weak be capable of defeating him and his armada?

"Take the irons off her," he said. "There is no reason to fear her. So said the amulet of the gods."

The guard removed the chains from Amanda's arms and legs and pushed her down to the floor. "Kneel in the presence of royalty," said the guard.

Granthaxe watched as Amanda fell to the floor. "Enough! Leave us." The guard and Kyron bowed and left the room.

Granthaxe looked down at the delicate female and offered his hand to her. She looked frightened, and was staring at him in shock. "You are safe for now," he said. "Why do you stare at me?"

"I'm sorry, I didn't realize you looked like . . . like—"

"Never mind what I look like. I have questions you must answer."

Amanda looked at him. She seemed strong and determined despite her size. "I will answer all of your questions to the best of my ability," she said, "as long as they are not of a military nature or about our fleet."

"Your loyalty is admirable but unnecessary. If I wanted answers concerning your military, I can assure you we would obtain them from you one way or another. That is not why you are here. Why did you not tell me that you had assisted our queen?"

"I didn't," she said. "I've never met your queen."

"You wore the amulet around your neck. The gemstones were aligned to trust the wearer. Unlike humans, the gemstones do not lie. And yet you betray this trust."

"It was given to me by my father," she said. "Our family has had it for over one hundred and twenty years. My great-great-grandfather was its original owner."

"Ah. The bloodline."

"Bloodline?"

"You are a blood descendent of the wearer. It explains the gemstones. They will not hold their alignment for any others. Where is this great-great-grandfather of yours now, Amanda Williamson?"

She gave the giant a peculiar stare. "Not to be rude," she said, "but if he was my great-great-grandfather over a hundred years ago, where do you think he would be?"

Her answer caught him off guard. "How would I know where he would be? That is why I am asking you. I have no time for puzzles."

"He's dead, Supreme Commander. We're talking over one hundred and twenty years ago. He was eighty-nine then."

"So. That would make him only two hundred and nine. Was he killed in battle?"

She dared to laugh at his question. "Supreme Commander," she said, "our people only have a life span of eighty to a hundred years."

"A hundred years?!" he said. "Our pets live longer than that. Then I fear we have little to talk about. All that could have been helpful to us would have perished with your ancestor. This is not good news for your species, Amanda Williamson."

"Not necessarily, Supreme Commander. Inside the amulet there were information chips. I am sure my great-great-grandfather would not have put them in there unless there was useful information on them."

"What sort of . . . information chips, as you call them? Do you eat them to gain these insights?"

"They store information. Recordings. Our people are trying to read them now. They were inside the amulet. But we're having trouble reading them."

"If you value your people, we must know what is on these . . . information chips."

"Supreme Commander, if I could get to Earth with them, I could open them. We have the equipment there."

"Ha! Your leaders would never allow this. They undoubtedly plot my demise as we speak. I cannot trust them. Even your good intentions will be consumed by their hatred. I thereby decline your request."

"Supreme Commander, the captain of the ship I came from, he cares very much about me. If he knew I was going to Earth, he would cease fire. I know it."

"He cares about you, you say? Enough to stop an army?"

"Yes," she said.

"Then you can be useful to me in another way. Very useful."

"That's great," she said. "Tell me what it is."

"You will be my last bargaining piece, Amanda Williamson. I will demand that your people cease attacking us and give us the answers I seek, or we will execute you."

"Execute me?! Can't you see that I'm trying to bring about a peaceful resolution? They can't read the chips without going to Earth. That's where you'll get your answers. I was hoping your kind might have a bit more common sense than ours and work with us. You're proving me wrong with your actions."

"Silence! If you were an Altarran and spoke like that to me, I'd have you beheaded." He looked toward the door. "Guard! Take her away!"

Just as the guard entered the door, a high piercing sound went off, followed by a message.

"Supreme Commander," said the disembodied voice, "our scanning system has detected twelve Earth vessels heading our way. They will be in range in two minutes."

"Battle stations. All ships arm weapons and prepare for combat. Do not, I repeat, do not fire weapons unless fired upon first."

The reply was immediate. "Message received and understood, Supreme Commander."

Granthaxe called his guard over and gestured at Amanda. "Bring her with me to the battle bridge."

He glanced down at the little red-haired human. "Perhaps when we show your comrades that you are still alive, it will give us some leverage."

"I thought your amulet said I could be trusted," she said.

"Yes, and it also said your leaders could not."

Granthaxe left his quarters with his guard and Amanda at his side. This could very well be his final battle. If so, he would see to it that it would be a memorable one, worthy of the Prince of Altarra— a battle to the death.

Chapter 43

Final Stand

Ryan approached Tanner at the weapons console. "Did you contact the weapons officers on the rest of the ships?" he asked.

"Sure did, Ry. Every one of them have my children locked and loaded in their torpedo launchers. Did you let the rest of the captains in on our dirty little secret?"

"They know. And not one of them had an issue with it."

Jill looked at the two of them. "Well I have an issue," she said. "Do you know what kind of collateral damage this could do? I can't believe I'm actually going to be part of this . . . this . . . bravado stupidity. Two hundred and seventeen years since nuclear weapons have been used, and I have to be involved with the schmucks that actually want to use them again."

"What did she call us?" said Tanner.

"This is a last resort only," said Ryan. "Trust me, if I have any other choice, I'll take it. Do you think I'll risk losing Amanda? You just make sure that *all* ships acknowledge that *nobody* fires their weapons without my orders."

"I'm holding you to that," said Jill. "Sending message now . . . sir."

Ryan sat back and waited for the rest of the fleet to check in. They had less than fifteen minutes before they would come face to face with the Altarrans. He was hoping they'd be able to arrive at some sort of peaceful resolution. They'd have to if there was any chance of sparing Amanda. That is, if she wasn't already dead.

Paul called from engineering. "Ryan, I'm still trying to figure out how to open those microchips. It looks like one of them isn't really a chip. It's a little bigger than the other one and feels heavier. I think there's something inside it. I'm going to open it up and see what it is."

"Interesting. Any ideas what it might be?"

"I'm hoping it's a microfilm. If it is, I can probably blow up the pictures using the radiology systems in the infirmary."

"Great idea. Stay on it, Paul. We're running out of time—and options. This info is probably our last shot."

"Tell me about it," said Paul. "These engines are on their last legs. Once we shut them down, that's it. All we'll have left are thrusters."

"Captain," said Jill. "All ships have responded. They understand that nobody is to fire weapons until we do."

"Great. Nicole, how much longer until we reach Earth?"

"Two minutes."

Ryan sat up in his chair. "Jill, call all hands to battle stations."

Jill hit the automated system. Alarms sounded throughout the ship.

Nicole called to Ryan, "Preparing to cut engines and fire braking thrusters."

"This is it," said Ryan. "Shut down the engines. Engage braking thrusters."

The UEDF Churchill slowed down. The sounds of the engines sputtering, along with the groaning of the ship's hull, made Ryan wonder if the ship was about to burst apart at the seams. By the looks of everyone on the bridge, they were feeling the same. He was hoping the ship would hold together long enough to finish their mission.

"Open a channel to the Altarrans," said Ryan. He could see the Altarran fleet in clear view on the monitors.

"Channel open," said Jill.

Ryan cleared his throat. "Supreme Commander Granthaxe, this is Captain Ryan Thompson of the United Earth Defense Fleet. It is my understanding that one of my officers is on your ship."

It didn't take long before the static subsided and the booming voice came through.

"Yes, Captain Thompson. I have your Amanda Williamson. She is in healthy condition and under our guard."

"Supreme Commander, I am asking that you surrender. If you release Amanda and surrender, I will allow your fleet to leave Earth and return to your planet."

"Captain Ryan Thompson, it has come to my attention that you have something of mine as well. Release it to me and we may talk of what will come next."

"And what is it that you think I have?"

"Information. It is in your information chip. If you think we have come this far only to retreat without learning the truth about our envoys, you are greatly mistaken. And so, this is my ultimatum to you. Find my missing envoys, or I will order my ships to fight to the death. If you want your Amanda Williamson, this is my offer."

Ryan looked around at his crew. Tanner had his hand on the firing mechanism just in case. Ryan turned his attention back to the Altarrans. "Supreme Commander, I believe that your people did visit our planet, but we have no knowledge of it happening. Plus it occurred well over one hundred and twenty-five years ago. There isn't a human being alive from that time period. Even if we could find out what happened, there's no one to talk to. And your envoys would have been long gone by now, too."

"What would you know about our envoys?! Our life spans more than three hundred years, so unless your ancestors killed them, our envoys are still alive. I warn you Captain Ryan Thompson, we will not leave here without answers."

Still alive? Ryan thought about the implications of that. He wasn't sure which would have been worse; having them still alive on Earth or finding out the government tortured them. He thought he'd try another tack.

"Supreme Commander," he said, "I acknowledge that your envoys may be alive, or something may have happened to them in the past. And I promise I'll do what I can to help find out. But to wage inter-galactic war over a few missing envoys would seem foolish for both sides. Thousands have died already. Isn't that enough?"

"Enough?! Billions upon billions are not worth these four! I would destroy entire planets for them, because our queen, Captain Ryan Thompson—my *mother*—is among them!"

"Your mother? I'm sorry, I—"

"What would an insensitive species like yours know of sorrow? I am doubly bound as an Altarran and as her offspring to either save her . . . or avenge her. And I will not leave here until one or the other takes place."

"Supreme Commander, it's obvious—"

"The only thing obvious is your ignorance. If it is a fight you want, then by the gods of the ancient ones, a fight you shall have. Stand ready. By my count, we outnumber you twenty-three ships to twelve. If you think your weapons superior, then come face us now. Amanda Williamson shall perish, but what is one person compared with thousands?"

Ryan couldn't believe it. The queen was the commander's mother. His mind was racing. All this time, in talking with Granthaxe he was looking at his mirror image. Is this what it was to be? An eye for an eye? A tooth for a tooth? And soon they would all be blind and toothless? Amanda had always used that Gandhi saying to drive her point home, but this was the first time it had really sunk in. Ryan stumbled back into his chair. His body and mind were numb. There was dead silence on the bridge. All eyes were focused on him.

Rawlings turned to Ryan. "Captain, sensors are picking up nine ships. It's the remainder of the fleet."

"Of what fleet?" said Ryan.

"The United Earth Defense Fleet," said Jill. "Your father's fleet. I have audio. Putting it on speakers now."

"This is Fleet Admiral Ben Thompson ordering you to surrender immediately, Granthaxe. The numbers are just about even now. And we all have the ability to disable your shields now. You have five seconds to stand down or be destroyed."

Suddenly, the doors to the bridge opened. Ryan turned to see Paul running towards him gasping for air. "Ryan! Hold your fire. I have proof . . . the missing Altarrans—"

Ryan jumped up. "Jill, patch me through to my father."

Jill nodded. "You're on."

"Dad! It's Ryan. Stand Down. I repeat, STAND DOWN!"

Just then, Ryan could see on the monitors the Altarran ships getting into position to fire.

Chapter 44
Search For The Truth

Ryan waited for his father to respond. It probably took only a couple of seconds, but it seemed like an eternity before he heard his father's voice.

"Ryan? What the hell are you doing out here? Where's Admiral Williamson?"

"It's a long story, sir. Hold one sec."

From the view on the monitors, it appeared that the Altarrans were about to fire.

"Jill, patch me through to Granthaxe, quick."

"You're on."

"Supreme Commander, hold your fire."

Without waiting for a response, he had Jill patch him back.

"Ryan, what's going on?" said his father.

"Now is not the time to talk about it, Dad. I need you to trust me."

"Who's in command of your fleet if Admiral Williamson's not with you?"

"I am. Listen. I need a few minutes to talk to the supreme commander. Just have your fleet hold on standby and listen in."

"Ryan, I don't know what twist of fate brought you out there, but you're an eighteen-year-old cadet in over your head, and you're giving orders to a Fleet Admiral. Let me take it from here, son."

Ryan felt his face turning red, but he knew now wasn't the time to get into a war of words with his father. He took a deep breath and continued to make his case.

"Dad, I know you're the fleet admiral but it's been Amanda, me, and the rest of the senior cadet class risking our necks out here. We've lost three ships. Two complete cadet crews dead, and one ship with some survivors out there somewhere, but we may be close to a deal with them. Now, I'm asking you—*begging* you—as my commander, but more important as my *father*, to have some faith in me, this one time. How about it, sir?"

There was silence—nothing but dead air and static for at least ten or twenty seconds. Ryan glanced at the monitor and wondered how long the Altarrans would hold off. He could see beads of sweat pouring down Tanner's face. Jill looked grimly determined, and Nicole's hands were shaking. Something had to give, and it had to be soon.

Finally, he heard a noise on the other line that indicated his father was back.

"Fair enough, son," said the admiral, in a subdued voice. "You want some time? I'll give you five minutes. You've certainly earned that much. After that, I call the shots. Are we clear on that, Captain Thompson?"

"Fair enough, Dad." Ryan had to admit it felt oddly gratifying to have his father call him Captain.

Ryan looked at Jill. "Get the supreme commander back on the com. And make sure my father is patched into the line in listen mode. I need him to hear everything."

He looked at Paul. "Show me what you have. Then I want a copy of these pictures forwarded to the Fleet Admiral."

Paul handed him a collection of still photos. He examined them, trying to make sense of what he was seeing. American government officials were standing around with a few of the largest upright-walking creatures he'd ever seen. They were at least twice the height of any human. It was hard to tell from the photos, but they looked hairy, like giant beasts, only they carried themselves more like people. He couldn't see their faces. But a military officer who looked a hell of a lot like someone in a photo in Amanda's living room was leading one of them onto a large military helicopter. "What the—"

"Switching frequency now, Captain," said Jill, bringing him back to reality. "I also have your father's channel piggybacked so he can hear everything. You're on."

Ryan took a deep breath. This was it.

"Supreme Commander," he said, "I have some very important information for you. Information about your mother."

Ryan waited, as the seconds ticked by. *Come on, you thick-skulled ogre. Answer me already.*

"Speak to me then," said Granthaxe. "And bring me no tricks, as my patience has already worn thin. It is strange, is it not, that you wait until the moment before battle to find the information I ask? By my word, nothing brings success like the final seconds of a festering tempest."

"Who the hell taught him English," said Tanner from the weapons console, "William Shakespeare?"

Ryan shot Tanner a look, then returned his attention to Granthaxe. "I have proof, Supreme Commander. Pictures that prove Amanda's family helped your people escape from captivity. Her ancestor must have hid them somewhere to keep them safe."

"Somewhere? The Earth is full of somewheres. You've proven nothing but what I already know—that my envoys were captured. I need to know where they are."

"It's not that easy. But I have an idea. If you and Amanda can come to my ship, I'll show you the pictures. Maybe you'll spot something we didn't. We could call a truce and work together to find them. You want your envoys back, and we want to save our planet. We both want the same thing, Supreme Commander."

"You offer me nothing! Tell me, Ryan Thompson of Earth, why, after all that has transpired on your planet, and against the everlasting truth of our gemstones not to trust your kind, should I abandon all I stand for to submit to such an offer? For if I do, what kind of fool am I?!"

"Did he really just say that?" said Tanner.

"Do you think we're so different?" said Ryan, ignoring Tanner. "We've both been fools. I didn't want Amanda to come to you. But she did anyway, while I was unconscious from an injury. All she wanted was to stop the needless killing. I mean, haven't enough of your people and my people died already? We've both made the same mistakes, Commander."

"The very first one of which was when you captured our envoys. And so it shall be your last. You speak well, but the time for negotiation is long past, and your sentiment mere words. Your ancestors—"

"I'm not talking about my ancestors, Commander. I'm talking about you and me. Please hear me out. I also lost my mother. She was killed by an evil man, right in front of me. And my anger was just like yours. I was mad at everyone. I blamed my own father, because he wasn't there. I watched her die right in front of my eyes. They wouldn't let me save her, Commander. They wouldn't let me save her. But maybe we can still save yours. I want to help you do that. Please, let me help you do that. Think about it. There's nothing to lose and everything to gain."

Ryan paused. He felt as if a thousand pounds had just been lifted off his shoulders. He felt a lump in his throat knowing his father was listening, and thinking of his mother, who could be watching over him at this very moment. If he could save Granthaxe's mother, in a strange sort of way it would be like getting her back. Out of the corner of his eye he could see Jill wiping her eyes. He only hoped his words had hit home with Granthaxe.

There was silence for a few moments, which was a good sign.

"Captain Ryan Thompson," said Granthaxe, who then paused. ". . . if you are sincere, then time shall bear witness to that. I accept your offer."

Ryan exhaled, and everyone on the bridge began cheering quietly and high-fiving each other. Jill and Nicole were especially emotional.

"We shall call a truce for seven of your days," continued Granthaxe. "The terms will be simple. I must check in with my fleet every four hours. In the event that they lose communication with me, then they'll have orders to commence attack. I must warn you, Ryan Thompson, I have already sent a message to Altarra calling for reinforcements should they be necessary. If these terms are of acceptance to you, then I shall come to your ship with your Amanda Williamson. If not, then let us do battle as warriors."

Ryan looked around the room and gave a thumbs up.

"Great, Supreme Commander," he said. "Those terms are most acceptable. We await your arrival."

"I leave momentarily. One more thing, Captain Ryan Thompson. While I appreciate your reference to me as Great Supreme Commander, it is most unnecessary. I do not require flattery. Supreme Commander is more than sufficient. I leave you now."

Ryan looked at Jill, then to Nicole, and last, Tanner. All at once, they broke into laughter. Just then a beep sounded.

"Your father is on a private line for you," said Jill, still chuckling. "Patching you through."

Ryan picked up his com device.

"Dad, did you hear it all?"

"Hell yes I heard it. That was one hell of a job you did there, Ryan. I mean that. I know I haven't been there for you, and God help me I wish I could do it all over. Maybe now you can see how my job doesn't allow me—well, I hope you know."

"You don't need to say anything, sir."

"No, I need to say a lot. But for now, keep me up to date on your talks with Granthaxe. I'll work with you on this. I just want you to remember one very important fact."

"What's that?"

"Don't make any promises without running them by me first. Even I have people to answer to. You got that?"

"I do, sir. Though rumor has it you've been known to break a few rules now and then."

He could hear his father laughing. "Yes, I have," said his dad. "And from what I'm seeing here, it's pretty damn obvious you're my son. You did good today, Ryan."

"Well, that means a lot, coming from you. I also have a request though."

"Of course you do. What do you need?"

"We have a microchip here. Separate from the microfilm with the photos. It was inside the amulet. We'll need to get it read as soon as possible. I'd bet anything there's probably more information as to where the missing Altarrans might be."

"Agreed. We'll have to get back to the base for that. Let's take this one step at a time."

"Yes, sir. I'll keep you updated."

Rawlings called out from the sensor array. "Captain. Our sensors are showing activity coming from the Altarran vessel. It appears that their cargo bay doors are opening. I'll alert our people we have an incoming transport vessel."

"Well, time to greet our guest then. Tanner, Paul, care to join me in the cargo bay? Jill, you have the bridge."

"Yes, Captain!" said Jill. She looked genuinely excited to be manning the bridge, if only for a few minutes.

Ryan left the bridge with Tanner and Paul at his side, cautious but optimistic. Things were certainly looking better than they had a few hours ago, but this was anything but over. Now the trick was to figure out where the missing Altarrans were. He only hoped they were still alive. He didn't even want to think about what would happen if they weren't.

Chapter 45

Truce

Upon entering the cargo bay, Ryan hit the communications device on the wall to contact the bridge. "Jill, what's the story? Any sight of them?"

"They just left. Estimated time to arrival is four minutes. When they're at one kilometer out, I'll contact you."

"We're here and ready," he said.

Ryan had the file in his hands and noticed that Tanner kept glancing at it. "Curious what they look like?"

"Does a cat like peanut butter?" said Tanner.

"I'm not sure," said Ryan. "Does it?"

"Of course I want to know what they look like," said Tanner. "Everyone seems to know but me. Amanda sure as hell knows."

"Tell you what, Tan man. When they get here, you'll have a front row view."

"The transport is one kilometer out," said Jill.

"Paul, open the cargo bay doors and turn on the landing lights," said Ryan.

He watched as Paul entered his code on the wall console. Red lights started flashing as warning sirens acknowledged the opening of the outer doors. A computerized voice blared over the loudspeaker, *Cargo bay depressurizing.*

Ryan watched through the double-sided, six-inch carbonized glass window as the transport ship deftly entered the landing area and touched down perfectly. Immediately after the transport landed, Paul closed the cargo bay doors. In a matter of minutes, oxygen had been pumped into the landing area inside the cargo bay.

Ryan waited patiently until the red light on the monitor turned green. "All clear," he said. "Let's get in there and greet our guest."

The door to the transport opened. Amanda stepped out first and ran toward Ryan. He put his arms around her and held her. "You did amazing," he said, holding her tight as she sobbed into his shoulder. "You really—"

He stopped mid-sentence, and if she answered, he didn't hear it, because over her shoulder he saw the huge, hulking figure of Granthaxe exiting the transport.

He glanced over at Tanner and Paul who were standing there with their mouths open. Although Ryan had seen the photos, nothing could have prepared him for the sheer awe of a creature so large and powerful. It was amazing Granthaxe had even fit in the craft, and as he squeezed out of it slowly, it resembled a Chihuahua giving birth to a dinosaur. The real shock, though, was when Granthaxe fully emerged and stood tall. As the supreme commander stood towering over them, it occurred to Ryan that the Altarrans bore an eerie resemblance to such mythical creatures as Sasquatch and Yeti. He hadn't expected Granthaxe to be so . . . hairy.

Tanner apparently had the same thought. "I'll be damned," he said. "If that isn't Bigfoot, I don't know what is."

Granthaxe looked down at his own feet, then at Tanner with piercing red eyes. Everyone jumped back a few steps. "My feet," said the large creature, "are proportionate to my body. Did you expect I should walk on feet the size of yours?"

Ryan suppressed a laugh. Fortunately, Granthaxe didn't notice. "Supreme Commander," he said, "it's a pleasure to meet you. I'm Captain Ryan Thompson. If you will, please follow me to our conference room, where we can review the photographs."

"I await with great interest, Captain. According to Amanda Williamson, you have much to show me."

"Let's hope," said Ryan. "Tanner, you head back to the bridge and hold down the fort while Amanda, Paul, and I go over these files with the supreme commander."

"Will do, Ry."

Ryan watched as Tanner walked up to Amanda first. "Good job not screaming," said Tanner. "By the way, I stand corrected. You really were dealing with King Kong."

"No!" said Granthaxe, who had apparently overheard. He leaned down toward Tanner. "Supreme . . . Commander."

Tanner looked up at Granthaxe. "You guys really need to work on a sense of humor."

The supreme commander stood tall again. "A human characteristic no doubt," he said. "I will research it."

Ryan wanted to smack Tanner on the head, but Amanda beat him to it.

"Ow," said Tanner.

"Your species is most peculiar," said Granthaxe.

"You have no idea," said Ryan. "Now let's get going."

Ryan could hear Granthaxe's heavy footsteps next to him as they walked. "There are some pictures you won't want to see," he said, "but I'm afraid we have to show them to you in the interest of good will."

They approached the conference room on the right and entered. There was a long table in the center. All but Granthaxe sat down. There was nothing big enough, or strong enough, for him to sit on, and even standing, he had to duck his head. He was lucky to have made it through the double doors. As they looked at the sequence of pictures spread out on the table, it was obvious that the Altarran envoys and the queen had been held captive at the former Area 51 for many years. A number of them showed the Altarrans in chains in a bare room with several laboratory tables. Ryan braced himself for the supreme commander's reaction. As expected, Granthaxe practically growled as soon as he saw them, making everyone step back a few paces. The table started to buckle from the pressure of his fist, but then he eased up.

They moved on to the next few pictures, which showed Amanda's great-great-grandfather, Captain Robert Williamson, loading the four Altarrans one by one into a huge military helicopter. "That's him," said Amanda. "He was later made a general, but somewhere along the line they say he went crazy or senile or something."

Granthaxe wasn't listening though. He was staring at the final picture on the far right. Ryan knew exactly which one it was. It was the one that showed the queen giving the amulet to Williamson.

"My mother," said Granthaxe. "Our queen."

"Look at what is says, though," said Ryan.

Everyone stared at the photo. Written on the picture in sloppy handwriting was an odd phrase:

Look to the Sentinels.

"What do you suppose that means?" said Paul.

Ryan shook his head.

"Nobody ever said anything about that to my family," said Amanda. "I'm also wondering who took the photo of him with the queen."

"It would have had to be someone he trusted," said Ryan. "He must have at least had some help, not that it does us any good now." He turned to Granthaxe. "Supreme Commander, do the words 'Look to the sentinels' mean anything to you?"

"In your language, a sentinel is a guard, a watchman. These are the people we must find."

"That doesn't help us, though," said Ryan. "It could be anybody. There are millions of guards of all kinds. Supreme Commander, if none of this means anything to you, then I'm afraid we're at a dead end as far as these pictures are concerned. Unless the other chip has more."

"There is another chip?" said Granthaxe.

"Yes. Well this one's actually what we call a microfilm. We also have a microchip that we found in the amulet, but we need to go to our base on Earth to read it."

"Then Earth is where we shall go, Ryan Thompson."

"I'm glad you agree. But *we?*" said Ryan. He could just imagine Granthaxe walking around on Earth.

"We. The plural of I. It seemed a clear statement."

"I know that, but it would probably be faster if I—"

"I must accompany your people with any search. That, Captain, is not negotiable."

Ryan rubbed the back of his neck, a habit he had when he was uncomfortable.

"That may not be so easy, Supreme Commander. My father's the Fleet Admiral. He's the one who would have to make that decision.

Of course, it would help if I could give him a good reason for your request."

"A child could understand my reason. If my envoys have been able to hide from your people for all these years, do you think for a moment you would have the slightest chance of finding them without my help? You could search for an eternity and not find but a ghost of their existence, even if you found their domain. But by my words, upon sight of their supreme commander, and my mother of her son, they will show themselves."

Ryan had to admit, the supreme commander's rationale was sound. "Okay," he said. "It may complicate things, but I think even my father would agree."

"If I may ask a question, Supreme Commander," said Amanda.

"As you wish, Amanda Williamson."

"Over the course of many years," she said, "there have been reported sightings of creatures . . . sorry, *beings* . . . that resemble Altarrans. One is called Sasquatch—or Bigfoot, as Tanner mentioned. Another is Yeti, or what we called the Abominable Snowman. But they're usually spotted on opposite sides of the world. Bigfoot's in warm climates, while Yeti's in the ice cold mountains of India. Bigfoot's brown, Yeti's white. Could there be a connection?"

"Our kind is most adaptable. These 'creatures' you speak of may well be our envoys or they may know of them. For millennia, our kind endured the wrath of your planet, from the fiery pits to the icy caves. Despite our size, we could hide in the deep snow or take shelter behind a forest tree. We could change color to suit our needs. Our hides are as strong as—"

"Wait a minute," said Ryan. He couldn't believe what he was hearing. "Did you say for millennia? Altarrans have been here before?"

"Altarrans," said Granthaxe, "is the name we take from the planet we fled to, the namesake of our most revered leader from our scriptures, Altaraxe the Great. He has long since joined the gods, but Altarra lives on bearing his good name."

"Fled to?" said Ryan. "Fled from where?"

"From Earth," said Granthaxe. "Our home, long before humans. Did you think you were the first seedlings of the gods? Well, the first you were not, nor will you be the last."

Ryan's mouth dropped. He was speechless. Amanda and Paul looked equally shocked. "The gods?" said Ryan. "And what do you know of the gods?"

"Captain, it was the gods themselves who taught us science and the study of the stars and the land. But when the great flood came, even we could not survive. You see, it was our celestial and aquatic friends who helped us flee to the skies. We scoured the stars searching for a suitable planet. With great fortune, we found one."

"Celestial and aquatic friends?" said Amanda. "Great flood?"

"Jesus, this is like a frickin' fairy tale," said Paul. "Tanner will have a field day with this."

"Who were these . . . gods?" said Ryan.

"Ha, we speak of them no more, except in our hearts. There is little that survives in our writing, and a million lifetimes have since endured."

"So, let me get this right," said Ryan. "Your people fled our planet tens of thousands of years ago using advanced technology, and then came back all these years later? Why so long?"

Granthaxe looked down and let out a big sigh that sounded like a hydraulic press.

"You must understand, Ryan Thompson, it was a lifetime mission of our people to once again visit our homeland. Every king and queen has dreamed of this. Then, through our advances in communication, we could watch, and we could listen. For two centuries we've known your signals and deciphered your languages. But we still could not venture to Earth within a single lifetime. And we had long since lost the technology of the gods. "

"And so you had to wait for your technology to catch up. I understand now."

Granthaxe nodded. "Many have failed," he said. "Only the voyage of the envoys I seek was able to reach our homeland once again. Our queen—my mother— was to be the first the first to fulfill the dreams of our race."

"I'm sorry," said Ryan. "I do apologize, Supreme Commander, on behalf of our people. But now we'll help you find her. Our leaders—"

"Your leaders," said Granthaxe, getting angrier, "proved even more barbaric than was foretold."

Ryan could see Amanda shaking her head. Ryan thought for a moment in the nervous silence. Something wasn't adding up. "There's one thing I don't get," he said, hoping also to change the subject. "Your ancestors—they left Earth as an advanced civilization. There would be evidence of this, right? But there's none. At least not from that long ago."

"We had glorious cities," said Granthaxe, "but they have long since washed away. If you search the depths of your seas, you will find all the evidence you speak of."

Ryan started having thoughts of the lost city of Atlantis. That would be too bizarre for words—not that this wasn't.

"There's only one problem with all this," said Amanda.

Everyone looked at her.

"If the first time your people returned was with your missing envoys," she said, "then it doesn't explain the sightings I spoke of. These sightings happened way before then. And they were also long after your people's supposed evacuation from our planet."

"There is another explanation, Amanda Williamson."

"There is?" she said.

"Legend says that when our ancestors fled Earth, some chose to remain. They lived as nomads in large sea vessels. It is possible that when the waters subsided, generations endured, hiding in caves and forests, and in your mountaintops. Perhaps our envoys have joined them."

"Well if that's the case," said Ryan, "then I'm afraid we're back to square one. I mean, what chance do we really have of finding them?"

"We still have the microchip," said Amanda. "It may explain who the sentinels are."

"Yes we do," said Ryan. "Now if you'll excuse me, Supreme Commander, I'm going to discuss our meeting with my father. If you would wait here with Amanda and Paul, I'll be back shortly."

"Where else would I wait? I shall continue to converse with Amanda Williamson. She is a wise female."

Ryan smiled. "Yes, Supreme Commander. She is very wise, for a female."

Amanda smiled crookedly at Ryan. "And so are you," she said, "for a male."

As Ryan left, he realized he had quite a challenge ahead of him. He needed to convince his father that it was imperative to bring Granthaxe along for the search, if for no other reason than to ensure that nothing went wrong should they somehow locate the missing Altarrans. The last thing they needed would be to find them and not be able to communicate with them. And who knew what that could lead to?

Chapter 46

Return To Earth

Ryan was in his quarters. He wanted privacy for his conversation with his father. After he thought for a few minutes about his approach, he called the bridge.

"Tanner, have Jill get my father on a secure channel and route him to my quarters."

"Will do, Ry."

Ryan cut the com link and waited. With all the ups and downs of the last few weeks, he wondered if he was headed for another high or the lowest depths of failure. For some reason, he thought back to a particular moment in his old history class, a viewing of a documentary film about the founding fathers of America. On the screen was a deep orange sun, half covered by the distant horizon. He remembered wondering whether it was a sunset or a sunrise that he was looking at. And just as he'd been thinking that, wouldn't you know it, a voiceover, representing Benjamin Franklin, had appeared with great drama: *Was the sun rising, or was it setting on this great nation?*

In this case, here and now, the fate of the whole planet was at stake, and Ryan wasn't sure where things were headed. And even if this situation was resolved, Pandora's Box had been opened. It made him realize how Franklin must have felt.

His com link beeped. After hesitating a few seconds, he pressed the button to open up the line. His father's face appeared on the monitor by his desk.

"Can you hear me, Dad?" he said.

"I read you loud and clear, Ryan. Any progress?"

"Well, yes and no. That's why I'm calling. We've reviewed the photos, and it's pretty clear Amanda's great-great-grandfather helped the Altarrans somehow. Granthaxe seemed to buy into that. But we can't get any further unless we can read the microchip. We need your blessing to move forward."

"What exactly was on those photographs?"

"Well, they showed pictures of all four of the missing Altarrans, some of them with government officials. There was a picture of their damaged spacecraft, too. It appears they were held captive for quite a few years. They're huge, by the way. And hairy. And at least twelve feet tall. If I didn't know better I'd say they were the same race as Chewbacca, only they're a lot bigger. There are photographs with them in chains over different time periods in the early part of the twenty-first century. The last two photographs were what sold the deal, though."

"Sold it how?"

"Well, one shows the queen placing the amulet around Captain Williamson's neck. The second picture shows the four Altarrans being loaded onto a helicopter. It seems Williamson did help them."

"And how is that news? Seems to me we knew this already, though I suppose this supports that theory."

"Yeah, but who took the picture? It appears Captain Williamson had help—maybe some other officers who helped him get the Altarrans off the base safely."

"Still, that doesn't help us much," said the admiral. "We don't even know who these other officers are."

"We do have one other thing though."

"What's that?"

"There was a sentence handwritten on the last photo. It said, *Look to the Sentinels.* Does that mean anything to you?"

"Look to the sentinels? Hell, just what we need, another riddle."

"Another one?"

"Yes indeed. Our friend Williamson left another message in his desk, and it's even more cryptic than this one."

"What did it say?"

"Let me see, I have it here." Ryan watched as his father took out a folded piece of paper. "Here it is. It says, 'The queen is with her loyal subjects.'"

"Could that be the sentinels?"

"Maybe, but there's more. The next line says, 'Inside the truth is sealed.' It doesn't say inside what."

"We found the microchips inside the amulet," said Ryan. "Could it mean that?"

"Could very well be. You may be right on the money there."

"What does the rest say?"

"It says, 'Only the worthy who see the ten shall have the truth revealed.'"

"The worthy who see the ten?" said Ryan. "Well, hopefully we're worthy. Granthaxe did say the amulet said to trust Amanda. And he seems to trust us. But what could the ten mean? Unless it means ten sentinels. Maybe that's who we have to find."

"Again, you could be right, but we're just guessing. We need to see what's on that microchip."

"Yes, about that," said Ryan. This was the part he was delaying for as long as he could. "It seems the supreme commander has some demands, but he can probably help us if we meet them."

"Demands? I should have known you'd save the most important issue for last."

"Well, sir, I remember a certain career officer once telling me to always save the most important negotiations for the end of the discussion."

"So we're into negotiations now. You know something, Ryan, your mother was right about you."

"About me, sir?"

"She always said you'd end up being just like me."

Ryan had to laugh. It felt surprisingly good to be talking to his father about his mother. "Well," he said, "I guess there could be worse people in life to be like."

"That's debatable. Now about Granthaxe, what does he want?"

"He wants to be involved in our search. Before you say no, understand that if the Altarrans are hidden, they're not going to come to the surface with a bunch of humans carrying guns searching for them. Plus, Granthaxe says they have the power to camouflage their fur. In all honesty, we need his help."

"Ryan, what you're saying makes sense, but how the hell are we going to hide an eight-hundred-pound gorilla, literally. I can tell you that the defense ministers will argue from now to next week. And I can just imagine Ian Rupert going for this. He and I don't exactly see eye to eye."

"I realize it's not easy, sir, but this isn't a normal situation."

Ryan waited as his father seemed to me mulling it over.

"Luckily, the president owes me a favor," said the admiral. "This might be the time to call it in. Meanwhile, tell Granthaxe we'll make it happen. Leave the rest to me."

"It's a wise decision, sir."

"Of course, it is. I made it. I'll talk to you as soon as I hear from the president. And, son?"

"Yes?"

"It's good to be working with you."

"Thanks, sir . . . Dad. Same here."

Ryan headed back to the conference room. He couldn't wait to tell the supreme commander that they'd soon be heading to Earth.

Upon entering the conference room, he could see Granthaxe and Amanda having a discussion. Granthaxe turned and addressed Ryan.

"Amanda Williamson tells me that on your planet females command warships. I find that most fascinating. On Altarra, only males can command. And yet she assures me that your females are superior at command."

"They also have great imaginations, Supreme Commander."

Amanda smirked at Ryan.

"Not to change the subject," he said, "but the Fleet Admiral has agreed that you should come to Earth with us. In fact, he insists on it."

"Ah, this is indeed good news," said Granthaxe. "Tell me, Ryan Thompson. This Fleet Admiral, is he the father you spoke of, from which you sought permission?"

"He is."

"Then he should be proud of his son. You are a true warrior. Now, if you will please take me back to my ship. I must prepare."

Ryan looked at Amanda, who shrugged.

"Wait a minute," he said to Granthaxe. "Your ship? I was thinking you'd come with us."

"My ship comes with me, Ryan Thompson. Surely you do not think I would leave my ship alone in orbit unattended."

Ryan tried to imagine an entire ship of Altarrans coming to Earth, not to mention his dad's likely reaction. For now, though, he decided to play it cool with his formidable guest.

"Of course not, Supreme Commander. I'll have Amanda fly you back, if that's okay with you."

Amanda looked at him as if he'd just lost his mind.

"Of course, Captain Ryan Thompson," said Granthaxe. "Amanda Williamson is a most accomplished pilot. Not to mention she is a good conversationalist. As you say, she has an excellent imagination. As soon as you are ready to return to Earth, please inform me. We shall follow you."

"I'll contact you as soon as we get the orders, Supreme Commander." Looking at Amanda, Ryan said, "I guess you can go to the cargo bay and see to it the supreme commander gets back to his ship."

He leaned in and whispered to her. "Just go along. I'll worry about my father."

"I'll use my great imagination," she said.

Ryan laughed and made his way to the bridge. He knew he wouldn't be laughing in a few minutes though. Somehow, he had to bamboozle his dad into having the president authorize a whole ship of Altarrans to land on Earth. Hiding one Altarran was bad enough, but a ship the size of an arena was another story altogether.

Chapter 47

Earth Defense Fleet Headquarters

"Are you out of your goddamn mind?" was the reply on the other line that got Ryan trying to muffle the com speaker with an empty folder. He didn't even need to see the video screen to know his father's face must have been a deep scarlet color by now.

"Dad, there's no choice. When a twelve–foot-tall creature tells you he needs his ship, you just don't argue. It was the only way he'd help us."

"There's always a choice, Ryan."

"You don't need to remind me."

"What's that supposed to mean?"

"Nothing. It's just that I need you to trust me. We can mask their ship on radar. We can just say we're bringing in our ships for repair. Battle damage and all that. That could work, couldn't it?" Ryan knew it could, but he wanted his dad to feel a sense of control over the final decision.

"I suppose it could, sure, but . . . aw, hell, give me a minute. I'll call you back."

The line went dead. Ryan wasn't sure if something else had suddenly come up, or if his father was actually taking his advice and contacting the president.

Ten minutes later, the com line beeped again. Ryan pressed the button.

"I spoke with the president," said Thompson.

"And?"

"And he was pissed as expected. But your old man has some clout. He went for it, with some stipulations."

"That's great news!"

"Yeah? Wait till you hear the stipulations, and then say that. The president says this mission has to be completely unauthorized."

"Unauthorized? So is he giving his approval or not?"

"Officially, no. This means the operation must be totally silent. Even our own government can't know about it. Not even Rupert. As far as everyone's concerned, we're bringing in damaged ships for repair. If there's a slip-up, it'll be considered a rogue action by the fleet commander. In case you haven't been following, that's me. I don't have to tell you the consequences for that."

Ryan was confused about how all this would even work.

"But sir," he said, "how do we hide it from our own people? We'd need their help to even carry out this kind of mission."

"Leave that to me. Meanwhile, you have an even bigger job. You've got to convince your giant friend to go along with this. This is a silent operation, not a welcoming ceremony. Can you handle that?"

"I'll try, sir."

"Trying is for cadets. You're a captain now, son. Make it happen. Over and out."

Ryan sat contemplating as the line went dead. He wondered what he'd say to Granthaxe. He thought back to his father's words. A silent operation, not a welcoming ceremony. He hadn't thought of it, but a welcoming ceremony was probably exactly what Granthaxe was expecting. This wasn't going to be easy.

He made his way to the bridge. Amanda had probably already returned by now. And Granthaxe was no doubt already preparing his ship for departure to Earth.

When he entered the bridge, Amanda was there waiting.

"Welcome back, oh superior one," he said, smiling. Amanda smirked back at him. "I take it our guest was returned safely," he said. "What's our status?"

"All systems are operating, some barely. Course and angle of descent for Earth are locked and loaded. The fleet's ready for departure."

"Okay, just keep everyone put. I'm awaiting instructions from my father."

"What did he say? Are we authorized?"

"Sort of."

He could see Amanda and Tanner looking at each other in bewilderment.

"Captain," said Jill, "I have the Fleet Admiral on the encrypted channel. Putting him on monitor now."

Ryan watched as his dad appeared on the monitor.

"That was fast," said Tanner.

"Ryan, crew," said the admiral. "I think you'll agree that I'm not exaggerating when I say that we're about to undertake the most important mission in the history of mankind. Code name is Operation Trojan Horse. As I've briefed Ryan, this is a silent, I repeat, silent operation. I trust the Altarrans are on board with this. You will have your cadet fleet flank the Altarran ship on all sides for a nighttime arrival on Earth. We will commence operation immediately. Six of our defense fleet ships will join you. We need to form a perfect square around the Altarran ship."

The admiral paused for a moment, no doubt to let everyone digest what he had said. Ryan wasn't about to reveal anything about his lack of progress with Granthaxe yet, but he did have a nagging question.

"What about the arrangements down on Earth?" he asked.

"I was getting to that," said the admiral. "I've arranged clear airspace for our trajectory under the guise of allowing us a safe path to bring our damaged ships in for repair. On Earth, the base has already been locked down. The cover story is that they need to keep our damaged ships in a secure hangar. In reality, that's where we'll hide the Altarran ship. A fleet of supersonic fighters will escort us in. I can't stress enough, this is an unauthorized and silent mission. Any help we're getting is from people that are either personally loyal to me or do not know the full details of the mission. Now, are there any other questions?"

"Sir," said Ryan, "the defense fleet is international. How can we assure they won't alert their nations to what's going on?"

"Blood is thicker than water, Ryan. You should know something about that. And these soldiers are my blood. The Altarrans, well, they're a different story. Are they on board with this?"

"They are, sir." He was lying, but soon enough, he'd make sure it was the truth.

"Then let's proceed. If there are no further questions, I'm signing out. And God bless us all."

Ryan looked around the room at the blank stares.

"No further questions, sir," he said.

The line went dead.

"What the hell are we going to do now?" said Tanner.

"Don't worry," said Ryan. "I've got this."

"Well that's good," said Jill, "because I have the supreme commander on the com. He wants to talk to you."

Ryan had hoped for at least a few minutes to prepare his approach, but no such luck.

"Put him on speaker, Jill."

"Okay," she said. "You're live, Captain."

"Supreme Commander," said Ryan, "are you ready for our mission?"

"I am. I have but a single question for you, Ryan Thompson."

"Sure, what is it?"

"What are your ceremonial customs to greet my arrival? After all, I do not want to destroy one of your kind if they are making a pleasant gesture unknown to me."

Ryan looked at Tanner, who was pointing an imaginary gun at his own head. Wow, did his dad ever call this one.

"I'm glad you asked that, Supreme Commander. I was about to contact you with those very instructions."

"Ah, synchronized brains at a great distance think alike."

Tanner almost lost it, and even Amanda was trying to keep from laughing.

"Supreme Commander, we have a certain ritual that you might find unusual. I hope you will accept this as our custom."

"Reveal it to me then."

"Whenever we have important or illustrious visitors, it is our custom to surround their vehicle on all sides, whether by air or by land. And they must travel in complete radio silence. It's our way of saying that they're revered and protected. It signifies that we're not worthy of viewing them until they're received. And so we ask for complete silence."

"This is an unusual request indeed, Ryan Thompson."

"It's purely symbolic, mind you. But it would do us a great honor if you accepted these conditions. In fact, some of our people believe their souls will be damaged if they hear a revered person's voice while still in transit."

"Strange that we have never observed this custom of your people."

"With all due respect, Supreme Commander, you wouldn't have."

"Damaged souls, indeed," said Granthaxe. "Well then Ryan Thompson, if their souls are damaged, then my big feet will prove useful."

What the—

"Supreme Commander, are you referring to soles on the feet? That's a different spell—"

"I know the double use of your word soul. You may tell the Tanner human that I have now mastered what he called a sense of . . . humor. As it is, I graciously acknowledge your honor and your custom. On behalf of the Altarran people, we accept your great tribute. I will await your instructions."

"Thank you, Supreme Commander. Our people will be deeply appreciative."

Ryan signaled to Jill to cut the transmission.

"Well then," he said. He glanced over at Nicole. "Let's go home."

"You bet your ass, sir," she said.

As soon as she made the announcement that they were commencing Earth trajectory, echoes of cheering could be heard throughout the ship as they left orbit.

He noticed Amanda and Tanner staring at him.

"What?" he said.

Amanda looked concerned, but then he noticed a slight smirk on her face. "You know, Ryan," she said, "I find it really disconcerting that you can make up such a complete fabrication on the spot. How am I ever going to be able to trust you?"

Tanner, on the other hand, was now kneeling on the floor. "Ry," he said, "I humbly bow down to the undisputed, revered, superlative, and lest I forget, glorious champion of everlasting bullshit. How in the hell did you pull that off?"

"Knock it off," said Ryan laughing. "The both of you."

"Look," said Nicole, pointing to the external monitors.

Ryan watched as the Earth Defense Fleet ships arrived. Majestically, they joined the cadet fleet as they moved into formation. Together, they proceeded slowly and steadily toward the Altarran ship. Within minutes they had engulfed the gargantuan vessel like a swarm of slow motion bees surrounding a honeycomb.

Ryan shook his head thinking about all the strings his father had had to pull to make this happen. He had probably called in just about every favor owed to him. It wasn't every commander who could secure that kind of loyalty, and it was no wonder so many people idolized him. Ryan was beginning to understand that the Fleet Admiral had a ton of responsibility, and when the chips were down, victory or success depended upon his decisions. Maybe even more so, upon his relationships. And the chips were most certainly down.

Fortunately, the rest of the flight went off without a hitch. The entire journey took less than thirty minutes. Before Ryan knew it, they were approaching Earth's atmosphere. It had been far too long since he'd seen the blue planet. He'd almost forgotten how beautiful it looked.

He watched the radar screen as Nicole brought up the coordinates of Fleet Headquarters. The ship rocked as they penetrated the thick air, but it was a welcome feeling if there ever was one. As they descended into the evening skies, right on cue, Ryan could see the lights from the supersonic fighters arriving to escort them the rest of the way. After a few more minutes, the hangar could be seen from the front window.

The touchdown was tricky, as the battleships beneath and in front had to scatter, but it went off as well as could be expected. Once they'd landed and the remaining ships were inside the hangar, most of the crews left for debriefing.

Ryan decided to wait with Amanda outside Granthaxe's monstrous ship. As he stood there watching people scatter to their destinations, he felt a hand on his shoulder. It was his dad.

"Good work, Ryan," said the admiral.

As soon as the door to the Altarran ship opened, the imposing supreme commander stepped down to greet them.

"Quite a big guy, huh, Dad?"

"You're damn right. I want him on my basketball team. He must be about thirteen feet tall."

"Just about."

Granthaxe stopped in front of Ryan. "Is this your father, Ryan Thompson?"

"Yes, Supreme Commander. I'd like to introduce you to Fleet Admiral Ben Thompson."

The hulking figure gazed down at Ryan's father. "So, I greet the man who destroyed a third of my fleet."

Ryan felt his pulse quicken, wondering how his father would react.

"We've all suffered losses, Supreme Commander," said the admiral. "Let us both look to better times."

"Better times indeed," said Granthaxe. "You and your son make formidable enemies. Perhaps one day you will make formidable allies."

"I hope you're right, Supreme Commander. Let's get going to the computer stations I've set up. If you'd follow me."

Ryan exhaled. He noticed the guards in the hangar. They were wearing lab coats so they'd appear to be members of the ground crew, but he knew who they were really were. Still, they stared at Granthaxe as if he were a polka-dotted unicorn. Luckily, Granthaxe didn't seem to notice. That was all Ryan needed, Granthaxe asking them to bow in respect.

When they got to the computer station, Ryan noticed an attractive female officer in her late thirties.

"Hello," she said. "I'm Commodore Laurent, the head of Research and Development."

"Pleased to meet you," said Ryan.

Granthaxe stood silent, but nodded.

"Professor Laurent?" said Amanda. "Is that you?"

The commodore smiled at Amanda. "Amanda! We've got lots to talk about."

Ryan watched as the two women hugged each other. "You know each other?" he said.

"This is the professor I did the report on solar flares for," said Amanda.

"Ah," said Ryan, "the one who said it couldn't work without blowing up our engines? Well, Commodore, I'm glad for all of our sakes you weren't right." He smiled to let her know he was half kidding.

"You are most certainly your father's son," said Laurent. She looked up at the admiral and grinned.

"Okay, now about this microchip," said Ryan. "We don't exactly have a lot of time."

"And he has your patience," she said to Thompson. She held out her hand for the microchip, which Ryan handed her.

"This is the piece we're talking about," said Ryan. "Can you read it?"

Laurent took the chip and looked at it. "This is definitely a microchip. Late twentieth century. We have a device here that can upload the data to our computer."

Ryan watched as the commodore put the chip into a strange triangular reading device from the military archives. Within seconds, data started appearing on the screen. All he could see were a series of zeroes and ones, a whole page of them. He looked at his father. "Binary?"

"That's how we used to store encrypted codes," said the admiral. "We'd mix up the binary representation. That's even before my time, but I spent years in special ops and we had to know the old codes. If I'm correct, we need to reverse the two rightmost and two leftmost positions and read every other line. Then it's just a matter of translating it."

"That sounds easier said than done," said Ryan.

"Watch," said Laurent. In seconds, she was able to switch the columns and remove the extra lines. "Now I'm going to run it through our decryption program and convert it."

When she was done, the screen read:

```
00000000
00000000
00000011
00000011
01001110
00001001
00000010
00000001
00000100
01100101
```

"I still don't get it," said Ryan. "There's ten lines of numbers."

"Ryan," said Amanda. "That's interesting in itself."

"How so?"

"Didn't you say one of the hints said 'only the worthy who see the ten'?"

"I'll be damned," said Ryan. "You could be right."

"And you were right as well, Ryan Thompson," said Granthaxe, with his booming voice. "Females do indeed have great imagination."

"Guys," said Laurent, ignoring Granthaxe. "I didn't convert it yet." She pressed another series of keys. Now the screen read:

```
1133N9214E
```

"Is that another code of some sort?" said Ryan.

"No," said the admiral. "See the 'N' and the 'E'? I'll bet you anything those are coordinates. Commodore, bring up the navigation system. Look for 11 degrees, 33 minutes north, 92 degrees, 14 minutes east. Let's see what it shows us."

Ryan watched as Laurent's nimble fingers flew across the keyboard. He couldn't help noticing his father's hand resting softly on her shoulder as he peered over her head at the screen. Good for him, he thought. In an instant, a map appeared on the computer display. Amanda let out a gasp.

Then Ryan spotted what she was looking at. On the screen was a smattering of tiny islands just below Burma and east of India. The following words sat just below one of them, in small type:

North Sentinel Island

"Look to the sentinels," said the admiral. "I'll be damned. Williamson was a damn genius."

"My envoys," said Granthaxe. "We must go there at once!"

"Not so fast, Commander," said the admiral. "I happen to know of this particular island. It's not the kind of place you just go at once."

"Do not delay me, Admiral. It would be unwise."

"Can we just cool it for a second?" said Ryan. "What is this island, anyway? Why can't we go there yet?"

Ryan's father shook his head. "It's in the Bengal Bay. Part of the Andaman Islands. And it just so happens to be home to the most isolated and dangerous tribe on the entire planet. A people we call the Sentinelese. The island's been under constant surveillance for centuries. In fact, not a single soul has ever visited there without immediately fleeing or being slaughtered upon arrival."

"But we have modern weapons and shields," said Ryan. The most they could have are bows and arrows, right? How many of them could there be?"

"And I have my Altarran warriors," said Granthaxe.

"It's not that easy," said the admiral. "There could be anywhere from five hundred to a few thousand of them, but we don't really know because all we have are heat signatures. Mostly, they're under cover of trees or caves. But that's not the point. First of all, the Indian government has made it illegal even to visit. We're talking about a civilization that's the same now as it was tens of thousands of years ago, probably even predating known human history. If Williamson took any Altarrans there, he would have been the first to make it out of there alive, unless of course he never landed."

"Yeah, maybe the Altarran envoys went there alone," said Ryan.

"Doubtful," said the admiral. "They would have hardly been accepted there. Besides, like I said, the island was under constant surveillance and the last known visitors arrived in 2006, a couple of lost fishermen. Nobody could make it in or out."

"My people could," said Granthaxe.

"How?"

"We have the power of camouflage. We've survived on your planet for millennia unseen. And yet there is another—"

"Wait a minute," said Thompson. "Did you say millennia?"

"Sorry, Dad," said Ryan. I kind of forgot to tell you that little detail. The Altarrans lived here long before we did."

"Little detail? When the hell were you going to—"

"Admiral Ben Thompson," said Granthaxe, "I was about to say that there is another way our people would have been accepted by this tribe you speak of."

"Another way? How?"

"As a child, my mother would tell me stories of ancient times on Earth. Legends passed down by our people. There were small island creatures that worshipped our kind as gods. They would call us 'tree shadows' because of our ability to hide among the trees. They would bring us fruit and pigs as offerings, and they would always paint their faces and bodies red when doing so. Red was the color of fire and lifeblood, while green was reserved only for nature or the gods. Perhaps these are the people of which you speak. Perhaps my mother sought out the ancient ones through a spirit journey and alerted your ancestor."

"Spirit journey," said Ryan. "Couldn't you do the same thing then to find her?"

"How I wish that were so, Ryan Thompson. Only the seekers are versed in the old ways. And one of our envoys that accompanied my mother was our seeker. As I stand here, I tell you that they are with these island people."

Ryan studied his father's face but couldn't make out was he was thinking. Finally, the admiral sighed.

"Supreme Commander," he said, at this point, almost anything wouldn't surprise me. But that still doesn't make our situation any easier."

"Speaking of easier," said Amanda, "what happened to those fishermen you were talking about?"

"Killed, of course," said the admiral. "A helicopter was sent in to get them, but even that was driven away by arrows. After that, there's been no further contact. None. If the Altarrans are there, then they're damn good at hiding, and our chances of finding them are even less than I thought."

"But it's all we have," said Ryan. "All the clues point there."

"Ryan, we don't know that island. We can't even observe the terrain. It's all trees and brush. The only thing we have to go on is heat signatures. And even there, we can't get true readings because according to the patterns, they have volcanic caves on the island. From the heat scans, we believe they live within those caves. I'm telling you, these people are one with the terrain. They're like damn ghosts. They'll be under your feet and you won't even know it until that poison dart hits your neck. Besides, if the Altarrans are actually there, and if they're worshipped as gods like the supreme commander says, the Sentinelese will perceive us as a threat and will try to protect them."

"That proves it, then," said Amanda.

"Proves what?" said the admiral.

"That they're there. The queen is with her loyal subjects! Everything points there."

"Amanda Williamson is correct," said Granthaxe. "We must go there. If my mother is on that island, then I will lead the way. It is the only way."

"I think he's right, Dad," said Ryan. He couldn't believe he was siding with an alien commander over his father.

The admiral paused for a moment and glanced at Laurent, then addressed the group. "To see what is in front of one's nose," he said, "needs a constant struggle."

"Huh?" said Ryan.

"It's something George Orwell once said. A great twentieth century writer. In any case, I suppose you're right," he said. "I'll get a team together. We'll go tomorrow night. If we have any chance at this, it'll have to be by nightfall." He looked at Granthaxe. "We're banking on your popularity there, Supreme Commander."

"I am popular everywhere I go," said Granthaxe. "And where I am not, a thousand deaths surely follow."

"Good way to win friends, "said Ryan. Turning to his dad, he said, "By the way, what about the Indian government?"

"Leave that to me," said the admiral.

Ryan laughed. "I knew you'd say that."

"Okay everyone," said Thompson. "I suggest we all get a good night's rest. We have a very long day ahead of us."

"And an even longer night," added Ryan. Before he left, he turned to Commodore Laurent. "Night, ma'am. It was a pleasure meeting you. I get the feeling I'll be seeing a lot more of you." He looked at his dad and smiled.

After everyone said their goodbyes, Ryan headed with Amanda back to the ship, which was still in the hangar. In a way, he was excited at the prospect of finally reuniting Granthaxe with his mother and ending the planetary conflict. But at what cost? Once again, he was left wondering what the future would bring. In some ways, they were heading into an even greater unknown than their first meeting with the Altarrans. And wouldn't you know it, it was right here on Earth all the time. After all this, it would be a cruel injustice to die on Earth at the hands of a so-called primitive culture. Still, he had to wonder. Was the sun rising on this mission? Or was it setting?

Chapter 48

An Island Lost In Time

Ryan must have been exhausted because he didn't even hear his alarm beep. As he looked at the clock, he was already a few minutes late for the big briefing with his father and a team of special ops officers. He scrambled to get dressed as quickly as he could and then ran out the door toward the briefing room. As he approached the room, he paused to catch his breath. Then he entered as inconspicuously as he could. As soon as he walked in the room, he noticed Granthaxe and another Altarran at the far end. They were hard to miss.

He was surprised to see Amanda near them. Could his father have really authorized her for the mission? Then again, maybe he hadn't and she was just here seeing them off. He prayed that was the case, because there was no way he wanted to risk losing her on this island. She didn't need to go. It was bad enough *he* had to go, but he'd established the relationship with Granthaxe so he managed to convince his father it was safest he join them to keep the peace.

Nonchalantly, he made his way up to her.

"Nice of you to join us," she said.

"Join you?" he said. "So you're going?"

"Oh, you're not going to start—"

"Amanda," he said, "there's no need for both of us to risk our lives."

"I'm afraid that's not an option," she said. "I'm going. Besides, don't worry about me. I'm as trained as you are."

"That's not the point. It's not what I meant. It's just that—"

"It's a moot point, anyway. Just ask the supreme commander."

Before Ryan could get the words out, Granthaxe approached. "Amanda Williamson speaks the truth," he said. "She wears the amulet of the gods. Only one who is bound to the amulet may approach the queen."

"Can't Amanda give it to her when we return?"

"Negative, Ryan Thompson. It would offend the gods themselves. The queen must never be seen without her amulet by her people."

"Not even her son?"

"Especially not her son."

"What about the other Altarrans then? Your missing envoys. I'm sure they'd have to look at her."

"They know our ways, and I assure you they abide with honor. Amanda Williamson must come with us."

"Supreme Commander, the Fleet Admiral will never permit both Amanda and me—"

"The Fleet Admiral," said Ryan's father, who had arrived from behind, "has already discussed this issue with our esteemed guest, and the issue is closed, Ryan. Amanda is going. Now, if you're concerned about the both of you being put in harm's way, you have my permission to remain on the base."

"No, sir," said Ryan. "That won't be necessary."

Ryan walked away. He understood the reasoning and knew Amanda was as well trained as he was, but he still didn't like it. He couldn't help feeling protective of her, especially after all that's happened.

"Do not be concerned, Ryan Thompson," said Granthaxe. "I shall personally see to it that your beloved is kept safe."

Ryan wanted to crawl under a desk and hide. The supreme commander had a booming voice, and he was sure that the entire room, including Amanda, had heard him.

"Thanks a bunch, Supreme Commander," Ryan said, as he felt everyone's eyes on him. "Maybe you can have your ship send a message to my fleet and let them know as well."

"Of course I can do that," said Granthaxe. "It is a most easy thing to do. I shall personally see to it before we leave."

At that moment, everyone around broke into hysterics, and even Ryan had to laugh.

"If I could have everyone's attention," said the admiral, who had now moved to the front of the room. "I'd like to direct your attention to the overhead monitor."

Everyone quieted down and faced the screen.

"What you see here," he continued, "is an aerial view of North Sentinel Island. We will be coming in at 2200 hours island time using a directional glider. It is imperative that we make a quiet entrance. These tribesmen may look primitive and their weapons crude. Do not let that fool you. They are fierce and tenacious and have the tactical advantage. From what we know, their weapons consist of spears, poison darts, and bows and arrows. But never forget that they've successfully driven away armed men and helicopters. Our mission is to get in, find the missing Altarrans, and get out. There are some specifics, but you'll get further instructions en route. When we've accomplished our mission, there's a carrier ten miles out waiting for our signal. They'll have ships waiting for us at the extraction point. We will use force only as a means of self-defense. Grab your gear and head to the transport. Wheels up in thirty, ladies and gentlemen."

Ryan grabbed his equipment and started out toward the ship along with a squad of eighteen special ops forces, his father, two Altarrans, and Amanda. They had a two-hour flight ahead of them, flying at Mach 3. Once they were twenty-five miles from the island, they would board the glider and make landfall.

The large transport took off at precisely 1900 hours. Most of the officers were either catching a nap or sitting quietly. Ryan, on the other hand, was a bundle of nerves. Looking at how calm the special forces soldiers were gave him a newfound respect for his father and the men under his command.

He couldn't sit still, so he made his way over to Amanda. She was also wide awake.

"Listen, Amanda, you know I didn't mean any disrespect about you coming along on this mission with us. I just don't want anything to happen to you. Not after all we've been through."

"I get it," she said. "But I'm not some helpless little girl. And you, of all people, should know that. So please relax. I'll be fine."

Kyron, the Altarran science officer, put her huge hand on Amanda's shoulder. "It appears," she said, "that there is a constant throughout the universe, Amanda Williamson. The male of the species truly believes that females would fail to survive without them.

Sadly, it is the male grid-like brain that limits their capacity to make decisions, and they would hardly survive without our superior multi-lateral processing."

Amanda looked at Ryan and smiled.

Ryan wasn't about to add fuel to this fire. It was bad enough debating with Amanda. But with a ten-foot female ape sitting next to her, it was out of the question. He decided to change the subject.

"So tell me, Science Officer Kyron, what do you know of this Sentinelese tribe?"

Kyron smiled, which was a frightful sight. Her teeth were razor sharp, and she had two large fangs, each about three inches in length.

"First of all, Ryan Thompson, you do not have to call me by my title. Kyron will suffice. As for the tribe, if this is the tribe from our stories, their legend goes back to our days of living on Earth."

"Do you have any factual information on them, or is it all stories passed down through the generations?"

"We have many stories, but it is difficult to separate fact from legend. My mother spoke of the little island beings when I was young. It was a story told for generations. She said they arrived from other lands on Earth and had fled from great beasts and horrible famine. On the island, they encountered our kind and believed us to be gods. We lived in peace for many years."

"So, they're a peaceful people."

"Only as the cobra is peaceful to the forest. I'll tell you another story. One day a large beast arrived on the island, shaking the ground with its fury. It was the size of ten Altarrans and a thousand times as strong. Its body was covered with armor. Our people hid in the trees, but somehow the little humans defeated the creature. They thought of us as their gods, and we thought of them as our protectors. They defended us fiercely that day. It is said that from then on, no creatures ever dared to visit the island again."

"Until other humans made the attempt," said Ryan. "And we know how that went."

"Indeed we do, Ryan Thompson."

Their conversation was interrupted by the pilot of the transport. "Five minutes to release point. All hands to their stations."

Ryan and the rest of the squadron hustled to get ready. It was time to make their move. He hadn't been thrilled about the prospect of arriving on this island anyway, but now, after his conversation with Kyron, he really wasn't looking forward to it. Just what he wanted to face: an ancient, mythical group of nasty, antisocial tribesmen hell-bent on protecting their gods. And if it was true that they'd defeated an armored beast, whatever it may have been, who knew what they were capable of?

Chapter 49

The Land Of The Gods

Ryan finished strapping himself into his seat on the long dark red glider. The sleek glider was docked in a built-in hangar area at the rear of the transport plane. According to the countdown on the monitors, the craft would be dropped into the atmosphere in sixty seconds. He made sure his night vision goggles were handy, as they'd be landing in the dark. Amanda was seated behind him, and to their left were two officers he didn't recognize. The rest of the crew were behind them, except for the admiral, who was up front in the co-pilot's seat with the pilot.

As he clenched his armrest, Ryan prayed that the admiral and the pilot were up to speed on their glider skills. Just the thought of being in a ship with no engines was unnerving. He'd read up on gliders and had even flown them in a simulator during training, but he never thought he'd end up flying in a real one. Still, there was no other choice. They certainly didn't want to alert the Sentinelese tribe to their presence.

Ryan held his breath as the countdown reached zero. With a jerk, the bottom section of the transport opened downward, and the glider slid straight down into the night skies. Ryan felt his stomach flutter as the glider shifted violently to the right and then dropped quickly. It was much worse than the simulator. He remembered reading that a glider has to fall at a downward angle in order to gain enough speed to generate lift. As they nosedived, he hoped the lift would happen soon.

After what felt like mile-long, white-knuckle freefall in the dark, the glider finally caught the wind currents and began to level out. Ryan could feel his dinner trying to erupt from his stomach. He made a mental note that if he somehow survived this mission, he'd never set foot in a glider again.

Traveling at least a hundred miles per hour once they'd leveled out, they had an eight-minute flight until touching down on the southern side of the island. Occasionally, the glider would slip to the side while flying forward, like an out-of-control sled, but eventually it straightened out. Every so often, there'd be a huge drop. As their altitude lowered, things started to become smoother. Thank God. Another minute of that and he definitely would have puked.

In the moonlight, he could see the island coming up fast as the glider zeroed in on its approach. He wasn't sure what to expect, but within minutes, they were close to the beach at the south side of the island. He held on tight as the glider settled down on the soft sand, jumping a few times before coming to an abrupt halt just short of a row of trees. The touchdown was a little bumpy, but overall, it didn't feel too much different from the few single engine landings he'd experienced.

He put on his night vision goggles and exited the craft with the squad. Amanda was right beside him. It was pitch black out, and it was jarring viewing everything through the green hue of the goggles. He felt like he was in a dirty fish tank. He watched as the squad of special ops forces readied themselves with all sorts of equipment. He already had his protective gear on, as did Amanda.

The admiral addressed everyone quietly prior to moving out.

"I want a three-wide formation," he whispered. "Evans, Livingston, and Jones, take the point. Byrnes, Ryerson, and Hawthorne, you've got our six. The rest of the team follow suit. Ryan, Amanda, Kyron, and Supreme Commander, take the middle positions, three through six. Okay, boys and girls. We have to make it five miles in under an hour to get to the nearest heat signal. And remember, we're in unfamiliar terrain. I want to be in position while we still have a few hours of darkness for cover. Let's move out."

Ryan knew exactly what his father was doing. He had purposely put him, Amanda, and the Altarrans in the middle of the squad. They were the most valuable, had the least experience, and they'd be safest with someone on either side of them.

"It's awfully quiet out here," Ryan said softly to Amanda. "All I can hear are our footsteps and those damn crickets."

"Tree frogs," said Amanda. "And it's too quiet as far as I'm concerned. They're bound to hear us from a mile away."

As they moved deeper into the jungle, Ryan felt more and more uneasy. The only thing he heard besides the frogs was the occasional scampering of small lizards and the rustling of leaves. It hadn't even dawned on him that there could be poisonous snakes. In a way, that creeped him out more than the Sentinelese.

Almost an hour had passed in silence when Lieutenant Evans on the point stopped and held up his hand. He turned to face the admiral. "Sir," whispered Evans. "I have multiple heat signatures one-half click to the north."

"Can you tell how many?" said the admiral.

"No sir."

"Keep moving," said the admiral. "Ready the concussion grenades. I'd like to avoid a massacre if at all possible."

Ryan was still on edge as they continued moving forward. Every footstep sounded like a giant alarm in the darkness, alerting the Sentinelese to their presence. Not to mention that heat signatures were just ahead, which meant arrows could be heading their way any second. Maybe this wasn't such a good idea after all.

Without warning, one of the officers in front of them grunted in pain, and another yelled, "Hit the deck!" A branch smacked Ryan in the face and he fell back. From all directions, it felt like the trees were attacking them. He looked ahead and it appeared some of the officers were already down. Branches were flying everywhere, and there was nowhere to take cover. He turned to see Amanda crawling toward a large boulder with a couple of the other troops. Just as he got up and lurched toward her, he heard the sound of something whiz by his ear. As he turned his head, he could see an arrow sticking out of the tree next to him.

Turning back toward the boulder, he was hit in the chest by what felt like a sledge hammer knocking him back to the ground. As he hit a pile of crushed branches, he looked up to see that it was Granthaxe who had pushed him down. And it was a good thing he had, because a large spear was embedded in the tree he'd just been standing in front of. Ryan crawled over to Amanda. She looked shaken but seemed to be uninjured. He looked out from behind the boulder. At least half of the team was down. He could see a few of them taking cover behind the trees and boulders.

Then, from every direction he could see tribesmen encircling them. They were falling from trees and coming out from under the ground. Ryan was startled when a bloodcurdling, bellowing howl pierced through the air just ahead of him. He looked toward the noise and realized it had come from Granthaxe, who was standing with his weapon drawn. Kyron was at his side, also holding her weapon. It must have been some sort of Altarran battle cry. A fruitless gesture though, as the tribesmen were all around them with their arrows pointed. Some were holding torches.

"Fire concussion grenades," ordered the admiral.

Ryan and the remaining forces fired into the first wave of tribesmen in all directions. The explosion rocked the ground and most of the first wave of Sentinelese warriors fell to the ground. Ryan wasn't sure if they were unconscious or dead. Unfortunately, the rest were standing behind the fallen ones, and they were unfazed. They began to move closer.

"Lock and load," said the admiral. "But hold all fire until they're within fifty feet."

The tribesmen closed in. Ryan raised his pulse rifle, as did Amanda. His fingers were braced against the trigger as he watched them approach. He felt like a sitting duck, as he half expected the next round of darts to hit any second. How many of them could there be, and what other tricks did they have up their sleeves? As slow as they were moving, it seemed an ambush could happen at any moment. He couldn't help thinking of his father's words: none had ever escaped this island alive.

Chapter 50

The Showdown

Ryan stood frozen, waiting for his father's signal as the tribesmen continued their agonizingly slow advance. It dawned on him that some kind of trap might fall from above. He glanced up, but didn't see anything. Then he noticed out of the corner of his eye that Kyron had moved in front of Granthaxe and was standing firm with her weapon down. He wondered what she was doing. She placed both her arms in front of her and crossed them, bringing them to her chest. Then she let out a howling sound, similar to the one Granthaxe had made, followed by a series of chants in a language he'd never heard before.

The Sentinelese tribe stopped for a moment. Could they have understood her? If only it would be that easy. He watched in anticipation as one of the Sentinelese tribesmen turned and spoke with some of the others. This was a good sign. They must have understood her and were probably debating what to do. Ryan said a silent prayer, even though he wasn't the praying kind. He thought back to the old saying, *There are no atheists in foxholes.* The tribesman gave a sudden look toward Kyron. Then they all began approaching his way again, taking small deliberate steps, like a cat stalking its prey. So much for prayers. He wondered why the ones in the trees hadn't begun attacking yet.

He looked again to Kyron and Granthaxe. "What's the problem?" he said. "I thought these people worshipped you guys."

"As did I, Ryan Thompson," said Granthaxe. "Perhaps these are not the island people my mother spoke of."

"They have to be," said Ryan. "All the signs."

Ryan couldn't understand why the tribesmen didn't back down at the sight of the Altarrans. Then it dawned on him. The tribesmen couldn't see them! They must have thought it was a trick, that someone was coming to attack the queen. He grabbed a flare from his backpack.

Amanda grabbed him. "What are you doing?" she said.

"I'm an idiot. A complete idiot."

"And you're about to prove it," she said. "What the hell are you doing?"

"We can see them, but they can't see us. That's *not* an advantage." Turning toward Amanda and the two other soldiers, he said, "Wish me luck, guys."

"Wait!" said Amanda, "Don't—"

He didn't have time to let her finish. He began walking very slowly toward Granthaxe and Kyron.

"Ryan, what the hell are you doing?" said his dad.

Ryan was relieved his father was still alive but knew he couldn't respond or he might trigger a reaction from the tribesmen. If he moved slowly enough, they might not take it as a threat. At least that's what he figured.

As soon he felt a searing pain in his left shoulder, he knew he figured wrong. He grunted in agony and made a desperate lunge toward Granthaxe and Kyron, grabbing onto Granthaxe to hold himself up.

"You are wounded," said Granthaxe.

"Never mind that," said Ryan. "Both of you, remove your helmets and goggles now."

"Why would—"

"Do as he says," said Kyron, removing her headgear. Granthaxe followed suit.

Ryan felt another sharp pain in his shoulder. He didn't know if it was the same arrow digging in or if he'd been shot again. "Close your eyes, quick," he said to Granthaxe and Kyron.

"But how will we defend ourselves?" said Granthaxe.

"Just do it! Now!" he said, losing patience. He grabbed his flare and ignited it, holding it up toward their faces.

He looked toward the Sentinelese, who'd stopped dead in their tracks. He could feel warm liquid running down his back, and the pain was intense. At least it wasn't poison or he'd be dead by now, though he was feeling awfully dizzy. After a few seconds, one of the tribesmen began to approach Ryan and the two Altarrans. He held a spear in his right hand and a torch in his left. As he moved closer and passed Ryan, it seemed obvious he was either their chief or some kind of spiritual leader. He looked older than the others, and was the only one wearing a shawl, which appeared to be made of sticks.

"Everyone, hold your fire," said Admiral Thompson.

Ryan looked around. He could see many of the squad members on the ground. Thankfully, his father wasn't one of them.

The elder tribesman stopped directly in front of Kyron. He put his spear on the ground and knelt in front of her and Granthaxe on one knee. Almost immediately, the rest of the tribesmen followed suit. Ryan looked around, and in all directions, hundreds of Sentinelese had dropped to one knee and placed their weapons in front of them on the ground. Even the ones in the trees had climbed down and joined them.

He could hear his father calling for the medic. There were many injured in need of attention. By his count, there were twelve men down. Unfortunately, he felt like he was about to be one of them as he dropped the flare to the ground and fell face forward onto the hard dirt. Suddenly, he felt another jarring pain in his shoulder. Son of a—! Had they seriously shot him again?

"It's out," said Amanda from above him, holding the small arrow near his face so he could see. "Just be glad there was only one arrow. Hold still, this may sting a bit." Ryan braced himself as he felt her rubbing the antibiotic salve onto the wound. Then he felt her press gauze to the wound and bandage it. "What the hell is wrong with you?" she said. "You could have gotten yourself killed."

"I saw the light," he said, as he got up.

"Very funny."

"How about a 'flare' for danger? Better? No?"

"Quit while you're ahead," she said.

Ryan noticed Kyron talking to the elder tribesmen. He approached them. "What's going on?" he said.

"I am conversing with the esteemed chief of the tribe," said Kyron. "Fortunately they still speak our ancient language."

"And fortunately," said Granthaxe, "I had the wisdom to bring Kyron with us. The old tongue has not been spoken by our people in thousands of years. But our science officers have a duty to be versed in the ancient ways."

As Kyron continued speaking with the chief, Ryan noticed the chief pointing to him and the other soldiers. Kyron said something in response. The chief looked at her, then replied and began laughing. Another nearby tribesman laughed as well. Ryan tapped Kyron on the shoulder. "I'm glad the chief is finding us so damn funny," he said. "What was it he said, anyway?"

"The chief wanted to know who you and your people are. I told him that you were our guards."

"And?" said Ryan.

"The chief said we should find better guards."

"Real funny," said Ryan. "Tell the chief I said to keep his day job. How about the queen? Is she here?"

"Indeed she is," said Kyron. "Back at the tribe's village, there is a hidden cave near the volcano. It is there we can find her."

"Great," said Ryan. "I'm going to check with my father and see about the injured. We may have to evacuate some of them. Be sure to tell the chief, when the big flying machines come not to shoot their arrows at them."

"I shall be sure to inform him," said Kyron.

Ryan motioned to Amanda to join him, and they headed toward his father. The admiral was surveying the situation. "Sir," said Ryan, "how many injured?"

"Twelve. Mostly broken bones, possible concussions, and a few are showing signs of internal injuries. If not for the body armor, they'd all be dead. We'll have to get a MedEvac ship in here to lift them out. Maybe Kyron and Granthaxe can let these tribesmen know not to shoot it down."

"Already done, sir," said Ryan.

"Great work. And by the way, quick thinking with those flares. If I knew you were planning that I might have stopped you. And I'd have been wrong."

Ryan just nodded and smiled. This was one time acting on his instincts had paid off. Feeling vindicated, he walked back to Kyron to make sure she knew about the MedEvac. He explained to her that it would be arriving shortly to take the injured men to a nearby carrier. He then waited while she relayed everything to the tribal chief.

"The chief is now aware that you are summoning your flying medical ship," said Kyron. "But he has extended an offer to use the tribe's medicine man."

Ryan tried to avoid laughing. He didn't want to insult the man.

"Please inform the chief that we have our own medicine man, but thank him for his very generous offer. Also, tell him that as soon as we get all of our injured off the island, we'll be ready to proceed to their village."

Ryan noticed that his father was being treated by the medic. He hadn't noticed any injuries when he was talking to him. He went to check on the status.

"Are you all right, sir?"

"It's nothing I can't handle, Ryan. A couple of cracked ribs. I'll be fine. How's the shoulder?"

"It's sore. Amanda did a great job patching it up, though."

The medic, Lieutenant Jenkins, piped up. "Sir," he said to the admiral, "it's more than likely your ribs are broken. I highly suggest you return to the ship with the wounded."

"Suggestion ignored, Jenkins. Tape them up and get the others ready to leave. The medical ship will be here in less than five minutes. If I start coughing up blood, then you can have me shipped out. Until then, I'm not going anywhere. Is that clear?"

"Yes, sir. Loud and clear, Admiral."

"Stubborn as an ox," said Amanda, who just walked up behind Ryan. "Like father, like son."

The deafening sound of the incoming medical vessel put an end to the conversation. Because of the dense trees and brush, the ship couldn't land. Instead, the injured had to be hoisted up with a pulley as the ship hovered two hundred feet above the ground. Within thirty minutes, the last member of the injured officers was on board, and the MedEvac took to the skies.

Now came the fun part. If they could just get to the village and find the queen, the nightmare could finally be put to rest—hopefully once and for all. Ryan couldn't wait to get back and tell Tanner and

Paul. Then again, it wasn't over yet. After all that had transpired, nothing would surprise him. In fact, he'd always had a queasy feeling when things seemed to be going too well. It was sort of a sixth sense—the same feeling he had had when his mother was driving him to the academy on that fateful day. And he was feeling it now.

Chapter 51

Finding The Queen

Though it didn't help his nerves any, Ryan was glad that the last two hours had passed in silence. The odd collection of Sentinelese tribesmen, Altarrans, and special forces had made their trek toward the village without incident, though he felt like was in *The Wizard of Oz*, marching with a misfit cast of cronies toward the Emerald City. Finally, he could see the village ahead through the tropical foliage.

The heat and humidity were getting to him, and the helmet he was wearing didn't make it any easier. Still, he felt more comfortable with it on, as he used it as a battering ram whenever he'd encounter thick brush. At least it was getting lighter out now and he didn't need the night vision goggles. Some of the tribe still carried their torches though.

Before long, everyone had stopped. Ryan looked ahead to see what was going on. The chief was walking to the side toward a large wall of rock that appeared to be part of an immense boulder. As Ryan looked more closely, he could see they were actually at the foot of a huge mountain, or perhaps a volcano. He looked up and guessed it was nearly 400 feet high. He noticed a strong sulfur smell in the air, which indicated it was more than likely volcanic.

The chief approached the huge stone wall and seemed to be pressing random sections of it. Then a tremendous rumbling sound began. Ryan jumped back a few steps as it nearly shook him off his feet. The stone wall was moving! Somehow, with the Altarrans' help no doubt, they had created a door of stone, built right into the volcano. But how, with no tools and only a few Altarrans? Could they have been *that* strong? It made him think of the Great Pyramids at Giza and the countless other ancient sites with inexplicable stone formations that seemed to fit together like a jigsaw puzzle.

Ryan saw Granthaxe up ahead, talking with Amanda and Kyron. Seconds after, Kyron left them and approached the chief. The science officer and the chief seemed to be discussing entry procedures. At Granthaxe's prodding, Amanda joined them and stepped to the front of the entrance. She knelt to the ground. Kyron seemed to be getting her into position. Then Kyron joined Granthaxe behind her. The two Altarrans dropped to the ground with their heads down.

The chief uttered a strange language, similar to what Kyron had spoken to him earlier. It was almost chant-like, and it grew louder as it went on. Ryan could hear heavy footsteps approaching from inside the cave. Everyone else was dead silent. He noticed they were all dropped to one knee, and his father was motioning to him to do the same, so he did.

Ryan stared in amazement as three huge figures appeared in the darkness of the cave. As they approached, between the emerging daylight and the light of the torches, he could begin to make out their features. They resembled Granthaxe more than Kyron. He was wondering which of them might be the queen. But then the answer became obvious, for behind them, a much larger figure emerged, with an open mouth and large fangs resembling the science officer's. The three Altarrans in front exited the cave and bowed to the ground. Only the queen remained standing. Ryan glanced over at Granthaxe and Kyron, who still had their heads down. Then, out of the corner of his eye, he saw Amanda get up. He watched as she slowly approached the gigantic Altarran queen, who was now staring down at her with a combination of awe and curiosity.

Amanda held up the amulet and uttered a few words in the same bizarre language the chief had spoken. The queen took the amulet and held it up high. She bellowed out a chant in the same language, and suddenly the other three Altarrans stood. Ryan looked around and saw that Granthaxe and Kyron were now standing, so he stood as well. Little by little, everyone rose to their feet.

Ryan watched as the queen put her hand on Amanda's face in an almost loving way. "Daughter of Williamson," she said to Amanda, dragging out the last name. Her voice was soothing, like Kyron's, though much deeper. "You have fulfilled my greatest hopes for our two worlds."

"It was my great-great grandfather's wish too, Your Highness," said Amanda. "I know that now."

Just then, Granthaxe approached the queen, and the mother and son embraced. As Ryan observed them swaying in joy, he imagined being reunited with his own mother. He looked up at the blue sky as if to acknowledge her—the kindest, most loving soul he'd ever known. He felt his eyes welling up, but it wasn't from sadness. On the contrary, his heart was as full as it had ever been. It was as if, in this one moment, he had become whole again.

The queen held her son back to look at him. "There is no greater pride a queen has," she said, "than the love of her people—and a mother the love of her son."

"I would never have abandoned you, Mother," said Granthaxe.

"I knew you would not. My greater wish was that your pain and your fury would not lead you astray. And I see it has not."

"It has not been without loss, Mother. Many of our brave warriors have fallen to bring this day."

The queen held up her hand. "And we will honor them justly," she said. "All that I see here pleases my heart, as the ancient ones gather with the humans and our own. There will be much to discuss later, my son, of their honor and yours."

They embraced again.

Ryan looked over at his father, and then at Amanda, who was looking back at him with a big grin on her face. Just a few short weeks ago, he could never have dreamt that he'd be with Amanda and his father together. And not just together, but getting along and truly supportive of one another. His anger toward the two of them seemed like a distant past. In fact, his whole opinion of the world had changed. For the first time, he realized something. Peace was worth fighting for, and no amount of pride or hatred should ever stand in its way.

His career sure hadn't suffered any. He'd now successfully commanded an entire fleet of ships, and with the help of his classmates, had staved off the destruction of the entire planet. But now he'd lead with new eyes, and a new purpose. Sure, it had taken a strange set of events, but he finally felt worthy to be his father's son—worthy and proud. But there was something else he'd gained that was even more powerful than any of that. He looked over at Amanda, who was now coming his way.

She raced toward him and into his open arms. "Well that went well," he said, holding her. "And in case I haven't said it, thanks. I mean that. You made all this happen, and I, for one, am sure glad you were here."

Amanda looked up at him. "I've always been here, Ryan. And I always will be."

He was basking in the moment when he felt a heavy pressure on his shoulder. He turned around. It was the queen.

Ryan wasn't sure what to say or how to greet her, so he just went with his gut. "It is my pleasure to meet you, Your Majesty. I'm Ryan—Ryan Thompson, and this is my friend, Amanda Williamson."

The queen smiled at them. Ryan tried to suppress a shudder as a pair of giant fangs protruded from her mouth. It must have been a trait of the female Altarrans, and not one of their better ones.

"Good day to you, Ryan Thompson and Amanda Williamson. I am Queen Darthaxe of Altarra." She looked at Amanda. "You do indeed resemble your ancestor, my dear Robert Williamson. He was kind and generous and wise. You should be most proud of him."

"I wish I'd met him," said Amanda. "He died long before I was born. But from what I've heard from my family and others that knew him, he was a great man."

"His spirit lives in you," said the queen. "Like you, he risked his life and everything he had to do what is right. If only his leaders were of the same heart. I pray yours are better."

"I pray too," said Amanda.

"They're much more enlightened now," said Ryan. He didn't want the queen to get the wrong impression.

"Then let us go drink and dine to the future," said the queen. "Our hosts are preparing a feast."

Just as she said that, Ryan noticed the smell of cooking in the air. Meat of some sort. He was almost afraid to ask what they were cooking.

He and Amanda followed the queen toward the fire pits, which were nestled in an open field in a village of small, thatched roof huts. The men of the tribe were carrying a huge wooden spit with what looked like a roasted pig or boar. A large bamboo mat was spread out on the ground, and tribeswomen were arranging a wide variety of colorful fruits and vegetables. There were also several large green buckets placed in the center, carrying some sort of fish. He wondered where they got the buckets from, as they appeared to be made of metal.

For the first time, Ryan got a good look at the Sentinelese people. Nearly all of them, the men and women, wore a handmade necklace or scarf of one sort or another. None of them wore much else, other than a small strip of cloth around their waists. Some wore makeshift shorts, but most just had a row of small vertical wooden sticks guarding their private parts. Nearly all of the women wore rope-like headbands made of bamboo or wood.

Ryan took off his helmet, and Amanda did the same. Suddenly, all the tribesmen and women started talking in hushed tones and kept glancing their way. They looked upset, and some of them started slowly moving away, chattering to one another. Ryan wondered why all of a sudden the Sentinelese people were spooked. He turned around to see if perhaps there was a lion or something behind him that was causing the ruckus. But there was nothing unusual. He looked at Amanda, then saw the chief sprinting toward them and motioning for the queen to come.

The chief stopped in front of Amanda and looked closely at her face, examining it as an artist would a model. He then shielded his eyes as the queen approached. He spoke rapidly to the queen in his native language—unless it was the Altarran tongue he was speaking.

Whatever language it was, it was obvious that something about Amanda had spooked the Sentinelese villagers. After talking with the queen, the chief bowed in front of Amanda, then walked away to speak to other villagers.

"What was that all about?" said Ryan. Then he realized who he was speaking to and added, "Your Majesty."

"You must understand," said the queen, "the Sentinelese tribe have never set eyes upon a white female, and especially one with red hair. They feared that Amanda Williamson was a demoness, sent to bring evil. But then the chief saw her eyes."

"My eyes?" said Amanda. "How would that make a difference?"

"Oh, but it makes all the difference," said the queen. "They have never seen a human with green eyes. To their people, green is reserved for the gods and red is for fire and the blood of life. That you have both red hair and green eyes caused the chief great confusion, Amanda Williamson."

"And what did you tell him?" said Amanda.

"I informed him," said the queen, "that you are the one true goddess of fire, and that if any harm had come to you here, their people would have been incinerated."

"That's amazing," said Ryan. "Our very own goddess of fire. It's a good thing they didn't kill her first."

"I'll say," said Amanda.

"Fear not," said the queen. "Observe."

Ryan turned around to see all the Sentinelese people on their knees looking at Amanda.

"Raise your arm slowly," said the queen to Amanda. "And look out at the people."

Amanda did as the queen suggested, and the tribesmen and women all rose to their feet.

"If your people ever wish to visit the islands again," said the queen to Ryan, "Amanda Williamson will have to be the one to make contact with them."

Amanda lowered her arm and turned around, and the Sentinelese people went about their business.

Granthaxe approached and put his hand on Ryan's shoulder. "You see, Ryan Thompson," he said, "even the women of *our* kind have great imagination."

Ryan laughed and looked at Amanda, who burst out laughing as well.

"That's all we need, Supreme Commander," said Ryan. "Amanda already thinks she's superior. Now you've made her a goddess."

Ryan's father came to join them. "I heard something about a goddess in our midst. Between Amanda and the queen, I'm surrounded by real royalty. I guess a fleet commander is small potatoes these days."

Ryan turned to Amanda. "You know you're never going to live this down," he said.

"Bow down when you say that," she said.

Ryan smiled. "Come on," he said. "Let's eat and get back to the carrier." He held his arm out for her to go ahead of him. "Goddesses first."

Amanda elbowed him. Everything seemed to be falling into place. By the end of the day they'd finally be on their way back to Fleet Headquarters. He couldn't believe they'd actually pulled it off. Maybe his superstitious hunch was wrong after all.

As soon as the thought left his mind, Ryan noticed the Altarrans looking around them with quizzical expressions on their faces. "What's wrong?" he asked.

"I hear something," said Granthaxe. "Above us, in the sky."

Ryan looked up. "I don't hear any—wait, I do hear something." High above them, he could hear a slight buzzing noise. Then it grew louder. What was it? The sun was shining down through the trees, but soon it was eclipsed by a shadow. The sky grew darker and the noise got louder.

He turned to his father. "Is this one of ours?"

But his father wasn't paying attention to him. He, too, was looking up at the sky. All of a sudden, as the sound grew deafening, Ryan spotted something heading toward them from above. His father yelled out, "Incoming! Hit the deck!"

Ryan dove toward Amanda to shield her, but in mid-dive a huge explosion shook him to the bone. He felt his body being thrown in the air, and just as his back hit a tree, everything went black.

Chapter 52

Dazed And Confused

Ryan slowly opened his eyes. His head was throbbing and his ears were ringing. He felt like he'd been hit with a baseball bat. He tried to stand, but his feet gave out from under him. Shaking his head, he looked around, trying to figure out where he was and what the hell had happened.

He saw Amanda, his father, and five of the special ops soldiers on the floor. They all appeared to be unconscious. There was no sign of the Altarrans, and Lieutenant Evans, who'd seemed the strongest of the lot, was missing.

He crawled over to Amanda and could see that she was breathing. Thank God, she was alive. He heard shuffling and turned to see his father waking up. "Dad," he said, "are you okay?"

"I'm alive," said Thompson squinting at him. "Not really sure about anything else at the moment. Any idea where we are?"

"Not a clue," said Ryan. "I came to about a minute before you did. It looks like we're inside a brig on a ship. The last thing I remember was a loud explosion. Then I woke up here."

The admiral struggled to sit up. "That was a concussion bomb. And it was a damn big one. Probably took out the entire village."

The rest of the soldiers were coming to. Ryan felt Amanda move and turned to see her sitting up. She had a glazed look in her eyes. "How are you feeling?" he said.

"Like an elephant sat on my head. My ears are ringing. Other than that, I'm okay. What happened?"

"We're trying to figure that out," he said. "We're locked up somewhere."

The sound of footsteps coming toward them caught his attention. "Someone's coming."

Ryan felt a huge sense of relief when Lieutenant Evans appeared. "Evans!" said Ryan's father. "Thank God. Get us out of here!"

"Now why on Earth would I do that," said Evans, "when I went through so much trouble to get you in there?"

Ryan was dumbfounded. Even his father was speechless. Almost.

"Evans," said the admiral, "I don't know who or what brainwashed you, but I'm your commanding officer, and you're dangerously close to a court martial."

"I'd think you'd have trouble arranging that from in there, Admiral. Now, I'd back away from those bars, as *you're* dangerously close to, well . . . dying."

Ryan watched anxiously as Evans took his pistol out. Ryan tried to distract him. "Where are we?" he said.

"Where you need to be," said Evans.

"You can't go rogue, Evans," said the admiral. "The ministry will come looking for us, and trust me, when they find you, they'll be all over you like a cheap suit."

"Oh, I'm not rogue, Admiral. And I think the ministry will be quite okay with my actions."

"Oh they will? I think you're in for a surprise."

"Did I hear something about a surprise?" said another voice from the other end of the room. Ryan turned to see who it was, and nearly fell over in shock. Amanda gasped.

It was the defense minister, Ian Rupert—Ryan was sure of it. And his father confirmed it when he walked to the other end of the cell to face the man.

"Rupert," said the admiral, "what kind of game is going on here? Our mission was sanctioned. Not officially, but it had to be done. And it worked."

"You've never been more right, Admiral," said Rupert. "It did work. It worked absolutely spectacularly, and I commend you for it."

"Then why are we in here?"

"Because, my dear Admiral, you failed to blow your simian friends to pieces while you had the chance. Their most important leaders were all on that island, and vulnerable. And you call yourself a military man. I'm disappointed."

Ryan had had enough. "You're a lunatic, Rupert," he said. "In case you didn't notice, we were able to end this peacefully, dumbass."

"Ah, the prodigal son speaks. And so eloquently."

"How the hell did you even find out about this mission?" said the admiral.

"The question isn't how, my crude friend—it's when. I told you the mission went spectacularly. Much better than even I could have imagined it, I might add." Rupert grabbed a chair from the corner and placed it in front of the cell. "Do you mind if I have a seat?"

Nobody answered.

"I'm sure you don't," said Rupert. "Anyhow, let's go back a little. Let's say to the mid twentieth century. Around the time of rumored incidents such as Roswell, and a few others I'm sure you know and love, there was a little government organization—we'll call it an off-shoot—known as IC-12. The IC stood for *inner circle*. Clever, I know. And just like your mission, theirs was 'unofficially sanctioned.'" Ryan cringed while Rupert made quotation marks with his hands. "And also like your mission," he continued, "the government looked the other way while the IC-12 made sure that our nation was safe and secure, through whatever means necessary. Sound familiar?"

His sing-songy tone was incredibly annoying.

"What's this got to do with us?" said the admiral.

"Nothing, my friend. Absolutely nothing. But it has everything to do with me. Because the IC-12 is still very much alive, and yours truly . . . runs it. You see, ever since Miss Williamson's dear ancestor decided to go against orders and assist a dangerous species, our organization has been searching for them."

"They're not dangerous," said Amanda. "And my great-great-grandfather was ten times more patriotic than you'll ever be."

"He was a traitor, Miss Williamson, very much the same as all of you. He let wounded enemies go free, and wounded enemies make very poor neighbors."

"They were only enemies because of your idiot group," said Amanda.

"Rupert, I'll see you burn in hell for this," said the admiral.

"Oh, do you have pull there?" said Rupert. "Anyway, before I was rudely interrupted, I was about to tell you how I suspected, from the moment we received the level two alert from Pluto, that the incoming visitors and the missing species were, in fact, one and the same. We even had warnings of such a visit, left by my predecessors."

"And you didn't tell me about them?" said the admiral.

"I did more than tell you. I practically led you straight to the general's cryptic little note, a note my predecessors found many years ago, I might add. So you see, Admiral, I had faith in you about one thing. I knew if anyone could decipher that code, you could. I, for one, could not. And so, I commend you. Excellent job."

"Wait a minute," said Ryan. "So that means Evans told you where we were heading when we finally cracked the code." He stared at Evans, who gave him the finger.

"A bright son you have, Admiral," said Rupert. "But just in case, I had the note treated. We've been tracking you ever since."

"Listen to yourself," said the admiral. "You've been chasing a peaceful species. They intended no harm. They can help us."

"Oh, they have helped us," said Rupert. "A great deal. When they first crash-landed here, we escorted them to our friendly private facility. You'd be amazed at the technology we learned from them with a little prodding. In fact, many of our weapons and engine designs are a direct result of their teachings."

"Yes, we saw pictures of your facility," said Thompson. "More like a torture chamber. I can't believe Hawking would support a group like yours. He'd never be behind this."

"How right you are. That is if he knew about us, which he doesn't. We've been privately funded for the last fifty years. Not like the old days. And besides, who's going to tell him? You? Your ape friends? You should know more than anyone, Admiral, when it comes to national security, all bets are off."

"What did you do with them?" said Amanda. "You and your coward friend."

Evans walked up to the cell with his gun pointed at Amanda. "Don't make me kill you a day early," he said.

"Now, now," said Rupert. "Let's not get them all stressed. After all, they'll be heroes soon."

The admiral glared at Rupert. "What do you mean 'heroes'? We're not doing anything for you."

"I second that," said Ryan.

"None of us are," added Amanda.

Rupert laughed. "Oh, but that's the beauty of it. You don't have to do anything at all. You've already done it."

"Done what?" said the admiral.

"Found the missing apes, of course. But then, sadly, they turned on you, as did the vicious islanders. You and your men fought valiantly and even managed to kill the apes and half the tribe. It's just unfortunate that the only survivor was Lieutenant Evans, who barely escaped the island. And there it is, Admiral. Tomorrow's news today."

"You're insane," said Ryan. "You can't kill them. They have thousands more that will come."

"And thanks to all of you, we know how to disable their shields, so again I must commend all of you on a job well done. I hope you understand why I can't let you live."

"Did you kill them?" said Amanda. "Did you kill the Altarrans?"

Rupert put a finger to his lips as if he was about to share a secret. Then he turned around. "Bring the admiral to my office," he said to Evans as he left the room.

With his gun pointed, Evans ordered them to all back away from the bars. Two other guards came in, cuffed the admiral and took him away. Oddly enough, they cuffed him from the front. They were either the dumbest guards in the world, or they had a good reason.

Evans leered at Amanda before joining them. "I'll be back for you later."

She spit at him.

He grinned as he wiped his face. Then he turned and left to join the others.

Ryan hoped his father would be okay. If anyone knew how to handle himself in tough situations, the admiral did.

"The fleet will probably send help, right?" said Amanda. "We're supposed to report to our backup team every four hours."

Ryan shook his head. "Evans is the communications officer. They knew what they were doing by placing one of their men in that position. He's probably reporting like clockwork. And it's probably why they need us alive another day, so he can stop the reports at the last minute, since he's supposed to be the only survivor. Otherwise the forensics would show we died earlier."

"Damn them!" said Amanda. Her face looked like she was ready to explode.

"Listen," said Ryan. "We need to keep our cool. We can't get out of here with force, so we have to use our heads. Try to think of ideas and I'll do the same."

He looked at the remaining five special ops soldiers. He knew that every single one of them understood the dire situation they were in. And special ops soldiers weren't the type to sit still and wait to die. He could see them all scoping out the ceiling, as well as all the corners of the cell. But he could also see in their eyes that they knew it was a fruitless cause. He realized then, that if there was any way out of this, it was going to be up to him and Amanda.

Chapter 53

Wounded Enemies

Ryan was pacing the cell when he heard footsteps. Two guards rounded the corner dragging his father with them. The admiral looked bruised, but at least he was walking upright and had the usual unyielding expression on his face. The guards opened the cell doors and threw him to the ground. Ryan tried to rush the door, but all he got for his trouble was the butt end of a rifle in his stomach, knocking him down as well. He crawled over to check on his father as the guards exited the cell and locked it.

"I'm okay, said the admiral, waiting for the guards to leave the area. He got to his feet slowly, as did Ryan. "They wanted information about the Altarran fleet and the amulet. They have no idea what was in the amulet, only that there were microchips we were studying. They also know it means something to the queen, but they're not sure what. They must think it's some kind of beacon or signal device. I assume you know what this means."

"I'm not following," said Ryan.

"It means they need us alive, for one. I couldn't tell if the queen was alive, or any of the Altarrans for that matter, and they sure as hell weren't about to tell me. But the more we can string them along, the more opportunities we'll get."

"This gives me an idea," said Amanda. "That Evans creep keeps staring at me. If I can somehow get them to bring me and Ryan together for interrogation, we might have a chance of distracting them."

"Too risky," said the admiral. "These aren't soldiers to mess around with."

"What do we have to lose?" she said. "We'll be dead anyway soon, and we won't get too many opportunities like that."

"I hate to day it, Dad," said Ryan, "but she's right.

Just then they heard footsteps again, as the two guards emerged from the hallway.

"Just go along with me," Amanda whispered to Ryan.

"You need a plan," said the admiral.

"I have one," she said. Then she looked at Ryan. "Whatever I say, argue with me."

The guards approached the cell and made everyone back off. "You," said one of the guards to Amanda, "come with us."

As the guard fiddled with the lock, Amanda stepped forward. "I know what you want," she said. "But I only have half the information. Ryan here has the other half."

Ryan remembered what Amanda had said about arguing, but he wasn't sure if she meant now or later. He decided to go for it.

"Amanda," he said, stepping forward, "there's no way we're giving them anything. Not from me, anyway."

"We have to, Ryan," she said. "Now isn't the time for your stupid pride. They need us both. If we help them, they may let us all go."

"Are you nuts?" he said. You actually think they'll—"

"Enough, you two," said the guard. "The girl comes alone."

The guard aimed his rifle at Ryan. Ryan yelled to Amanda, "Don't tell them anything. They'll kill us all."

"Wait!" said a voice from the far end of the room. It was Evans. "Bring them both. I think the admiral's son needs some incentive."

Ryan didn't like the smirk on Evans's face. He sure hoped Amanda knew what she was doing.

The guard turned to Ryan. "You heard him. Step forward."

Ryan did as he asked, and the guards opened the cell again. They cuffed him and Amanda, again from the front, and led them toward the corridor, locking the cell behind them. Ryan tried to turn to see his father, but the guard knocked him in the back of the head with his gun.

As they proceeded up the corridor, Ryan could tell for sure he was on an airship. And it was apparently docked, because it certainly wasn't in flight. He wondered what kind of interrogation tactics awaited them. He'd find out soon enough. If there was one thing he'd learned, though, it was to trust Amanda's instincts.

They approached a room on the right, and the guards led them inside. It was empty, except for a few chairs and a metal table. The guards left and shut the door, which automatically locked with a hiss. Only a few seconds had gone by when the door opened and in came Rupert, along with Evans.

Ryan's fists tensed.

"Please," said Rupert. "Have a seat. We have much to talk about."

"We have nothing to talk about," said Ryan, still standing. "So you can take us back to the brig and save your time and energy."

"Don't speak for me, Ryan," said Amanda. I don't know about you, but I'm not ready to die." She sat down.

"She's much wiser than you," said Rupert. "Better genes, I suppose."

"Ryan wasn't quite sure what to do, so he continued arguing. "What the hell are you doing?" he said to Amanda.

Amanda looked at him and motioned with her eyes to the chair next to her. Ryan shook his head.

"Evans, call the guards," said Rupert. "I think our friend needs convincing."

"You won't torture it out of me," said Ryan. "I'm as stubborn as my father."

"Oh, we're not going to torture you, Mr. Thompson. We're going to torture *her*."

Amanda stared daggers at Ryan. He paused for effect, then relented.

"Okay," he said, as he sat next to Amanda. "I'll hear what you have to say. But that's all I'm promising."

"You know," said Rupert, "you're not exactly in the driver's seat. We can obtain those microchips at any time. But that amulet. It means something. What does it mean?"

"We don't know," said Ryan. Only the Altarrans know that."

Rupert looked at Amanda. "Miss Williamson, is that your story as well? Because it's not a very believable one."

"It's true," said Amanda. "They wouldn't tell us. They said it's a gift to them from their gods."

"A gift from their gods?" Rupert said, laughing. "So now we're in *that* territory, are we? Well, I'm afraid that doesn't bode well for you, unless their gods come and save you. But I'll give you another opportunity. What can you tell me about their fleet?"

Ryan jumped in. "They're a lot more powerful than you think. There are thousands of them. And they're headed to Earth."

"Oh, I doubt that," said Rupert. "At least not in my lifetime. You see, you're not the only ones watching the distant stars. I'm talking more about their capabilities and their status. I know you can give me more than that."

"You think we'd tell you that?" said Ryan.

"Well, it *is* the only reason you're alive, and it would make our jobs so much easier. Of course, if we come to realize you have nothing for us, then we'll just have to take our chances against them. And you, my friend, will no longer be needed."

"You'll kill us anyway if we tell you."

"Wait," said Amanda. "They may not if we join them. I mean their group. I'm sure they could use us, with our knowledge."

"The fairer and wiser sex, indeed," said Rupert.

"As if you'd trust us," said Ryan.

"Trust . . . is overrated, my friend. But over time, it can be earned. Beginning with the information I ask."

Just then the door opened and one of the guards entered. "I'm sorry to interrupt, sir" said the guard, "but Agent Barkley is online for you. He wants to know whether to send another ship with a second team."

"Tell him . . . tell him I'll be right there."

Rupert turned to Evans. "Watch them. Closely."

He began to leave the room. Then he turned around. "Oh, and in case either of you have delusions of grandeur, I have guards stationed in our corridors."

"That won't be necessary," said Amanda. "We're not going anywhere."

"As I said, trust," said Rupert, looking directly at Ryan, "needs to be earned." With that, he turned and left.

Ryan looked at Amanda as Rupert left the room. He wasn't sure where she was headed with her plan. They were both trapped here, but at least they were together. He wondered what was going through her mind.

Evans approached. "So," he said to Amanda, "our little girl wants to come over to the dark side."

Amanda smiled at him. "Maybe I do," she said. "But if I do, it'll be with Rupert, not a bottom feeder like you."

Evans grabbed her shirt and lifted her off the chair. "We'll see about that," he said, pushing her toward the wall.

Ryan jumped up to grab him, but Evans quickly turned and gave him a roundhouse kick that knocked him to the ground. It felt like a train had hit him. Evans approached him, grinning. Ryan inched back along the floor, looking up at his attacker. He'd never be able to get up with his handcuffs on. Then he saw his opportunity. "So," he said. "How does it feel, Evans?"

Evans looked down at him and laughed. "How does *what* feel?"

"This," said Amanda pounding her handcuffed fists up into his groin from behind. At the same time, Ryan jumped up and charged him, knocking him over Amanda's kneeling body.

Ryan slammed the center of his handcuffs into Evans's face as Evans tried to reach for his laser pistol. Amanda grabbed it just in time.

Evans, dazed, slid back against the wall.

Amanda stood pointing the pistol at him, her hands bound together by the handcuffs.

"You don't have the guts," he said.

"Neither do you," she said, as she shot him in the stomach twice.

Evans screamed in horror, rolling violently on the floor. His hands turned red as he held them to his midsection.

She approached him and looked down. "Your boss said never to leave wounded enemies," she said. Without hesitating, she aimed the pistol and shot him in the head. Evans's lifeless body fell back as a pool of blood formed next to him. His arms were grotesquely spread out like a fallen eagle. She spit on him for good measure. "That's for my great-great-grandfather," she said.

Ryan put his hands on her shoulder. "Remind me never to get on your bad side," he said.

"Your last three years were on my bad side," she said. Then she smiled.

"Let's get those keys off him," said Ryan. "We need to get out of here."

They quickly grabbed the keys and unlocked each other's cuffs. As they took the pulse rifle and concussion grenades out of Evans's holster, Ryan wondered something. "By the way," he said, "what would you have done if Rupert was never called out of the room?"

"My original plan," she said, "was to tell Rupert I'd only talk to Evans. But when Rupert left, I just reversed it."

Ryan shook his head and laughed. "All I can say is it's a good thing they handcuffed us from the front. Some agents."

"I know why," she said. "Look on the table."

Ryan looked and saw an oversized graphics tablet.

"They wanted us to draw schematics," she said. "I knew that as soon as I saw how they cuffed your father. But now we have a bigger problem. How do we get past those guards?"

"Leave that to me," he said. He realized he was starting to sound like his father. "You take the laser pistol, since you seem to like it so much. I'll take the grenades and the rifle. We'll need to make like you're still cuffed and I'm leading you from behind. They won't see me at first. Are you ready for this?"

"Ready as I'll ever be."

"Let's go then."

They unlocked the door and swung it open slowly. Amanda walked ahead of Ryan.

"Put your hands behind you," he said.

"But we were cuffed in the front."

"Well then let's hope they don't notice the difference."

"I don't see anyone," she said.

"They're there—you can bank on it."

They proceeded up the corridor toward the brig, where Ryan's father and the others were held. Ryan could hear voices ahead.

"They're up ahead there," he said. "Keep your pistol ready behind your back. I'm right behind you."

"Hey, why am I in front?" she said.

"You're less of a threat."

"Hey!" she said.

"Sorry, I'm just trying to think like them."

Just then, two guards emerged from the brig. They spotted Amanda.

"Who's leading you?" they asked. "Where's Cadet Thompson?"

"Right here," said Ryan, as he jumped out with the pulse rifle and fired, killing the guard on the left. Amanda was quick to the draw and shot the other guard, who fell back.

Ryan and Amanda rushed forward. "Grab their keys and unlock the cell," he said. "I'll watch the door."

Ryan opened the brig door as Amanda snatched the keys from one of the dead guards.

"What the hell happened?" said the admiral from inside the cell.

"We'll explain later," said Amanda, as she slid the cell doors open. "Rupert's still alive though."

Ryan watched with one eye on the door, as his father and the five special ops officers exited the cell and ran to the dead guards to grab their weapons.

"Hawthorne," said the admiral. "Take the rest of the team and find out if the Altarrans are still alive. If they are, get them out safely."

"With pleasure, Admiral," said Hawthorne.

"Sir," said Ryan. "I'm not sure if anyone's in it, but there's a secondary brig. I heard the guards talking when they took us into Rupert's office. Something about it being easier to guard."

"Well I'm sure this ship's designed like ours," said the admiral. "There'll be another brig down the corridor on the right, with an armory just past it. Hawthorne, try and get into it and grab as many weapons as you can. See if they have any explosives. I'll get a message to the carrier to send reinforcements. I'll bet anything this ship is docked on the island. We'll meet just outside in thirty minutes."

"Got it, sir."

"And Hawthorne," said the admiral.

"Yes, sir?"

"Shoot first. If they're still alive after you shoot them, then you can ask questions."

Hawthorne smiled. "You don't have to tell me that, sir. Payback's a bitch."

Ryan kept an eye on the corridor while Hawthorne and the other four special ops soldiers headed off to find the Altarrans. He hoped they were still alive.

"What's the plan, sir?" he asked his father.

"We've got to get to the bridge. They're going to know soon enough that we're on the loose. I need to get to their communications console and call the carrier. Do you have any idea how many guys they have with them?"

"All I know," said Ryan, "is that they only have the one team. I can't imagine they have more than eighteen men with them. And we've killed three of them already, including Evans."

"Good work, son. Let's move out."

"You can thank Amanda. She may have a new career as a mercenary."

Amanda elbowed him as they took off with the admiral down the corridor toward the bridge. Just as they turned the corner, they saw two more guards coming their way. They all opened fire, catching the guards by surprise and killing both of them.

Ryan kept alert as they continued on. His father was right. This *was* the same ship design. When they arrived at the bridge, the admiral said, "I'm gonna open those bridge doors. As soon as I do, I'm opening fire. You and Amanda toss in the concussion grenades. Ready?"

Ryan handed Amanda a grenade. They both had their hands on the pins. "Ready, sir."

"Now as soon as that door opens, toss them." The admiral moved in front of the door. The motion sensors immediately opened the double doors. He hit the floor and opened fire.

Ryan and Amanda tossed the grenades and took refuge behind the bulkhead. There was a muffled explosion. "Let's move inside," said the admiral.

They entered the bridge. Three of the bridge crew were out cold. Ryan and Amanda combed the corners looking for any others. There didn't appear to be anyone around.

"Bridge is clear, sir," said Ryan.

"Keep me covered just in case," said his father.

The admiral went directly to the com unit and started sending his message to the carrier ten miles off the island. "Amanda, you cover the bridge doors," he said.

Ryan kept on the lookout and Amanda guarded the doors while the admiral finished sending his message. After a few tense minutes, there was a loud beep, indicating that they'd received a response. "That's it," said the admiral. "We'll have two transports with a hundred troops in thirty minutes. Let's get back to the rendezvous point."

The three of them bolted out from the bridge and headed to the main exit. As they turned the last corner, Ryan was startled by a voice from behind them.

"Drop your weapons, my friends, and slowly turn around."

Ryan froze in his tracks, as did his father and Amanda. It was Rupert's voice. He must have been waiting on the other side of the corridor.

"Do as he says," said Ryan's father. "No sudden moves."

Slowly, Ryan, Amanda, and the admiral placed their weapons on the ground in front of them and stood. They turned around. Rupert was there with four of his men, all pointing weapons at them.

"You're done, Rupert," said the admiral. "Two transports will be here within fifteen minutes. You can kill us, but you're done. Of course if we're alive, you might be executed less painfully."

"And so the fly tries to negotiate with the spider," said Rupert. "You have no communication facilities, admiral."

"I used your bridge."

Rupert looked concerned. He glanced quickly at one of his soldiers. "Go check the bridge," he said.

As the soldier ran off, Rupert began laughing.

"I'm glad you find it funny," said the admiral. "So do I."

"I find it amusing," said Rupert, "that you're all in such a precarious position and yet you're so defiant, as if you've won a great victory. You see, even if what you say is true, you won't live to see your supposed retribution. And if my last act is to rid the planet of a dangerous species and its traitorous allies, then so be it."

Now Ryan was trying to avoid laughing. Because he couldn't believe his eyes. He began to move to his left, toward the wall. He could tell that Amanda and his father had the same idea, as they began moving toward the other wall.

"Oh, that's not necessary," said Rupert. "I'm not going to shoot you just yet. I'm waiting for a report from one of my agents first. You see, I want you to be the last to see your ape friends. One big happy family. You won't have to wait long, I assure you. It'll only be a matter of minutes."

"You're wrong," said Ryan. "It'll be more like seconds."

Just then the weapon fire came like a hurricane from behind Rupert and his guards. They didn't stand a chance. Ryan watched as they fell to the floor dead. Behind them came Granthaxe, Kyron, and Hawthorne.

Ryan and Amanda ran forward to greet them when Ryan spotted Rupert's other guard to his left coming up the corridor from the bridge. The guard had his weapon pointed right at them. Without a weapon, Ryan could do nothing other than tackle Amanda to the ground. He braced himself when the guard suddenly stopped. The man was still pointing his weapon, but seemed frozen in place, as if he were trying to decide whether to shoot them. Then he fell forward and dropped to the floor.

Ryan couldn't believe it. At the far end of the corridor, behind the fallen body, was the Sentinelese chief, with three of the admiral's soldiers walking with him. The chief was holding some sort of blowgun. Ryan turned to Amanda. "Talk about a silent killer," he said.

Slowly, everyone gathered together, like warriors after a hard-fought battle—the Altarrans, the admiral, Ryan and Amanda, the chief, and the special ops agents.

"Where's the queen?" said Amanda.

"She's already off the ship," said Hawthorne. "She sent the chief in with a few of our men. Seemed to think we could use some help."

"Damn if she wasn't right," said Ryan. He bowed his head to the chief, who bowed back.

"She'll be wanting this," said the admiral, as he pulled the amulet out of Rupert's pocket. He stood and looked down at Rupert's body. "They don't let you bring amulets into hell."

"Sir," said Hawthorne. "That's all of them. We've killed all their crew. We also found the tribe. They were scattered in the trees. I have to say, sir, Rupert's men wouldn't have stood a chance against them."

"I tend to agree," said Thompson. "Good job, all of you. Now what do you say we get outside and wait for the reinforcements?"

"I second that," said Ryan. "They can clean up this mess. I think we've done enough for one day."

"For a lifetime," said his father.

Ryan and Amanda joined the admiral and the ragtag group of Altarrans, special ops forces, and one brave chief as they made their way to the exit ramp. Ryan never thought he'd be so happy to be setting foot on North Sentinel Island again, home to the most isolated, dangerous, and mysterious tribe on Earth. But luckily, they were also the queen's loyal subjects. And besides, this time he'd be arriving with the one and only goddess of fire.

Chapter 54

Going Home

Ryan stood back to watch the Altarran queen saying her goodbyes to the Sentinelese tribe. The transport ships had landed just outside the village. Everyone except for Ryan, his father, Amanda, and the queen were already on the transport.

The Sentinelese chief bowed to Amanda and handed her a feather from his headband. Then he straightened and walked away.

"The feather is an invitation," said the queen. "You are welcome here anytime. There was one more thing he said, though I thought it peculiar."

"What was that?" said Amanda.

"The chief told me that he takes back what he said earlier to Kyron. His words were, 'Never mind getting better guards. These ones are good enough.'"

Ryan laughed. "Tell the chief he's not so bad either," he said. He turned to Amanda. "Looks like we have a nice vacation spot if we ever want to get away."

"Who said I'd bring *you*?" she said. Then she smiled at him.

The admiral approached them. "Queen Darthaxe," he said. "On behalf of our people, I want to personally apologize for what you and your comrades have gone through. I hope we can look forward to better times ahead."

"Indeed we shall, Admiral," said the queen. "There is much we can learn from one another. Especially those foreign to us. The wondrous cave of rock is such an example."

"Yes," said Ryan, "I'd love to learn how you were able to teach the Sentinelese to build that. I mean, it's not something we'd even have the technology to do."

"Oh, but you misunderstand," said the queen. "It was they who taught us."

Ryan was dumbfounded. He could tell his father and Amanda were equally surprised.

"They taught you?" said the admiral.

"As I have said, Admiral," said the queen, "there is much to learn from those who are foreign to us."

Hawthorne came running up to let them know it was time to go. Ryan, his father, Amanda, and the queen said their final goodbyes to the Sentinelese people and followed Hawthorne to the transport. They had a three-hour flight to UEDF Headquarters ahead of them.

After everyone boarded, the transport took off. Ryan looked out the window as they ascended from North Sentinel Island. He wondered what other mysteries the island and her ancient people had kept hidden all these years. Maybe one day he'd find out.

Exhausted, he collapsed in his seat and dozed off. After what seemed like mere minutes, he awoke to the sound of the transport touching down at Fleet Headquarters, just outside the hangar where the Altarran ship was hidden. It was hard to believe they'd finally reached the end of the road. All that was left was getting the Altarran ship into space and back with their fleet.

The transport taxied into the hangar. When they had deplaned, Ryan approached his father. "What's next, sir?" he said.

"Everyone needs to get checked out by medical," said the admiral. "Then we have a debriefing. I'll see you in the hangar at 1900 hours. Get cleaned up and have something to eat. We're repairing your ships. Since we only have nine active ships from our fleet, until we can build more, we're going to overhaul yours."

It seemed like a lifetime ago that Ryan was with his crew on the Churchill. He was looking forward to seeing Tanner and Paul. Even Jill and Nicole would be a sight for sore eyes. He didn't think he could have said that a few weeks ago.

"Those ships served us well, sir," he said. "We even used their x-ray labs for our microfilms. By the way, did you find anything in the files about the IC-12 unit, or an inner circle?"

"Not a damn thing," said the admiral. "The president knew nothing about it either. Hell, there could be more of them out there for all we know, but we got their leader. We'll be launching a world-wide investigation."

"I wouldn't mind being part of that," said Ryan.

"You'll have plenty else to do, starting with heading down to medical and getting checked out."

Ryan saluted his father. "Will do, sir."

He went to medical, where he received four stitches in his left shoulder, as well as a couple of injections. Then he and Amanda went to the mess hall. As they entered, he spotted Tanner, Paul, Nicole, and Jill sitting at a table, waiting for them. They all stood up and applauded. Nicole and Jill had tears in their eyes. Even Tanner looked pretty touched.

Tanner was the first to speak up. "The buzz around here," he said, "is that we all now have a goddess to worship."

"Damn, Tanner," said Ryan. "We just got out of debriefing. Where are you getting your information?"

Tanner pointed to the corner of the mess hall. The area was cordoned off for the crew from Granthaxe's ship. "The big guy whose head is scraping the ceiling told me all about it."

Ryan looked over at Granthaxe, who spotted him.

From the corner of his eye, Ryan saw his father heading his way with a female officer by his side. At first he thought it was Commodore Laurent. As they came closer, he realized who it was. Could this be? And if so, how?

He looked over at Nicole, who had taken a seat, and smiled, shaking his head in disbelief.

She looked confused, but gave a slight smile and waved to him. "What are you smiling at?" she said, obviously not realizing who was behind her, walking with the admiral.

Ryan looked over Nicole's shoulder at her sister, Tara, who, for all intents and purposes, should have been dead, since the Lexington had been destroyed.

"C'mon, Nikki," said Tara. "I taught you better than that. What are you smiling at, *Captain*?"

Nicole froze, looking as if she'd heard a ghost. Tears welled up in her eyes as she jumped up and turned around. "Tara?! I thought you were dead!" She threw her arms around her sister and the two embraced.

"How did you survive?" said Nicole. "We heard your ship was destroyed."

"It was awful, Nikki. We'd already taken heavy damage, and Captain Ramsey ordered us to abandon ship. We were leaving in the escape pods when I saw the Lexington speed up, right into the path of the missiles headed for Admiral Thompson's ship. The last I saw, I . . ." Her voice trailed off. She was obviously upset by the event.

"He's a hero," said Admiral Thompson. "And I'll make sure that nobody ever forgets that."

Hawthorne approached. "Admiral," he said, "it's time."

Ryan looked at the clock and realized it was time for them to go to the hangar so the admiral could address the fleet. He motioned to Amanda, who came to join him. His father went ahead.

As he walked with Amanda, two hulking figures, the queen and Granthaxe, came to greet them.

"Ryan Thompson and Amanda Williamson," said Granthaxe. "You have both done a great service to the Altarran people. True warriors you are, putting your own lives at risk to rescue our queen . . . my mother. We came close to destroying one another. But now, I give you both my personal pledge to bind our races as kin."

"Thank you, Supreme Commander," said Ryan. "Though I have to give most of the credit to Amanda. She never for one moment gave up hope for a peaceful resolution. A wise man once told us we were better together than apart, Amanda and I. And I guess he was right."

Ryan looked and Amanda and smiled.

"And maybe the same can be said for humans and Altarrans," added Amanda.

The queen had the amulet in her hand. "Amanda," she said. "You have fulfilled my wishes even more than I could have ever hoped for. And for that, the amulet of the gods belongs with you, to keep as a sign of friendship between our two people."

Amanda started to protest. "Oh no, I can't accept that," she said. "This is such an important piece of your history. I appreciate it, but please, take it with you."

"No, my child," said the queen. "Your family has kept it safe for many years. Without your beloved Robert Williamson, I would not be here today. Even worse, a terrible war would have occurred, at great loss to both our kind. No, my dear Amanda. The gods themselves would want this with you—for what greater bond is there than our greatest treasure?"

Ryan realized something. "But what about the rule," he said, "that Altarrans must not lay eyes on the queen without her amulet?"

"Who do you think made the rule?" said the queen. "And a silly rule it was. It exists no more."

"Then thank you," said Amanda, holding the amulet to her heart. "I'll cherish it and keep the family tradition of passing it down through the years."

"It does us a great honor," said the queen. "And speaking of honor," she said, turning to Granthaxe. "My son, just how many of our ships were lost in this battle you forged against the humans?"

"Twenty-seven battleships, mother," said Granthaxe, "though greater than half our crew members were able to evacuate in escape crafts. But I fear we lost three troop carriers as well. It was a great loss."

"We lost three full troop carriers?" said the queen. "That's over three hundred thousand warriors!"

Ryan thought now would be a good time to tell Granthaxe the good news before all the joy turned sour. "Hold on a minute," he said. "About those troop carriers. They're still in one piece. At least they were a few days ago when we left them."

"Left them where?" said Granthaxe. "They live?"

"Yes, they live. They were too big for us to destroy, so we disabled their light-speed engines and destroyed their communications array. They should be somewhere between Pluto and Neptune. So you see, Queen Darthaxe, there's no need to demote the commander or beat him to death."

The queen looked oddly at Ryan. "Why would I beat my son to death?"

"You know," said Ryan, "I've learned to love you and your people, but you really do need to work on your sense of humor."

The queen looked at her son, confused.

Granthaxe smacked Ryan upside the head, almost knocking him off his feet. "Thank you, Ryan Thompson. That is very good news."

Ryan held the back of his head. "What was that for?"

"Did I do something wrong?" said Granthaxe. "On more than one occasion I have seen both you and Amanda Williamson do the same to close friends of yours. I assumed it was a gesture of friendship."

Amanda laughed. "No problem, Supreme Commander. But you—"

"Amanda Williamson," said Granthaxe. "Humor . . . achieved."

Ryan and Amanda both laughed.

"And now," said the Supreme Commander, "we must prepare to leave. We have much to do and a long journey ahead. And we must stop to assist the damaged ships."

"I'll talk to my father about sending some engineers out to help you repair them," said Ryan.

"You are most gracious," said Granthaxe.

The queen smiled that hideous, fanged smile at Ryan. For some reason, that still unnerved him. He kept waiting for her to bite his neck.

"Farewell, dear friends," said the queen.

Ryan and Amanda hugged the two giants that they'd probably never see again, and turned to join the cadets and the UEDF personnel as they made their way to the large hangar bay.

As they entered, Ryan watched his father step onto the makeshift stage at the front of the room. He felt a sense of pride as the admiral addressed the room of approximately two thousand officers and cadets.

Thompson cleared his throat and everyone quieted down.

"I wanted to take a few minutes," he began, "to thank everyone in this room for their help in bringing this volatile situation to a peaceful end. It took a little wrangling and a lot of sides coming together to make this happen. As for our Altarran friends—and yes, we can consider them friends—I've already spoken with them about communication methods and protocols. Negotiations to reach a lasting peace agreement between our collective governments on Earth and Altarra have already begun."

As Ryan joined the crowd in applause, he couldn't help shaking his head and smiling. Leave it to his father to have already begun secret negotiations. And with all the chaos, he hadn't even thought about how they might stay in touch with the Altarrans. He'd assumed it was an impossibility. But then, when it came to Benjamin "Flash" Thompson, nothing was an impossibility.

"I'm not going to keep you any longer than necessary," said the admiral. "It's been a grueling two weeks, and I know most of you would very much like to relax. Before concluding, there is one more thing I'd like to do. I'd like Cadet Amanda Williamson and my son, Cadet Ryan Thompson, to come up to the stage."

Ryan looked at Amanda with wide eyes. He had no idea they were going to be called up, and neither did she, apparently. He stood up and followed her to the stage.

They walked up the portable metal stairs and stood next to the admiral. As Ryan looked out toward the audience, he noticed a man enter the rear of the hangar. He knew right away who it was. He nudged Amanda, whose eyes lit up. Her father had come a long way for this event. Somehow, his visit must have been arranged prior to the outcome being known.

Admiral Williamson stood in the back of the room and saluted them. Ryan and Amanda saluted back.

Ryan's father acknowledged his lifelong friend with a nod, and then turned to Ryan and Amanda.

"As Fleet Admiral of The United Earth Defense Fleet," he said, "it gives me great pleasure to bestow a special award on both of you."

The admiral slipped behind the podium and returned with two Golden Cadet trophies. "After a long discussion with Admiral Williamson," he continued, "it has been decided that for the first time in history, two cadets will win the coveted award. Both the admiral and I couldn't be more proud, not only because you are our legacy, but because you've both exceeded our wildest, and already high, expectations. Congratulations to both of you."

As the two of them accepted their awards, their hands trembling, Ryan could see that Amanda was as astonished as he was. He choked up as the crowd stood and applauded. Amanda turned toward him, her face beaming. He couldn't help thinking how fortunate he was. She was compassionate, smart, and beautiful. It killed him to think of how many times he'd nearly lost her. But he knew one thing for sure. He was never going to let anything come between them again, least of all, his own fears.

She looked nervous as she put out her hand to shake his, as was customary for the winner of the Golden Cadet Award. But he refused to extend his hand, instead giving her a serious look. As could be expected, she looked confused as he shook his head no. But he couldn't keep the ruse going any longer. He smiled as he pulled her close and kissed her.

He could hear everyone cheering wildly as he whispered in her ear, "I love you, Amanda Williamson."

About the Author

Edward Miller

As chief editor for a sci-fi gaming website for over fifteen years, Edward Miller has crafted hundreds of stories designed to take readers to new places and immerse them in mind-bending situations. His debut novel with co-author J.B. Manas, *The Kronos Interference*, was named to Kirkus Reviews' Best of 2012. Kirkus called the book, "impressively original" and a "tour de force."

In a former life as a musician, Edward toured the United States with such acts as Foghat, The Allman Brothers Band, Edgar Winter, 38 Special, and others. Edward resides in Willow Grove, Pennsylvania with his wife and family, along with their dog, Lady.

Acknowledgements

First and foremost, I would like to once again thank Paula Berinstein for her expert advice and keen editing eye. Also thanks to Jerry (J.B.) Manas, my friend and co-author on *The Kronos Interference*, who contributed many insights to this book as well. Thanks to Brian Thompson, veteran film actor and valued friend, for his thoughts during the writing process. Thanks also to Joseph Dilworth of Pop Culture Zoo Press.

Thanks also to my test readers for their candid and helpful feedback: Mary Keaser, Phil Fisher, Nancy Cutler, Robin Goldblum, Ann Beth Goldblum, Mary Kate Gillespie and Jonas Sosa, Jr. Thanks also to Tom Goldblum for his unending support.

Special thanks must go to my wife, Heidi Miller, for watching the back of my head as I wrote for months at a time. Also to Alfie and Geri Myers, Carl Miller, Stuart Goldstein, Nicole Gordon, Becki and Ben Gomez, and the next generation, Sophia, Gabe, and Alicia Gomez. And last but not least, to my dog, Lady, who may be old, but never complains about it.